Whose hearts are in alignment?

***Miranda Jones* is perfectly aligned with the man of her heart.** She'd gotten it wrong about relationships a few times, but now she has it right. Her hopes and goals, values and dreams, all align not only within herself but with the amazing man who is now her fiancé. Being an astronomer, he knows all about alignment and feels exactly the same way about her and the life they're planning.

But that has left Miranda's sister Meredith hurt, their parents confused, her artist's rep concerned, and even some of her friends skeptical. Why did Miranda and Cornelius keep things secret for so long? Did they have something to hide? Has their own happiness come at the expense of misery for others?

California's Central Coast is **growing explosively.**
Now, in the late 1990s, tourism is up, but so are environmental regulations. Housing is on the rise, but so are water restrictions. Gambling is limited, but the Chumash tribe lobbies for a gaming casino. Crime is low on the quiet Central Coast, but a murder born of greed has yet to come to light. The stock market is booming, the upwardly mobile are pouring out of Los Angeles in search of a fresh start or a weekend getaway. In these affluent, pre-9/11 days, it's a time of infinite possibilities.

Milford-Haven is a **town full of characters.**
Escapees from San Francisco and Los Angeles, New York and Arkansas, Montreal, Australia and South Africa, have come here with their own hopes and expectations, agendas and shadowed pasts. The stakes are high: create a new life from scratch. The opportunities are dazzling: own a piece of the California dream.

It's a town of buried secrets and a dangerous mystery, quaint shops and breathtaking vistas, peaceful solitude and spontaneous conversations.

What delights people here is the unique perspective this part of the coastline offers. Once they see the sign to **Milford-Haven** and pull off Highway 1, their heads begin to align with their hearts and they never want to leave.

Come discover for yourself . . . ***Whose Hearts Align.***

Book Two – *Where the Heart Lives*

"In *Where the Heart Lives*, Mara Purl strategically presents a glamorous alternative to big city vibrancy. In the second installment of her already popular Milford-Haven series, the California Central Coast is once again the locale for her magnetic cast of characters. Purl's success is based on her ability to appeal to readers on a more elevated level than traditional romance fiction generally prescribes. Though she never loses the common touch in her storytelling instincts, in every potential stereotype emerges a well-developed character with a standout personality."
– ForeWord Reviews

"[In] the second volume of this ongoing saga . . . Purl returns to picturesque Milford-Haven. The town is filled with back stories—dark secrets, hidden agendas, failed romances and budding love, not to mention the unsolved mystery. Skillfully interspersing the moment-to-moment thoughts of her characters with their actions and dialogue, Purl effortlessly moves from one personal story to another. Like visiting friends and catching up. . . ."
– Kirkus Review

"Part small-town confidential, part mystery, part romance, the story is cozy in the best sense of the word. Steeped in California charm, the setting plays host to a wide variety of characters from across the social spectrum. High society rubs shoulders with artists and diner cooks, providing a snap shot of an up-scale village. Despite the town's air of quaint charm, the people are refreshingly realistic."
– Bookwire

"[In] the second Milford-Haven novel, award-winning writer Mara Purl deepens the intrigue in this captivating window into the little battles, victories, successes, and failings of ordinary people in [the] complicated world [of] Milford-Haven."
– Midwest Book Review

Book One – *What the Heart Knows*

"Former *Days of Our Lives* star Purl presents the first novel in her Milford-Haven series, which . . . features a setting of unadulterated beauty—the small coastal town of Milford-Haven, CA in the prosperous mid-'90s—and a cast of successful, sexy, sometimes quirkily independent characters. . . . Readers will find details galore . . . and the novel's many inner monologues reveal scheming, secretly confused, or flawed personalities. . . . Milford-Haven offers depictions of daily life, hints of possible future romance, the threat of scandal, and carefully parsed out mystery. . . . the novel is poised to convince readers to continue with the series."
– Publishers Weekly

"Former *Days of Our Lives* actress Purl imbues her soap opera finesse into the fictional setting of Milford-Haven, a sleepy California coastal town. This may be Apple Pie, USA, but hearts are on the line, professions are at stake and a possible murder has tainted the landscape. A whirlwind of juicy drama with dangling-carrot closure."
– Kirkus Review

"*What the Heart Knows* is an upbeat novel . . . the first book of Milford-Haven. The book opens powerfully . . . Purl does not use external paraphernalia to bring her characters to life. Multiple love stories, friendships, crushes. . . . Purl's characters are well-traveled, educated, and street smart."
– ForeWord Magazine

". . . in Mara Purl's enchanting novel *What the Heart Knows* . . . although the picturesque, seaside setting of Milford-Haven plays an important role in the novel, the cast of interesting and eccentric characters is what really draws the reader into the book."
– BookWire

"Mara Purl's *What the Heart Knows* is a first class novel by a very talented writer with strong believable characters, a rapid pace delivery of story, and very tight writing that make this novel such a delight to read. I look forward to seeing other titles in this impressive series."
– Gary Roen, Nationally Syndicated Book Reviewer

"I read Mara Purl's *What the Heart Knows* and loved the book—just devoured it, in fact—and can't wait to read the next installment." *– Anne L. Holmes, APR*
National Association of Baby Boomer Women

"You can't escape the pull of Milford-Haven, the setting for *Days of Our Lives* actress and award-winning author Mara Purl's enticing new novel *What the Heart Knows*. This fictional, coastal California town offers a simpler life. . . . My kind of romance, this [is a] juicy, take-me-away-from-it-all read . . . plus, the inviting story makes you *think*." *– Charlotte Hill, Boomer Brief*

The Milford-Haven Novels Series

"In Mara Purl's books the writing is crisp and clean, the dialogue realistic, the scenes well described. I salute her ingenuity." *– Bob Johnson,*
Former Managing Editor, The Associated Press

"Every reader who enjoys book series about small town life has a treat to anticipate in . . . Mara Purl's *Milford-Haven Novels*." *– Dee Ann Ray,*
The Clinton Daily News

"Mara Purl's characters have become old friends and I keep expecting one of them to give me a call!" *– Nanci Cone, Ventura Breeze*

". . . an intrigu[ing] cast of diverse characters."
– Fred Klein, Santa Barbara News Press

ENDORSEMENTS FROM OTHER AUTHORS

"Mara Purl is a skillful storyteller who has written a charming and tantalizing saga about the ways in which lives can intersect and be forever changed. The first novel in the saga is not-to-be-missed." *– Margaret Coel*
New York Times Best-Selling author

"I found a kinship with . . . your heart for character . . . and with your truly fine unveiling of story events." *– Jane Kirkpatrick, Author*
Wrangler Award, Willa Award

"I so admire Mara Purl's writing style. The pictures she paints are just glorious, her characters and attention to detail inspiring." — *Sheri Anderson*
Emmy Award-winning writer, Days of Our Lives

ACCOLADES FOR *MILFORD-HAVEN, U.S.A.* the hit BBC radio series

"Mara Purl's mix of a soap-opera format . . . is a smash hit in Britain." — *The Los Angeles Times*

"A sudsy look at today's toughest issues." — *The Hollywood Reporter*

"A slice of life in 'small-town U.S.A.' includes well-known cast members and music artists like the Doobie Brothers." — *Billboard*

AWARDS FOR *WHOSE HEARTS ALIGN*
National Indie Excellence Award
Winner – Fiction: Romance

ForeWord Book of the Year Award
Finalist – Fiction: Romance

EVVY Award
Winner – Fiction

Beach Book Festival Book Award
Winner – Fiction: Romance

AWARDS FOR *the Milford-Haven Series*
National
American Fiction, Authors Show, Benjamin Franklin,
Book Excellence, Elite Choice, ForeWord Indie,
Global E-Book, International, Independent Press, Literary Titan,
Maincrest Media, National Indie Excellence, Pinnacle,
USA Book News Best Book

Regional
Beach Book, Beverly Hills, EVVY, Holiday, Los Angeles, New York City
Big Book, San Francisco, Southern California, USA Regional

AWARDS FOR *the Author*
The Authors Show Top Female Author – Fiction
Los Angeles County Commission for Women – Woman of the Year

Whose Hearts Align

Mara Purl

Whose Hearts Align

Book Four
A Milford-Haven Novel

Milford-Haven PUBLISHING, RECORDING & BROADCASTING HISTORY
This book is based in part upon the original radio drama Milford-Haven ©1987 by Mara Purl,
Library of Congress numbers SR188828, SR190790, SR194010; and upon the original radio
drama Milford-Haven, U.S.A. ©1992 by Mara Purl, Library of Congress number SR232-483,
broadcast by the British Broadcasting Company's BBC Radio 5 Network, and which is also
currently in release in audio formats as Milford-Haven, U.S.A. ©1992 by Mara Purl. Portions of
this material also appear on the Milford-Haven Web Site, http://www.MilfordHaven.com
© by Mara Purl. All rights reserved.
978-1-936878-24-6
Portions of this work were published in early editions
Test-Marketing Novelization Edition Copyright © 1999 by Mara Purl
Library of Congress Txu-846-611
Cause & Conscience Edition Copyright © 2008 by Mara Purl

Publisher's Cataloging-In-Publication Data
Purl, Mara.
Whose hearts align / Mara Purl. — New ed.
p. ; cm. — (A Milford-Haven novel ; Book four)
Based on the original radio dramas Milford-Haven and Milford-Haven U.S.A.,
broadcast by BBC Radio 5 Network.
Portions also appear on the World Wide Web at http://www.milfordhaven.com
ISBN: 978-1-936878-24-6
LCSH: Man-woman relationships—Fiction. | City and town life—California—Fiction.
Women artists—California—Fiction. | Energy industry executives—California—Fiction.
Restaurateurs—California—Fiction. | Missing persons—Investigation—California—Fiction. |
California—Fiction. | LCGFT: Romance fiction.

PS3566.U75 W456 2024
813/.6—dc23

Published in the U.S. by Bellekeep Books, New York www.BellekeepBooks.com
Distributed by Ingram

*This book is dedicated to
my mother—
elegant, generous, complex and devoted.
And to my mother-in-law—
sweet, kind, and wise.*

Acknowledgments

Thanks to my publishers: Patrice Samara, Kara Johnson and Tara Goff at BelleKeep Books. Thanks to my gifted editorial team: Derra Moyers, editor & proofreader; Vicki Hessel Werkley, development editor. Thanks to Mary Helsaple for exquisite watercolors for my book covers, to Reya Patton for cover concept, and to Rebecca Finkel for superb interior design and cover adjustments.

Thanks to my marketing team: Jonatha King at King Communications in Santa Barbara for PR and marketing; Don McCauley for PR distribution; Kelly Johnson and Sky Esser for internet design and wizardry. Thanks to Judith Briles for superior marketing programs and events.

Thanks to those who provide expertise during my research: to artists Mary Helsaple, Caren Pearson for inspiration and depth of detail; to Dr. Laurence Doyle for astronomical specifics; to Pilulaw Khus for Chumash wisdom and for her book Earth Wisdom co-written with Yolanda Broyles-Gonzalez. Thanks, always, to the SLO County Sheriff's Department. Thanks to both Stan Waterman and Al Giddings for many years of friendship and for valuable oceanographic research. Thanks to Al for including me as a crew member in the Yellowstone shoot for his Discovery Channel documentary *In Celebration of Trees*.

Thanks to dear friends in Cambria who've supported Milford-Haven for many years with such enthusiasm, including Elaine Traxel Evans, Kathe Tanner, Susan & Brent Berry, Judy Salamacha and Dennis Eamon Young. Thanks to Mary Lou Belli, Verne Nobles, and Frank Abatemarco for seeing the potential of the Milford-Haven Television project.

Thanks for special events: to dynamic organizations in several parts of the country for working with me to produce the community-based Milford-Haven Chari-Teas® (Possibili-Teas, Generosi-Teas, Hospitali-Teas, Creativi-Teas, and our list continues!)

Thanks for organization support: WWW (Women Writing the West), CLAS (California Literary Arts Society), IBPA (Independent Book Publishing Association), SLO NightWriters, Sisters in Crime, the Author's Guild and Author U/ Author You, Colorado Authors Hall of Fame, and Publishing at Sea.

Thanks to the many independent bookstores who participated in my program #SendIndieBookGift, started during the pandemic. It was wonderful supporting you and reaching new readers all over the U.S.

Thanks to Bill Berkuta and all at Haven Books Audio for award-winning audio books. Thanks to my mentor Louis L'Amour, who believed in my project and told me to keep going with it.

And most important of all—thanks to you, my readers! I'm thrilled to welcome those of you who are new to my books. And I extend a special heartfelt thanks to the core group of readers who began with the novels' early editions. I appreciate your steadfast support during my publishing journey.

The Radio Drama

Milford-Haven had its first air date in 1987, and my thanks go to KOTR, in Cambria, California, our first radio home. In its next incarnation *Milford-Haven, U.S.A.* was broadcast on the BBC, thanks Ms. Pat Ewing, Director of Radio 5—a maverick network that launched a maverick show, and celebrated with us when we reached 4.5 million listeners.

Before there were any shows to broadcast, there were the cast members, and my thanks go to both the original cast of *Milford-Haven* and to the cast of *Milford-Haven, U.S.A.*, seasoned professionals who brought my characters so vividly to life that their work is inextricably woven into the fabric of the characters themselves.

Before there were cast members to record, there had to be a studio, and my thanks go to Engineer Bill Berkuta whose Afterhours Recording Company became our studio home, a workshop in which we created one hundred episodes of the first show and sixty of the second, and where we now create audio books of the novels.

Thanks to the late great David L. Krebs, our foley master, a gifted sound artist who created our aural reality. Thanks to Marilyn Harris and Mark Wolfram, who composed the haunting *Milford-Haven* theme and all the music cues that support the emotional ebb and flow of the story. Thanks to Warren Talcott for the intriguing *Milford-Haven* poster, and to Caren Pearson for the compelling *Milford-Haven* logo art—each of which gave our town its visual reality.

Before I created my own soap opera, there was *Days of Our Lives* and my thanks go to the producers, writers, directors and fellow cast members with whom I worked, and from whom I learned so much.

And before there was a *Milford-Haven*, there was a young woman who had always lived in cities—Tokyo, New York, Los Angeles. I spent a summer performing in a play at Jim and Olga Buckley's Pewter Plough Playhouse in Cambria, and became fascinated with the life in and of a small town. With Elaine Traxel Evans's help, I immersed myself in this new culture—admittedly seeing it through the eyes of an environmentalist—and began to realize that it was not only a local drama that was being played out in its quiet streets, but a universal one as well.

Listeners in the U.S. and in the U.K. agreed, writing to me about their own lives, their own towns, and the commonality of the situations we face globally. My thanks go to my listeners everywhere. Several years later the link with listeners was to be vividly demonstrated, when the original Milford Haven in Wales embraced me as an honorary citizen and showed me those same streets, those same dramas, uncannily alike in the multi-cultural parallel universes we all inhabit. Thanks to Bruce Henrickson of the Belhaven House Hotel. Special thanks to Jim and Anne Hughes, who shared my vision even before we met, who welcomed me into their home, and with whom I continue to forge a unique town-to-town relationship.

My thanks go to my family and friends—helpful, discerning and, above all, supportive—Ray Purl, Marshie Purl, Linda Purl, Larry Norfleet, Erin Gray, Miranda Kenrick, Vickie and Bob Zoellner.

And finally my thanks go to my characters, among whom are—Jack, Zack, Miranda, Cornelius, Samantha, Rune, Meredith, Connie, Rick, Emily, Kevin, Joseph, Sally, Tony, Zelda, Notes, Susan and Cynthia, who are building, buying, painting, observing, planning, rehearsing, flirting, traveling, dealing, reporting, cogitating, dominating, dishing, healing, conniving, playing, sneaking and seducing, respectively.

Dear Reader —

Welcome back to Milford-Haven! And if this is your first visit—it is my pleasure to introduce you to my favorite little town and to its many residents, all of whom are described in the Cast of Characters at the back of the book.

Naturally formed openings in large offshore rocks occur all over the world, and California's Central Coast is no exception. Formed as rock is eroded by water, wind, and sometimes ice, these arches always make me think of windows. They offer glimpses into unique perspectives—but only if we align ourselves to see what's on the other side. Rarely, these natural openings are heart-shaped, as is the case in this book.

Relationships in Milford-Haven include various kinds of alignments, as they do in all small towns. Who has chosen sides on important issues like environmental compliance? Who believes in volunteer organizations and educational projects for local youth? And perhaps most importantly, who has found a true heart-connection with the right partner? Sometimes the very person we hope to find isn't visible, until we bring our own heart into alignment with what we value most.

My protagonist Miranda has found the man of her heart, but now must create a new life with him while staying aligned with family and friends, some of whom don't see what she sees. Her sister Meredith has also found someone special and embarks on gaining a new vision of what's possible.

You may read these books out of sequence, but I think you'll enjoy them most reading them as I wrote them. _Whose Hearts Align_ is the fourth novel, with novellas and novelettes expanding and enhancing the saga.

Through the novels, each Prologue proceeds with the investigation of journalist Chris Christian's disappearance. The heart of the story is seen through the artist-eyes of Miranda Jones. And each novel's themes are concluded by environmentalist Samantha Hugo in her ongoing journals.

In each novel, we leave Milford-Haven to follow Miranda Jones to destinations that fascinate her painter's eye and her restless heart. This novel takes her just up the coast to a rustically gorgeous spot perfect for a wedding. This book references a trip to the stunningly rugged beauty and drama of Alaska, told in the novella _Where Eagles Roost._ But then it brings her back to a deeper sense of home than she has ever known, one her heart recognized from a drawing done much earlier—a home she will share forever in Milford-Haven.

As the story unfolds, follow my footsteps over the inter-connected pathways of those who inhabit Milford-Haven, and come to understand . . . whose hearts align.

Mara Purl

"If you align expectations with reality, you will never be disappointed."   – Terrence Owens

"It is only with the heart that one can see rightly; what is essential is invisible to the eye."
                    – Antoine de Saint-Exupery

"When you find alignment, the conditions will not matter."   – Abraham Hicks

"We can see our true goals clearly only when our head and heart are aligned."
                    – from Samantha Hugo's Journal

Prologue

S enior Deputy Delmar Johnson was not eager to read the journal of a dead woman.

Presumed dead, he corrected himself, hoping it wasn't so. He almost felt he'd gotten to know Chris Christian in recent weeks, watching videos of her special reports, piecing together elements of her interrupted life

But all day he'd put off reading her journal—even to the point of lingering over dinner at the Bird's Nest. Now just outside the restaurant, he delayed for a moment longer, taking in the view.

The customary coastal chill of late spring was settling over the Central Coast as it prepared to bed down for the night, almost ready to pull a foggy blanket over its shoulders. *Those hills do look like shoulders,* he thought, still reveling in his good fortune at having moved here. *I'm a long way from South Central Los Angeles.*

He worried that his reflexes had slowed in an atmosphere no longer charged with nightly drive-by shootings. And he rejoiced that he could now go several hours thinking about something beyond survival of the fittest.

Gravel crunched under Del's boots as he crossed the parking lot, and he felt comforted by these surroundings, enjoying a new sense of belonging. Tempting though it was to head for his cozy studio apartment, he could no longer avoid his self-appointed task of reading the journal.

Though he'd had orders not to treat the missing reporter's case as an active one until—or unless—something concrete turned up, he was free to pursue whatever he wished during his time off, and he'd done just that.

As of yesterday morning, all that had changed. Hikers—lost while trying to make their way through a local canyon—had used an abandoned wreck of a car as their reference point when calling Park Rangers for help. When the car's plates had later been called in, they matched those of a missing woman: Christine Christian.

After getting the hikers safely out of the area, the department had processed and towed the car. Though the forensics team were still going over the vehicle, what had come to light was the owner's purse. Its discovery seemed—at least for now—to lead to only one logical conclusion: that Ms. Christian survived the crash, then crawled out of the damaged vehicle to find help.

Next the team discovered a velcroed pouch under the carpet of the rear seat. In it was tucked the reporter's notebook, which proved to be a journal. Delmar imagined the diary contained some leads, or perhaps at least one smoldering clue. And it waited for him now, its information potentially hot enough to burn a hole through his desk.

Pulling into his assigned parking spot at the San Luis Obispo County Sheriff's station, he turned off the motor and let the

Suburban begin to cool. As he stepped down from its high running board, he let the heavy door slam and heard all four locks respond synchronously as he pressed the remote and headed up the stairs to the front entrance.

The SLO County Sheriff's office shared a building with the Department of Forestry, perhaps signifying that trees were every bit as important as people—a sentiment with which Del was beginning to agree. The two species stood toe to toe in a necessary symbiosis, each literally creating the other's air to breathe. Experimental programs in inner cities proved third-generation welfare families who'd never seen a tree began to overcome depression and hopelessness with the planting of a single sapling.

Del opened his office door, his gaze flying to the journal to disprove his theory of spontaneous combustion. Still intact, the unprepossessing volume contained the full weight of what was almost certainly the last months of a dead woman's soul.

Lifting it, he ran his hands over the nubby, black, syntheticover-cardboard, perfect-bound book. Not an expensive item—she hadn't chosen leather or raw silk for her memoirs. Yet, it had a simple elegance about it—classy, understated, functional. He asked himself for the hundredth time whether or not he had the right to read someone else's private writings.

Of course, he could rationalize that it was his *job* to read it. But it surprised him what hesitance he felt. Perhaps it was the very nature of self-reflection that bothered him. Now he knew of at least two local women who wrote journals: Sally O'Mally and Chris Christian. There might be others. *Do women tend to write the same sorts of things, or are diaries as distinct as the personalities of those who write them?* What would happen, he wondered, if he started to write his *own* journal? He'd never done that much soul-searching, if that was its primary function. And when it came to recording the daily events of life, they seemed far too mundane to bother. Of course, he kept a log of work-related activities, but that came with the job.

Could I write down personal thoughts—how it is to be one of the few African Americans living in a Caucasian stronghold? Or how I might feel about a particular woman? Involuntarily, he found himself resisting the idea of committing anything to paper. It wasn't so much the inability to frame his thoughts and feelings in words; it was that he didn't trust what would happen to the journal itself.

What was a private diary but a dangerous little emotional time-bomb that sooner or later was bound to go off? Full of betrayals, heartbreaks, and all manner of things best left unknown, it seemed to him a bad idea ever to keep one. Unless . . . unless something happened to the owner.

And here I am, the follower of clues. Thinking back to Christopher Darden's book, he remembered what the former D.A. had written —that Nicole Simpson had left those photos of herself battered and bruised . . . had left them for him. *Did Chris Christian leave this journal for* me?

Del sat in his desk chair and picked up the book. One of the last things he knew she'd planned was her dinner date with Joseph Calvin, which had been scheduled for Tuesday, October 20. He flipped to that page, hoping something written in her own hand would provide a clue.

Each page of the diary was devoted to a single day, with numerals indicating time printed down the left column. The capital letter "J" was written twice on that day, first, in the morning. The printed 6 a.m. numeral was circled, and next to it a small heart and several hastily sketched stars were added. Also 11 p.m. was circled, the "J" appearing again, this time with a question mark.

Between the two, the 6 p.m. was circled. Opposite it was the cryptic notation "MM." He didn't really expect to find she'd named her own killer. *Yet, it was possible she did.*

Del closed the diary. Logically, the next thing would be to read from the beginning, but he squirmed at the idea. Not only did he still balk at intruding too soon. He also believed there was more to her life than could have been captured in a layout of printed days with minimal notes added.

He thought back to his mother Ruby's practice of opening her Bible at random. "God will lead you when you let Him," she'd say. Though intellectually this made him feel foolish, as though he were following an old wives' tale, in his gut he sometimes trusted the old ways and felt now was a good time to employ the practice. He flipped open a page. *"Good date with Joseph last night. He still refuses to be called 'Joe.'"*

What was startling in reading the words was their immediacy. Chris didn't seem dead at all, or even missing. Her voice was here-and-now in present time, and he felt transported not only back to that moment but also into her particular reality, as convincingly as if she'd taken his hand and walked him into her life.

Shuddering at the thought, he reminded himself for the hundredth time that Chris wasn't necessarily dead at all. Yet, he couldn't shake the feeling he was trespassing on someone's unfinished life.

Part I

Cause & Conscience

"Conscience is the heart of Heaven."
– *Chinese proverb*

"Your own heart, your own conscience,
must tell you why I come."
– *Jane Austen, Pride and Prejudice*

Chapter 1

May-gray cloud cover enveloped California's Central Coast like the plastic mulch-films carefully tented over the nearby strawberry fields. Like the berries, the town of Milford-Haven ripened, patiently awaiting emergence from its protective blanket.

It was only 6 a.m., yet already residents were walking along the beach, watering flowers, or sipping their morning coffee. Despite the immanent approach of summer, this was not a sunny season. May cloud cover would likely be followed by June Gloom, but in July and August summer sun would brighten the skies and warm the air. Meanwhile, farther east and away from the coast, the days were already heating to a simmering point.

Miranda Jones had an important call to make. In fact, it would be one of the most important ever.

The previous month, the man of her heart had proposed and she'd been living on cloud nine ever since. Their engagement, and indeed their entire courtship, had been a well-kept secret and they'd been treasuring their private joy.

It was time, though, to share the news at least to their nearest and dearest. They could've remained incommunicado longer, except for their upcoming plans. Discovering they'd both been invited to work at the University of Alaska, Fairbanks, for a month this coming summer, they'd realized that magnificent state would make a perfect honeymoon destination. But in order to embark on a post-nuptial vacation, they'd first have to have the nuptials.

Accordingly, it was time for Miranda to call her parents. Oh, what a fuss would ensue. Mother would exult, then take out her Cross pen and red leather Gump's refillable notebook, and start to make plans. Father would pepper both her mother and herself with questions.

Am I ready for all that? Well, I have to be.

Showing absolutely no bravery whatsoever, Miranda placed the call. At this early hour, she knew her father would be out on the links and her mother would have the answering machine silenced until 8 a.m.

She heard their cheerful, electronic voices announcing who they were and what the caller should do.

"Hi, Mother and Dad. Guess what? Well, no, you can't possibly. I have wonderful news! That is, I have important news to share and I've missed you, so um, here it is. I've met the most terrific man. We've been dating, in between his trips overseas, and . . . he, um, works for NASA, but he also travels a lot. So when he got back from Tokyo—that's where his last trip took him—he um, he asked me to marry him. And I said yes! So, uh, well, we're engaged! So when you get this, uh, call me back. Oh, his name is Cornelius Smith. Did I say that? And this is Miranda, by the way, which I guess you already know. Love you!"

She hung up the receiver. *Oh no,* she worried. *I didn't do that right. Well, at least I did it. What date is today?*

She glanced down at the calendar on her desk. She had just flipped to a new page and put her finger on the numeral 1. But it was when she pronounced the date that she got the joke and had to say it aloud.

"May Day! May Day!"

Miranda knew it wouldn't take long for news to spread through her family like wildfire. Sure enough, her mother had called later that day, thrilled at the news, but chagrined to learn the wedding would take place just under seven weeks hence. While Dad made comments in the background and Mother shushed him, she said there was no time to waste and that she wanted to plan the shower for May 10 at the homestead in Belvedere.

Whatever plans I thought I had next weekend, I'll have to cancel. Otherwise Mom will be crushed. Her parent had also suggested that she take both her daughters shopping for the wedding dress the following day. Mother would do some advance reconnaissance on the gown, sort out the catering and the guest list for the shower, and generally manage every detail.

None of this was a surprise. Veronica "Veri" Jones could step up to play the part of General at a moment's notice. All this brought up the question of her sister Meredith.

Miranda'd let a day go by, but now she needed to talk to her sister and worried how it might go. They hadn't been on the best of terms ever since Miranda had moved out of the home they'd shared in San Francisco. Things had improved after Meredith made the effort to come to Milford-Haven for Miranda's art show last spring. But that'd also been a busy time and one filled delightfully with the distraction of Cornelius' attentions.

She'd thought at first she might try to surprise Meredith with a quick birthday visit tomorrow but had learned her sister'd made plans with girlfriends for a spa weekend—a weekend that did not include Miranda. Now, Miranda had an important question to ask her only sibling. She dialed her sister's number and waited to hear the familiar voice.

"Wondered when you'd get around to calling," Meredith had said in an acerbic tone.

"Oh. You've been waiting for a call from me?"

"Well, duh! You're getting married, aren't you?"

Miranda paused. "I am."

"Good for you."

"Wow. You sure don't sound happy about it," Miranda noted.

"I might be happier if you'd chosen to inform me," Meredith groused.

"As a matter of fact, I was calling to ask if you'd like to be my maid of honor." *Maybe that'll get us back on track,* Miranda thought, disappointed that she'd had to present her question defensively rather than joyfully.

"Great. You were, but now you're not?"

"Meredith, I do not understand where you're coming from."

"You would, if you thought about someone else for two minutes. You told Mom and Dad. You evidently told what's his name's parents. But me, you just ignored."

Miranda sighed. "You're right. I did avoid calling. I guess... I didn't know what to say."

"Since when has that ever been an issue between us? We've been frank with one another for years."

"We were. Or I thought we were, until Zack."

Miranda heard a sudden intake of air come over the phone and knew Mer was processing. But then, instead of a shift in tone, Mer shot back with another zinger.

"What about him? It's not like you cared about Zack one way or another."

"What an earth? Why would you say that?"

"It's the truth. You can't handle it?"

Miranda stretched her back, sat up straighter and took a breath. "Meri, do you want to hear the truth about Zack and me?"

"If I have to."

"You brought it up, so I think it's time we cleared the air," Miranda began. "He's a good person. But he never came clean with me."

"About what, pray tell?"

"About his job. About what mattered most to him. He led me to believe he was a music promoter. He took me to the Doobies concert, which you know about because I told you about it in some detail. I was backstage with him, met the band, met the crew. It was only much later that I discovered he only co-produced the concert as a favor, or as a lark. I finally found out not only that he works for an oil company, but is the heir to the firm."

"Oh, give me a break. You could have found out about him if you'd actually cared."

"I don't do research on people, Mer. That's your department. And in your line of work, that's fine. For me, I have very little reason to suppose someone is not who he represents himself to be. However, that's only one aspect of what happened between us."

"From what I know, basically nothing happened between you. I don't know why you're pretending it did," Mer criticized.

"I am not pretending anything," Miranda protested, beginning to feel pushed toward the edge of anger. "Anyway, another issue was that Zack blew hot and cold."

"Actually, that's more your department," Mer flung back.

Miranda, pressing her lips together, chose to ignore this. "He was interested in my paintings. He wanted a particular piece, which was already on hold for another client. So I took him on a hike to the location of the piece he wanted and offered him options for a commissioned work, something that would be exactly what he wanted. He seemed excited about this. And then . . . nothing. No follow up. And this became a pattern. He'd call, and—"

Meredith began to laugh.

"Mer? Something's funny?"

"It is, actually. His call. It became a turning point, and you had no idea."

Confused, Miranda suspended the sentence she'd started. "Sorry, I seem to be missing something."

Meredith huffed. "Exactly. You seem to go through life in a sort of fog, unaware of what's going on right under your nose. And since you don't investigate or confront, you never get to the truth. This is just what I mean."

Miranda felt awash in anger, hurt, and confusion. But what she sensed that, under the bluster, her sister was trying to tell her something. "What, Meredith? What is it you think I don't know? Out with it."

"That's the spirit. Okay, here it is. Months ago, when I was at your house, your phone rang. I answered. I don't know why, but I think it's because I thought it might be you. You'd left your door unlocked as usual, and you'd put a note for me on your hall table. So when the phone rang I figured you were calling to let me know when you'd be coming home. I mean, you did have a visitor; you did know I was coming. Yet, you weren't home when I arrived. Weird."

She's playing for time, still not able to spit it out. Must be a big thing. "And what does all this have to do with Zack?"

"It was Zack calling. That's what. He was playful, direct, and hot."

"Zack was?"

"Of course. That's who he is. That's what he likes. Everything was right there—his quick wit, his jibes and jabs, his eager passion. We flirted like mad. It was the most fun I'd had in years. He was irresistible."

Miranda began to laugh.

"You find that funny? Jesus, no wonder he felt so hurt."

"Hurt? No. Confused. That's what he was. And now I know what he meant that night at the gallery."

"At the gallery . . ." Meredith began, sounding unsure for the first time.

"He and I had it out that night. Not a fight, but a clearing. He told me he'd come to my show to figure out what had happened during that phone call. Of course, I had no idea what he was talking about. I did, however, share my feelings, and told him I felt he and I could be friends but nothing more."

"And then I arrived," Mer said, her voice softer.

"The moment you did, his confusion ended, and I don't just mean about the call. He recognized you, even though you'd never met." Miranda paused, and they both waited in silence for a long moment. "It would never have been right between Zack and me, Mer. But it's probably always been right between the two of you."

Meredith huffed again. "Zack said you were being generous to be his friend. I see what he means, now."

"Oh, Meri. That's kind."

"It's just the truth. Which is what this call is about, isn't it?"

"Totally."

She heard her sister inhale, exhale. "So, you want to ask me again?"

Miranda chuckled. "You mean about the wedding?"

"Yes."

"Meredith, would you please be the maid of honor at my wedding?"

"I would love to be your maid of honor!"

Both women began to laugh, though Miranda felt her eyes fill as they did.

"Okay," Mer said. "Now tell me about what's his name."

Miranda, the laughing abating, sighed deeply, thoughts of Cornelius flooding through her. "Oh, Mer, it's the most magical feeling I've ever had in my life. It's like being a child, building a sand castle, and believing that once it's built, you can move into it. That's basically what I will be doing—moving into a castle with the man of my dreams."

"Well, forgive me, but that doesn't sound very realistic."

"Okay, here's some realism for you. The man makes my toes curl. My whole middle turns to jelly when I just think about him, and when he's close, my body starts humming."

"Oh my God. Sounds like true love to me."

Miranda giggled.

"But . . . he's kind of strange, right? I mean, a physicist? A professional nerd? Who'd have thought he had passion?"

Miranda did her best to stifle a groan.

"Oh, girl, you got it bad."

"Hopelessly. We have the best time. We have this . . . depth of understanding. He gets me. I get him. I don't even know why sometimes. Or how. I'd say it's like magic, but it's more spiritual than that."

"So how did he propose?"

"Ohhh, it was amazing. Took me totally by surprise."

"Yeah?"

"He had gone to Tokyo for a few days, he had—"

"Tokyo? Oh, my. Fits right in with the family mojo. And he's quite the jet setter, for a physicist."

"He is, actually, though not in the usual way. Anyway, he went shopping for a ring."

"In Tokyo? So this was after you said yes?"

"No! Before he asked."

"Wow, that takes confidence," Mer said admiringly.

"And faith, I think. So when he got home, he arranged this elaborate evening for us," Miranda went on.

"Champagne and fancy restaurant?"

"Actually, peach tea and fancy campsite."

"No!"

"Sooo *not* your cuppa."

"And so perfect for you."

"Yup. Exactly. You'd hate the stuff we do. Well, not all the stuff we do."

Miranda burst out laughing and so did her sister. "It's going to be so wonderful, Mer."

"I get it, kiddo. I get part of it. But the important thing is, you're happy. And he's the real deal, isn't he? Not fooling around, not stringing you along with . . . string theory or something."

Miranda chuckled. "Not stringing me along, no. Building with me. Creating the life he's always wanted, which happens to be the life I've always wanted."

"Whew. So where's the wedding going to be? Promise me you're not going to hang from bungee cords or something. Mother would faint."

"No bungee cords. But we'll be at Ragged Point for the ceremony and the reception. We can't move into our new house yet."

"New house? You have a new house?"

"Not new, really, but being renovated. It's a lighthouse. And it's amazing. You'll love it. Or not."

Meredith laughed this time. "Uh, it does sound interesting. But what about a party at Mom and Dad's?"

"A party, sure. We'd enjoy that. After the wedding. Maybe on our way back from our honeymoon."

"Well, no matter that you'll have gone on your honeymoon, she'll call it a reception. That'll make her feel better. She's longing to celebrate you some more, you know. She's about to bust a button, she's so proud. And Dad seems to have come around, too."

"Not a moment too soon."

"Go easy on him. He's trying."

"I know. Cornelius is strong. He'll stand up to Dad easily. "

"Then he is strong. So is Zack."

"So . . . you've progressed that far?"

"Meaning?"

"Far enough that he's met the folks?"

"Yes. He wanted to. And then Dad was . . . I don't know, weird. In fact, so was Zack's dad."

"Mr. Calvin was weird?" Miranda queried.

"Each of them admitted to being old friends. But neither would give details," Mer explained.

"Really? Hmm. Well, maybe they played golf or something. Not too far-fetched to imagine their paths crossing," Miranda suggested.

"I suppose not. Anyway, it was fine. Fun, actually. Dad had approval written all over his face," Mer exulted.

"Naturally. He saw the money."

"Ouch. That's really harsh, coming from you, Mandy."

"Yeah, I know. Sorry. Cornelius has me working on that," she admitted.

"On what?"

"Not being so judgmental of my dad. He keeps pointing out it's a two way street. And he's right, damn it," Miranda confessed.

Mer chuckled. "Good for you. Good for him. Cornelius, I mean. Good for everyone," she said more softly.

"It really is, Mer. All the way around."

Chapter 2

M eredith rose early on Saturday morning, eager to begin her weekend getaway.

This wouldn't be one of her secretive assignations with Zack. Nor would she travel far—only to the far side of the Golden Gate Bridge. But it would be a delightful indulgence, none the less.

Her actual birthday didn't arrive until the twelfth, but she'd booked a two-day stay at Cavallo Point for this first weekend of May and invited her most fun girlfriends to join her. They'd begin their stay at the Healing Arts Center & Spa.

Three hours later, traffic a distant memory, her weekend wardrobe put away in her room, she lay stretched out on a plush, high-thread-count covered table, allowing herself to relish every stroke of the masseuse's hands.

Marcille moaned from the next table.

"Keep it down over there, will you? " Meredith complained.

"But this is almost better than sex," Marcille explained.

"Speak for yourself, woman," Meri countered.

Marcille's head popped up. "Really? Do tell!"

"Yes, do," said the drowsy-sounding voice of Chao.

"Maybe later, during happy hour."

"You mean, we're gonna get happier than this?" asked Valentina.

"I certainly hope so," Meri confirmed.

"Whatever you say, Birthday Girl," Marcille said.

Meredith giggled. *I deserve this*, she thought, inhaling the heavenly lemon-verbena scent. *I've been wanting to get together with my girlfriends and my birthday is the perfect excuse.* After the spa, they'd be heading to the property's restaurant, where a prix fixe dinner with wine pairings awaited. *They run a well-known cooking school here, so I know the food will be superb.*

Cavallo Point was a historic property within view of the Golden Gate and almost within sight of Meredith's own house. But tucked into a treed box canyon on the edge of Marin, it had a far-away feeling while being easily accessible for city-ites like Meri and her pals.

Originally built as a complex for soldiers serving at nearby Fort Baker, the horseshoe-shaped housing area was ringed with historic structures, but she'd chosen two of their contemporary suites where the women would pair up as roommates. Sleek wood and fireplaces, tall windows and beautiful views, nice living rooms where they could spread out, all fit the bill—a rather hefty one, but well worth it, as she seldom gave herself a treat like this, and her friends were most appreciative.

She'd felt more than a little exhausted and really needed the rest. She'd been working even longer hours than usual so she could spend time with Zack Calvin, an emotional investment she considered to be well worthwhile. But she tried not to make herself too available—so the girlfriend weekend was a good strategy.

But this little trip was more than just tactics. Mer needed to work on her *ikigai*, a favorite Japanese word that stood for everything important: one's reason for being, personal passions, values, vocation . . . a general sense of feeling centered.

Being honest with herself, two things came to mind, both connected to her sister. First, she recalled a conversation about *ikigai* they'd had when they still roomed together in the city. Miranda had not only grasped the concept readily but had embraced it more quickly, even when it caused a disruption that led to her moving away.

The other was her own perennially competitive nature. Really, not *all* the May celebrations could be focused on her sister. Mer had wanted this one for herself.

Mother would throw Miranda a bridal shower next weekend, as though she'd had months instead of days to plan it. Of course, it would be predictably elegant and beautiful. And of course, Mandy would chafe at all the attention and the expensive gifts the guests would bring. The modesty and gratitude she'd express would only further impress Mother's friends. It all stuck in Meredith's craw just a bit.

Why? She'd wondered again. She moaned, hoping the masseuse's deft hands might dig out these pockets of toxicity from her sinews. *Why should it matter so much? I've never been jealous of Mandy!* But if she were honest with herself, she did know what was bothering her so much. It had to do with who deserved what, and it was somehow out of whack.

Dismissing these intrusive thoughts, she'd stepped from the table to the sauna, then to a cold plunge. By then she was floating on air, as were her friends. They all drifted off to their suites to dress in comfortable slacks and sweaters, grabbing pashminas or jackets against the chill fog rolling in as they walked to the dining room.

Sea air riffled their hair and shawls as they strolled, then delightful cooking smells greeted them as they arrived at their table. While they mmmed and ahhed at the scrumptious seafood and sauces, grilled vegetables and freshly baked bread, they went around the table providing work updates, as was their custom.

Part praise, part competition, these friends had been keeping pace since college days, and each was a high-performer in her field. Journalism for Marcille; owner of a string of workout gyms for Chao; travel planning for Valentina; and of course finance for Mer. *I'm so proud of each of them*, Mer thought, swallowing the last of her perfectly seasoned brussels sprouts.

Two hours later, they were back in Meri's suite, where a lovely gas fire warmed the space and where they all decided to share a second bottle of wine. The stories during dinner were a good start, but now that tongues were loosened, the friends began to spin a few more tales.

"Okay, Meri, spill it," Chao demanded. "Who's the mystery man? I haven't seen you out and about with anyone. Where are you hiding him?"

Mer laughed. "He doesn't live here."

Valentina groaned. "Not a long-distance relationship!"

"They're the worst!" Chao agreed.

"Aha!" Marcille pronounced. "That's why you're never around on weekends anymore!"

Mer chuckled again. "Guilty," she admitted. After another sip she added. "He lives in Santa Barbara."

"Oh, my God. That's a hellova commute," Valentina observed.

"At least it's not New York," Marcille said, drawing a laugh from everyone.

Meri decided it was only fair to let her nearest and dearest know at least *something* about the man, but she was careful to omit the part about his having dated her sister first—"dated" being a relative term that didn't strictly apply in this case.

For the next hour, the women took turns lauding or complaining about previous or current boyfriends, all except Marcille, who had to endure teasing about her too-perfect marriage.

"Okay, okay," she finally said. "There is absolutely nothing as good as married sex. Mark my words. One of these days, you'll know exactly what I mean."

A hush fell over the room.

"Seriously?" Chao asked. "That's not a myth?"

"Not if you marry right," Marcille said, her tone dreamy. She glanced over at the birthday girl. "You already know what I mean, don't you?"

Meredith just smiled, holding to a hope she could confirm that status sooner rather than later.

Meredith awakened in her childhood room on the following Friday morning, delighted at the faint aroma of coffee reaching her from under the door.

Despite the much-needed relaxation of her spa weekend, she'd gotten wound up again by another stressful, busy work week. Now, she was here to help with her sister's bridal shower. Just because she was being dutiful didn't mean she couldn't enjoy the comforts of her parents' home.

She stretched, then pushed up against the double layers of pillows to take stock of the room. *Mother's done it again, made the room even lovelier.* Most of the renovations had been done a few years earlier, transforming the cozy space yet again.

This was where Meri used to hide as a child when she didn't feel like answering her mother's calls. "Meri!" Mother's voice would come from downstairs. Keeping silent, Meri would play a game with herself to see how long she could hold out before replying. "Meri!" Would come the call more insistently, her voice pitched a little higher. *Hee-hee,* Meri thought. *I'm still hiding!*

"Meredith Yoko Jones!" Mother would call.

"Uh-oh," Meri would think, realizing she was now in trouble. *Mommy never says my other name! So* the child version of herself would answer at last, explain that she hadn't heard her mother's cries, and watch her parent roll her eyes in disbelief.

It'd been a naughty game, but mostly innocent—unlike the teen years where she'd actually barricaded herself in this room and one time even dared to climb out the window. *Good thing I didn't fall and break my neck, as Dad said I would if I ever tried a stunt like that again.*

Through all its transformations, the walls of her room had been blue—Meri's favorite color then and now. Back in the day, it was powder blue; as a teen, she'd been allowed to have one electric-blue wall. Now the room had found its ultimate expression in Imari blue, that spectacularly sophisticated tone painted onto beautiful pottery in ancient Asia, then adopted by Delft in Europe.

Given Mother's propensity for collecting all things Japanese, it'd been a simple matter for her to populate Meri's room with selections from her collection: ginger pots, plates and platters upended on carved wooden stands, everything from tiny pickle dishes perfect for holding rings, to a giant platter balanced atop a heavy wooden armoire.

To show off these treasures, Mother had assembled a selection of throw pillows in varying shades and fabrics, from pale blue watered taffeta to deep Prussian blue velvet. The duvet currently gracing the bed mimicked an Imari pattern, though sometimes a plain blue was in use, depending on the season and the need for warmth.

But Meri hadn't come to her folks' home to lollygag in bed as if she were on vacation. She'd come to help, and it was time to show up for "work."

Veri Jones gathered their small plates and cups and carried them from the kitchen island to the sink. "I do appreciate your coming early to help, Meri dear." Her thanks were sincere, but she wasn't sure her elder daughter's heart was really in the tasks at hand. "Would you rather I did the napkins and you did the gift table?" she asked.

"No, I can do the napkins, Mother." She paused a moment then added, "I'm just a little distracted."

"Let's have another cup of coffee, shall we? We can go sit in the den and I'll turn on the fire. It's awfully chilly this morning." Veri poured from the still-hot coffee pot into the cups they'd just been using and led the way to the den. After flipping the switch to start the gas logs aglow, she pulled a soft throw over her daughter's lap, then grabbed one herself to sit opposite. "Everything alright at work?" she began.

"Excellent, as a matter of fact," Meri said. "A full complement of clients—a couple of interesting ones, too," she added, sipping at her drink while she looked into the fireplace.

"Wonderful. And how is Zackery?"

Meri seemed to jump a little at the mention of the man, but then a smile tugged at her lips.

"Mm-hmm, I gather that's wonderful as well," Veri observed.

"Oh, Mom, he's . . . it's . . ."

"You don't have to explain, dear. It's still early days, and I imagine you're both figuring out a lot of things. From what I can tell, he's a very fine young man. And you know your father has always thought highly of Joseph."

Meri nodded. "I'm glad. I like Mr. Calvin too, though we don't see much of him. Between Zack's schedule and mine, it's a bit crazy."

"I can imagine," said her mother understandingly. "All that added travel. And will he be coming to the wedding?"

Meri put down her cup. "He will," she said with a sigh.

"Hmm. Still uncomfortable about Mandy?" Veri probed.

"I don't think so, no."

"Good. He needn't be. Our Mandy is over the moon with her astronomer." Veri couldn't help but laugh at her own joke. "I imagine she'll be hearing that quite a lot."

Meri smiled. "I'm sure she will."

"What's the hesitation, Meri dear? Do you not like Cornelius?

Meri paused for a moment. "I . . . like him well enough. I like him for *her*. It's just. . . ."

Veri waited patiently for her daughter to continue, knowing it would be best not to put words in her mouth.

"It's just that it's so unfair!"

Startled, Veri put down her cup. "What's unfair?"

Meri's cheeks began to color. "From the few details Mandy's mentioned, I gather the man is wealthy."

Confused, Veri stared at her daughter. "Well, he has apparently worked hard and come into some very good fortune. Isn't that a good thing?"

Meredith sighed, her eyes squinting as she seemed to consider what to say next. "You know, after that conversation Mandy and I had when she still lived on Russian Hill with me, we did better. We might only have found a few feet of common ground, but we did find it. She convinced me that she really was working hard, and it's been great to see that over the past few years she's had some decent commissions."

"I couldn't agree more. She's both gifted and deserving."

"Spoken like her mother," Meri whined. "But here's the thing. Now she'll never really have to work. And she never has to pay back the loans you've given her. Don't deny it—I know you've helped her."

"Of course we have, from time to time. As a matter of fact, she did pay me back for a large piece of furniture," Veri bragged.

"Aha. Must be that fabulous stair-step wall unit. Your favorite taste: Asian."

Veri felt herself blush. "It was her favorite piece too, and it suited her decor."

Meri sighed. "Okay, she paid for something. But I bet she'll never have to pay back her share of the Russian Hill house. You and Dad will probably give it to her for a wedding present."

Annoyance chipping at the edges of the calm she was determined to maintain, Veri said, "We had not planned that as her gift from us, no."

"I worked myself to the bone to be able to afford that house! And you bailed her out! Once again, she skates by while you fill in the gaps."

Veri sighed and shook her head. "Meredith dear, you've still got things mixed up. You and I have discussed this before—what it's like for artists. I know this from my ballet board work."

"That's different."

"No, it's not," Veri countered.

"Those dancers rehearse till they bleed! They never stop working!"

"And you still maintain that Miranda doesn't? How many paintings a year do you think she turns out?"

"I don't know, ten?"

"It's more like a hundred. But Meredith, dear, that's not the point."

Meri blew out a mouthful of air. "Then what is?"

"She has her path, and you have yours."

Meri had no reply to this, and the two women sat in silence for a long moment.

"One day your father and I will be gone," Veri continued.

"Mother!"

"You girls will have each other. You'll probably both be stuck helping your old parents for a while, then you'll put us to rest and we'll only stare at you from the pictures framed here and there. Then you'll have your memories, and God willing, you'll have one other person with whom you share many of those memories. It'll be reassuring, comforting. But in order for that to happen, you'll have to have a relationship. You'll have to learn to forgive the slights, real or imagined. You'll need to be flexible as you realize she won't do things the same way that you will."

"No need to be so dramatic, Mom. Geez."

Veri could feel water pooling in her eyes.

When Meri looked up, she saw it too. "Mom!"

Veri reached both hands across the coffee table to grasp both of her daughter's. "Be happy for her, Meri. Life is too short for anything less."

Meredith spent the day doing anything and everything her mother asked. By the end of it, the two of them, plus their faithful Pilar had completed everything on the list, except for making the finger sandwiches, which would have to wait for tomorrow, at which point they'd create a three-woman assembly line in the kitchen and turn out egg salad, cucumber, and ham with brie and apple.

On the dining table, Veri's monogrammed napkins were pressed and displayed in a spiral stack; her other Imari plates—the ones that included reds and golds—were ready in three stacks. Waterford crystal stemware stood lined up to receive either white wine or refreshing cranberry spritzers. On the sideboard, Mother's gleaming tea service waited to be filled with boiling water, sugar, milk, or lemon slices. And in the foyer, the guest book lay open with a gold pen.

Veri had decided pizza would do for their dinner tonight, and she'd told Pilar to leave for the day and get some rest. Charles had returned from his golfing hours earlier, to sequester himself with his stamp collection. Sinking into the living room sofa, Veri said, "I don't know about you, Meri dear, but I'm pooped."

"Same."

Charles appeared in the cased opening. "What's for dinner?" he asked.

Both women burst out laughing.

"I was about to ask the same thing," Miranda said.

"Mandy dear!" Veri jumped up, her fatigue temporarily forgotten. "We didn't hear you arrive!"

After hugs all around, Miranda said, "Oh, Mom, everything looks gorgeous!"

"Thank your sister. She worked harder than I did."

"Not really," Meri put in. "It was fun, though. Pizza for dinner in twenty!"

Chapter 3

Miranda enjoyed her bridal shower more than she'd expected to. Her mother had outdone herself with a surfeit of elegant details, to be sure. But it was the spirit of the event that'd touched her heart.

It'd been completely unselfish, a supreme effort to choose everything that Miranda would enjoy and nothing that she wouldn't. Though her mother could sometimes be overbearing, on this occasion she'd held in check any overt sense of trying to control her daughter, speak out of turn, or bully her.

Why? She wondered. *If I had to compare her to any other creature, I'd say she was like a mama bird, eager to push her chick out of the nest to fly on its own.* Yes, it was as though her parent realized all at once that her daughter was now a separate and independent being, capable of making major decisions and of facing the consequences, whatever they might be.

We'll see how long this lasts, she thought ruefully. *Hate to be a cynic, but Mother is still Mother, after all.* In spite of this, she laughed at the bird image and reveled in the lovely hours they'd spent celebrating.

Miranda could hear a couple of voices in the hallway, so she slid out of bed, pulled on her robe and opened her door.

"Oh, good morning, dear," Veri said.

"Hi, kiddo," Meredith added, also still in her robe and pajamas.

"There's breakfast downstairs. And then we should probably get going," Veri pronounced.

Miranda thought for a moment. "Get going?"

"We do have to find your dress today, Mandy."

Mandy and her sister looked at each other and burst out laughing.

"Oh, honestly. You girls!" their mother complained.

"What?" Meri put in. "It's only eight o'clock and none of the stores open till ten."

"Yes, but by the time we eat, get dressed, and get into town, it'll be at least ten."

"I suppose she's right," Mandy said.

Miranda relished the wonderful Sunday French toast prepared by Pilar and spent the hour lavishing her mother with thanks and praise for yesterday's spectacular party. She'd also made a side trip to the kitchen to do the same for Pilar.

After showering and dressing for the day, she knocked on her sister's door.

"Yes!" Meri called out. "Come in!"

"Hey, Mer. I just wanted to thank you for yesterday. I'm thrilled you're my maid of honor. I appreciate all you're doing."

"Took your time telling me about it, didn't you?"

Miranda was stunned at the almost hostile tone. "Sorry?"

Meredith, now dressed as well, sat in the window seat and looked out the mullioned window. Meri turned to face her sister and took both her hands. "I'm glad, Mandy. I really am. I'm also a little jealous. I mean, I am the older sister, and all."

"Older and wiser," Mandy confirmed. "You'll help me, right? I mean if I'm doing something stupid and fail to follow protocol at the wedding. I'm so besotted, it's hard to focus these days."

"Oh, you'll do fine," Meri affirmed.

Miranda sighed. "Hope so." She paused, then asked, "So, um, how are things with Zack?"

Meri's eyes flashed toward her, then glanced away out the window again. Then, if Miranda wasn't mistaken, a smile played at her lips.

"Aha. Good, eh?"

In a tiny voice, Meri said, "It is."

Mandy leaned in and hugged her sister. "Oh, Mer. I'm so glad!"

"Really?" Meri asked.

I so seldom see her soft like this. Miranda thought for a moment, then said, "It would make so much sense if Zack were right for you. Maybe that's why he met me, so he could meet you. How else would it have happened?"

Meri shrugged. "I don't know."

"From what I've seen, he may be complicated, but I think he's also very good. I have the feeling that if anyone can understand him, it'll be you." Miranda paused for a moment. "And there's something else. I think if he plays his cards right and really pays attention, he might be the one to understand you too."

"There does seem to be a wavelength thing," Meredith allowed.

"I wish you every great and good thing with him, Mer."

"Thanks. So. Ready to get a wedding dress?"

Veri stepped out of the family car after their twenty-mile drive through slow traffic from Belvedere, across the Golden Gate and into the city. She was exulting in the notion of having a shopping day with both of her daughters. *When was the last time? When they were both in school? Too long to count.*

"I'm not sure how long we'll be, Mr. Milovich," Veri said to the family's personal driver. "A couple of hours at least."

"Iz not problem, Madame. Please use car phone if you need me earlier."

Her daughters following as they crossed the street, Veri couldn't help but smile. *I imagine we look like a bevy of swans heading for a pond*, she thought, wishing Charles were there so she could share the private joke, since he often referred to his graceful group of pens with himself as the cob.

Neiman Marcus, Veri's second-favorite store in town after Gump's, stood resplendent on its corner. Its famous rotunda, with its stained glass ceiling, gleamed from within. They stood for a moment like a group of tourists, gazing upward. "Let's go inside and see it properly," Veri suggested. A few minutes later, the three women stood at the railing that circled the space, taking turns looking up at the spectacular ceiling and looking down to the floor below.

"You know the history, don't you girls?" Veri asked.

"Not really," Meredith replied. "I don't think I paid much attention when we used to come here years ago."

"Same here," Miranda added, "as far as historical details, though I do have sketches of the stained glass that I did as a girl."

"Well, of course it's Neiman's now, but this used to be a department store called City of Paris," Veri explained.

"See the ship, Meri?" Miranda asked. "It has big white sails."

"So that's what those are," Mer said.

"The ship brought the store's founders from Paris to San Francisco in 1850," Veri added.

"Check out Mom the historian," Meri commented.

"It is gorgeous. Thanks, Mother," Mandy said.

"Perhaps we'll come back here for lunch in a little while," Veri suggested, then she headed off in the direction of the bridal department.

A short while later, Miranda emerged wearing an off-the-shoulder confection made of floral lace and pleated chiffon.

After a moment, Meri piped up with, "I can see the gown, but I can't see Mandy."

Veri glanced at their sales associate, hoping Meredith's brusque tone didn't offend. "You're right, Meri dear. It's not quite simple enough," she agreed.

Miranda disappeared into the dressing room and came out a few moments later wearing a strapless, double-breasted A-line gown. Already, she was tugging at the upper edge of the fabric to keep it from sliding down.

"That's just odd," Meri said, again with a bluntness that made Veri wince. "I mean, it looks like the designer took a white tuxedo jacket, chopped off the sleeves, and added a long skirt."

Mandy burst out laughing, her pitch slightly manic.

Oh dear, Veri realized. *Mandy is reaching the end of her shopping tolerance.* "Why don't you move on to the next one, dear?"

Miranda seemed grateful as she stepped back into the private enclosure, and somewhat distressed when she displayed a third gown, this one sleeveless with a back drape. "Uh . . . this one is nice and simple from the front, but the back . . . feels too fussy for Ragged Point."

"*Point* taken," Meri observed, making a face that had her sister chuckling. "It might work for me, though."

Veri and Mandy darted looks at her.

"I mean, some day! Not now!" Meri insisted.

Veri held a hand to her chest. "Gracious! You gave me a start. Well, let's keep that dress in mind, then. When Mandy takes it off, look at the tag and get the details."

When the girls emerged, she said, "Let's have some lunch."

Veri could see Miranda had calmed down while they savored delightful shrimp Louie salads, but they hadn't yet found the dress.

"I have an idea," Meri said. "In my capacity as maid of honor, may I suggest a little boutique I know?"

"Splendid!" Veri exclaimed. "You have something up your sleeve!"

"Well, it might be something sleeveless."

They all chuckled, Veri paid the bill, and they met Mr. Milovich at the curb. In short order, they were delivered to the iconic Mission District Meri had recommended. On the self-named Mission Street, the car moved past multicolored facades and multicultural murals. Veri spotted the vibrantly decorated front of a theatre at one end of the block and a small hotel at the other. But while it seemed her girls were quite comfortable here, Veri found it a bit unnerving, hardly dressed for a romp through the bohemian neighborhood. *Mandy can scarcely take her eyes off all these wild pops of color on the walls, but Meri seems quite focused on her goal.*

They turned the corner onto Valencia, a tree-lined avenue with outdoor cafés and its own fair share of murals. Sure enough, the architectural style was "mission," derived from early Spanish structures, at least in terms of their exterior features: nicely maintained stucco and tile, with shaped parapet rooflines or dormers on the front elevations.

"Here it is!" Meri called, causing Milovich to pull to the curb.

Veri followed her daughters out of the car, by which time their patient driver had a chance to offer her his hand. "The Artistic Bride," read the sign over a quaint front door done in watercolors Miranda herself might have painted.

"Perfect!" Mandy exclaimed.

Meri, looking smug, led the way inside.

Not exactly couture, Veri thought, *but the place does seem to be a match for my artist daughter.* "Shall we?" she suggested. She headed for one rack, while her daughters each took another. Veri looked closely at a few selections, moving the hangers along the bar as she went.

"Oh!" Mandy said from the next row of gowns.

"Find something?" Meri asked.

"This might be the one," Mandy said.

Veri had already walked toward the main counter. "May we have a dressing room?"

"Oh, absolutely," said a pretty red head. "Follow me."

A moment later, Veri found herself in a surprisingly spacious area set aside for private fashion shows, complete with a three-paneled mirror and a private changing room. It wasn't long before Miranda appeared on the small platform, draped in a creamy satin gown that outlined her shapely waist, clung to her slender hips, and offered a V in both front and back revealing just enough skin to make her groom's mouth water.

"Oh, my," Veri uttered.

"Yes, yes, yes," Meri agreed.

Mandy herself was speechless, her eyes wide and round.

"Brilliant, Meri dear," Veri pronounced. "You get the maid of honor prize."

Meredith had basked in that moment of parental appreciation last weekend. Now, she stood to get a fresh cup of coffee, then returned to her desk. When she wasn't reviewing recent events, she had successfully settled her nerves by plunging into work, the one thing she could always count on, pun intended.

It was a math thing and always had been for her. Good at numbers, all the way through private school and college, she'd reveled in every aspect of the subject from arithmetic to calculus.

Of course, to make a career of it, one had to add chariness, because without scrupulous integrity, the numbers wouldn't work, nor would the trustworthiness allow for a pristine reputation.

Bottom line, what was investing but simple arithmetic? One had to be able to add, subtract, multiply, and divide. That's how she calculated returns, profit margins, and dividend yields. Figuring out price-to-earnings ratios wasn't much more complex. Then there was the comparing and contrasting of percentages. Next there was compounding, which was really just algebra. Linear algebra was dealing with multiple variables. Differential calculus dealt with rates of change.

Meredith could easily stay in her head for hours at a time, running mathematical scenarios and generating reports. She'd also learned, however, that dazzling clients with fancy print-outs didn't necessarily create trust. There was another whole aspect to her job, and it lay in the realm of psychology, and even sometimes veered into the world of acting—not to hoodwink but to convey the strength and calm she herself didn't always feel.

I better start feeling it right now, because I want to talk to Zack later. He'd be at work now, so she'd leave him a quick voice mail, promising to call him right about the time the work day ended. Just the thought of him increased her heart rate, but she told herself again to play it cool.

Cool, cool, cool, kiddo. You can do it.

Could she though? When it came to Zack Calvin, she wasn't so sure. Dating for her was usually a game, one she knew well how to play. Flirt outrageously, hint at sex, promise nothing. That kept a man on his back foot, ready to spring forward but not sure he should. That was the ticket, keeping a guy off balance.

But with Zack, it was more often she herself who felt her world could tilt at a moment's notice. All he had to do was train those baby blues on her and she could feel her cool reserve begin melting, like a scoop of ice cream plopped onto a hot sidewalk.

God, she couldn't even think of a sophisticated metaphor but was reduced to a childish image. Yet, she was no child and neither was he. He was a grown man with a deep center of gravity, and she was in danger of sinking right to the bottom of this emotional ocean in which they found themselves.

Their developing relationship had had two starts, in a way, adding a complexity to their situation. He'd been dating her sister. Mer had heard bits and pieces about this guy but few details. One day while visiting her sister, Mer had answered the phone. *Why did I do that? Maybe it was fate.*

Mer had flirted with the disembodied voice on the other end of the line, playing that game she enjoyed. What she hadn't expected was how vividly he'd responded, almost to the point of saying he'd drive right over. *Oh no! He can't do that! This must be the guy Mandy's been dating, and he thinks I'm her!* Mer had disengaged from the call as quickly as possible, but it'd left her with two things: a feeling of guilt and a wicked curiosity bordering on longing to reconnect with that man who'd been able to awaken all her senses in one short phone call.

She'd been willing to let the memory of the call drift off to become a fantasy, one she'd never act upon. Until she decided she had to attend her sister's big art show, her first in this town of Milford-Haven where she'd moved.

Mer shouldn't have been surprised that the telephone man was there at the art show too. In the intervening weeks, he'd obviously figured out he'd gotten his wires crossed—or had them crossed *for* him. And there the two of them stood, formally introduced at last and confronted with the very voices they'd heard over the phone lines.

Even if I hadn't recognized his voice the moment he spoke, I would already have been riveted to the spot by those eyes and by his vivid presence. Lean but muscular, handsome as a model, yet shadowed with some sort of brooding discontent, the man had danger written all over him—danger to *her* if to no one else. As if that weren't enough, he angled for a private moment with her and challenged her as though to a dual. "That was *you* on the phone, wasn't it?" He'd boldly asked.

Well, what was a woman to do? Of course, she'd challenged him right back later that same night. She'd asked if he'd like to take a moonlight drive. Once alone with him in his car, she'd asked him point blank whether he'd be interested in being with a woman like her.

I mean, why fool around? If this guy wanted to play the game with her, fair enough. But knowing, now, who he was, what position he held professionally and socially, realizing he'd probably played the field quite enough to know his way around both the board room and the bedroom, it was time to put up or shut up. Suddenly, she'd felt she had no more time to waste. She needed to know whether he felt the same and might be willing to really give things a try.

Meredith thought back to their first night. Well, their first night of physical intimacy. The emotional intimacy had come first. That'd started the very evening they'd actually met in person for the first time.

It'd been after her sister's art show in Milford-Haven. Zack had started it, by confronting her head-on. *Talk about throwing down the gauntlet. I had no choice to admit it. And I wasn't about to back down, either!*

She smiled, remembering how the energy crackled between them. But they were in the middle of a big social occasion, both of them with family members present, and various other important players. So she'd waited for him at the motel where most of them were staying. When he arrived, she climbed into his car. *How did I ever have the nerve? But of course, I did. I couldn't have stood not knowing for one more hour.*

He took her for that moonlit drive and parked at a turnout overlooking the ocean. "Would you ever want to date someone like me?" She'd been brazen as hell, but courageous too.

After commenting that she didn't pull any punches, he said, yes, he would.

So they talked and talked. After that, they talked on the phone nearly every night, laughing, telling stories, flirting. She'd invited him to San Francisco. He'd invited her to Santa Barbara. But there were memories in both those places, so they'd decided to meet in the middle. He'd found them a beautiful cottage for rent in Avila Beach and booked it for two nights.

She'd arrived first, tired from the long drive. She'd brought nothing but some bottled water for the kitchen, and only one change of clothes, some walking shoes, and a bathing suit. As it turned out, she'd only needed the water.

Nervous as hell, she'd waited for him in the living room. When he arrived, she rose and turned to face him. They stared at one another, pulses racing. Then he'd come for her, grabbing her in a powerful embrace. She didn't remember how they got upstairs to the bedroom, but she laughed later at the clothes strewn along the way and across the floor.

He'd taken her fast, which was just what she wanted. But her own reaction surprised the hell out of her. *I started crying. And I never cry!*

"Did I hurt you?" he'd asked. "I'm sorry! I should have been more gentle. I just got so carried away—"

She'd shushed him and crawled into his arms. He had done nothing wrong. He'd done everything right, offered her the full spectrum from passion to patience, from power to tenderness. And he'd done all that in one night.

Meredith had the inescapable feeling that she'd never want anyone again as much as she wanted Zack Calvin.

That had been the second start to their relationship—the real one. So now, here they were months later, seeing each other as often as they could, given that they lived in two different cities. As though they had a long, resilient cord connecting them that stretched taut when they were apart and yanked them back together, the current structure included frustration but also a longing that led to some very exciting times when they could finally be in person.

But this arrangement was hardly sustainable. She wanted to just trust the process, feel confident that she intrigued him enough that he'd be the first to suggest ways to close the gap. But would he? Would it ultimately be up to her to think of some ingenious way to rearrange her life?

That brought another set of worries. What if she moved herself —lock, stock, and barrel—to Santa Barbara and then their relationship didn't work out? Would she want to live there if she didn't occupy the top position in his heart, his bed, and his life? *No. If I have to go back to being alone, I'd rather be in San Francisco where I have my own support system.*

For now, she'd have to continue to play the game. She reminded herself, though, that she was playing for keeps.

Chapter 4

Meredith sat with her feet up, alternately gazing out her two living room windows as the lights of San Francisco twinkled. The diamonds and rubies of head-and-tail lights streamed across both the Golden Gate and the Bay bridges in the distance, and between them, a cozy gas fire kept her feet warm against the chill fog of the season.

She'd put in another long Friday at her office, then come home for a tasty bowl of ramen. Now she nursed a Nespresso cappuccino and tried to keep at bay the loneliness that was a new arrival in her life, thanks to Zack. With plans to spend the long Memorial holiday together, they'd opted to have this one to themselves to catch up on their own things. But she missed him.

She could feel herself becoming more vulnerable. At first it'd ticked her off. She'd worked so hard for so many years not to be. It'd been the only way forward in her career, where men tended to challenge her to duels, as they would with any of the other boys.

Either that or they made incorrect assumptions about her compe-
tence or her drive. She handled all that quite well these days, thank
you very much.

Meanwhile, in the personal romance department, the only time
she'd opened her doors wide enough to succumb to the wiles of a
handsome, dynamic man had turned disastrous. After his protracted
and successful pursuit, she'd gotten herself into big trouble. Un-
beknownst to her, the man had been married, as the wife had
announced in no uncertain terms by confronting her in her own
office.

That had been infuriating, humiliating, and even potentially
dangerous legally. She and her mentor had called in the legal guns
and their investigators to find out whether the couple had been
running a scam. Mer had never learned the results of that inquiry
because she didn't want to know. She just wanted to steer clear,
which is exactly what she'd done.

Now, however, she actually had a man of her own, and the
vulnerability was something that cut both ways. She could see that
he cared, perhaps even as much as she did. But they were doing
their best to take it slow, that being a relative term.

She'd been feeling the shift gradually, from solitary self-
reliance to companionship, or to companionability, she corrected.
She was moving from a stolid certainty that no one could or would
understand her, to a startling realization that she made sense to
someone else. He saw through her defenses and called her out on
her manipulations. Well, he questioned some of the workplace
maneuvers she mentioned in a way that was diplomatic, but stunningly insightful. *I can't put anything over on him. I never could,
right from the start.*

He'd laughed and whistled when she'd revealed her real estate scheme, the one she had kept secret from her sister and future brother-in-law. Of course, that really hadn't worked, because Cornelius had found out and confronted her. But Zack had warned her first that hoodwinking her own sister might come back to bite her. Ultimately, though, he'd said, "Don't let me get on your bad side," with a rather admiring glint in his eye.

She didn't really want to be vulnerable. Except with him, God help her, she did.

Meredith had taken a big plunge into the vulnerability pool one weekend they'd spent again at their little rental in Avila.

She'd felt it important to have a "cards on the table" session. Most of the time, a liaison didn't last long enough or go deep enough to make this kind of conversation necessary. But she and Zack had started with a secret and she didn't want any more of them.

So here it was. Meri had reveled in one of their spectacular love-making episodes, then gathered plates of fruit and cheese they could enjoy in bed. While sipping sparkling water and feeding him some grapes, she'd paused to pull the covers up a bit higher, then pulled back the heritage curtain.

She had a more complicated background than what appeared on the surface of things. She'd never known the woman who'd given birth to her, she explained, and never would. Mariko Imaizumi had married Charles Jones in some sort of clandestine ceremony in an official office in Tokyo. Mariko's disapproving parents had offered no support, not even when the couple's infant came along.

"Your . . . your mother was Japanese?" Zack asked.

Meredith feigned nonchalance, but inside she felt the distant rumble of an earthquake. *Is this it? The end of our relationship?*

"That's fascinating," Zack said. "And what about your . . . your other mother?"

"Veronica. Veri. Mom. The only mother I've ever known, the woman who raised me."

"And she loves you? You love her?"

This is what he's asking, about love. "Yes, she does. Absolutely. We're close actually. I mean, she annoys me in the way a good mother does. And she understands me, supports me. So does Dad."

"God, I'm happy for you to have that. Not everyone does." Zack pulled her close. "Okay, so tell me the rest. So your dad was living in Japan?

"Yes."

"And he gets divorced, leaves Japan?"

"No, my birth mother died."

"Oh. Sorry."

"From what they've told me, my parents that is, it was a bad situation anyway. First of all, Mariko's parents hated the idea that their daughter had married a barbarian, and one with blue eyes, no less. All they could talk about was that maybe the baby would have the dreaded blue eyes. And then, I did."

He turned her head to gaze into those orbs. "You do. The most incredible blue I've ever seen."

She blinked, touched beyond words.

"So," he continued. "Your own grandparents didn't. . . ."

"They didn't accept me, wanted nothing to do with me, and were probably just as happy that their only daughter died, and the shame with her."

"That's about the most heartless thing I've ever heard."

But Charles Jones had later found happiness with Veronica Merit, who in turn had been the mother who reared Meredith.

Meri had the long limbs and high cheekbones of her Caucasian ancestry, along with the blue eyes that left no question in anyone's mind. When people met the Jones family, they saw two tall slender daughters with dark hair and brightly colored eyes, which matched the parental Joneses quite closely.

"So, now that you know, is it weird ?"

"Is what weird?"

"That I'm Asian. Part Japanese."

"Uh, only if you think it's weird that I'm half Scottish."

She burst out laughing. "Oh, yeah, that'd be a real deal breaker," she commented.

"Meri," he said, touching her face, "you're very special to me. You already know you are. Whatever has made you who you are, how you are, I'm fascinated, okay? I wouldn't have guessed the Asian heritage. But I did always know you were exotic and way out of my league."

That comment had led very smoothly to their next round of intimacies in their cozy getaway place.

Zack felt his usual sense of satisfaction at the end of a busy Friday, had enjoyed dinner at home with his dad, and then begged off early to spend the rest of his evening in his cottage. Though he missed his beautiful companion, he wanted the time to reflect, sort through his feelings, check his impulses.

Right now his impulse was to catch a flight for San Francisco so he could lose himself in bed with Meredith. But he'd spent enough of his life succumbing to that kind of impelling force without considering its implications. She deserved better. So did he, he was finally beginning to realize.

That's not to say sex wasn't a key component of any relationship he hoped to have. It'd been decent with all the women he'd dated. It'd been great with Cynthia. But with Mer, it was off the charts.

Is it the emotional connection? That's what women always claimed and men usually denied. He figured the only way he'd know for sure was to continue the journey with her.

He thought back to their first time in bed. They'd wanted each other for weeks, but because of their lives' complexities, they'd managed to keep the brakes on, more or less, until that night in their rented seaside condo.

Afterward, he lay on his back, panting, his heart beating so fast he could hardly catch his breath. *Yeah. Breathtaking. That's how I'd describe being with Meredith.* He remembered laying still, splayed on the sheets, wishing the ceiling fan were spinning.

His breath began to slow, his heart rate return to normal, while images and sensations continued to flash through his mind. The fierce passion in her eyes, the lithe strength in her limbs, the plunge, the deep acceptance of being inside her.

Worth the wait. Her beauty and spontaneity, the intensity of their connection. *And here I thought I'd already experienced all of that. Not really. Not until her.*

When his own breathing quieted enough to hear, he realized Meredith was crying. He rolled toward her, cradled her, drew covers up over their shoulders. "Did I hurt you?" he asked quietly. "I'm sorry! I should have been more gentle. I just got so carried away—"

She put a finger to his lips. "Shh," she interrupted. "You were perfect. That's why I'm crying."

Baffled, he nevertheless smiled and knew enough to just hold her till the tears abated.

Zack hadn't shared this with Meredith yet, but he knew dating her was causing a profound stir in his psyche and knew he'd wanted to talk with someone about it.

He returned to the offices of the wonderful Dr. Rosenbaum, whom he'd seen a couple of years earlier. He'd shared a review of his relationships. He'd dated Cynthia for quite a while . . . though he doubted his heart was ever really in it. Though beautiful and vivacious, Cynthia had also been needy both emotionally and financially, a toxic blend that had led to unintended harm.

Then he'd dated Miranda—or at least made some attempt to date her—a relationship that was never consummated, thank goodness.

When he met Meredith, he'd had to assure her he was free and clear of all previous entanglements before she'd agree to see him. He respected that boundary she'd set. He'd agreed she was right.

With his insightful therapist, he'd been able to be honest, acknowledging there were still ghosts in the room. The doctor'd asked, why? Because Zack still carried guilt about both those relationships, not least because they had overlapped.

This in turn revealed a worry moving deep in the waters of his consciousness, an angst about his own worthiness, and a vague sense that he didn't belong, hadn't earned his place in the world, something that likely traced from what had been his long-forgotten adoption.

But something bright and hopeful had also surfaced. Life was for the living. He had an opportunity with this woman that might not come again. And even if he'd wanted to turn away from the powerful attraction that'd drawn them together, he doubted he could have suppressed it for long.

Zack thought back to that second weekend at Avila, where by then he and Meredith felt comfortable enough to feel they shared a vacation home.

She'd revealed her Asian heritage—something he found endlessly fascinating. He'd left Meredith a note while she napped, taken off for run down the beach, then come home and taken a shower.

All during his run he kept thinking about what she'd shared. A complex childhood, she'd said. But his was no less so. He had accepted Meri's trust in him as a precious gift. Could he do less?

Turnabout is fair play. It was his turn to reveal what he could about his own background. But there was more. They hadn't gotten to the point of discussing previous relationships yet. *Is this the moment?* Despite his wish to be honest, for the most part, he already had been.

No doubt Meri had been involved with others before him. Did he really want to know? And did he want to mention anything about Cynthia to her? That seemed a distant memory now. He cherished this private time with Mer and hated the idea of bringing others into it.

After he dressed, Mer took a turn showering. Zack suggested they walk down the street to a little bistro they'd discovered. They enjoyed an early evening meal of fish and chips with coleslaw, then strolled back to their condo.

Though he enjoyed the meal, the walk, and certainly the company, he kept thinking it was his turn to reveal some complexities of his own.

Zack had felt the need for something sweet and had known Mer'd brought a small stash of cookies to their condo. He'd also wanted the cozy setting of their bedroom for this next conversation, so they'd pulled on comfy sweats to sit cross-legged on the covers, doing their best not to let crumbs scatter.

"Last Christmas, I received an unusual letter," he began.

Meredith sat in utter silence, her eyes on his.

"It was from my mother."

"But I thought—"

"You're right. She's been gone a long time. But she'd left—"

"—a letter for you. Oh, my goodness," Mer said quietly.

"Yeah. It was sweet. It was sad, of course, her goodbye message, wishing me a good life."

Water began to pool in Mer's eyes.

"But also, she came clean about the adoption."

"What?"

"I'm adopted," Zack said. "I think I'd known for a long time, but no one had ever spoken about it."

Meredith reached for a cookie and began to chomp.

"Dad had always known, of course. So had James. I mean, in a way, he was my surrogate mother." Zack huffed a small laugh. "Dad was busy working, James was always there for me."

"Okay," Mer said, after taking a sip of water from her bedside bottle. "What happened?"

"They tried, my parents. Joseph and Joan, that is. They tried to have a kid. When they couldn't, Joan wanted to adopt. In those days, all of this was handled in secrecy."

"Oh, tell me about it."

"Yeah, you already know. But in this case, it wasn't a multi-cultural taboo, just a cultural one. The idea was the child wouldn't bond properly if a thread of lineage was left dangling."

Mer considered for a moment, then asked, "So, do you know who your birth parents were? Or rather, are? Have you ever researched it?"

"No. No clue. I mean, presumably they gave me up for a reason. And I couldn't have a more devoted dad. So why hunt trouble?"

Mer sighed. "I don't know. I've asked myself the same. Would I want to go searching around in Japan for a family who didn't want me? Like you, I've got people who do love me."

Zack felt himself smile. "What's not to love?" he asked. "Anyway, I just wanted you to know."

"Curiouser and curiouser," she said.

"How so, Alice?"

She chuckled. "Parallel worlds."

Part II

Hearth & Home

"Have nothing in your house that you do not know
to be useful, or believe to be beautiful."
– *William Morris*

"Home is the place where, when you have to go there,
they have to take you in."
– *Robert Frost*

Chapter 5

Miranda awoke in a cuddle. Curled on her side in the dim pre-dawn, she felt the warm fur of her cat curled against her stomach and the comforting thighs of her fiancé pressing against the backs of her knees. This is perfection, she thought, reaching around to run her palm down the length of manly leg.

Cornelius made a soft grunting sound, which made her offer a soft moan, which then inspired Shadow to utter a "Meh," as if completing a domestic chorus.

Miranda chuckled to herself, enjoying the little rustle that rippled through her family and feeling utterly pleased that her nearest and dearest, Shadow and Cornelius, had adopted one another as though born to be together.

Born to be together. That's exactly how she felt about herself and her soon-to-be-husband, her beloved, her intended, her one and only.

Time for them had become fluid. It seemed it had taken forever to find each other, but now it felt as though they'd always been together. Yet, with multiple projects—their upcoming wedding among them—it seemed they were always busy, which made this time together all the more precious.

She lay there hoping for another few minutes of sleep, but the bright light of dawn crested over the edge of the high bedroom windows, and her eyes blinked open. Rolling carefully to her other side, she freed her arm from the covers and had to look again at the shiny ring sparkling on her hand, then saw where sunlight was shining onto the objects in the bedroom she now shared with him. Life itself seemed shiny and new. She'd been smiling so much since last March, she was surprised her jaw didn't have a perpetual ache.

She spent another moment looking at his ruggedly handsome face, now slightly shadowed with his overnight whiskers. *Like a charcoal drawing*, she thought. She was tempted to grab her sketch pad and capture the image while he slept but could already see he was stirring, and their day was about to begin.

With summer soon to arrive, one thing didn't seem so shiny: the chaos of their home. Though not even this could dim her joy, she did recognize that the list of tasks seemed to grow longer rather than shorter.

They would be moving, but that was at least a year away. Cornelius had purchased the land where their new home was being renovated. But until that rather huge project was completed, they'd combined household belongings in her rental. He'd had a rental of his own in northern California, near his NASA Ames job. But since he'd made arrangements to continue working remotely, he'd been able to move back to Milford-Haven, where he'd grown up.

This house had worked perfectly for her when she lived here alone. A large enough master suite downstairs; an open concept main floor with a separate artist's studio for her. But Cornelius had clothes, furniture, books, more books, lots more books, equipment, and a desk. All of this had been crammed into her space, but this was hardly satisfactory.

Just yesterday, they'd had the brilliant idea to ask Miranda's landlord whether they might also rent the adjacent house. Actually, the two "houses" were connected with a common wall, but the two dwellings were offset, which provided more privacy for each. The next-door space was intended for short-term rental but had been nearly always empty as long as Miranda had lived here, so she didn't think it'd be a problem to rent it themselves. Then Cornelius could have ample office space; they'd have room for guests; and Cornelius could even host some of his colleagues, should they need to meet in person. All in all, it seemed ideal.

Cornelius had offered to approach the landlord, and she appreciated that he'd volunteered to take on a task she didn't relish herself. To what she knew would already be a busy day for him, he'd added one more thing.

Cornelius kissed Miranda and sped out the door that led into the garage.

It's not that he'd wanted to hurry their kiss. He just knew if he didn't, he wouldn't get out the door at all or at least not until much later. As he closed the door, he could still hear her giggling, still taste her. He chuffed out a laugh and hit the garage opener, then moved to his Durango, which took up far too much room in the space it now shared with her Mustang. *All the more reason to get on with today's task.*

Before leaving, he'd surveyed again the jumble he'd made of her previously tidy great room. Her dining table had disappeared under his stacks of file folders, desk lamp, computer tower, disk drives, reference books, and whatever else he'd deemed indispensable and not suitable for storage.

The lovely mural she'd painted on the one large wall was now mostly obscured behind several low shelving units he'd shoved into the room. She'd created a scene that extended the real one visible through her sliding glass doors, a style that'd become a signature for her. He'd even watched her create one in Lompoc last spring.

Through her mostly glass wall, the view extended through a thick stand of pines and down to the ocean. Her mural did the same, but it offered a night-time view. To it, she'd added a huge, hovering moon in burnished gold, with pale silvered walls alternating between dark tree trunks. The ocean-horizon continued at the same level that the real one did.

"Why did you paint the moon?" He remembered asking her one evening when he'd been invited over for dinner.

"Why? Oh, I love the moon. I've painted it scores of times. I thought about that wall for a long time, and one day I knew it would be right here."

"I did my thesis on the moon," he offered. He'd seen a moment of confusion flash through her eyes. "No," he continued, laughing. "Not *on* the moon, but *on,* or *about the moon.*"

"Oh!"

"I'm a spaceman, but not that kind of spaceman."

They'd had a wonderful laugh about it, which recurred through dinner and beyond.

"There's a branch of study in astronomy called selenography, mapping the moon's topography," he explained.

"Well, we both love the moon," she'd said softly while they snuggled on her couch. Another sweet memory with this woman he now loved so much. *That mural . . . another in a long series of signs that our lives were already connected.*

During his reverie he'd driven the ten minutes to his parents' home, where the aromas of a wonderful breakfast greeted him. They sat cozily at the kitchen table, enjoying his mother's signature French toast with warmed syrup and fresh berries. He ate too much, as he usually did when she served this dish, and they continued catching up on their news while the meal concluded over extra cups of coffee.

They'd been delighted with the progress he and Miranda were making, though his mother had seemed just a tad anxious for their wedding date to arrive. She'd stopped short of saying the two fiancés were "living in sin," but he felt a frisson of disapproval.

Accordingly, he'd provided a few more details about their ceremony and asked his mother to take charge of the rehearsal dinner arrangements. That had caused a charming flutter of joy, and with her eyes brimming, she'd said enthusiastically, "'Leave it with me."

He'd then planned to spend an hour or two in his old room. True, he wanted to use his desktop computer to take care a few things. But he also wanted to be on the premises long enough that if either parent actually needed help with something, they could ask without hesitation. He'd noticed lately that they claimed they "didn't want to bother" him. But one of the great things about moving back to Milford-Haven was that they could call on him for projects large and small, even something as trivial as reaching to a high shelf.

Once at the desk in his old room, Cornelius dug into his long list of emails, deleting immediately those he knew were junk. Then he went back through the list and replied as needed. In particular, he was looking for a response from Miranda's landlord, hoping it would be a simple matter to rent the next door unit as well. He was prepared to negotiate and to be generous. He and his bride-to-be had enough on their plates right now without taking on any sort of hassle over their accommodations.

"Ah," he exclaimed aloud when he saw that a reply had indeed arrived. But his relief was soon replaced with confusion.

> To: Dr. Cornelius Smith <csmith@seti.org>
> From: Beth Weisner <eweisner@BluewaterRealty.com>
> Dear Mr. Smith,
> We appreciate your interest in 29 Pine Ridge, Unit B. However, as we no longer own the property, we refer you to the new owner whose information follows:
> M. Jones
> 2060 Jones Street, San Francisco CA
> Should you have any further questions, we will do our best to answer them.
> Yours Truly, Elizabeth Weisner

Cornelius ran fingers through his hair. "Oh, for heavens sake," he muttered. "They've got this all screwed up. That's Miranda's old address." Too frustrated to try sorting this out via email, he glanced at the bottom of the message, picked up his parents' extension phone and dialed the numb er listed below the email's signature.

"Blue Water Realty," a receptionist said.

"Yes, may I speak with Ms. Weisner, please?"

"I'll see if she's available," the woman said. But then a moment later, another voice chimed, "Beth Weisner. How may I help you?"

"Ms. Weisner, this is Dr. Smith. I'm interested in renting one of your properties."

"Marvelous! Here in San Luis Obispo?"

"Just up the coast actually. But there seems to be some confusion. Your email said it was owned by the current renter. I thought we'd get to the bottom of the confusion more quickly by phone."

"Oh . . . you received an email from me?"

"I did. Dated last week, reference number 1439."

"That is so helpful!" She said in an obsequious tone. "Let me just look that up."

She placed him on hold while Cornelius ground his teeth to the saccharine sound. Then she was back.

"No confusion, Dr. Smith. We sold that property to M. Jones, who resides in San—"

"No, she doesn't."

"I beg your pardon?"

"M. Jones does not reside in San Francisco. Not any more. She is the tenant in the other side of the property I'm trying to rent. M. Jones is my fiancée and—"

"Congratulations!"

"Thank you. But you see my point, I do know where my fiancée resides. And now that there are two of us at said residence, we need room to expand. Thus, the desire to rent the second unit, which has remained mostly empty for the past few years."

"My, this does sound confusing," the woman admitted.

He overheard some paper rustling and then she said, "Hmm, yes, I see the most recent renter was M. Jones. But that makes perfect sense. She liked living there and decided to buy it."

"But she didn't."

"She didn't like it? But—"

"No, she *does* like it. But she didn't buy it. She's still paying rent."

More papers rustled.

"Oh, yes, I see in the files that the new owner requested the renter's checks continue to be sent to us, then forwarded. Probably because she's in the middle of moving."

"Let me get this straight," Cornelius said, keeping his tone as slow and deliberate as if he were speaking to a ten year old. "You are receiving checks from M. Jones. And you are sending these checks to M. Jones at a San Francisco address. Do I have that right?"

"Yes, sir. Makes perfect sense, doesn't it?"

"Uh, not to me. Why would M. Jones write checks to M. Jones?"

"To create a transactional paper trail."

"That sounds . . . Never mind how it sounds. Let's try something else. Do you have the actual documents in front of you? The deed for example?"

"No, we wouldn't have the deed. That would be with the owner."

Cornelius wiped a hand down his face in frustration. "Okay, do you have the rental agreement?"

"Probably not, since we're no longer the owners. But maybe there's a copy of the old one. Let me check."

Suddenly, the irritating hold music was once again being piped through the phone, and Cornelius had to press his lips together so as not to slam down the receiver. But while it played, a possibility was starting to form in his mind, one about which he really hoped he was wrong.

"Dr. Smith?"

"Yes," he answered through clenched teeth.

"I did find the old agreement."

"And the name on it?"

"M. Jones."

"There's no first name?"

"There is. It's Miranda."

"Excellent. She is the tenant, who is still paying rent, and she is my fiancée."

"So then everything is clear, yes?" Ms. Weisner said brightly.

"Possibly," he allowed. "Let's just research one more name."

"And what name would that be?" The woman's tone revealed her utter confusion.

"The name of the new owner."

"But . . . as I've explained the new owner is M. Jones."

"Yes, but what I'd like to confirm is her first name."

"Well, I don't see how her name could change from one document to another, but fine, in the interest of putting this matter to rest, I will see if I can find the original sales agreement."

Paper rustled, and he heard the distinct sound of a file folder being slammed down on the desk. Then the woman's voice said, "Uhhhh. . ."

"Yes?"

"Well, the name on the sales agreement is actually Meredith Jones. Might that be a middle name, or a legal name, or—"

"No, it's a first name. But it's the first name of a different person."

"But how—"

"I'm sorry, Ms. Weisner. It seems someone has. . . well, never mind. I have the information I needed, and I'll take it from here."

"Dr, Smith?"

He heard her say his name when the receiver was already halfway back to its cradle. "Yes?"

"I apologize for the confusion! Goodness, I'm not quite sure how that happened here, but I can assure you all these papers are in order legally."

"Oh, I'm sure they are. Thank you for your help."

This time he hung up without further hesitation.

Chapter 6

Miranda was still giggling as she watched Cornelius' Durango drive away. *That man,* she thought with a sigh. She headed to the kitchen to make herself a cup of tea, then took a breath, doing her best to take advantage of being on her own for a few hours to focus on her work.

She stepped into her studio, followed closely by Shadow, who promptly leapt onto the wide desk.

"Want to work with me?" Miranda asked.

"Rrrrow," the cat answered, rolling the consonant sound in her throat.

"Good," Miranda confirmed. "Have a seat."

Shadow tiptoed over to the window, performed a careful pandiculation, surveyed the outdoor scene replete with her favorite tree, then chose a sunny spot on the desk and curled herself into it, wedged between a book end and a ceramic mug, disturbing neither.

Miranda opened her HandBook notebook, the one labeled CAT for Commissioned Art Tracking to review current projects, always her favorite way to begin a work week. Though her projects always inspired her, lately she'd found herself drifting off into romantic reveries. One moment of remembering Cornelius' arms around her and she would feel herself start to melt from the inside out. Desire would rise like heat from a hidden flame, and she would feel her heart thudding, her face flushing. Then her vivid imagination would begin painting images to rival Renoir.

"Whew, kitty, is it hot in here?"

"Meh," the cat scolded.

Miranda cleared her throat and returned her gaze to the notebook, where she quickly reviewed her current and upcoming jobs, which included a very exciting commission and teaching session in Alaska.

But in addition to her work-for-hire, there was the personal project she wanted to start. She'd asked Cornelius what he wanted for his wedding present. She'd known what he'd say, and they said it simultaneously: a painting. Accordingly, she'd been thinking about this awake and asleep for weeks now. And with the wedding only a month away, she had no time to waste.

One image that'd been coming to her was an ocean-and-landscape with a full moon hovering. Its golden light would limn the escarpment, trees, and ripples below. *That'd be similar to the mural I did here, which I know he likes. But that new work would belong upstairs, a wide piece hanging over the bed.* She'd have time to complete that one later.

Meanwhile, there was this immediate task, and as if that weren't pressure enough, he had already chosen the spot where the painting would hang in their new home. It was a tall, narrow space, so she wouldn't be able to create a landscape piece—literally the definition of the shape. Usually her only vertical pieces were the small ones that Zelda arranged to have made into postcards.

The new painting would have to be vertical, and large, as it would hang in their foyer, itself a somewhat unusual fan-shaped space. A door off the foyer would lead up the spiral staircase to their bedroom, and a wide opening would lead to their living room. The new piece would hang in between, welcoming one and all.

So it wouldn't hang in a public location, yet she wanted it to hold a private message. Ideally that meant she wanted a message that would work for friends and family but also contain a message only he could decipher.

As yet, no clear idea had surfaced, except one: she wanted it to include a heart. Whether it would be subtle or obvious, she didn't yet know. Now she pulled out another notebook and reviewed some of her recent sketches. This was where her intuitive mind would often show itself, offering guidance to which her logic had no access.

She'd lately become intrigued by large window-like holes in offshore rocks known as sea stacks. These coastal formations were natural sculptures to her artist's eye, colossal pillars of rock carved by forces of wind and water, having started as volcanic out-croppings along faultlines.

Indeed, just a few miles farther south stood a related cordillera of geological marvels with Morro Rock rising from the ocean as the first of the Nine Sisters, though these volcanic mountains were not permeated with any holes.

She returned to considering the window rocks and inspected her drawings more closely, noticing there was usually an object visible through the hole: a tree, a house, a flower.

A realization struck her. She'd have had to be in exactly the right position in order for that object to be visible through the hole. One step right or left, and nothing would be in the frame offered by the drilled-out rock. And that's what had created the fascination, pulling the gaze into the image.

She remembered where she'd done the first sketch. She'd been hiking the coastal trail, standing on one promontory, looking at the next one. In the distance, a boat had crossed the water, passing for a moment through the rock-window.

The idea caught her attention, so she started looking for other examples. Up the coast stood the Piedras Blancas lighthouse, the structure and the surrounding rocks glistening white. And at a different location, she knew there was a rock standing out from shore, washed and pummeled by the Pacific. From most perches along the shore, the rock and the lighthouse were interesting but separate elements.

But would there be a vantage point where the lighthouse might be visible through the hole in the rock? She'd have to hike a somewhat treacherous trail along the rocky coastline to discover whether or not that might be true. But in her imagination, she could see the possibility.

Alignment. That's the underlying idea.

Her perspective, the rock, and the lighthouse would all have to be aligned in order to be visible. Miranda sat back, her eyes widening. She could see the painting now and began to sketch the image. The lighthouse would be quite small in the distance, the rock appearing fairly large in the middle distance. Perhaps the image would include a path—similar to the ones she hiked—as though the viewer had paused during a walk to notice the unusual sight.

Lighthouse . . . that always stands for guidance, illumination. But what does the hole signify? An opening, true but. . . .

The hole—why not make it heart-shaped?

That would mean that it's only from the heart perspective that alignment allows you to see the guidance you need.

The image presented it in her mind as clearly as a photograph, its interpretation printing out as a line of text.

Now she knew exactly what her wedding present painting for Cornelius would be.

Cornelius sat still for a long moment after concluding his call with Ms. Weisner.

He considered his next steps. *What are you up to, Meredith?* He hardly knew his future sister-in-law but had looked forward to spending time with her. *Beautiful, exotic, and somehow fierce.* Those were among his first impressions when they'd met at Miranda's art show last spring. The rest of what he knew about her came mostly from sibling stories.

From these, he'd learned at least two important things: Meredith's value system was tied to money and she went after what she wanted. That much he'd observed himself, watching the way she'd made a head-on approach to Zack Calvin, whom she now dated. *Well, since she favors the direct approach, I should probably do the same.*

Even as he tried to script the phone call he'd have to make, he couldn't quite imagine leading with, "Hi, Meredith. Why did you buy your sister's building without telling her?" No, he'd have to have at least one graceful tactic up his sleeve.

What about wedding plans? That really was his fiancée's purview. He could, however, ask Meredith's advice about what sort of gift to choose for his bride. *Yes, that's it.*

Cornelius drew a hand through his hair, looked up Meredith's information on his Palm Pilot, picked up the desk phone handset, and dialed her home number. *Miranda said she works at home on Mondays, so I . . .*

"Meredith Jones," came a clipped, professional tone over the wire.

"Meredith, it's Cornelius." There was no reply for a long moment, so he continued. "Your sister's—"

"Fiancé! Yes, of course! Sorry, I was expecting a call from a client."

"If this is a bad time, I can—"

"This is fine. What can I do for you?"

"You sound busy." *Maybe I should have waited till evening, when I hear she enjoys a glass of wine. Or waited till the weekend.* But he pressed on. "Two questions."

"Shoot."

"Need your advice about a gift for your sister. Is there something you know about? Something she's always wanted? Or is there a family tradition about what the groom gives to the bride?"

"Ohhh, that is so sweet!"

Her tone had shifted so dramatically he almost didn't recognize her voice, which suddenly sounded a lot like her sister's.

"No wonder Mandy's in love with you," she continued, the softness in her comment revealing a side he'd never seen. *Maybe this is part of what Zack sees in her.* "Well, I'll have to give it some thought. And I will, I promise. I've never heard anything so thoughtful. Okay if I get back to you?"

"Absolutely. Thanks," he said.

"Okay, what's the other thing?"

Cornelius took a breath. "The other thing is a mystery I'm hoping you can solve."

"Uh, well, I'll do my best."

"I'm trying to rent the other half of Miranda's building. As far as I can tell, you're the new owner."

He could hear a sharp intake of breath over the line. It was followed by a burst of nervous laughter. "You found me out!" she exclaimed, a little too cheerfully. "Talk about wedding gifts, I figured she and you . . . I mean, her place is cute and all, but . . . You're not staying at your parents' place these days, are you?"

He let her sputter on for another moment.

"You two must be so crowded so I thought. . . ." At last the rambling petered out.

"You bought it as an investment?"

Again, he heard a small gasp, then, "Like I said, you found me out." This time the tone was resigned.

Suddenly, he felt they stood on an even playing field. He knew instinctively the purchase had not been a kind gesture, nor a secret gift, but a strategic move, and likely one she had planned before he came into the picture. *This has to be some sort of convoluted payback for the San Francisco house.* He knew Meredith felt cheated because Miranda had never paid for her share.

"Tell you what. Rent it to us, and we'll call it even."

"Even? I'm not sure what you mean."

"For now, I'll tell her the owner agreed to rent the rest of the building to us for a year, while our new place is being renovated. Then, when you decide the time is right, you can reveal yourself as the owner in question. You can explain it was your wedding gift to us—buying it so we didn't have to, then arranging with me to rent it to us."

"At a reduced rate, I assume?" she queried.

"Not at all," he said. "Whatever's fair."

"I see," Meredith said, sounding stunned. "You'd . . . you'd do that? And keep it from her?"

"In the interest of good family relations. And only for a short time."

He swore he could hear the wheels turning in her head while he waited for her reply.

"You drive a hard bargain," she intoned.

"I'd do anything for her."

"I get that." Meredith sighed. "Lucky woman."

"I'm the lucky one. You'll let the property manager know?"

"I'll call her."

"You'll call her now, yes?" He pressed.

"Right away."

"Great. We'll see you soon, right? By the way, I hear the shower was quite the event."

"Mother was in her glory. But that'll be nothing compared to the show she'll put on at the wedding. You'll be dealing with the entire complement of Jones women. Obviously, nothing you can't handle."

Cornelius chuckled. "I don't know about that."

"Well, if this conversation is any indication—" Her words trailed off. "I—" she began, apparently struggling to say something. "Thank you, Cornelius."

"You're welcome," he said quietly. "Let's not do it again."

"Right."

Cornelius spent a few minutes tidying his desk while he reviewed the phone call. He hated the idea of keep anything secret from

Miranda. *But this is a delay, not a secret,* he told himself. *One thing that counts as a good secret is a gift, especially when it's for a bride.*

He stood, stretched, and headed out to the kitchen, where he figured he'd find his mother.

"Oh, good, dear. I was hoping to speak with you about something. Have a moment?"

"Of course."

"Want a refill on your coffee?"

"Thanks."

He sat at the kitchen table while she poured some freshly brewed java into his cup and did the same for herself. After pulling out the chair facing his, she sat. "One thing is about the car. Your car, I mean. Your father and you can sort out the details, but we wanted you to know you can take it any time."

"Mom, I don't—"

"Now that you'll be living in Milford-Haven again," she continued as though he hadn't spoken. "After you're married. I don't know what you'll do about the charger. Maybe you'll want to keep it here for when you visit us. Or maybe you'll—"

"Mom. Stop."

"What?"

"The car is yours. It's nice you let me borrow it sometimes when I'm here, but it's your car. I'll be getting another one next year, after our house is ready. Meanwhile, I've got the Durango."

"But I know how you hate driving a gas guzzler."

He laughed. "Well, I do and I don't. It's as comfortable as a living room, and it gets me where I need to go in the mountains. The EV-1 can't pull that kind of duty."

His mother sighed. "Well, all right, when you put it that way." She took a sip of her coffee and leaned back in her hair.

He could see the relief in her body language. *Wonder how long she's been carrying that concern around?* "There's no need to worry, Mom. It's all going to be good."

Her face lit up. "It is, isn't it? Oh, my goodness, you have found yourself the most wonderful girl. Sweet as can be, pretty as a picture, and crazy for you."

He felt himself blush. "How . . . how can you tell?"

"Oh, a mother knows," she said with a grin. "But anyone can, when it comes to her feelings. The way she looks at you . . . like all her planets have aligned."

Cornelius laughed out loud. "Did she tell you that?"

Now his mother laughed. "She did! I couldn't have come up with that myself, but she gets you, dear. Who'd have imagined it was the artist who would understand the astronomer?"

Meredith had given herself a couple of hours to recover. The phone call from Cornelius had knocked her off center.

Her future brother-in-law was far more formidable than she'd imagined. *Wow, I really didn't see that coming.* Not only had her secret real estate ploy been uncovered, but he'd collapsed her position in a kind of Machiavellian pincer move.

Rather than confronting her head on, which would have given her a chance to flank him, he'd been the one to approach from two sides at once. She should have expected the vice grip of guilt coming at her from the right: he'd caught her in a suspected betrayal. The blind side had come out of left field: researching the records at the real estate management company, which erased any white lies she'd tried to spin.

She'd figured that if—or when—the fact that she'd bought her sister's rental building came to light, there were two likely responses. Her sister would see it as a loving gesture: her sibling wanting to spend some time closer. The fiancé might see it as a family matter he should leave alone. But she'd been well and truly outfoxed. *And I'm the fox in this family!*

She felt herself getting annoyed again, and pushed back from the desk in her home office to stand and head downstairs to the kitchen for a fresh cup of coffee. But when she got back, she found herself staring out the window and thinking back to her conversations with Zack.

Their relationship, like most of Meredith's, had started with strategies and maneuverings. But in the relatively short time they'd been seeing one another, they'd progressed beyond the gamesmanship that'd colored her past and likely his as well.

Was there really any point to being irritated with Cornelius for seeing through her? Could there be a clearer, brighter path ahead? Was Zack already helping her to be a better person?

Chapter 7

Ralph Hargraves bent over the boxes that had arrived with his latest order, his glasses slipping down his nose.

His store, which he'd loved running with his late wife, had become too much for him, and he'd finally admitted it. *Not a moment too soon.*

"Well, glory be," his wife would've said if she were still here. But she wasn't.

Life had been tough since her passing but was starting to shape up. That gal Sally who ran the place next door was sweet as the pies she made and kind as a daughter might be. He'd eat his breakfast at her counter and lunch most days, and she often sent him home with a boxed-up dinner.

The main thing was, his store was now in good hands. He paused a moment to recall that last call before Tony'd arrived two months ago.

He'd heard the phone ring, winced as he'd straightened his back and shuffled to his front counter. "Hargraves Hardware," he'd answered in a well-practiced tone.

"Uh, yes, Mr. Hargraves, it's Tony Fiorentino, from New York."

"Tony from New York! Yessir! How's the weather there?"

"Not too bad, not too bad, sir. A little rain yesterday."

"Oh, yes, well, that's just the thing, you know."

"Just the thing, sir?"

"To make the spring flowers grow! We're getting a few of those here too, don't you know."

"That's good," said Tony, with a chuckle in his voice. "I'll have to get over to the Park and have a look."

"Too much concrete over in those parts for me. Gotta have my flowers." Mr. Hargraves noticed a spot of dried paint on his wooden countertop and worked on it with his thumbnail.

"Have to agree with you there," said Tony.

"Got your check. Put it in my account," Hargraves declared.

"Yes, sir. My accountant mentioned it'd gone through."

Ralph pulled his tall stool closer and sat down. "Long as you're satisfied, then I am too, young fellow. I think you'll do just fine with the store." He paused for a moment, listening to the silence, and let the news sink in. "Now, I'm not publishin' this forth just yet. Thought we'd ease folks into it."

"Yes, that's how I'd like to do it," Tony agreed. "I'm gonna need to be your apprentice for a while, learn the ropes, you know."

"Smart fellow like you, won't take long. Even after you take the reins, I don't plan to be moving anywhere. I'll still be in town. Expect to see you soon, then?"

"Yeah . . . yes. I have a few more things to close up here. And I've got a realtor looking for a place for me in Milford-Haven."

"Nothin' but nice places here," Mr. Hargraves said with conviction. A customer walked into the hardware store, ringing the door chime. "Gotta run now—got somebody browsing."

"All right, sir. I . . . I want to thank you—"

"No need."

"I . . . I'm looking forward to—" Tony tried to continue.

"Just holler when you get here." Mr. Hargraves hung up the phone. "Be right with you," he said to his new customer. Walking to the storeroom, he reached deep into his back pocket for his oversized handkerchief and dabbed a tear from his eye.

Sally O'Mally hummed the little tuneless tune that always played in her head when things were going well. This morning, she was almost convinced she was humming a recognizable melody.

"We're good for now, Sal," her wait person said. "Wanna take a load off?"

"Thanks. Maybe I will." June Magliati was her primary employee. But Sally'd come to trust her as a dear friend—and had grown accustomed to her Brooklyn accent too.

The early breakfast crowd in Milford-Haven consisted mostly of hard-working locals. As usual, they'd swept through her restaurant like a swarm of locusts. But she never begrudged them their healthy appetites. It was a sign of well-being and prosperity for her and for her adopted hometown.

The tourists typically arrived later—"late-comer sleep-ins," as she called them out of earshot—straggling in with the well-rested look of folks on vacation, eager to treat themselves to fresh pancakes, warmed cinnamon rolls, or eggs with homemade biscuits.

In her twenty-seventh week of pregnancy, it was all Sally could do to stay on her feet through the morning. Now to give her body a brief respite, she would take advantage of the momentary lull before the daily lunch onslaught. She stepped into her tiny private office. *I can barely fit myself in this room,* she complained, bracing herself as she lowered into the one easy chair.

One more thing Jack failed to do, she sighed. *After all those promises, he never did build the addition.* She pushed back in the chair, then hoisted her feet up to the padded stool whose cushion Mama had needlepointed for her years ago. The stool had grown wobbly with one leg coming loose—until Tony fixed it for her a couple of weeks ago. *So thoughtful.* She sighed again, growing calmer.

The pieces of Sally's life all seemed to be fitting into place. She just wished they'd be doing it a little faster. The restaurant was thriving. The baby was growing. *Lord knows that's the truth!* Sally groaned. *And the right man is finally in my life again.* But the fact remained: in a few short weeks she'd be giving birth as an unwed mother. *The very thing I tried so hard to avoid all those years ago.*

Tony Fiorentino, her high school sweetheart, had been deeply in love with her, and she with him. They'd wanted to marry, but the Vietnam War interfered with their plans. When Tony was sent overseas, Sally'd been too afraid to tell him she was pregnant. Under the crushing weight of internal overwhelm and external shame, she'd ended the pregnancy. By the time Tony returned home to the States years later—a veteran who'd taken a bullet in the spine and was now paraplegic—Sally'd been unable to face him.

Meanwhile, she'd left Arkansas and made a new life for herself here on the Central Coast of California. Using some of the money from her late father's life insurance—which Mama had insisted she share—she'd started her own business and managed to put down roots of her own. She'd discovered a confidence she'd never found before, built up her restaurant till she trusted herself, and her fellow townsfolk accepted her and her restaurant as permanent fixtures.

Then she'd met Jack Sawyer; successful as a builder-contractor, he was an aggressive, confident man who seemed delighted by her company and her good cooking. He'd courted her for a while, during which time he'd promised to build an addition onto her restaurant at cost. Now that dream—and every other one she'd once entertained about Jack—had been dashed by his utter rejection, delivered in angry outbursts. *As if he had anything to be angry about! Funny how the man's true colors didn't show until the pregnancy.*

Though she'd been hurt and devastatingly disappointed by his cold lack of interest, she couldn't pretend she'd been anything but thrilled at the prospect of bearing a child—even one unwanted by its father. Her temper still spiked when she thought of Jack. Sally remembered how during her visit to Arkansas last spring, Mama had seen the anger flash through her like heat lightning. *Is that how Mama knew I was carrying a child?* Sally had asked, but Mama'd simply answered, "Three things a woman knows: when to get food on the table; when she's pregnant; and when her daughter is." Shaking her head, Sally marveled at her mother's intuition, a gift so powerful everyone came to her for her insights.

Something else Mama had said too. "The closer you get to happiness, Sally girl, the more you run from it. I were you, I'd work on learnin' to accept the good things trying to come your way."

She smiled at that sage advice and thought of Tony. After so many years apart, their lives were coming back together quickly. It had all started when he called her last winter, inviting her to a special concert at the Central Coast Bowl. The Doobie Brothers had arranged a fund-raiser for veterans, and Tony had been honored. Knowing she lived somewhere in the area, he'd tracked her down. He wanted her there with him, and what a proud, touching moment it had been!

After he returned home to New York City, they'd had wonderful phone calls. While Sally was at Mama's, she'd called him at his apartment. They'd reminisced, they'd laughed, they'd caught up. When she'd returned to Milford-Haven there'd been a note from him. *No, not a note. A real letter—polite, respectful, but more—with words like "longing" and "remember" and "special."*

The letter had buoyed her. For one thing, it suggested he'd forgiven her for not responding to the letters he'd sent from Vietnam all those years ago. Most important, that letter had reopened the door between them that'd been closed for what seemed a lifetime.

But once that door was open, she next had the prickly task of sharing her biggest news: she was pregnant; no longer involved with the father; and planned to keep her child. She imagined every kind of reaction from shock to disappointment, from hesitance to withdrawal. *Well, I'll just have to come out with it,* she'd ordered herself. *That'll jar his preserves.*

What she hadn't predicted was his actual response. "Are you healthy? Are you happy about it?" When she'd said *yes,* he'd replied, "Good, then so am I." The very next thing he'd said was that he'd like to help, if she'd let him. She remembered the joy and relief of that moment, unable to say much through her tears.

That's the thing about Tony, she reflected. *Sometimes small things are big. But the big things . . . he has a way of making them small.* With that issue hurdled, they'd moved forward like a thawing river in spring.

In fact, her next worry was at the sudden strength of their reconnection. Wasn't it possible Tony was actually responding to some lost version of herself, some fantasy he'd augmented and cherished through the years? Though it'd been within the bounds of etiquette, already he'd shifted to small terms of endearment in his letter, and she loved it. But how real was this? Starved for affection, she worried she shouldn't trust herself. *Mightn't he be just as hungry? How far should I let this go?*

But soon anticipation hung in the air between them no matter the physical distance. Their phone calls became virtual visits, long rambling conversations that both reassured and titillated. One night Sally was shocked to realize they'd been talking for four hours. When she expressed alarm about the bill, Tony simply said, "Don't worry, Sweet. We need the time."

Wonderful as their calls were, both of them seemed to agree that touchier issues would have to be discussed in person. Tony accelerated the process by making plans to move to Milford-Haven. Taken aback at first, Sally quickly recognized in him the same urge she'd had herself to own a business and put down roots somewhere new. He was tired of the big city, he'd explained, tired of the cold winters, and had been looking for a new location. Because of the Doobies invitation a few months earlier, he'd fallen in love with the promise of Milford-Haven.

Once he'd bought old Mr. Hargrave's Hardware—which happened to be for sale and was next door to Sally's—it'd seemed the obvious choice. She and Tony were business-neighbors on Main Street and couldn't avoid seeing each other. Beyond that, neither of them could resist the attraction, and they began dating. Soon it was clear they could no longer avoid facing the old hurts that had kept them apart.

The weekend before last, Tony'd offered to cook dinner for her. She should've suspected he had something up his sleeve. Like most important conversations in their lives, it had started in a kitchen.

On Saturday they'd met at her restaurant to cook. Tony started on their dinner, fixing his baked ziti while she prepared a fresh garden salad and a homemade apple pie. Cooking side by side, they'd rediscovered that the paths of their lives, divergent for so long, were coming together, lining up till they were as parallel as railroad tracks.

After dinner, she'd gathered her courage. She would never forget telling him about the child he might have had with her, the pregnancy that'd ended when she was hardly more than a child herself. She'd risked it all to share that heavy secret. But when she opened her heart, Tony shared her sadness. They wept in each other's arms as she sat across his lap, letting go of their judgments and fears, rationalizations and expectations.

Then, in one sentence, Tony had handled the next question that loomed. "Seems like the new baby brings it all right again." Sally's tears of sadness were then replaced with tears of joy. Gratitude welled, not only for his words but for the truth of what he said.

As they washed their dishes after supper, they both knew it was their own hearts that had been washed clean, and they'd embarked on a new chapter. That was only six weeks ago; yet it seemed as long as six months, or even six years, they'd grown so close. *We're movin' like greased lightnin'*, she thought, *now that nothin's in our way.*

At this point, they usually spent part of each day together, and being alone in a room with the man set her pulse thumping. She wanted to go to him, lose herself in his embrace, kiss him till his eyes rolled back in his head.

Is it possible he's somehow gotten sexier over the years? she wondered, blushing at the thought. *I don't hardly ever think of the wheel-chair. Everyone says when you lose one sense you develop the others. Is it like that for Tony?* Losing the use of his legs, had he unconsciously compensated with a heightened sensuality, an increased sensitivity? Or was she just fantasizing? Breathing hard at the thought of his wide lap, his enveloping arms, the silk of his hair, the spice of his scent, she closed her eyes, sank back and reveled in the sweet remembrance.

Life is like a river, Sally reminded herself, letting the rising warmth of the day seep into her bones. The idea of the river soothed her, and as she imagined the sound of its flow shushing against lush banks, she dozed, a smile playing across her lips.

A river . . . that's what the baby's hearing too, she thought, drifting off. *Row row row your boat, gently down the stream.* She sang the well-known song like a lullaby to her unborn child. *Merrily merrily merrily merrily, life is but a dream.*

But the baby's father . . . where was he? Why wasn't he a part of this special time? The boat seemed harder to handle now, and up ahead, some danger lurked.

A memory began to blend itself with the dream. "The father's name is Sawyer?" Mama had asked, pinching her mouth.

"Why, Mama? Somethin' wrong with that name?"

"Well, Sally girl, it ain't the best, on account o' its meanin'."

"But it just means a man who saws wood, and since Jack's a builder, it seems like a good fit."

"Ye-yus, but it means somethin' else too. It's when a big old branch gets stuck in the bottom mud of a river. Can be right dang'rous for folks comin' through on their boats."

Whether it was the memory of the conversation, or the image of a treacherous branch stuck mid-river, Sally came full-awake with heartburn forming a lump in her chest. "Jack Sawyer," she spat. "Can't live with him. Can't shoot him."

How could I feel so peaceful one minute and so all-fired het up the next? Surely the hormones couldn't be completely to blame, but these days Sally sometimes found herself vacillating between calm and rage.

Most days she enjoyed a newfound strength, an increased capacity to meet the challenges of the day, as though everything was now minor compared to the very miracle of life expanding itself inside her.

She focused on Jack for another moment. What if he offered himself to her now? She imagined again what she'd pictured when he first deserted her: his groveling return and abject apologies. *Would I take him back?* It only took a second for her answer to surface. *Not even if the cow jumped over the moon.*

She realized with some relief that a great distance had opened between them. Jack had only wanted convenience, where Sally wanted commitment; he wanted companionship, where she wanted a soul mate. The realization rang true like the clear tone of a bell. She squeezed her eyes shut and said a prayer of gratitude. "We're free, Baby," she whispered. "We don't have to be angry anymore."

A distant but boisterous laugh broke the silence. Opening her eyes, she hefted herself out of the comfortable chair and waddled into the restaurant's kitchen where she turned on one of the large faucets in the industrial sink and splashed cold water on her face.

"You doin' okay, Sal?" asked June.

"Ye-yus! Just had me a little nap."

"That's good, Sal. Sure you're up to doin' lunch?"

"No problem." And as Sally patted her face and hands with a paper towel, her body—so heavy with child—felt suddenly light.

Chapter 8

Samantha Hugo, director of the Environmental Planning Com-mission, had gone to bed with a migraine and been dismayed to discover she still had a headache when she woke this morning. The hot shower and a vigorous shampoo-massage had helped, and her morning meditation managed to diminish it, but opening her eyes, she realized it was seeping back like water under the door, and she had a sinking feeling this would be a three-day fight to stay afloat.

Doing her best to ignore the pain, she started her morning reading—*Milford-Haven News, San Francisco Chronicle, Los Angeles Times, Wall Street Journal*—eating a bowl of oatmeal and sipping strong coffee while she flipped pages. Working with a green high-lighter, she circled headlines of articles she wanted clipped. The research files at the EPC had grown extensive, expanding beyond the present capacity of the file cabinets. *Must remember to buy one more.* Patting the pile of newsprint, she felt for her sticky-note holder, pulled one small yellow sheet and jotted a reminder.

Once the articles were marked, they had to be clipped, trimmed and pasted onto standard-sized paper. She bought reams of gray-looking recycled sheets for the purpose, running them once through the printer so that "EPC Archives" would appear across the top of each.

Sam used to love prepping for the cutting and even now found it meditative when she had time to perform the simple, repetitive task. She'd developed a technique of laying a metal ruler alongside the articles she wanted, then lifting the paper and tearing against the straight edge. When she got into the flow of it, the work was fast and the feeling of accomplishment immediate. *If only I could get Susan to feel that confidence and gratification.* Sam realized this was one of Susan Winslow's most dreaded jobs—clipping the papers and filing the articles. But *everything* that touched the girl set off some sort of emotional explosion, as though her nerve endings were always raw.

Staring across her cluttered kitchen counter, Sam considered her ward. The Central Coast Mentoring program had paired her with Susan—who'd graduated two years ago from the high school on the nearby Chumash Reservation. A private grant had paid a stipend toward additional training, and Sam, herself, then matched it. Between the classes at Central Coast Community College and her EPC job, this was one young woman who was really being given a boost. Yet, she never seemed grateful. *Hell,* thought Sam, *Susan is better known for insouciance than for gratitude.*

Irritated, Sam stood, rinsed out her oatmeal bowl and carried the still-hot mug of coffee to her bedroom. Dressing was usually a simple matter, as she stuck to colors that complemented her golden-toned skin and red hair, and chose fabrics that kept their shape without ironing. Today she paid even less attention than usual, grabbing a sleeveless olive top with matching slacks. Her makeup, though understated, was another of her meditations, and she applied it with care, using the time to let slip away the minor irritations of the morning, hoping the headache would slide away as she did. But as she combed her hair into place and clipped on a pair of silver earrings, a vice seemed to compress around her skull.

She pressed her thumbs into her temples. *Better take something for it before I leave.* Reaching for a mild over-the-counter pain-killer, she stopped in the kitchen for a glass of water. Into her brief-case she folded the newly marked newspapers, then she grabbed her purse and headed for her car. Five minutes after she pointed her Jeep Grand Cherokee down the steep incline, she rolled into the back parking lot of the EPC. After ten more minutes, the pill had done nothing to alleviate the pain, and Samantha flinched as Susan slammed the office door behind her. "Susan, you're late again," Sam called out, instantly regretting she'd used any volume.

"Yeah, well, we can't all be perfect like you, Samantha."

That tone again. Sighing, Sam put down her pen and again dug her thumbs into her temples. "I put the circled papers on your pile, Susan. You're falling behind."

"So I should drop all the correspondence and play cut-outs with old newspapers, right?"

That does it! Sam stormed to the outer office to confront her employee. Towering over her, Sam felt suddenly like a school bully who should go pick on someone her own size, particularly now that she noticed how skinny Susan looked. "Have you lost weight?"

The question surprised them both. "What?" Susan demanded.

"You don't look well, Susan. You're getting much too thin."

"Maybe by *your* standards, Samantha. I happen to *like* the way I look. And anyway, it's none of your business."

"Fine," Sam replied. "Try to work with efficiency today. And don't disturb me. I'm in no mood." Turning on her heel, Sam retreated to her office and, to avoid another loud noise, closed the door as quietly as she could. Moments later, Susan burst in.

"I thought I told you I didn't want to be disturbed." Sam's tone was quietly menacing as her thumbs dug into her temples.

As though she hadn't heard her, Susan continued, "So I've been thinking about Jack Sawyer."

"How sad for you."

"You know," she continued, "how you're always trying to *get* him breaking rules and everything, and I figured out how."

"I find that highly unlikely."

Ignoring her, Susan pressed on. "So, like, the thing is to actually *catch* him in the middle of something."

Sam looked up. "Good luck," she smirked. "I've been trying that for years."

"The most substantial project he has going is that Clarke house. It's the biggest house ever built in this town. The way people talk about it you'd think they never saw a mansion before."

"How many mansions have *you* seen?" When there was no reply but a sullen expression, Sam asked, "What's your point?"

"That we should go over there and check it out."

"*We*, Susan? Don't you mean, *you?* Go check out all the men in their tight T-shirts, sweating in the noonday sun?"

"Well, if you'd rather go yourself, Samantha, I'm sure you could give yourself a thrill."

"Quit wasting time and get back to work."

"Not till you hear my idea. I think we . . . or rather *I* . . . should give that building a real careful look."

"Not even professional inspectors have been able to catch Jack at his little games, Susan. What makes you think—"

"We don't *know* that. He could just have paid them off."

Sam looked up sharply, then replied, "As a matter of fact, you're right. I wouldn't put it past him. All right, so what makes you the expert?"

"You don't know this," she bragged, "but I got Kevin to show me the plans to the Clarke house, and then, like, I checked out other plans in my textbook."

Dumbfounded at this, Sam concentrated on keeping her jaw from dropping as she looked at her assistant.

Susan continued, "I've gotten pretty good at figuring out how houses get put together. So something came up in class that got me thinking."

Sam now brightened and asked, "You mean to say you paid attention in one of your classes?"

"Well, yeah. This class is kind of cool. It's about compliance and—"

"'Compliance and Cooperation.' I know." Reflecting on the girl's sudden interest in something relating to her job, Sam considered her options. *Best not to dampen such spirit as there is.* "All right, you can go to the Clarke house and take a look around. But this is strictly off the record. Get it? This is *not* an official EPC inspection. And *don't* let Jack know what you're up to. Make him think you're just—"

"...just there to flirt?"

Sam regarded the young woman in front of her with a mixture of regret and respect. "Exactly."

With a spin that seemed triumphant, Susan tossed her long black hair and strode out of Samantha's office.

Miranda heard Cornelius' key in the lock and felt that now familiar thud in her chest. *Will it always be this way?* she wondered. *Probably not. But oh my, how he makes my heart pitter-patter.*

"Honey, I'm home!" his voice rang out.

A huge grin split her face as she answered, "In the studio!"

She listened as his footsteps approached. Giving up any notion of taking the moment for granted, she slid off her high stool and into his arms. Their kiss started off gentle but was quickly going deeper, when she felt the gentle pressure of his arms pressing her away. "Whew," he said, his dark blue eyes twinkling. "I've only been gone for a few hours."

"Missed you, none the less," she said quietly.

"Me too. Can you take a break?"

"Yeah, good timing. I made us some tuna salad sandwiches. They're in the fridge."

They spent a few moments in a surprisingly synchronized series of domestic chores, with Cornelius grabbing some chips from the pantry cupboard, Miranda plating their sandwiches along with a couple of sliced dill pickles.

"Iced tea okay?" She asked.

"If it's that peach concoction you make, then yes."

She smiled while pouring the chilled tea over ice and bringing their glasses to the dining table—the half that wasn't currently in use as his "office."

Cornelius took a bite, then a sip, then sighed as he wiped his mouth. "How's your work going? You were in the studio all morning, right?"

"Yes," she replied after a bite, which concealed a secret smile. *I don't want to tell him about the painting idea. It has to be a surprise.* "I didn't get any actual painting done, but I made it through my whole list, put deadlines and timelines on my work calendar, made a couple of calls. I feel more organized, even though life is still moderately controlled chaos."

Cornelius chuckled then took another bite., "This is delish, by the way. You add stuff to the tuna."

"Mm-hmm," she confirmed. "Chopped celery, lemon pepper, fresh lemon. But no peppers. That's what your mom adds, right?"

"She does. That's good too, just different."

"Too spicy for me," Miranda mumbled.

"I know. For now."

"You're gonna spice up my life, are you?"

Cornelius put down his sandwich and gave her one of his penetrating looks. "I certainly hope so."

Miranda felt her cheeks heat and a tingle travel through her center.

"Good," he said quietly, reading her like a book.

She cleared her throat, took a sip of tea, and asked, "What were you up to all morning?"

"A bit of research and some good conversations. I stopped by my folks'," he reported, then looked a bit sheepish. "Had a second breakfast with them."

Miranda chuckled. "They're good?" She asked.

"Oh, yeah. After a brief catch up, I checked my mail—a few things had arrived, since the change of address hasn't come through yet. But I also used the computer in my old room to clear out some emails. And there's some good news."

"Tell me!"

Smiling, he said, "First, I got the permission from the county to go forward with the planetarium."

"Cornelius! That's huge!"

"Yeah, it's good."

"It's exciting!"

"It is. But it adds to an already very long list of construction projects. We have that meeting with Jameson coming up, so we can discuss it with him. But the planetarium has to be further down the list."

Miranda rose from the table.

"Something I said?" He asked.

"No. Yes! I need a pad and pencil." She placed her plate in the sink, then grabbed the memo pad she kept on the kitchen counter and lifted a pencil from the pottery jar that held various writing instruments. "Okay," she said, sitting down again. "Main house. Studio. Planetarium," she wrote in her fluid cursive.

"Right. Main house plans are close to being complete, from what he tells me. We haven't seen them in a while, nor the site, so we'll get a tour."

"Can hardly wait," Miranda commented.

"I know. Still, the addition, the finishes . . . it'll take a few more months or longer. I think your studio building has to be next, once the house is done. Remember the studio building is going to have that first floor with public access, a place to exhibit your work, teach classes, hold workshops, invite other artists. All those things you told me about."

Miranda felt her gaze drift as she pictured it all, then she brought herself back to the present. "Meanwhile, I'm okay working here. But we have to figure out your work space."

"Well, we'll both continue working here, because there's more good news."

"Tell me," she said.

"The owner agrees we can keep this place for at least another year. And next door, too."

"Really? Fantastic! Oh, wow! When can we do a walk-through? We need to plan what goes where. It's more or less the same as this side, but reversed, right? Do you want the space that mirrors my studio to be your office?"

Cornelius laughed. "Not sure, yet. But I think we can get in there this week sometime and measure things. With your eye, you'll have me sorted out in one visit."

Miranda sat quietly for a moment, her pencil creating a doodle of climbing ivy. "I can draw it out, after we measure. See where your bookshelves fit, your desk. . . . it'll be more functional than being crammed in here. And the new property, it's so incredible to think we'll be there." She looked up, fixing her gaze on him. "All that was for 'someday,' you know? And now it's . . . it's here."

He reached for her hand. "Nearly here," he said. "Near enough to be planning for it."

She nodded. "Yeah. Amazing. So . . ." She began to sketch the property, drawing squiggly lines to represent the ocean it faced. "At one end we have the lighthouse home. The studio building is at the other end of the land, as far away as it can be."

"Jameson suggested it so the public access is as distant as possible from our private house."

"Right, I get that, but that's a lot of empty space in the middle."

"It will be for now. And that'll mean less noise at the house. For a while."

"True. And it'll give you time to plan the planetarium."

He huffed out a laugh. "Those drawings have been done for years."

She smiled at her fiancé. "Of course they have. That's coming off the 'someday' list too, isn't it."

They sat together, fingers intertwined, looking at the sketch on the table, a rough drawing of their future.

Chapter 9

Miranda cleared their dishes and kissed Cornelius goodbye again. *I could get used to this,* she thought with a chuckle.

While he drove off to Cal Poly for a meeting with an astronomy professor there, Miranda stepped into her studio to grab what she'd need for the morning: outline of the class she'd teach at the local kindergarten next autumn, postcards for the gallery, fliers for the playhouse. Stopping by the kitchen counter, she picked up her grocery shopping list, then headed for the garage where she placed everything on the passenger's seat of her Mustang.

She drove first to the school and left the class outline she'd promised in the kindergarten teacher's cubby in the faculty lounge. She'd also promised to create a poster for the Playhouse's upcoming production, and she left the original with the box office manager, who promised she'd see the director of the show received it later that day when he arrived for rehearsal.

The next item on her to-do list was a stop at the stationers, where she had fun picking out a looseleaf binder and several inserts.

Then she stopped at Finders Gallery, where Nicole greeted her warmly. "Bonjour Miranda!" She exclaimed in her lovely Montreal accent. "Ca va?"

"Tout va bien," Miranda replied. "Et toi?"

"Bien. Good. But we could use a bit more traffic, tu sais?"

"Feast or famine," Miranda said with a nod. "Well, maybe these will help a little."

"Oh, you're one artist who always follows through to reach out to the public! So smart."

"I have to give Zelda the credit for initiating the process. But once I started, I kind of fell in love with creating my postcards."

"They're beautiful! Miranda Jones miniatures. That's what I call them, tu sais? Everyone loves your paintings!" Nicole paused, looking down to review the postcards, then holding up the first one to inspect it more closely. "Love this one. I know, I say it every time, but the colors . . . the juxtaposition of the wildflowers on one side, the ocean on the other . . . makes me feel like I'm right there on that bluff."

Miranda felt her cheeks heat at the praise.

"And my very favorite part is that sand castle! It almost looks too perfect to be made of sand," Nicole enthused.

"Blame that on my dad," Miranda divulged. "He's the one who taught me how to dribble the wet sand so it makes those turrets."

"Ah, so perhaps you inherited some of your talent from him."

Miranda pressed her lips together, never having considered her business-minded father as possessing even one atom of artistic inclination. "Perhaps so," Miranda said quietly. "Zelda does a good job getting these printed," she added deflecting the attention away from her private musings.

"Oh, la la, that Zelda. She is something else!"

Miranda laughed. "Oh, for sure."

"Will she be visiting again?"

"Well . . . she'll be here for the big day."

"Quoi? What big day?"

Miranda grinned and thrust her left hand toward her friend.

"Oh Mon Dieu! You're engaged?"

Miranda nodded, letting the joy rise through her as it always did at the thought of marrying Cornelius.

"So when is this big day?"

"You'll get an invitation of course, but it'll be soon."

Miranda did her grocery shopping, then decided to walk the short distance to her final errand. Shell Shock was just down Main Street, and even from here, she could see where the breeze tickled at the mobile hanging near the front door, its flat Placuna shells tinkling delightfully.

A chime rang as Miranda stepped through the door, and she heard the owner Shelly call out "Welcome!" In her distinctive Australian accent.

"Miranda!" She exclaimed as she drew close and offered a hug. "How are you, girl? Excited, I bet!"

Miranda nodded. "Excited, overwhelmed, ready, nervous, you name it, I'm feeling it."

"I can imagine! But I mean, really, you two . . . Well, you were meant to be. It's obvious as the sun on a bright day."

"Aw, that's sweet. Thanks, Shell."

"So, what brings you in? Time to do the next shell painting, right?"

"It is. Zelda's been on my case about it, wanting me to get it done before the wedding. I was too distracted to figure out what shell to paint for a while, but I finally had a breakthrough."

"Love it when that happens!"

"Me too. Um, this has to stay confidential for now, okay?"

"Confidential? From Zelda?"

"From everyone for now, because it's about my gift for Cornelius."

"Aha! Okay, my lips are sealed."

"It's not done yet, but I'm going to do a painting that includes a rock with a hole in it."

Shelly looked at her as though she might have rocks in her head.

Miranda laughed, then said, "Trust me, it's a good thing. But I have to find a coordinating shell."

"Right, as you did with the Placuna lens shell to go with the lens on the map image you did for an earlier postcard."

"Yes, exactly," Miranda confirmed.

"Okay, so I gather you need a *shell* with a hole in it?"

"You're too quick, Shelly."

Her friend just smiled and said, "Follow me."

Miranda walked behind the store owner as she made her way past elevated trays of seashell collections, each more fascinating than the next. She stopped next to one labeled "Limpits." At first, all Miranda could see were dark oval shaped shells that didn't seem to spark any interest.

"Strange, right? But pick one up," Shelly instructed.

When she did, Miranda could see daylight through a central hole from which striations radiated outward, making the shell look something like a sunburst. "Oh! This is perfect!"

Shelly crossed her arms and smiled. "Thought it might be."

"Light comes in, but it also goes out. Fascinating," Miranda muttered, more to herself than to her friend. Then she said to Shelly, "I know I'm always going to get this synergy thing when I step into your store."

"Maybe it's because both of us believe in synchronicity, eh?"

"That must be it. Okay, um, can I buy ten of these? I have a feeling I might even want more, but that'll work for now."

Nodding, Shelly offered, "I'll just wrap them to keep them safe, and be right back."

As the store owner walked away with the box of shells, Miranda shook her head, marveling at how well the universe seemed to answer her every need.

Miranda sat at her studio desk to assemble the loose leaf notebook she'd purchased.

Oh my. This is real! She couldn't help but let a small squeal escape, which caused her cat to look at her quizzically. "Sorry, Shadow. I'm just so excited!"

She began unsealing packages of dividers and several types of paper—graph, lined, sketch, even a few in different colors. Picking up a fine-point pen, she labeled the tab inserts, The first thing she thought of was bridesmaids, which took her back to that conversation she'd had with her mother a month earlier, when she'd asked Veri's reaction to color swatches she'd sent.

"Oh!" Veri's voice had brightened. "They're all lovely, with your excellent eye for tonalities. I know the greens are your' favorites, and they're quite beautiful. Your bridesmaids dresses will have a tendency to blend into the surroundings, though, don't you think? Since you insist on having your ceremony outside."

"We'll be under a pergola, with a view of the coastline winding northward. There will be trees, but the gardens will be in bloom. I was thinking each woman could wear a different shade."

"What an interesting idea," Veri remarked. "Like Sergei Diaghilev's 1921 production of 'The Sleeping Beauty' where all the ballerinas were in light pastels. He started a fashion trend with that production, you know."

"Oh my goodness, Mother. You're a ballet encyclopedia! But yes, that would be the idea. I'm not sure we would go for pastels, exactly. The dresses should be a little more vibrant, or else they may look a little washed out . . ."

". . . in the bright sunlight. Yes, I see. You're right about that. Well, dear, how can I help?" Very inquired.

"This may be a lot to ask, Mom, but how would you feel about pulling samples from magazines? You could mail them to me, and I can scan them, send them out to bridesmaids. Of course, send them to Meri. She gets first pick."

"I would love to do that for you, Mandy dear! I'll start today."

That was a sweet conversation. Mother's probably been waiting for years to be able to participate in wedding plans for her daughters.

Miranda returned her attention to the tabs she still needed to label: florals, catering, guest list, gifts. She paused, trying to think of what else needed to be handled. *Rehearsal dinner? No, that would be managed by the groom's parents.*

She carefully labeled the tops of the pages, used her three-hole punch to place the needed strategic holes, then clicked the sections into place. *Now it needs a cover sheet*, she thought. She looked through her shallow printers' drawers to find a sheet of card stock, then cut it down to standard notebook size, and took her small cup to the kitchen.

She carried the water back into her studio, where she chose a brush, moistened it, then swirled it through her blue watercolor block. Sweeping the brush over the card stock until it resembled blue sky with a few drifting clouds, she set the image aside to dry.

She needed phone numbers, she realized, so she could call the manager at Ragged Point. Did they do their own catering? She wasn't sure. Would Sally want to contribute something in the food department? She would, of course, but they might not be allowed to employ the services of an outside caterer. In that case, maybe Mrs. Smith would like to hire Sally to do her hors d'oeuvres at the rehearsal dinner.

Mrs. Smith. That's going to be my name too! Well, not exactly. She planned to hyphenate her two last names. Still, some old-school people—like all the parents, aunts, uncles and. . . *Oh! Grandma Dorothy! I have to invite her! Well, first, I need to tell her. And it's already been too long since we spoke.*

That part of the family was a little complicated. Her grandfather, Charles the First, as they liked to call him, had married Dorothy, and they'd had Charles the Second—aka Dad. He'd been an only child, until Charles the First divorced Dorothy and later married Wilhemina, and they'd had Wiliam. So Dad had a half-brother. *They are real brothers, though, and have always treated each other as such. Should I invite Wilhemina? I'll have to ask Mom. I do want to invite her daughter Wilma, though. I've always liked my cousin. Maybe they'd make the trip from Colorado.*

Were there other relations on Cornelius' side she should invite? That would be an excellent question for his mom.

Miranda reached for the painted card stock, checked to make sure it was dry, then added lettering in a dark blue marker. Wedding Plans, she wrote in her lovely cursive, under it adding Miranda & Cornelius. June 21, 1997.

She loved the date they'd chosen: summer solstice, a celebration of alignment, transition, balance, nature, Earth . . . so many things they treasured. She felt a little wistful, though, that they wouldn't be marrying on the first date they'd chosen: September 29. Both of their birthdays were on twenty-ninths, and they liked the "nine two nine" idea. It sure had a ring to it. So they'd decided to make that date a private holiday no one else would know about. *No matter what date, we'll be celebrating for the rest of our lives.*

Chapter 10

Delmar pulled his SUV into the driveway of his cozy Milford-Haven rental. Exhaustion pulled at his limbs as he climbed out of the vehicle, but with his first inhalation of cool, coastal air, he already felt better.

He'd driven 160 miles today, from here to Paso Robles, then down the 101 past Atascadero to San Luis Obispo, farther south to Santa Maria, then north again to take the 1 to Morro Bay, and finally back home. Temperatures inland had risen to the low 100s, and he'd watched heat radiate from the asphalt, creating watery mirages that made him thirsty but also reminded him to keep an eye on fellow drivers who might be made either drowsy or irritated on the road.

He'd spent the morning working in his SLO office, reading parts of the newly discovered journal, stopping only when the forensic team called with their latest report. They'd found yet another item secreted, this time in a concealed trunk compartment. A blank mini-cassette was hidden there, together with some triple-A batteries. The tape recorder itself was missing. *Which means she has—or had—the device with her.*

Disturbed by the news, Delmar had sought temporary distraction, first in paperwork and then in a very worthwhile meeting at his headquarters.

His boss Captain Sandoval had looked up from his desk when Del walked in. "I take it you asked for the meet because you finally have something."

"Just enough, I think," Del confirmed.

"Take a seat," Rogers offered. "What've you got?"

Delmar presented facts; the Captain countered, which he did so well—his method for getting his people to clarify their thoughts. Ultimately, Delmar won the argument. It wasn't easy convincing his boss that the listening device should and could be installed at Clarke Shipping. Sandoval had done a good job playing devil's advocate.

In the end, permission was granted, and it had taken quite a team to ensure access in the middle of the night without alerting the firm's security guy. Two devices were placed, one in the conference room, one in Clarke's office. If they'd had more time, Del would have liked to add even more, but it'd been a matter of timing. The security man's rounds only permitted them a specific window.

Now that they'd have ears on the ground, it'd be a matter of monitoring the feed, something for which there wasn't actually much man power. Del had volunteered to spend some of his off hours listening to the tapes that would come into the office in SLO, and there were two others who would do their best to keep up with the rest.

How long it might take to hear something significant, nobody knew. But from Del's perspective, it would only be a matter of time before Clarke or any other bad actors in that place revealed their true colors.

For the moment, he was delighted that both the heat and the long miles of the day were over. *That doesn't mean I don't have work to do tonight,* he thought ruefully. Still, the comforts of his cozy home embraced him as he entered, hung his keys on a peg by the back door, and yanked his feet out of his heavily fortified work shoes. Next he removed his belt with its holstered weapon and hung it in the small rear closet, then locked it, finding even this ritualized sequence of tasks a comfort. He grabbed a quick shower, changed into the lightweight sweats he wore in warmer months, and skipped his thick socks in favor of a worn pair of slippers.

When his stomach rumbled, he headed for his freezer, where he saw a rather unappealing collection of frozen dinners lined up like books on a shelf. Choosing the Salisbury steak entree, he slit the plastic film covering, popped it in his microwave, then assembled a plate and flatware on the bar. While his food heated, he walked over to his stereo system and dropped the turntable needle on Keb Mo's recent album, "Just Like You."

Once dinner was served, he sat on one of the two barstools and tucked in to his modest meal, greatly improved by the music. He had to laugh when he heard the man sing, "I'm On Your Side." As if the singer had tuned into Del's efforts to understand the mysterious journalist whose disappearance he was investigating, the lyric said, "Just tell me what's wrong and let me make it right." *If only,* he thought, putting away his dishes and closing down the stereo.

Del grabbed a beer from his fridge and settled himself at the work surface that would likely never become a dining table again. He'd brought home the journal recovered from Christine's car. It matched the last journal of hers that he'd read: same small size, same elastic strap keeping it closed. This one was labeled 1996-D, which presumably meant it followed immediately after the previous one. *That should give me a good, consistent timeline*, he reflected, hoping to fill in some of the many gaps in her known whereabouts, though they'd yet to find notebooks labeled A or B. The C notebook had contained stamps from lighthouses, but the date function at the light stations must not have been working well, as the stamps seemed to be out of sequence.

Ignoring both the recognizable scent of lavender that rose from the pages, and the now-familiar handwriting, he focused on content. Flipping forward he found:

> *I feel as though I'm having some sort of clandestine love affair. The symptoms are all the same: my heart skips a beat when he calls; I can never call him back; I look forward to meeting him but am scared and worried about these meetings, and can't tell anyone about them. Last time I was due to meet with him, I remember glancing in my underwear drawer, thinking I ought to put on something naughty for our meeting. It was a strange thought, and I dismissed it, but the fact that it crossed my mind got my attention.*

At first he assumed Chris was referring to Joseph Calvin, but the references to being unable to call him didn't jibe with other notations: *call Joseph back.* Curious, he flipped pages backwards to see if he could anchor these comments to any person or appointment but found none that seemed to relate. Settling back in his chair, he picked up where he'd left off.

Meanwhile, I'm still dating Joseph. Most of the time I enjoy the man. He just "gets it" in a way that younger men don't. He's a gentleman in the old sense. What possessed the women's movement to decide having doors opened by a man was a bad idea? It feels positively luxurious, and I say that from the depths of my hypocrisy.

If Joseph were another schmo trying to bang out stories on the word processor next to mine or a co-anchor trying to beat me out for ratings, I'd claw and scratch at him as I would any colleague. Did I say colleague? Do I really have any colleagues? Don't they all become competitors? But since Joseph is above it all by virtue of (a) not being a distinguished fellow member of the press corps and (b) being richer than God, the only clawing and scratching we do is in bed, and both of us wish we could do a bit more of that.

The journal seemed to grow hot in Del's hands, and he dropped the book on his desk. *I don't want to read this.* The fact that his reaction to such intimate descriptions revealed some secret strain within himself of . . . what? Conservatism? Shyness? Inexperience? Hardly. It was the sense that he was being forced into becoming a prurient peeping Tom. Yet, if he didn't read the journal, wasn't he failing to do his job? Taking it up again, he soldiered on, skipping over further intimacies about Mr. Calvin.

Why did I ever start accepting calls from this mystery man? He's got one smooth voice, and I wonder if I'd have been so receptive if he didn't sound so sensual.

This, Del realized, must be the man Chris was referring to earlier . . . the one she could never call back . . . an informant? "Mystery Man" could be what she was signifying with the initials "MM." She gave him no name in her notes. But at least he had something to trace. A few minutes later, he'd almost decided the journal contained nothing but personal battles between the reporter and her conscience, when he opened it for one more glance and caught sight of a possibility that would fit the "MM" initials. He began reading again.

It was Mr. Man's theory that I'd find something at Sawyer Construction. I did—but only by dumb luck.

When I was an earnest student at journalism school, they sure as hell never mentioned I might be breaking and entering. My hands shook so badly I thought the local sheriff would hear me from the highway.

Del stopped reading as though he'd been slapped. *The local sheriff . . . that's me! Jesus, I'm in her journal. Well, yes and no.* He went back to the page.

But then the lock gave, and it seemed almost too easy. I had no idea what to look for, but there were a lot of plans in Mr. Sawyer's office. So I started separating architects' drawings—those huge sheets—and they kept curling. I used my nail to pin one edge down. Then I realized my polish had left a tiny red-pencil line. I used an eraser to try to get rid of it, and there I was, frantically trying not to tear the page, when something caught my eye. Under the "Clarke Shipping" line, a second line, with a second corporate name, "Sunomon Corporation."

I was curious about the two names . . . maybe a holding company? I checked all the sheets. Nothing unusual —they all matched. As quickly as possible, I rerolled the papers and replaced them on the desk. I couldn't wait to get out of there.

I took one more look around, and my flashlight streaked across something near the door, behind a file cabinet. Another roll of plans. Old ones, I figured. But when I touched them, they weren't dusty. In current use . . . but stuck out of sight? That got me going.

My instinct to open that second set of plans overcame my better judgment. My heart started to race when I saw the client designation. "Clarke Shipping" and under it nothing about Sunomon. Nothing at all. So now I start comparing both sets of plans sheet by sheet. The differences were hard to spot at first, so subtle that even a worker who'd been referring to them all day wouldn't have noticed the differences at a glance. But the differences were there: the depth on the poles; the date of contractor inspection on the concrete extrusion. And down in the corners on one set of plans, little tiny infinity signs. I did a pretty good job of memorizing what I saw.

Here the narrative trailed off. Apparently, she'd meant to continue. *Did she run out of time?*

Suddenly in sync with a woman he didn't know—and probably never would—Del felt his own mind spin as fast as hers must have, realizing the magnitude of the clue she'd just found.

He thought through the sequence again. Chris had had an anonymous informant she'd named "Mr. Man." He'd sent her to Sawyer Construction. That had led her to Clarke Shipping . . . which meant the plans must've been for the Clarke mansion currently under construction. She must have confirmed this with her contact, who then sent her not to the Clarke Shipping office, but to Clarke's private home. Why?

Had the informant's tip been a genuine lead from someone trying to help her get a good story? Or had it been a setup, sending Chris to a possible kidnaping, or worse?

This journal ties her case to Clarke Shipping. This should finally be enough to get a court order to install a bug ... find a way to trap someone there. A worker? Or even Clarke himself, if he knows about this.

Del now had something concrete to take to his superiors. He also had enough new information to construct the bare outlines of a puzzle. In his gut, Del knew he'd just stumbled across the very path he'd been searching for.

Delmar headed to Paso Robles for a meeting the following morning, then cracked the windows of his SUV on his way back to Milford-Haven. He glanced up at the orb burning high over the coast. *The sun is warm on my face—and I fear Chris Christian will never feel that warmth again.*

He shook his head as though he could dislodge the presence that still haunted him.

His car was still too warm, and he flipped on the air conditioning. Of course, this wasn't *real* heat. *If I were back in L.A., I'd be baking in my squad car,* he mused. But by now he'd acclimated himself to the relatively cooler climes of the Central Coast. Even so, the July weather seemed oppressive, and he knew it was only a prelude to the much hotter month of August. Already it was plenty hot just over the ridge of mountains he was driving through. Paso registered 109 degrees yesterday, setting a new record. *I'll be heading over into that heat again tomorrow, to go over the car with the forensic team.*

I must be spoiled, he thought. *What's the matter with me? Nothing a glass of Sally's sweet iced tea wouldn't cure.*

Lunch was in full swing by the time he pushed open the squeaky screen door of Sally's Restaurant, and he slipped onto his customary stool, then perused the menu. When he'd decided on the California sandwich—avocado-tomato-and-Swiss-on-rye—he glanced around at the crowd. It took discipline, but he managed not to do a double take at the sight of Stacey Chernak walking in the front door and taking a seat at the far end of the counter.

Quickly, his mind sorted the facts he remembered: she worked for Clarke Shipping in Morro Bay; she'd had bruises consistent with domestic abuse; and when they'd spoken some weeks ago, she'd known about the mansion being built here in Milford-Haven. *Maybe she's here to check on Clarke's property.* It made sense. And the injuries he'd seen on her several weeks ago had now apparently healed. With the practiced eye of a professional, he kept her in sight while June took his order.

Chapter 11

Stacey Chernak had made her way down Main Street to Sally's quaint little restaurant and been only slightly intimidated to discover how popular it was. Since she was on her own, it didn't seem right to take a whole table, so she'd opted for the counter.

Ze chilled gazpacho will be just ze thing for this hot day, she thought, finding she was hungrier than she'd realized. Once she ordered, it arrived quickly. Enjoying her soup, and the crisp salad that came with it, she lost track of her anxieties until she glanced to the end of the counter and saw Deputy Johnson. With an involuntary jerk, she dropped her spoon, and it clattered to the floor, the sound lost in the background din of the restaurant.

Trying to calm herself, she thought back to their previous encounter. He'd interviewed her at Clarke Shipping, asking questions about some missing woman she'd never known or heard of. *I am sure he noticed my injuries, though he did not ask me directly.*

She'd pushed her luck at the time, leaping at the opportunity to talk—only in theoretical terms—about the rights of victims of domestic violence. If he'd seen through her charade at the time, he hadn't let on. He'd been kind, informative, available. She wasn't used to that. It had scared her even more than gruff inconsideration might have.

Whatever the case—here he was. *Perhaps he vill not remember me. No, zat is not likely.* What would she say if their eyes met? What would she explain about her trip? Well, it was, after all, part of her job. Stacey slipped off her stool and stooped to retrieve the dropped spoon.

This is more than just doing your job, her guilty conscience whispered. *You know you also wanted to get away—away from Wilhelm.* She climbed back onto her stool and placed the soiled spoon near the counter's edge where her waitress would see it. *Perhaps it is even more,* her conscience continued. *Zis trip was so you could prove your trustworthiness to your husband, show him that you could drive somewhere on your own but remain obedient and loyal, and therefore no longer have to cause him to discipline you.*

She risked a glance in the deputy's direction. *Ze last time he saw me I had bruises. Fortunately, I have none today. Last spring I had even considered reporting Wilhelm to this deputy.* Now, once again in the presence of an actual law enforcer, she suddenly felt foolish. She could prove nothing. She'd stolen none of Wilhelm's papers—not even temporarily, to make copies of any of the documents she'd found. She'd overheard nothing concrete that she could report about his behavior. Yet, his entire profession of reuniting lost children with birth-parents had been called into question, as far as she was concerned. And his apparent obsession with one particular case—the Hugo case—seemed out of proportion.

In spite of her misgivings, her intuition was working, picking up traces of something unholy and dangerous. Pursuing this line of inquiry was hazardous to her, she knew. At best, she was asking for more abuse in what had now become a consistently abusive relationship. At worst, she was setting an explosive device that could be triggered in a final deadly episode. So far, Wilhelm had restrained himself from doing murder. Would he always remain on the razor's edge of control? *Perhaps he, himself, does not even know.*

Shuddering, Stacey did her best to come to grips with the fact that she'd committed to some inexorable course and that perhaps, in some way, she herself was somehow attracting the very elements to further it. *Is zat why Deputy Johnson is here at the same moment I am?* But then she chided herself, *Zat is foolish.* He probably ate here every day, and she'd just stumbled into the patterns of life in this small town.

The fact remained: they were both here. She had the feeling neither of them would leave Sally's Restaurant without having a conversation with each other.

Kevin Ransom parked his truck and heard the hubbub of Sally's Restaurant the moment he turned off his engine. Swinging his legs to one side, he rotated his body out of the truck and stood in a fluid motion, unconscious of his own grace. Hearing the screech of Sally's screen door, he hurried to catch it before it slammed shut behind the previous customer.

There were two things that topped Kevin's "least favorite" list. One was confrontation—and he went out of his way to avoid it. The other was being clandestine—which made him feel guilty, even when he hadn't done anything wrong. Though he didn't care to admit it, he resented being told to spy, and he wished Jack wouldn't ask him to perform these tasks.

Now, however, he'd followed Mrs. Chernak's trail to Sally's Restaurant's parking spaces. Conscience was telling him he should walk inside and tell her what he was doing. Instead, he ducked in the door and stood just inside to scan the room.

There she is, at the far end of the counter. Kevin watched as Deputy Del stood from his own stool, moving to one next to her. Then they began to talk. Jack would arrive at the restaurant soon, Kevin figured, so he waved at Sally and took their usual corner table.

He knew Jack would be anxious to hear from him. So once he was seated, he opened the cell phone his employer had given him, and called.

"Sawyer."

"Yeah, boss, it's me. She's here at Sally's. Want me to bring you something?"

There was a moment of static while Jack considered. "No. Save me a chair."

Realizing the phone had gone dead, Kevin closed it and craned his neck to read the specials written in multi-colored chalk on the blackboard he'd helped Sally fasten to her back wall. In bright green, "Gazpacho" was hand-printed under "Soup," which was printed in pink. Kevin always checked to read the specials and usually ordered whatever Sally was featuring for the day. He turned his head just in time to catch Sally's eye.

"Hey there, Kevin. Glad to see you're *alone* today."

"Not for long, though."

"Oh." Sally bit her lip. "Well, tell me what I can get for you right quick. I'll be sendin' June over to take *his* order."

"I think I'll have my *own* special today, Sally. Tuna—"

"—melt with extra pickles on the side?"

"Right," Kevin replied, then grinned. *Really feels nice that somebody remembers what I like.*

"Ice' tea?"

"Yeah!"

"Comin' right up." Sally smiled back at him warmly.

It took only a few minutes for Sally to fetch his iced tea and bring it to his table. As she did, Kevin watched as the smile fell from her face like a plate dropping to the floor. He glanced over as Jack strode into the restaurant. He seemed to look right through Sally as though she wasn't there, aiming his barrel-chested body toward the table where Kevin was sitting. Kevin's gaze went back to Sally, and he saw the hand holding the coffee pot start to tremble, then watched as Sally turned one rubber heel with a squeal and headed into the kitchen. His heart hurt for these two people who'd once gotten along so well, and now couldn't seem to say a decent sentence to each other.

Taking the seat across from Kevin, Jack sat as June approached their table. She put her coffeepot on the edge of table, pulled the order pad from her apron and licked the end of her pencil.

"Yuz ready?"

"I'll have the usual, June. Sally knows what that is."

"Why don't you tell me, just for fun."

Kevin noticed her Brooklyn accent had an extra edge of sarcasm today.

"Fine. I'll have the hero sandwich—hold the lettuce. And a cup of coffee."

"Cawfee. Got it. I'll be right back."

"You're carrying the pot, aren't you?"

"Pardon me?"

"Can't you pour me a cup right now?"

Glaring, she grabbed his clean cup and filled it, retreating before any further friction ignited a spark.

The tension's riding high today, Kevin considered. *At least I got our corner table. Jack hates it when he can't see behind his back.* From here, both of them could see everything that happened in the restaurant, so Kevin knew exactly when Jack noticed Deputy Johnson talking with Mrs. Chernak.

"Bloody hell," Jack muttered under his breath, wincing at a sip of hot coffee and swiping at his mustache. "A fine thing."

Playing innocent, Kevin asked, "What's that, boss?"

"You see who's talking to our client's Girl Friday?"

"Oh, yeah, saw them talking before."

"And I suppose you didn't think to mention it." Apparently disgusted, Jack squinted at him.

"Well, no, not really. I mean, Del's in here every day."

"And you mean to tell me he speaks with every customer?" Fury flashed through Jack's eyes, and Kevin wished he could make himself small.

The men sat quietly as June returned to place the sandwich plates, refill Jack's coffee, and hurry back to the kitchen.

"Think about it, Kevin," Jack fumed, his voice carrying a heavier rasp than usual. "What else *could* they be talking about?"

Puzzled, Kevin regarded his food longingly. "Other than what, Jack?"

"Other than the house!" Lifting the stack of soft bread and flavorful meat to his mouth, Jack sank his teeth into the sandwich, nearly biting it in half.

Sally pounded on a new batch of biscuit dough, doing her best to take out her aggressions within the inner recesses of the kitchen.

"Some reason you're doing biscuits in the afternoon, Sally?" June asked.

"Who wants to know?"

"Just curious," replied June, placing sliced dill pickles on a line-up of plates. "Those for tomorrow morning?"

"Might as well get a head start."

"If you say so." June ladled *gazpacho* into bowls.

"Well, I *do*," said Sally emphatically. Looking up at her colleague, she pursed her lips. "No offense, June."

"None taken." June lifted the two bowls and carried them out.

Samantha arrived at Sally's Restaurant, huffed when she saw Jack and Kevin at their usual table, then took a seat at the far end of the long room. June brought over a glass of water and a menu, at which point Sam explained Miranda would be joining her, and June returned a moment later with another water, menu, and setup.

I won't be surprised if Miranda's a bit late, given all that's going on in her life these days. Her friendship with the younger woman was certainly a special one. It'd started when Sam hired Miranda to paint a mural for the EPC the moment she'd arrived in town. Indeed, that job had helped Miranda make the decision to make Milford-Haven her home, though Sam took no credit for the decision, which had been entirely up to the wonderful young artist.

Sam had become aware, however, that the family did not approve this move and in many ways continued to recommend that Miranda reconsider, even though it was clear to people here in town that Miranda had made her choice. Though Sam was sure her parents were lovely people, she also felt for the young woman as she sometimes chafed at the not-so-subtle pressures to conform. *Am I Miranda's friend? Or a substitute mother? Maybe a bit of both. I'll need to tread carefully when her real mother comes to town for the wedding.*

Sam caught sight of her friend, waved, and Miranda headed over. The two women embraced and sat, and Miranda took a long sip of the water her friend had ordered for her.

"I'm so glad to see you," Samantha said warmly. "I know this must be a crazy busy time with all the wedding preparations."

Miranda smiled. "It is busy. And it is crazy. All the more reason I needed to relax for a few minutes."

"Yes, and eat something. If I know you, you haven't had lunch yet."

"You're right," Miranda confirmed, glancing up at the colorful chalk board displaying today's specials.

June arrived at their table. "Tea for yous?" she asked.

Both women nodded, and both ordered the soup of the day. June nodded as she scribbled in her order book and walked away.

"First, how did your bridal shower go? I'm sure it was elegant." Sam knew her mother Veri had arranged the event for her daughter at their family home in Belvedere.

Miranda smiled. "Oh, it was."

"Tell me all about it!" Sam enthused.

June arrived with two bowls brimming with fresh gazpacho and small plates of homemade cornbread. They thanked her, then resumed talking.

"Mother's garden . . . the flower arrangements inside . . . the doors all flung open . . . I'm not sure I've ever seen it look so beautiful."

"Oh, my," Samantha murmured, taking her first bite of soup.

"Of course, there was the usual disagreement over my dress. She and my sister insisted on taking me shopping, though. I was worried at first, as everything we saw was . . . well just not me. Ultimately, we found something simple and lovely."

"I can hardly wait to see it," Sam enthused, "when you walk down the aisle. And what did you wear for the shower?"

Miranda smiled. "Something simple, of course."

"What color?"

"Peridot green."

"Which matches your birthstone jewelry."

Miranda nodded. "Which were gifts from her."

"I'm sure it made her happy to see you wearing the jewels," Sam observed. "So, who all was at the party?"

"Friends of hers, and some friends of mine, women from the neighborhood, some school friends I hadn't seen in forever."

"How nice they all wanted to celebrate with you," Sam commented.

"They brought so many gifts, it was embarrassing. I think a lot of this was Mother showing off," Miranda added.

"She's proud of her beautiful, accomplished daughter. Of course she wants to show off."

Color rose in Miranda's cheeks as though she felt ashamed of her ungrateful attitude. "You're right. She went to a lot of trouble. It was all very sweet, really." Fidgeting with her spoon, Miranda stirred her soup absently.

"You're going to liquefy that chunky soup," Samantha noted with a smile.

"What? Oh, sorry."

"It's *your* soup. Enjoy!" Samantha paused, dabbed her mouth with her napkin, than asked, "What else is going on, Miranda?"

"There's something . . . I'm not sure what it is, but something's going on with Meredith. She won't tell me what. She just kept saying it's 'your moment' and that all the focus has to be on me because 'you're the one getting married.'" Miranda finally took a spoonful of soup.

"Hmm," Sam considered. "Think she's jealous?"

Miranda paused for a moment. "Yes. I think she is. Though it doesn't really make sense. I mean, she only started dating Zack a few months ago, and from I can tell, that's going really well." She broke off a piece of cornbread and said "Mmm" when she bit into it.

"Maybe it's because she's the elder sister and she figured she should be the first to get settled in a permanent relationship," Sam offered.

Miranda pressed her lips together. "Wish I could say I feel a little bit guilty about that. But honestly, I don't. I'm too happy!"

Both women laughed out loud.

"That's just the way it should be," Sam declared. "This really is your moment. Your ship has come in."

"Thanks, Sam," Miranda whispered, her eyes beginning to pool. "I love Cornelius so much I can hardly stand it."

Sam gave her a broad smile. "And it'll only get better. You'll see."

"Not sure how it could, but I'll take your word for it."

The two friends ate in silence for a few moments. Then Sam observed, "You do look marvelous. You always do, but now . . . there's something different."

Miranda nodded. "I feel it. I think with everyone I dated before, including Zack, I was sort of playing a role, I harbored this fear that I wasn't smart enough, desirable enough, pretty enough, talented enough, you know? So I tried too hard to be *nice,* to fit in, to do what they wanted. I hardly left myself enough room to figure out what I wanted. Except when it came to work. Putting that first saved me, in a way."

Sighing, Samantha patted her napkin to her mouth and said, "First of all, what would ever possess you to believe you're not gorgeous, talented and desirable, I can't imagine. But I do understand the *nice* factor. I used to do that myself."

"No way."

"Hard to believe I could ever be nice, right?"

"No, I didn't mean—!"

"Just teasing, Miranda." She laughed. "But seriously, I played the part of 'Pleasing Woman'—but not for very long. Rebellion came naturally to me."

"Oh boy, I wish it had to me. But now . . . I just get to be myself with Cornelius. He wouldn't have it any other way. And he can spot any less-than-authentic behavior a light-year away."

Sam closed her eyes for a moment, then said, "Talk about light-years. You've moved on to the next level, Miranda, if you already have that kind of honesty in your relationship. Pausing for a moment, Sam sighed again and looked over at her friend. "Miranda, every woman—maybe every person—has the desire to please others. It's not a bad thing. It can even be a beautiful thing. When it gets out of kilter—and believe me, I know it can happen—we go into what I call 'nicey-nice' mode. We think we're functioning in a kind of superior way: we're being patient, kind, even in the face of resentment or anxiety. It can be dangerous, though. Because we can agree to things we don't actually *want* to do. I've learned that we're only overly nice when we're afraid of losing something—or someone."

A slight smile of recognition crossed Miranda's face. "That makes sense. I *was* afraid of losing Zack, even though we were never really together. I have no fear of losing Cornelius. I'd do anything for him but not out of fear."

Finishing her soup, Sam pushed her bowl away and smiled at Miranda. "Now you're talking."

Miranda slurped a bite of soup, then said, "By the way, I know Sally isn't your favorite person, but she's hosting another shower for me right here in her restaurant next Saturday. I hope you'll come. It'll be a lot more casual than the one in Belvedere. And we're going to stuff envelopes."

Sam laughed. "Being practical while you celebrate? Well, of course I'll come. I wouldn't miss it, Miranda."

Cynthia Radcliffe had finished another punishing gym workout. But now that she was showered and almost dressed to go out, she gave herself a half smile, pleased with how she looked.

In the weeks and months since her break-up with Zackery, she'd run an emotional gauntlet. The first days she'd indulged in a series of crying fests, burrowing under the voluminous white pillows and comforter of her bed and weeping till her eyes were nearly swollen shut. *Thank God those days are over!*

The next phase had been anger. While she let it roil through her, she'd thrown breakables—not the *most* valuable ones—letting the fury rip through her and her condo. *Good thing I got past all that. I don't want to break any more of my stuff.*

Next, she'd cleaned her condo, sweeping up broken shards of glass and porcelain, then scrubbing everything in sight. She'd followed her domestic devoirs with a redo of her shopping habits, training herself to buy fresh fruits, salads and soups, skipping most of the sugar and carbs. She was more disciplined now, and that was all to the good.

In some ways, all that personal drama seemed to have happened years ago. The frightening sense of being so out of control, the ugliness of her dependence on Zackery, the stupidity of her assumptions. . . .

Most terrifying of all was the resemblance to her father when he'd been at his worst. *I can't go down that road. I think I stopped myself just in time.* But when she was honest, she knew she still had work to do on figuring out exactly what triggered her.

Meanwhile, she had a new-old hobby. After she'd been brave enough to ask Rune to listen to that tape of her singing, he'd come through for her. He'd arranged for a two-weekend gig at a little club up in Goleta. That'd gone well, and he had a few more things set up for her. "You sing like a bird, Chica," he'd said with that sexy smile of his.

That was another thing. Rune was sexy. *No wonder Zack was always jealous.* She'd suppressed the spark between them back in the day, but now there was nothing stopping her. Well, except that he didn't want this just to be a rebound fling, and neither did she.

Heading for her small, sunny kitchen, she decided to heat some milk for *café au lait*, and when it was ready, she carried an oversized white cup to sit on her tiny balcony. As she slurped a first steaming hot sip, she heard the call of a wild parrot from its branch on a nearby loquat tree. *Well, that's a bird, but I hope I don't sing like that!* She chuckled, in a better mood than usual these days.

She had to admit she'd earned the better mood. She'd finally gone to some Al-Anon meetings, where she'd started to recognize some her own patterns. Self-justification had been her standard operating procedure for as long as she could remember, imprinted early by her alcoholic parents. Reconsidering her actions from the point of view that *she* might be the cause of events in her own life—at least partially . . . this had been a startling new concept.

She'd even begun to ask herself what she might have done differently with Zackery. When the answer surfaced, it amazed her. *I could have been more honest!*

She could almost hear her mother's long-ago admonition to the contrary. "Never let a man know what you're thinking; never let him know you're smart; set a tender trap they can't help but fall into." She'd swallowed the advice as neatly as her mother had tossed back her gin. Cyn had even thought it'd worked for all those years.

But Cynthia herself had been caught in repeating patterns. Case in point: she and Zackery had the recurring drama of nasty fights followed by sexy reunions . . . just like her parents. Zackery used to beg her to calm down, say what she needed, share her feelings. Instead, she'd hide behind self-manufactured drama.

She thought back to the beginning of their relationship. *I started out trying to land him because he has money, power, and security.* There. At least she'd admitted that to herself.

Another thing she'd finally seen: she'd always considered passion to be the glue that held romantic relationships together. *If you don't have that, you don't have anything.* Or so she'd always believed, just as her mother had said.

Share my feelings? Baring her soul to a man had seemed like a suicide move on the chessboard of romance. Now she was experimenting with expressing herself, answering honestly, for example, when Rune asked her how she felt and what she wanted.

He was good at that, had always been good at calling her on whatever scheme she'd tried to hide behind. *That used to make me mad. Now I sort of appreciate it.*

Rune had asked her out over the Memorial Day weekend, a couple of weeks from now. He was away now, visiting his father in Mexico, but he'd be back by then. He wanted a casual afternoon of perusing the shops downtown, he'd said. And they'd follow it with a nice dinner.

"No pressure, Cyn. Just wear something nice. We'll have fun," he'd promised, giving her another of those sexy smiles. It'd been a long time, and Cynthia was looking forward to an evening out.

Chapter 12

Samantha sat in her desk chair but then popped out of it again as though she were a jack-in-the-box. What the angst was all about she couldn't figure out, but she felt as though ants were racing up and down her arms and crawling along the seams of her slacks.

Work folders lay stacked on every square inch of her desk, but this was nothing unusual. There was plenty of work to occupy her; yet she couldn't seem to focus on anything but a future she couldn't quite glimpse.

Was there something she'd been missing? Was it that report she read the other day? Both she and Stacey had agreed there was really no new information in the most recent report, but something kept ticking in the back of her mind. Deciding she had to set her personal concerns aside at least long enough to get some work done, she called out to Susan. "Bring me that soil report from the house on Wilson, will you?"

She called out again, but when there was no reply she decided to check on that report later. *Susan must be in the restroom.*

Stacey reached the outer door of the Environmental Planning Commission, her heart pounding loudly enough to sound as though she were knocking on the door.

She'd seen Ms. Hugo at the restaurant, but fortunately, she and her friend had been talking with one another and had left before Stacey had finished speaking with the deputy.

The golden afternoon light indicated her time was now limited: she *had* to arrive home before Wilhelm. Pressing her hand to her chest as though she could slow her heart rate, she inhaled and pushed the door open.

A young woman sat before a computer screen, but failed to acknowledge her visitor. Long, straight black hair draped over one eye and trailed down her back—Stacey couldn't see how far. The features were attractive, but the face was pulled taut almost in a grimace. *Is she Asian? No ... perhaps she is American Indian? Zis must be Susan Winslow,* Stacey reasoned. "Hello?" she ventured, but Susan banged away at her keyboard. "Uh, excuse me, I am sorry to disturb."

"Yes," the young woman snapped without looking up.

"I am wishing to meet, please, Ms. Samantha Hugo?"

"I'll see." Rolling her chair back, Susan stood, then clomped in heavy shoes to a private door, and banged on it.

"What is it, Susan?" The woman's voice, which Stacey recognized as that of Ms. Hugo, had annoyance in the tone, discernible even through the closed door.

"You have a visitor," Susan sang. "Want me to send her away?"

"Well, who is it?"

Without ceremony, Susan turned to face the visitor. "Who are you?"

"I am Mrs. Chernak."

As though coming out of a trance, Susan suddenly seemed aware. "Oh! It's Mrs. Chernak!"

Suddenly, the door to the private office opened. "Mrs. Chernak!" exclaimed Samantha. "Well, this *is* a surprise. Uh . . . why don't you come into my office."

Susan seemed annoyed by this, and Stacey watched as the younger woman turned on the heel of one of those big shoes and spun back toward her desk. Then, with some relief, Stacey followed Ms. Hugo into her private office, waiting while she cleared a stack of magazines off a chair.

"Please have a seat. As I said, I'm surprised to see you, Mrs. Chernak. Does this mean you have some news?"

"This is not exactly news, but I thought it would be good if we could meet in person."

"Frankly, I've been wanting to meet you in person since we first began talking, so I'm delighted."

Heartened by this remark, Stacey felt the knot in her stomach begin to unwind. "You see, although, of course, my husband and I work together, I vill now handle your case."

"Yes, I know. I thought we already discussed that during our last phone call."

Stacey shifted her weight in the chair. "Of course, we *did*, but in zis case I am having a personal interest."

Samantha looked at her skeptically. "Oh? Why is that?"

She does not believe me. Panic clutched at Stacey, and her eyes darted around the room. With effort, she folded her hands, forcing them to settle in her lap like two birds trying to escape their cage. *This woman is good with her instincts. I must give her substantial reasons and perhaps share with her more than I planned.* Inhaling, Stacey gathered her thoughts. When her eyes came back to Ms. Hugo, the woman still gazed steadily at her. "Your case interests me, Ms. Hugo. I feel perhaps I can imagine how . . . difficult it would be to lose a child."

"I didn't lose him, Mrs. Chernak; I gave him up. But you're right, it *is* difficult."

"I was thinking, sometimes we choose something early in life, then wish to change our mind later." Stacey saw her words had struck a chord. "Perhaps we could review the case together."

"You mean, go through all the details again? Surely you've already taken notes on all the information I've given you."

"I have." Reaching into her oversized purse, Stacey pulled out a plain manila envelope. "Would you like to read for yourself what we have found out so far?"

Samantha's eyes darted to the envelope avidly, as though it held blackmail negatives. "Yes!"

Opening the file, Stacey traced her finger across a form. "Gregory Hugo Sawyer, born May 5, 1960."

"*Cinco de Mayo,*" Samantha said under her breath.

"I beg your pardon?" Stacey's pencil was poised, ready to write.

"No, no, nothing. Continue."

"In 1963 the home adopting him was Santa Innocente in San Jos. Usually the records kept by Catholic homes are excellent but—"

"It burned down. You told me that."

"This is the report we received."

Snatching it from the hand Stacey offered, Sam scanned it quickly, as though afraid the words would disappear before she could read them. Stacey knew what she would see: the orphanage fire report, which concluded with "No fatalities."

"Thank God," she muttered.

"Then I found . . . that is, *we* found—my husband and I—that your son and two other children from Santa Innocente had been moved to Atascadero."

Ms. Hugo seemed to make an effort to keep her feelings controlled, gasping, "So close!" Then she added, as though thinking out loud, "Close in geography to where I live *now*, but, of course, distant in time."

Handing her another sheet, Stacey looked kindly at the pain in Samantha's eyes.

"This is just a microfilm photocopy—a little hard to read."

"Yes. I am sorry, the copier . . . that is, this is the only copy I could find." She'd made the copy herself, furtively, having "borrowed" the original from Wilhelm's desk. She hated lying to this woman, but for now she was taking as much risk as she could.

"It says *three* children."

Stacey fidgeted. "Yes, we . . . I am vorking on discovering where they are as well."

Closing the file, Ms. Hugo handed it back to Stacey. "I appreciate your showing me the file, Mrs. Chernak. I . . . well, I'm glad you're working on the case."

Feeling herself lighten at the vote of confidence, Stacey smiled and felt a bit more courageous. "There is one thing I would like to ask you, Ms. Hugo.

"Yes?"

"You are also continuing to try to find your son on your own, yes?" The client looked uncomfortable at this. "I do not criticize you—I ask because . . . if you find information, would you mind to speak to *me* about this case?"

"Speak to you?"

"Yes."

"And not to your husband, you mean?"

Her mouth dry, Stacey kept her gaze steady. "Zat is right."

After a slight pause, she replied, "I *prefer* working with just one contact, as I mentioned on the phone. So that's not a problem."

Relieved, Stacey returned the file folder to her bag, then stood. "Thank you, Ms. Hugo, for your time."

"Thank *you.* And do keep me posted."

"Posted?" Stacey paused. "Oh, yes, I vill keep you informed." She turned to go.

"There was nothing else? No other questions you had for me?" Ms. Hugo asked.

"Not for zis moment. But please, you could call me. I . . . you could reach me here." Retrieving a pen and a small note pad from her voluminous bag, Stacey jotted the number of Clarke Shipping.

Obviously surprised, Samantha looked at what was written. "This isn't the same number that I have."

"No . . . I have . . . this is my work . . . my other work."

"You have another job?"

"I do. Zis is why my husband is usually answering the agency telephone. But for certain cases, like yours, I prefer you should reach me directly."

Though she paused for a moment, the woman then seemed to accept this. "Well, thank you for the number. And for the visit."

"Thank *you.*"

Opening the door of the private office, Stacey nodded to Susan, who seemed to be hastily returning to her desk. *Was Ms. Hugo's secretary listening at the door?* Susan's smile seemed forced. But the young woman's attitude could not dampen Stacey's relief that her mission had been more successful than she'd dared to hope.

Samantha retreated to her office and closed the door. Something about the Chernak woman's visit bothered her, and she couldn't quite put her finger on it. Mrs. Chernak had shown a directness in coming to her office, which she liked. On the other hand, she'd seemed at times jittery and insecure, as if looking over her shoulder.

Though technically Chernak hadn't revealed anything new, Sam did have a clearer sense of the facts because now she'd read them and seen that they existed in a file. *It's all true, then. I really am looking for my long-lost son, and someone really is helping me to do so.* Yet—much as she wanted to—she didn't quite trust Mrs. Chernak, at least not yet.

Beginning her late afternoon ritual, Sam sat in front of the computer, clicked the Internet access icon and began scrolling through her regular list of environmental sites, thankful again for the new DSL connection. Though it was far more expensive than the old dial-up, she felt the time savings more than made up the loss to the budget. She no longer had to wait through the sign-on process—and she should call Del to thank him again for the advice. Come to think of it, Del would be a good person with whom to discuss the Chernak visit. Sam jotted a quick note to herself in her overcrowded calendar.

When she'd forced herself to read through the news items on each site, she began perusing one of her favorite eco-bulletin boards where she read the latest rumor—that some yahoo developer in Pebble Beach wanted to take down 33,000 historic Monterey pines. Shuddering at the thought, she stood to get one final cup of coffee. The very idea that someone would want to destroy these healthy trees, when they were already so vulnerable, showed either gross ignorance or just reckless disregard. The whole species was suffering from pitch canker disease, for which as yet no cure had been found, and trees all the way from the Bay Area to Santa Barbara's Hope Ranch were showing signs of the fungus.

She plunked down in her chair again, rubbed her temples to ease the persistent headache, and found herself succumbing to a sequence of thoughts, each crowding out the next. First, there was the upcoming Town Council meeting, where she knew she could expect more than the usual fight from Jack. *I have more preparation to do.* That was tonight's homework.

Wilhelm Chernak had instructed Russell Clarke to meet him at his office after hours. Of course, the man hadn't liked his tone, but that was immaterial. Yes, Russell Clarke was the CEO and owner of Clarke Shipping, a mid-sized firm that handled international oil delivery to ports all over the world. In his own domain, which included his attractive offices in Morro Bay, he was king. In his partnership with Chernak, however, he was subordinate, though he considered himself to be an equal. *He can think this for now,* Chernak muttered.

Wilhelm, who ran a small firm of his own in the pleasant coastal town, had considerably bigger fish to fry, as the Americans would say. For now, his agency for finding lost children was a perfect front for his actual endeavors as a successful trafficker. Not even his own wife realized what he was actually up to.

Stacey worked at his little agency part-time and worked nearly full-time at Clarke Shipping, acting as an efficient secretary four days a week, which allowed Wilhelm to keep eyes on Clarke and his employees in a perfectly subtle way. Stacey, whom he had wooed and married in their native Switzerland, was not the sharpest knife in the drawer—another American expression he enjoyed using—but she was loyal and useful, at least for now.

He was pleased she would not be at the office, nor would she likely to be home by the time he concluded his meeting with Clarke. He had planned it that way, contriving to have her sent to Milford-Haven to check on the mansion Clarke was having built there, and also meeting with their client, the Hugo woman. Of course, Stacey would be late getting home, which meant he had the perfect excuse to punish her, lest she suspect her limitations were being eased. He enjoyed their little contretemps, and smiled, remembering the last time he'd battered her for no particularly good reason.

Wilhelm entered the Clarke Shipping premises with his key, then climbed the stairs and made his way to the conference room, where he'd told Clarke to wait for him. He had evidently complied, because he sat in the darkened room now, his silhouette outlined only by ambient light bouncing off the bay beyond the plate glass windows.

"Hiding in your own establishment?" Wilhelm asked, his voice laced with insult.

"The better to see you with," Russell replied in a deep, sonorous voice.

"Vell, it is good to be seen," Wilhelm parried. He was instantly on guard, and immediately irritated. *Zis is alvays his attitude,* he complained to himself, the stress of the moment bringing out the Swiss accent he could never quite squelch, even in his own thoughts. "Zo," he said, slapping a file down on the conference table and yanking out one of the comfortable chairs to sit opposite Clarke.

"What did you need?" Russell inquired.

Zat deep voice . . . he must charm the women with it. "You know what I need. A complete update on this man you hired to take care of the journalist woman."

"Hmmph. That hardly seems a legitimate excuse for our visit. After all, we agree the less you know the better. N'est-ce pas?"

Wilhelm refrained from reacting to Clarke's use of French, which he knew he only used to irritate him further. "Pas," he responded with a tense grin.

Clarke crossed one leg over the other and touched a button on the wall, which turned on a soft glow emanating from the crown molding that decorated the top of all four walls. "Fine. What is there to tell? The man did his job and has been laying low, pending further instructions. Should we need him again, he'll be ready."

While he spoke, Clarke adjusted his cuff links and looked bored, or perhaps just impatient. *Does he have somewhere else to go? Is he keeping someone waiting?*

"As I said, I need ze details. For example, how did zis man arrange to meet with the journalist? Wasn't he told to warn her? Is zat what he did? Or did he do vorse? Did he thereby open us up for unwanted scrutiny? Zis woman was well known. If she does not reappear, what sort of connection vill they find zat might lead to Clarke Shipping?"

Clarke uncrossed and recrossed his legs, looking slightly uncomfortable. "I see your paranoia is showing, Mr. Chernak. What brought all this on?"

Now it was Wihelm's turn to feel uncomfortable. "There has been . . . a rumor circulating at your very own company about zis woman. I am surprised you do not keep better ears at your company."

Russell turned to face Wilhelm directly, his lips drawing back as though he were about to growl. "Of course I have good 'ears' at my own firm," he snarled, showing even more of his truculence. "You're making assumptions about you know not what."

Wilhelm sat taller in the chair. "Fine," he said. "Ven can you arrange transport for my next shipment?"

Clarke provided a weak smile as he said, "Thirty-nine days."

Wilhelm looked away, calculating for a moment. "Zis is good."

"By the way, I'm thinking of adding someone to this shipment. That so-called wife of yours. She's getting too inquisitive."

Wilhelm felt the blood drain away from his face, then rush back with the anger beginning to boil through him. "You vill not touch her," he declared in an icy voice. "I have her perfectly under control." Even as he said the word, he struggled to maintain his own.

"If that's the case, then perhaps it's her friend who needs to be dispatched, whether via shipment or some other means."

"Friend?" Wilhelm asked. "Stacey does not have friends."

"Oh, I see you're a bit out of touch, Wilhelm. She's become quite cozy with Gladys. And it's a shame, since both of them are good workers. But Gladys has been with the firm long enough to know where bodies are buried, at least some of them." Clarke chuckled.

Wilhelm thought for a moment, trying to recall where he'd seen the name. *Scheisse. Stacey had her business card, from that shelter organization.* "Yes . . .," he replied slowly. "Perhaps zat vould be best. I vill leave zat in your capable hands."

"Good. Was there anything else?" Russell asked.

"No. Ve vill meet again soon, no doubt." Wilhelm said, standing.

"No doubt," Russell agreed, tenting his hands and making no effort to shake hands.

Wilhelm turned on his heel and exited the building, forcing a deliberate slowness when he'd have preferred to run.

Chapter 13

Sally was so busy during her Wednesday morning breakfast rush that she'd nearly forgotten her irritation of the day before.

That was Tony's fault. His presence in her life had lifted her up beyond anything she'd been able to imagine in . . . well, she couldn't remember how long.

She'd done the prep work for the upcoming lunch hour, and glanced around at her gleaming stainless countertops. She hummed her little improvised tune now, as she looked forward to the afternoon she and Tony had planned. She was taking off the rest of the day, something else that was making her happy.

"Okay, June, I'm leavin' now!" she called to the far end of the kitchen.

"Right, Sal. Have a good one!" came the reply from her trusted assistant.

Sally squeezed herself into her yellow Pinto, grateful she could still drive, and headed to Tony's rental, where he had promised to feed her. *Well, he'll be feedin' both of us*, she thought, patting her swollen belly.

She arrived at his place and parked on the street, since his van occupied most of his driveway. The rental was modest, but he kept it as neat and tidy as her mama's sewing room. She was about to knock on his front door, when he swung it open for her.

"Welcome," he said, his eyes sparkling, his rich voice resonating through her.

"Well, thank you kindly, sir." She giggled.

"Hungry?"

"Enough for two," she confirmed.

"Excellent. Follow me."

As he rolled down a short hallway, she followed till they arrived at the kitchen-dining area where he'd set the low peninsula with two place settings. A basket with a paper napkin liner was hiding something—rolls, she imagined. And a wonderful aroma of tomato sauce filled the air.

Her stomach rumbled as he pulled out the one chair for her, then moved to the stove to start dishing raviolis.

"How many, Sal?" He asked.

Her stomach growled again before she could answer. "Well, excuse me!"

Tony laughed. "That's a good sign!"

"I'll have four, if there's enough."

"More than. Tomato sauce good?"

"If it tastes as good as it smells, I'm gonna want plenty."

"Comin' right up."

Sally waited patiently, entranced by watching the fluidity of his movements. His long arms reached for a ladle, his hands deftly managing the serving, and then the carrying of both plates on a tray attached to his chair.

"Dig in," he suggested when they sat opposite one another, fragrant steam rising from their food.

Sally took a first bite and closed her eyes in appreciation. "Mm mm mm," she intoned.

Tony chuckled. "My mom's recipe," he offered. "Can't go wrong. Worth its weight in gold."

Sally nodded. "Oh, ye-yus. My mama's too. Trick is to watch her make the food, cuz when she writes down a recipe, it jus' says, 'pinch o this, pinch o that.' Who knows how big a pinch is, anyway?"

"I hear ya," Tony agreed. "Only way I learned was looking over Mom's shoulder. Want a roll?"

"Don't mind if I do." She waited as he pulled back the napkin for her, and she lifted out a soft, warm bakery item.

"These ain't homemade, " he confessed. "Best I could find, though, without getting them at your own restaurant."

Sally laughed, took the roll and spread butter on it, then watched for a moment as it began to melt. "Tony, I—" she began. "It's so nice havin' you here. Feels like forever you weren't. And now it feels right as rain."

"Good," he said in a matter of fact tone. "Meant to be."

The words themselves were almost romantic, and she felt her pulse rise, along with a few misty ideas. But his tone sounded rather businesslike.

"So listen," he continued. "I've been thinking about something. Who owns that property behind your restaurant?"

Sally blinked. *So he is talking about business*, she thought, pulling herself back from the brink of embarrassing herself with some gooey, unwanted sentiment.

"Oh, Mr. Hargraves does. He owns that whole parcel, including your hardware store, my restaurant, and that empty storefront. Oh, and the parkin' lot too."

"What I figured," Tony said thoughtfully, pushing away his now empty plate. "I had an idea I wanted to run by you. It could be awfully nice out back, if we set up some tables, umbrellas, some potted plants."

"Oh, ye-yus, I've always imagined that!"

His expression growing more animated, Tony went on. "We could put pavers, set up a pathway between your store and mine, encourage folks to stop for a meal after they shop, or wander over to the hardware store after lunch."

Envisioning what he outlined, Sally nodded.

"You know, what with the baby coming and all, you won't have as much time; you'll have to hire an extra hand. Maybe this can make up some of the revenue."

"Some of the revenue?"

"More places to sit, a little shade. Your regulars might not break away from their favorite tables, but the tourists—they'll love it."

"Why, I believe you're on to somethin' there, Tony!"

He gave her a wide grin. "Good. Next thing is to check with Mr. H."

"Oh land sakes, he would never say no. Prob'ly what he's been wantin' all along anyway. And now he's finally got the right man for the job."

They each sat in silence for a long moment. *He must be imaginin' it, jus' like I am. He did want to talk business, but it's a dream too.* She watched as he glanced around, apparently searching.

"Need somethin'?" She asked.

"Yeah, a pencil."

While he rolled toward the far side of the kitchen, Sally took their plates to the sink, rinsed their dishes and placed them in the dishwasher. Tony was back at the table, but sketching something, and she returned to her seat to watch.

A rough sketch showed their two businesses, and he was mapping out a pathway and patio area. "If this works like I think it will, I'd like to ask Hargraves if I can rent that empty space too, turn it into a garden shop."

"Ye-yus! It'd fit right in with the hardware. You'd have the indoor goods folks need and then the outdoor things too."

"Exactly."

"You . . . you got buckets of money for all this, Tony?"

"I got a bucket or two. And these would likely fill right back up, if I do it right."

Oh, you're already doin' it right, she thought. Aloud, she added, "Jus' let me know how I can help."

Miranda had made a salad of crisp mixed greens, seasoned croutons and perfectly ripe tomatoes, a quick, tasty meal for two. Now she grew excited as Cornelius drove them to the architectural offices of Jameson Raymond.

The unusual building was nestled into a hillside, angled windows glinting in the sun, landscaping embracing the various modular units of the structure. Miranda stood for a moment, taking in the sight of it as though she might paint it one day.

"Beautiful, isn't it?" Cornelius offered.

"Oh, my," she replied quietly. "I shouldn't be surprised, after all the conversations we've had with him. But we always met at our property."

"Right. I'd forgotten you hadn't seen his office." He reached for her hand. "Ready?"

Miranda smiled and nodded, stepping through the door when he opened it for her.

"Come on back!" They heard Jameson's voice call out.

His conference room offered an ocean view through a trapezoidal plate glass window, and once again Miranda paused to admire what she saw. But soon her gazed drifted down to the table itself, at which Cornelius was already staring.

"You did it," he said.

"Well, it's a start," Jameson confirmed.

The long conference table was almost entirely taken up with a model of their property. But instead of the decaying structures, construction zone, and ripped out shrubbery on the actual site, here all the planned buildings stood in their perfection, if at an uninhabitable scale.

"Makes me want to swallow Alice's Drink Me and shrink myself to fit!" Miranda sang.

The two men laughed.

"In that case, I better get to work on power and plumbing," Jameson joked.

"Wow," was all Cornelius could add at the moment, bending over to peer more closely at the planetarium.

Miranda, meanwhile, couldn't decide which she found most fascinating: their lighthouse home, her studio building, the pond, the pool, the guesthouse, or the geodesic dome. "What—?" She began, pointing at the round structure.

"That'll come along later, along with the kids," he explained.

Miranda felt heat rise through her. "Children?"

Cornelius caught her eye, and the two shared a moment of virtual time travel.

Jameson cleared his throat. "You know how kids love funny looking buildings. This sort of looks like a jungle gym from the outside. Inside, it'll have comfortable rooms they can grow into."

"Whimsical," Miranda said quietly.

"Marvelous," Cornelius almost whispered.

"Probably on my mind a lot, given my wife's current condition."

Now all three of them laughed.

"I'm a visual person," Cornelius declared, staring again at the model. "I can't tell you how much this helps!"

"It's the first step of manifestation," Miranda observed. "It's how I always work, too. Oh, I love it so much. We're going to have to find a place to keep this forever, even after everything is built. It'll be better that doll houses, if we have girls."

"And better than model planes if it's boys."

"And good for everyone in the household who possesses an imagination," Jameson added.

Miranda took some time to peer more carefully at the small structures from every possible angle, hunched over as she circled the table, while Cornelius peppered his friend with questions, all answered in animated tones.

Half an hour later, Jameson asked, "Shall we go view the full scale model?"

Jameson drove his two clients to their property, unable to keep his enthusiasm from bubbling to the surface.

"Remember that section of the wall where we used to climb?" he asked Cornelius, who was riding shotgun.

"When we were seven year olds? Oh, yeah, I certainly do. And so do our mothers!" The two men guffawed.

"Hmm," Miranda said from the back seat. "Does your wife know about these naughty boy stories? I gather you two were doing something dangerous?"

"Of course!" Jameson reassured. Then he added, "Not!"

Another guffaw engulfed the front seats.

"What happens on your property, stays on your property," Jameson admonished.

Miranda thought about this for a moment, recalling the first night Cornelius had invited her there to enjoy a camp dinner and the most romantic night of her life in his tent. As though reading her thoughts again, Cornelius turned his gaze toward her. "Yeah," Miranda agreed, "You're absolutely right about that."

Jameson, smart enough not to ask exactly what she meant, pulled up alongside the front edge of their lot. "Here we are," he said, exiting the car as his passengers did the same. "Let's start at the main house."

The heart of their new-old abode was the stone tower that'd never been a functioning lighthouse, but certainly looked like it, if a bit smaller than most. Around its base, a semi-circle of new construction would fan out, then blend into a spacious new kitchen-dining-living area.

"The lighthouse is a palimpsest," Jameson explained.

Miranda and Cornelius looked at each other.

"Oh, sorry. Meaning it's something reused but still carrying elements of its earlier form."

"Exactly," Miranda now confirmed.

"Got it," Cornelius echoed.

Warning them to walk carefully, he led to the opening where the front door would be installed, then up the spiral stairs. He paid close attention to what each of them mentioned, using his own shorthand to make marks in a small notebook. Miranda focused on assessing wall space for murals and floor space for furnishings, and sizing up the windows for future coverings.

His pal Cornelius, on the other hand, asked questions about where the electrical panel would be located, which he would show him when they walked through the addition downstairs; whether the one solar array they'd planned would be enough for the whole property (if not, they could add to it later); and whether he thought painting the pool black would be a good idea. He replied yes, that it would absorb more heat and blend into the landscape.

This is my favorite thing, Jameson kept saying to himself. *Helping people realize their dreams, or manifest their vision, as Miranda would say.* He was liking her more and more, now utterly convinced she was indeed the right match for his buddy. Having found that perfect partnership in his own life, he'd hoped and even prayed that Cornelius would find this blessing for himself. He'd despaired for a while, with his friend being a science nerd, an introvert, and a night owl. Yet, the universe had conspired to bring these two together. They'd seemed an unlikely pair at first—an artist and a scientist. But he was wrong about that. They completed each other's sentences when discussing some topics, laughed about their different perspectives as they talked about others.

About the plans for the property, Jameson felt increasingly confident. These friend-clients were both good at expressing their design and function ideas, which of course made the process easier than most. And the fact that they had a virtually unlimited budget didn't hurt! But there was something more. These two people thought big and would soon be acting big. He was convinced of it. They would do important things in the world, and this would be not just their family home but also their global headquarters. And he, Jameson reminded himself, was building it for them.

Miranda lowered herself into the camp chair next to Cornelius and took the hand he extended. She looked into his eyes for a moment enjoying the light pressure when he squeezed one finger after the next.

"What an incredible day," she commented, suffused with a sense of fulfillment she could scarcely articulate.

"Getting hard to tell where the dream ends and the reality begins," Cornelius said, perfectly summing up both their sentiments.

They turned, then, toward the sea wall to enjoy watching the sun set over the ocean, casting its long rays across their property. The light glinted on the water, fragmenting into perfect puzzle pieces while at the same time remaining whole. *And that's how I feel about my life*, she thought, a shiver of delight shimmering through her.

"Chilly?" he asked.

"No," she said. "Just happy. So happy"

"Not as happy as I am," he said quietly. "You have no idea."

He took a deep breath, let it out, his sigh mingling with the evening breeze.

She inhaled then, gulping the rarified air of the property where they'd be building their lives together.

Chapter 14

Delmar had spent his Wednesday hunkered down in the SLO office, reviewing stacks of labeled file folders and noting progress on current cases: Felony Evasion; Grand Theft; School Threat; Scam Alert; Suspicious Death; Burglary Suspect; and Reckless Driving were among those being handled by the competent group of officers and detectives, with nothing falling through the cracks. His own job as a member of SPU—Special Problems Unit—gave him flexibility to set his own schedule and roster, but he made himself available to his colleagues when they needed him.

Thursday morning he enjoyed a quick breakfast at Sally's, the best place in town for keeping his ear to the ground. He chatted for a few minutes with Emily Wilkins, reporter for the *Milford-Haven News*, who chattered about a few upcoming summer events she'd be covering. But she did a good job keeping her finger on the pulse of the town, attending Town Council meetings, asking the right questions to keep the citizenry apprised of policies and developments. Though they'd only touched on the subject lightly so far, he considered her an important contact in the Chris Christian case. Even though their respective work took place in the two separate media of print and broadcast, still they were both journalists. Emily might hear something that Del wouldn't. As he moved toward his stool at the counter, he nodded at Lorraine Latimer, the doyenne of the council, affectionately known as the "Crone" for her wisdom, though he would never address her as such.

He enjoyed connecting with these locals, each of them contributing citizens, feeling a growing sense of belonging in this coastal enclave. But when his food was served, he found his thoughts returning to a particular passage in Christine's journal that kept repeating itself in his mind.

She'd chronicled that her contact had sent her to the Clarke house. Before going there, she didn't know much about it, but had done enough research to discover that its owner, Russell Clarke, owned Clarke Shipping, which was in Morro Bay.

Del, too, had followed his own leads to Clarke Shipping, where there were other cross-connections. One, Stacey Chernak worked there, though she was also ostensibly helping Samantha Hugo track down her son. Two, Stacey was being abused, a fact that both he and his friend Gladys had noticed. Three, the abuse put Stacey's husband Wilhelm in the frame, but Del still didn't know exactly how. The fact that he was an abuser did not yet mean anything legally, as Stacey had not pressed charges.

But why would Chris's contact send her to the unfinished house? What might have been there at the time that would cause Christine's investigation to take a leap forward? Since construction had continued, whatever it was might now be less accessible. Or, maybe he could still come across some anomaly.

Could Del justify a visit to the site himself? *I could claim to be a lookie-loo, not there in any official capacity, just curious about Milford-Haven's first bona fide mansion.* With no more than a hunch for guidance, he set off for the location just north of town.

Delmar saw a friendly face the moment he parked near the entrance to the property. His friend Kevin's height gave him away as he walked carefully across the rutted dirt of what would become the driveway.

"Hey, Kevin!" Delmar called.

"Hey there, Delmar," Kevin replied on the way to his vehicle, where he placed some metal pieces in the truck bed. "What brings you to our unholy mess?" he asked with a grin.

"Unholy, is it?"

"Well, I don't know why I said that," Kevin admitted. "It's just . . . something odd about this project. It's taking forever, for one thing. Maybe it's just cuz it's so huge."

Del nodded. "Seems likely. But, uh, what do you mean by 'odd'?"

Kevin looked at Del as if he might say something more, but then shrugged it off. "Nothing. Tired, I guess. Been a long week."

"At least it's Thursday. Almost done, right?" Del reminded.

"Yup. Can hardly wait. So, something I can do for you?"

"Just being a nosy neighbor, really. Thought I'd like to poke around, but I suppose that's not allowed without an escort."

"Must be the season for construction site tours," Kevin observed. "No problem. I'll grab you a hat, though."

Delmar followed as Kevin led him from the bright daylight into the darkened interior. While he let his eyes adjust, he accepted the hard hat Kevin offered and placed it on his head. Then he watched his own footsteps so as not to trip over debris, as Kevin led on.

"This'll be the kitchen," Kevin said, pointing to a large area where Sheetrocked walls defined a large open space, and where markings on the floor indicated "island," "cab" and other identifiers.

"Nice," Del remarked blandly.

"If you like that sort of thing," Kevin said under his breath. "This'll be the living room."

Now standing in a cavernous space with a gigantic opening facing the sea, Del said, "Nice view."

"Yeah," Kevin agreed, while shaking his head. "Might as well be sitting outside."

Del chuffed out a laugh. "No accounting for taste."

"Takes all kinds."

The two men continued down corridors to bedrooms, then in the opposite direction to a massive master suite. Del heard a scrape behind him, but when he turned, no one was there.

Kevin stared toward the same area where Del's gaze rested. "Nothing there, right? Happens a lot here. Like there's a ghost."

Del whipped his head around to look into Kevin's eyes. "What do you mean?"

"Oh, nothing. It's like I said before. Something odd about this place. But there's a lot of wind right here on the coast, you know? I'm not used to that. My place is up in the trees."

Not willing to discuss his own beliefs with Kevin at this point— and certainly not here—Del said, "Yeah, mine too. Cozy, right?"

"Cozy, beautiful, full of critters. Feels like I'm surrounded by friends, not all alone out here."

"Good point," Del agreed. "Anything to see downstairs?"

"Not much, just some empty rooms. But I can take you down there if you like," Kevin offered.

A few moments later they'd negotiated the planks that filled in where stairs would be placed. The rest of the bottom floor, though, was also Sheetrocked. The large room closest to the coastline seemed to be a second living room, or perhaps a den and screening room, with a walkout to a lower deck, again offering an incredible view of the rocky shore. "Depending how it gets finished, this could be on the cozy side," Del observed.

"I suppose," Kevin allowed.

As they headed back to the planks to get back upstairs, Delmar felt the hair on the back his neck stand up. He stopped walking, his senses alert.

"What?" Kevin asked.

"I don't know, I—"

Neither of them spoke for a long moment.

"Nothing. Go ahead," Del directed.

"What I'm talking about," Kevin muttered as he climbed back to the main floor.

Back in daylight and on solid ground, Del turned to thank his friend. "Appreciate the tour," he said. "Looks like it'll be quite the showplace!" he spoke with a cheer he didn't quite feel, in case anyone overheard. Suddenly, he heard footsteps and turned to see a worker heading inside. *That's a big guy. Not as tall as Kevin, but muscle-bound.*

"Hey Burt!" Kevin called to him. "Wanna take lunch now?"

"Sure thing, boss," the man called back. As he did, he turned his head just enough for Del to notice something on his face. *Just a shadow? No . . . a mark. A mole! Holy— That's him!* He was only able to keep his face implacable because of his years of training. "One of your regulars?" he asked Kevin as casually as his voice would allow.

"Sort of, yeah. He's a seasonal guy. Good worker."

"And his name is Burt? In case I see him around, I can say hi."

"Yeah, Burt Ostwald. German name, I guess."

"Sounds like it. Well, thanks again, Kevin. Hope you have a great weekend away from work."

"Thanks! I could use it."

Delmar climbed into his SUV and drove away, vibrating with awareness.

This is the link! This is the missing connection. I know it is.

He quickly drove home, where he could best collect his thoughts, forcing them to slow down enough to get aligned. Skipping his usual rituals, he walked directly to his small back patio and sat heavily in one of his Adirondack chairs.

Where had he first heard about the large man with the sizable mole on his face? In Santa Barbara. Yes, that's the man who had rented a kayak and failed to return it in time. But by morning, the kayak rested against the shack, so the owners had no reason to follow up with the guy.

Meanwhile, there'd been that strange case of the sea otter who'd been shot. The necropsy had confirmed the cause of death, and Del has asked the local Fish & Wildlife director to keep his apprised, should anything further surface about that case.

This "Mole Guy"—Del could make a call to the kayak rental to confirm his name—had then disappeared, but there was nothing unusual about a tourist passing through any of the coastal towns.

Neither might there be anything strange about a man working in Milford-Haven but taking a kayak rental in Santa Barbara—though he could've rented a kayak and enjoyed an excursion in Morro Bay, which was a good hundred miles closer.

If Ostwald were a seasonal worker, where did he live? Presumably, he was on Jack Sawyer's payroll. As a hired worker, he'd have access to the construction site any time. Would he have gone to the house at night? Could he be Christine's contact, the one to invite her there? If so, he had information he'd wanted to share. He'd be in the "good guy" column.

On the other hand, what if he had not been Chris's contact? What if he'd ambushed her at that house, carried her off somewhere, even disposed of her body? Then what had he done with her car? Could he be the one who drove it up into the hills by Lake Nacimiento? If any of this were true, he'd most definitely be in the "bad guy" category.

Delmar called the office to check on sound recordings that might by now have been retrieved from the new surveillance devices placed at Clarke Shipping.

The one tape that'd been transcribed so far had picked up a menacing references to two employees: Gladys Wilson and Stacey Chernak. Stacey's apparent ignorance of the larger picture would likely protect her for the moment; but Gladys, who'd been working as an informant, was at immediate risk of being exposed, if she hadn't been already.

Weeks earlier, he'd vetted an officer who could fill in for her, a trained operative who could pose as having been sent by the Temp agency the company used, but who also knew how to handle herself in dangerous situations.

Del called her, confirming she could step in quickly. Next, he had to extract Gladys carefully without raising suspicion about what would be her sudden departure.

He'd called Gladys to meet him for lunch in Milford-Haven. He'd chosen the Bluebird café, rather than Sally's, the charming hub that tended to have ears. The Bluebird, where he sometimes enjoyed dinner, was more private. In addition, it suited his purposes to have Gladys make the half hour drive north, so they would not be observed in Morro Bay, where she worked.

Gladys, whose job at Clarke Shipping told only part of her employment story, also served as one of the directors at the local domestic violence shelter, a post filled by a tight group of rotating experts. It was a way of keeping expenses to a minimum for the non-profit, and it also ensured extra security for its temporary residents seeking respite from abusive situations.

Because of her domestic violence training, Gladys was plenty savvy about presenting a pleasant face in public, while helping those in dire need with absolute discretion and secrecy. So today, if anyone did notice them having lunch, they would appear to be old friends exchanging jovialities as a cover for information they actually needed to share. It didn't hurt that both Del and Gladys were African American. He knew there was still enough polite but simmering prejudice that their Caucasian observers would dismiss two black friends having lunch as something normal—more normal than an interracially mixed couple.

Del had arrived first and chosen a table where he could observe the front door and the other patrons unobtrusively. When Gladys arrived, he stood to welcome her, and they shook hands warmly.

"Well," she said in a voice pitched just loud enough for others to hear, "How are you old friend? It's been quite a while!"

Del played along. "It has been. I'm so glad we could get together and catch up!"

Their waitress stopped by and they each ordered iced tea.

"I'll have the chili and some cornbread," Del said.

"That nice big Caesar salad for me," Gladys said, then added, "Got to watch my girlish figure, you know!" She then laughed.

The waitress nodded politely and left while she scribbled their orders.

"I don't have as much time as I thought," Gladys said, patting her face with her napkin to obscure the words.

"Okay. You're being watched?"

"No doubt," she said, as their glasses of tea arrived. "There is no doubt whatsoever that I am overdue for a vacation!" She said, full volume.

"I hear that," Del said quite audibly. Then quietly he added, "I finally got permission to install the bug."

"Bugs!" She called out as their plates of food arrived. "Can't stand them!"

"Thank goodness they're few and far between, compared to the south," Del agreed. "Thanks," he added, nodding to the waitress.

Once they were alone again, Delmar leaned over his food and brought his spoon close to his mouth. "I haven't had a chance to tell you, but we've been monitoring overnight. We've already heard enough to know it's time to pull you out."

"What?" Gladys asked, forgetting to say the word quietly.

"It's all arranged. We have an undercover woman in the department who'll fill in for you while you're gone. We've set it up so you can visit that sick aunt of yours, in case they check."

Gladys took a sip of tea and began to choke.

Del patted her on the back. "It's okay. You'll be safe."

"Are you all right, Miss?" The waitress was back with a concerned look on her face.

"Yes," Gladys said weakly.

"Her tea went down the wrong pipe," Del explained. "Don't you hate it when that happens?"

"Oh, it's an awful feeling," the waitress sympathized.

"If something were actually caught in her throat, I'm trained in the Heimlich." Del offered his most dazzling smile.

"Good to know!" The waitress said, returning to the kitchen.

"Sorry to spring it on you," Del said softly. "But I couldn't risk talking at your office, nor over the phone."

"When?" She asked.

"Soon. I'll call and ask after your aunt. That's when you can say she's feeling poorly."

The rest of their lunch was almost entirely a charade, as Delmar watched his friend's expression, convinced he could almost see the wheels turning.

Chapter 15

Susan found herself irritated by the gnawing rumble in her stomach. Alone in the EPC offices late Friday afternoon, she sat at her desk sucking up the last of the double café mocha drink she'd brought with her earlier today. But the high caffeine beverages had only served to give her a chemical high and a case of jitters.

With a nerve-induced jerk, her hand pushed the mouse across its pad, and she watched the computer screen where a series of pages were displayed on the *http://www.coastalawareness.com* relatively new website Coastalissues.com. Impatiently, she clicked on the link to another coastal erosion study for the EPC files. "Come on!" she yelled at the machine as, one by one, the graphics slowly popped into view.

When the report she wanted had finally loaded, she clicked the "print" button and rose to make sure there was paper in the printer, then clicked a print order and closed down the website. "So stupid," she mumbled. *The point of websites is supposed to be no paper, but Samantha wants me to print these reports and put them in the filing cabinet!*

With a final glance at the wall clock, Susan clicked the "shut down" option and bounced up from her office chair, sending it careening noisily across the wooden floor. It was time to close the office. She had an early dinner—or very late lunch—date with Kevin.

Stepping into the ladies' room, she bent over at the waist, then stood, flinging her hair over and back. Adjusting the long fall of the straight black strands, she added some taupe lip shine and one more splash of the men's cologne she saved for special occasions.

Susan had no trouble finding her tall friend sitting at a rear table next to the juke box, despite Wing Ding's being crowded and noisy, as usual.

In her customary short skirt and heavy shoes, she sashayed to the beat of Bob Seger's song "Old Time Rock and Roll" that blared through the room as she made her way past the bar and slid into the chair next to Kevin. "Hey." Even seated, Kevin was so tall she had to look up into his face to batt her long black lashes.

"Hi," he said amiably. "Hungry?"

"Starving," she admitted, grabbing one of the menus stuck into a small table rack. "Veggie burger," she pronounced, after a quick scan of the specials.

"I think I'll have a meatball sub," Kevin decided. A waiter they both recognized stopped at their table, taking no notes when they gave their order, only nodding to indicate he'd memorized their selections. A few moments later, he returned with tall glasses of fizzing Coke, and Susan braced herself, knowing he'd slam them down hard on the worn wooden table. He always did.

"How's work?" Susan asked, eager to warm things up as a prelude to today's discussion. She finally had Samantha's grudging permission to visit the Clarke house. Now she needed to gain access. *Kevin will help me. He always does.*

"Pretty good," Kevin replied. "Most of the jobs are running smooth. Jack wants me at the Clarke job site part of this week."

Bingo, thought Susan. The Seger song ended, allowing her to speak in a normal voice. "Now *that's* something I'd like to see." She smiled. "I guess I'd need a tour or something."

Kevin drew a sip of his drink through a fat straw, then put down his glass. "Funny, I already gave a couple of tours yesterday."

"Oh, yeah? Like, who for?"

"First, a woman who works for Mr. Clarke. You know, the owner of the house? She came to see it."

"Why?"

Kevin paused for a moment. "Jack thinks Mr. Clarke is checking up on him. Maybe he was."

Susan flung her hair to one side. *I'm getting more information than I thought I would. Cool.* "Who else?"

"Oh, it was just Delmar. He likes to keep an eye on stuff all over town."

"He's a snoop?"

"No, he's a cop. It's his job."

"Oh, guess so. Did you show them everything?"

"Oh, yeah. Not that there's anything to hide. It's a big house, though. Kinda hard to tell what room is what at this point."

"I *love* seeing unfinished houses," Susan crooned.

"You do?" Kevin seemed surprised.

"Uh, well, especially this one, 'cuz it's so big and all."

Their sandwiches arrived and were slapped on the table as unceremoniously as their drinks had been. A customer stepped to the jukebox, poured in some coins and made some selections. In a moment, the Doobie Brothers began to sing.

While the song's bass notes drummed through the table, Susan said, "So cool I got to see them in person." She picked up her knife and sawed through her fat burger until it was in several pieces. After a moment she realized Kevin was watching her, rather than eating his own lunch.

Stabbing one of the bites with a fork, she lifted it to her mouth and began chewing. After taking a sip of her Coke, she said loudly, "Anyway, I have time this evening. Since you're giving tours, any chance you could give *me* one?"

She watched as Kevin sank his teeth rapturously into his sub. While he chewed, sipped and swallowed, he seemed to consider her request. "I'd have to check with Jack, and he's gone for the day."

Susan pouted. "Oh." She pushed pieces of sandwich around her plate.

"But I can ask him tomorrow, though I'll have to call him at home." They ate in silence for a moment. "How's school going?" Kevin asked. "Wish I had time to take some classes."

Susan could feel a blush creep across her cheeks. "Uh, good, I guess." She took a bite, trying to quell guilt about the classes she'd skipped.

"What subjects are you taking?"

"Accounting," Susan choked out. "*So* boring. And A&C, which is the only class I like."

"What's that stand for?"

"Architecture and Construction."

Kevin was lifting the last half of his sandwich to his mouth but stopped its progress in midair. "Really? What do they teach you?"

"Well, like, what has to get built first, how an architectural plan has to be converted before construction, stuff like that. See, that's why I like unfinished house tours."

Kevin pushed away his plate with its uneaten pickle and chips, a sadness crossing his face.

Oh, shit, thought Susan. *Maybe I hurt his feelings.* "I bet you could even *teach* the class," she said, eager to smooth whatever feathers might be ruffled.

"Maybe," Kevin said, "but I'm not a teacher. I *do* know about construction, though."

"Right! See, all the more reason why if *you* give me the tour, I'll *really* learn something—not like the theoretical stuff I get in class."

"You're really lucky," he said, "that you can afford classes."

Susan gulped Coke. "I'm not paying," she mumbled. "Comes with the job."

"Wow! Even luckier! Jack would *never* spring for something like that."

"Yeah, well, Samantha *expects* it. It's not like I had a *choice* or anything. I *have* to take classes." She chomped another bite. "And as far as money's concerned, my job *sucks.* I can't even hardly afford my rent!"

Kevin looked surprised. "What do you mean?"

Shit! I didn't mean to tell him that! But . . . now that I have, maybe I should just— "Okay," she said, taking a breath. "I wasn't going to say anything, but I think I might have to move."

"Why?"

"Like I said, I could barely make the rent last month. Still trying to catch up. The Environmental Planning Commission is all talk, you know. When Sam gets around to it, she applies for grants. But the salary she pays me is pathetic."

"Have you told her?"

"I told her I needed a raise. Did she listen? No! She never does!" Resentment roiled through her, threatening to spoil her lunch.

Kevin looked at her thoughtfully for a moment. "Listen," he began. "I uh . . . I know the guy who owns that little cottage you rent. He wants me to do some maintenance work. I bet I can get him to reduce your rent for some of my time to get some maintenance jobs done. That'll solve it for a month or two."

Stunned, Susan felt her mouth dropped open as she stared at Kevin. "You'd do that . . . for me?"

"No big deal," he said quietly. "Could happen to anyone. Listen, about the tour, I can show you around the Clarke house tomorrow during lunch, when the workers are taking a break. Right now I better get to the office. Jack wanted me to catch up on paperwork tonight."

But I wanna go tonight! Susan whined to herself. She considered. Should she force the issue, see if she could make Kevin take her there now? *No*, she thought. *I'll go there myself right after dinner, then go again with Kevin tomorrow. That way I can look it over for myself and have time to figure out what questions I want to ask.*

"Sure," she said. "I'll check with Samantha, but I think that'd be fine." She batted her eyelashes again, then as an afterthought said, "Thanks."

On their way out of Wing Ding's, Kevin paid for both their meals.

Susan pulled her battered VW bug to rest on a quiet street near the Clarke property. She exited her car, wriggled into the straps of the small leather backpack she used as a purse, pulled down on her short T-shirt, then walked the couple of blocks to the construction site.

Arriving in time to see the last of the workers leaving, she noticed two of the men eyeing her hungrily. *I think I know that one at the entrance . . . the big guy with the mole on his cheek.* She vaguely remembered flirting with him some weeks earlier at Wing Ding's. Tossing her hair to the side, she smiled at him and walked over the rubble of the caked and rutted driveway toward him. Ignoring the *No Trespassing* sign and stepping through the entryway, she came toe-to-toe with the man's large construction boots.

"We're closing down for the day, Miss. For the weekend, actually."

Looking up into his face, Susan gave him a sultry pout. "Aw, I'll only be a couple of minutes. Can't you give me a peek?"

Hoping mole-guy would catch her double meaning, she watched as he perused her from head to Doc Marten-clad toe. Enjoying the attention—and glad Kevin wasn't here to see it—she shifted her weight from one hip to the other. She liked the rough, dirty look of the man, saw the glisten of sweat on his muscular arm, and inhaled his pungent odor.

"Can't do that, Miss. It's not safe around here for little girls."

Giving him another pout, Susan assured him, "Oh, I can take care of myself. And I *promise* to be very, very careful."

The man snorted. "I'll bet." Glancing at his watch he said, "Can't be responsible for what happens after hours. But it *is* dangerous around here when you don't know what you're doing." Towering over her, he continued. "Consider yourself warned."

"Oh, I *do*." She stood her ground.

The worker stepped around her and called out, "Better put on a hard hat!" then walked away without a glance backward.

"As if he cares!" she mumbled. She listened as his boots crunched across the rubble, watched as his truck bounced down the rutted driveway. When the growl of his engine had faded, she realized with a small jolt of nerves that she was actually alone.

Something creepy about him, she thought. Then she reminded herself of her mission. *This is my chance to find something useful against nasty Jack. Then maybe Samantha will actually* get *how smart I am.*

She was glad, now, she'd studied the plans with such diligence. Feeling a need to assert her independence, she saw this as a long overdue chance to prove her worth to an employer who thought of her as little more than a wayward child.

Picking her way carefully over the flooring that was strewn with concrete bits, discarded nails, and other debris, she ignored a hard hat that rested there, scoffing at it. She walked through the oversized main room, trying to picture how anyone could use such a large space. *This would be great for parties,* she imagined. *You could put pillows on one part of the floor and leave the rest of it free for dancing.*

There was a big hearthstone in front of the fireplace, which must have covered a large hole that would have gaped until the stone was in place. And over by the kitchen, there was an open hole that'd probably lead down some stairs to a basement. Though dark orange light still spilled over the open window frames, the sun would soon be low enough that only a pale glow would penetrate the house, which had no electricity yet. *Better have my flashlight handy.* She reached into her backpack to retrieve it.

For the next several minutes, Susan wandered from room to room, trying to recollect which spaces were designed for what purposes. Though the main level was a little confusing, nothing about it seemed unusual except its size. The more she wandered, the more agitated she grew. *What am I supposed to be looking for? I don't see anything weird or out of place here.* Then she remembered the hole where stairs would eventually lead down. Frightening though it was to consider heading down to the lower level, it might offer access to a hidden space.

Walking back to what she supposed was the living room, she took a careful look at the crude slatted plank leading down into the perfectly dark hole. Shining her flashlight into the basement, she couldn't see anything but unfinished wooden flooring. Still, unless she looked, she'd never know. *Maybe that's where nasty Jack is trying to hide something.*

Taking a first step onto the plank, she felt it sag under her weight. Holding the flashlight in one hand and clutching at the floor's edge with the other, she stabilized herself and waited for the board to stop swaying. Then, carefully, she side-stepped the rest of the way down to the lower floor.

A musty, dank smell rose up to greet her nostrils, and she had to steel herself not to flee her sudden sense of claustrophobia. Walking cautiously through relatively low-ceilinged spaces, she emerged into a corridor off which were three windowless rooms. The bare walls seemed to close in on her, and she forced herself to gulp air.

Where am I? Despite the flashlight, the disorientation on this level was even more extreme than it had been upstairs. *But I swear these rooms aren't in the plans. Or maybe these are closets?* Numbers were written in black marker on some of the support beams. She had no idea what they meant, but, placing the flashlight on the floor, she fumbled in her bag till she'd withdrawn a notepad and pencil. Walking from beam to beam, she wrote down the numerals —those she could make out. *I can compare them to the ones on the plans they had in the office.*

The incomplete wall she now faced had an opening in it that led outside to an area under the deck. The upright beams supporting the deck seemed okay to her. *Of course, I'm no expert.*

But turning back around to reenter the house, she saw what appeared to be a crack in the foundation, close to where the house and the deck were joined. With the shadows falling, she couldn't see too clearly, but bending down to touch the line in the concrete, she felt where it had separated. *This might mean something.* She jotted down its location in her notebook.

If Jack Sawyer is doing something wrong in the construction of this place, how the hell can I prove it? One thing she *did* know —it was getting dark and she'd taken all the notes she could. Putting away her pad and pencil, and clutching the flashlight, she made her way carefully back to the plank and started to climb up to the fireplace. Knowing the ascent would be easier than the descent, she made no special effort to walk sideways. After all, the men who worked here must clomp up and down on this thing as if it were solid stairs.

Not even the deep sag in the board broke her confidence on the first three strides. But as her Doc Marten came down for a fourth step, she lurched as the plank slid to one side. Fear clutching at her belly, she felt the board slide even farther.

She flung her arms upward to grab for the edge of the floor above, but as she did, her forearm scraped along something sharp. Calling out with pain, she just managed to keep her grip and scramble upward till she reached the main floor.

She gained her footing and bent over to catch her breath. Wind rattled through the structure sending a chill down her spine, and she shook as shock began to grip her. *Breathe,* she told herself, as the old symptoms of PTSD tried to intrude.

She stood, dizzy with pain, aware she had to get out of here. *Can't see . . . I must have dropped my flashlight.* It was down in the hole, no doubt, and she wasn't about to try retrieving it at this point. Walking as carefully as she could, she made her way to the front door opening, across the hard ruts of the driveway, and down the street to her car.

Hands shaking, she managed to unlock her vehicle. When the interior light came on, she gasped: her hand was bleeding. Reaching across the driver's seat, she grabbed a stack of paper napkins she'd swiped from the burger shack and pressed them against her palm.

Gulping air, she fastened her seat belt, started her car, and drove slowly out to the main road. *That might've been a rusty nail.* Heart pounding, she considered what to do. *I could drive to Samantha's . . . but then I'd have to tell her what happened. I could tell Kevin. But I just wanna get home.*

Delmar threw his legs over the side of his bed and gripped the edge of his mattress. *That same nightmare again.* He looked around his dark room, then out through the open window, where he saw a thin line of red etching itself across the top of an eastern ridge.

The frequency of his dreams about Chris Christian had slowly, but surely, increased over the past nine months. *Sometimes it's like she's trying to speak to me.* Of course, in a tangible way, she now *had* spoken to him . . . through her journals. Because that, in turn, had instigated some of his own journal writing, it now almost seemed they were in a dialogue. *If so, it's the weirdest conversation of my life.*

A shiver ran down his spine. *Most likely, I'm talking with a dead woman.* He stood, as if to shake free of the thought. Then, to the empty room, he said, "And most definitely, I'm now talking to *myself!*" He sighed, then muttered, "This is a *great* way to start my weekend."

He walked into the bathroom, relieved himself and threw cold water on his face. As if to cover his naked body from an unannounced guest, he pulled on sweat pants and a T-shirt, then headed to the kitchen for a glass of orange juice.

Sitting at his small table, he ordered his thoughts. *What are the facts? Chris has now been gone long enough to be* officially *missing, and that changes . . . what?* With the discovery of her car, he at last had authority to conduct a comprehensive search, both locally and nationally. That was good. *But . . . although we've found her car, we're really no closer to finding* her.

On his mental screen, Del watched again the possible scenario that played like a film whenever he imagined Chris climbing out of her damaged car after it hurtled down that lost canyon. His virtual camera always zoomed in on the blank mini-cassette. *She's out there somewhere—with her tape recorder. Where the hell is she?*

Susan tossed one final time in a tangle of sullied sheets, waking herself from a nightmare. Her hand hurt like hell, but she knew that wasn't the only thing making her angry.

The bright sunlight refused to be blocked, despite the sheet she'd hung over the window. She flung a hand overhead to yank it. But from the floor-mattress that passed for her bed, her hand instead hit the bottle of water she'd left close by, knocking it over.

She'd forgotten to replace the lid, and the water spread in the direction of the torn envelope. Clutching for the letter, she rescued the hand-written yellow-pad note just as the corner soaked up the edge of the puddle.

How dare he write to me? She'd never answered it. She kept hoping he'd take the hint, but her father was nothing if not dense. Of course, that's how he'd wound up in prison in the first place. That, and the fact that he was a *killer*.

He always maintained it was an accident. They said he'd been full of remorse in court. She couldn't remember any of that; she'd been too little. She just remembered watching her mother die. That was something she'd *never* forget.

They said he'd been a model prisoner through the years. Now they were letting him out. *That's the system for you. Commit a murder. Get out for good behavior.*

Words from his letter came back to her unbidden: "Of all the mistakes I made, drinking alcohol was one of the worst, because it led to all the other mistakes. I always thought I could control the drinking. I realized too late it was controlling me. From the depths of my own guilt I am finally starting to see a better way to live. The remorse is a heavy burden, one I will never shake. Don't make the mistakes I made."

He has the gall to offer me advice! As if a letter about guilt could explain it all away! As if he could understand anything about my life! As if he actually cares! He knows nothing, and I'll see it stays that way. I have no parents. I have no father. I don't need one! I don't need anyone!

The sound of the ticking clock on her floor irritated her only half as much as seeing what time it was. *Great, I'll be late for work again.* Throwing back the top sheet, she kicked shoes out of her way and noted the puddle of water had stopped spreading. *It'll dry on its own.* She went to inspect herself in the bathroom mirror. Though hunger gnawed at her stomach, she ignored the minor annoyance and pinched her waist and the backs of her arms, where she could still grab half an inch of flesh.

Disgusted, she waited for the water to heat in her tiny shower stall. Taking little satisfaction from her ablutions, she pulled on tight-fitting, faded black leggings and a cropped black T-shirt that showed off her midriff. Samantha hated this outfit—which pleased Susan no end. Sticking her tongue out at the posters of rock musicians glowering from her black wall, she grabbed her backpack and flung open her front door, slamming it behind her. But that only made her hand hurt all the more.

Kevin woke early as he always did, raised a long arm from under the covers, and used it to push aside the nearby blinds to glance out his bedroom window.

What I figured, he said aloud. Fog drifted past the glass pane, obscuring what would otherwise be a view through the trees to the ocean down the hill from his cozy little house.

Fog or no, the critters who shared the property with him would be expecting their breakfasts. As he pulled a warm sweatshirt over his head, his own stomach rumbled.

In his tidy kitchen, he gathered a couple of nuts from the glass canister on his counter. His resident squirrel Rocket—Rocky for short, of course—would eat any kind, but his favorite, reserved for Sundays, was pecans. Kevin deposited two on his balcony railing, chuckling as he heard the creature responding with his enthusiastic little barks.

The opossum who lived in the large Jeffrey pine across from the balcony did a good job taking care of herself. But since Kevin had noticed babies in her pouch, he figured she could use a little help. These creatures needed lots of calcium, which they got from eating the skeletal remains of rodents and birds. For these items, she'd be on her own. But she also liked fruits and eggs, so he put an apple, a peach, and a hard-boiled egg in the metal bowl reserved for her use, and carried them downstairs to the foot of the tree.

Before he could head upstairs to make himself some eggs and toast, he heard gravel crunching in his driveway. Walking around the garage level of his hillside house, he was surprised to see Susan's car coming to a stop in his driveway.

"Susan?" he asked, walking toward her. *This can't be good. Something must've happened.*

"Hey, Kevin," she said in a nonchalant tone, as she stepped out of her car.

Her face looks pale. "Are you okay?" As he asked, he noticed her hand—bandaged poorly, a wound having leaked, leaving behind a dark stain. "What happened?!"

"I—" she began. "I fell. Well, I caught myself, but my hand scraped across a rusty nail, and I—"

"Come inside," he interrupted. "Wait for me while I get dressed. Then we'll get you to a doctor."

"But I—"

Kevin sprinted up the steps to his front door, banging through it. In the kitchen, he filled a mug with hot water and placed it inside his microwave to heat. Then he dashed into his bedroom, pulled on a clean pair of jeans, a T-shirt, and grabbed his jeans jacket against the morning chill.

By the time he walked back into his kitchen, he found Susan, still looking fragile, sitting in one of his two kitchen chairs. He pulled the warmed mug from the microwave and tossed in a big spoonful of honey and a caffeinated tea bag. "Here, take this," he instructed. "You can bring it in the car."

Without waiting for her to agree, he led the way to his truck and opened its passenger door for her, helping her climb in while he held the mug of hot tea, then handing it back to her before slamming the vehicle's door.

He climbed into the driver's side, started the Ranger, and drove slowly down his driveway, along the streets, and out to Highway 1, at which point he hit the accelerator. "There won't be any traffic on a Sunday morning until we get to SLO," he explained.

"Where are you taking me?" Susan asked. She didn't seem concerned, just curious.

"You said a rusty nail, right? You need a tetanus shot."

Chapter 16

Sally was at her restaurant Saturday morning just as the sun broke over Milford-Haven like a freshly cracked egg, the yellow vivid and round, the white spilling across the awakening town.

Her homemade biscuits were lined up ready to go into the oven, the coffee set to brew, and the white sauce for this morning's special just needed a little more whisking. *Time to clean up my mess before the rest of the staff arrives.* Pulling on rubber gloves, she ran soapy water into the mixing bowls and dipped her sponge to begin work on the counters. She didn't look up as she heard June coming through the back door but just responded with a bright "Mornin'!" to her greeting.

After using a clean cloth to polish the stainless steel to a gleam, Sally removed her gloves, then reached up to put away her cleaning products. She pressed fists into the small of her back, drew fingers through her hair, then stood quietly for a moment as she moved her right hand to lightly rub in a circular motion around her expanded belly.

Her screen door screeched, which was no surprise, as she knew some of her early birds liked to read their papers while the first pot of coffee brewed. She started through the kitchen, out toward the counter, but it wasn't a customer, it was Tony. *Now there's a welcome sight*, she thought, her heart thumping. The baby in her womb seemed to do a little tap dance as Tony wheeled toward her.

"Mornin', Beautiful," he said, his smile revealing white teeth against his dark beard.

"Mornin', your own self." She beamed back at him.

"Got something for you," he sang.

"Is that so?"

But as he was about to close the distance between them, June called to her from the kitchen. "Sal? Your Aunt Ida's on the phone."

"The phone?" Sally asked, confused. "The phone rang?"

"Yeah, just now."

It's Mama, she thought. *Something's wrong.* Sally stood looking at Tony, watching his face as it suddenly mirrored her own worry.

"Go get the phone, Babe. I'll be right here."

Whirling, Sally rushed inside her small office and picked up the receiver on her desk. "Aunt Ida?"

"Hi, hon. It's your mama. She had a fall."

"No!"

"Now she *is* gonna be fine. Fact o' the matter is, she *says* she's *already* fine. If she knew I was callin' you, she'd skin me alive. But I just thought—"

"You did right, Aunt Ida. I'll come as soon as I can."

"Now don't you tell her it was me that—"

"I'll tell her it's about the baby and that I just *had* to see her one more time before it came. I'll make some calls about plane schedules, and then I'll call you back."

"Well, I'm relieved to hear it, child. I'll be home."

"Thanks, Auntie."

Sally hung up the phone and sank into her desk chair. Fear about her mother's health tried to engulf her, but she fought to keep it at bay.

Tony wheeled quietly into her doorway.

"Mama had a fall," she said simply. "They say she's okay, but I have to go home to her right away. I'm gonna fly out today."

"No, you ain't," he said.

"What?" Sally asked, rising. "Tony, it's *Mama*. She needs me, and I'm goin'."

"I didn't say you weren't *goin'*. I said you ain't *flyin'*. Not with you this pregnant. We'll take my van."

"But Tony, I got Miranda's shower today! I can't just waltz out on her!"

"It'll take me a little time to get everything ready. Everything's gonna work out. You'll see."

Before she could think of an argument, Tony used his strong arms to wheel himself out of her restaurant.

Tony rolled himself at high speed across the parking lot to his hardware store. *Gotta get the van serviced, first thing.* Shushing through his back door, he sped to the phone and called the mechanic Shop. When he explained the situation, the shop's owner, Art, said, "Anything for Sally." Immediately, he agreed to have someone pick up Tony's vehicle, have it checked over and fully serviced, then delivered to the hardware shop by the close of the business day.

Okay, that's handled. Art's a good man—one more Main Street neighbor. I'll have to thank him properly. Still holding the phone, Tony thought for a moment. *Better call Mr. Hargraves. He did say he'd fill in for me if I needed it.*

He dialed the number of the former owner and waited till the man answered. "Hello, this is Tony."

"Yessir," the elderly gentleman answered. "Glad to hear from you, young fellow. Everything going all right at the shop?"

"It is, but I have a favor to ask. I'm gonna have to make a sudden trip out of town. Would you be willing to mind the store while I'm away?"

"Well, I thought you'd never ask!" The man seemed cheered at the prospect. "When do you need me?"

"Sunday we're closed, so Monday morning till . . . I'm not exactly sure when. I'd say about a week. Very sorry to land this on you so suddenly."

"Since I retired, my wife complains I'm around the house too much anyway." He chuckled. "No, really, it's no problem."

"You still have your key, right?"

"I do."

Tony continued, "I'll leave you a list of pending orders and the phone number where you can contact me."

"Very good. I'll be there bright and early tomorrow. You just call me when you're heading home."

"Will do. Appreciate this, sir. I owe ya."

"Young fellow, you don't owe me a thing."

What a great old guy, thought Tony as he hung up the phone. *One of the many good things about this move to Milford-Haven.*

Now he looked around the office and workshop that comprised the back half of the shop. Though customers almost never saw this room, he kept his tools and workbench clean and ready for whatever carpentry or electrical work came in. He also liked being able to find things readily and couldn't abide a mess. On this point, as on many others, he and Sally agreed completely. Sally kept her place clean as a whistle, and his own spaces were almost always ready for inspection. *Once a Marine, always a Marine.*

Having confirmed everything was in good order here, he pulled a notepad from its rack and began a packing list. *Food... no, Sally will ask June to see to that. What do I need from home? A flat of water bottles, couple of decent shirts. And my suit. I want to look presentable.*

Sally sighed and surveyed the room one more time.

While Tony made all their travel arrangements, she and June and some other helpers had brought in all the special decorations, and now her restaurant did look adorable, if she did say so her own self.

Closed for regular lunch business this special Saturday, it was fixed up for Miranda's wedding shower and envelop stuffing. *Now that's the funniest name for a party I ever did hear,* she thought. But it was practical to get help from friends, getting all the wedding invitations ready to mail. And for sure, it'd be a lot of fun. *'Course, I'll have to put up with havin' Samantha here. But today ain't about me! It's about my good friend.*

She thought for a moment about Miranda's wedding, which would take place in nature rather than a church, and that sounded just perfect. Sally was thrilled to be a bridesmaid, but not so thrilled about having to get a dress big enough to cover her baby bump. *Oh, well, like I just said, it ain't about me!*

Thinking of her friend, Sally turned around to admire again the mural Miranda had painted for her across the back wall. On the front wall stood a hutch left to Sally by her grandmother, as was the set of dishes gleaming from behind its glass doors. The pattern of delicate flowers on a white background had been Granny's favorites, and Sally only used them for special occasions like today. She and Tony had discussed having the cabinet moved to her house, where he'd add earthquake safety straps and small door locks. If the hutch got moved, she could ask him to carpenter built-in shelves on that wall, styled to match the wooden booths in that far section. *That'd be a good idea. But not today!*

None of her guests knew that she and Tony would be leaving tomorrow for Arkansas. Though Sally hadn't expected to visit home again this soon, Sally wouldn't feel right till she'd seen for herself Mama was alright, like everyone claimed.

June would take over at the restaurant for the ten days or so that they'd be away. Her bags were packed. Pretty much everything was ready.

For now, she looked at the tables, each of which held small, individually wrapped seashell gifts Miranda and her friend Shelly had worked on for the guests. And on the long bar, Sally had an array of food she and June had fixed: deviled eggs, finger sand-wiches, brownies, and a big bowl of sparkling lemonade punch.

Sally gave herself one more moment to feel wistful at not being able to celebrate a wedding of her own. So many times through the years she'd imagined working with Mama on all the details, sharing laughter with her girlfriends back home, walking down the aisle with T— *Stop that right now!*

Those long-ago dreams had to be put away in a special little box best kept in the attic of the old homestead. True, she'd have rather had a husband before her little one arrived, but life had gotten a mite complicated.

Right now, it's all about Miranda, the bride to be!

Miranda stepped into Sally's Restaurant—one of the most familiar places in town—and her jaw dropped. The room had been transformed almost beyond recognition. *But I was just here yesterday! How in the world did they manage this?*

Miranda had recently completed the promised mural on the large wall to the left of the entrance. It depicted rolling hills to represent both Sally's original home in Arkansas, as well as her adopted home here along the Central Coast. Hillsides with rows of crops rolled through the scene, an idyllic depiction of farmland with a huge sycamore painted in one corner, its branches reaching to the adjacent wall and continuing along the ceiling. Cows of various sizes dotted the hillsides and in the foreground, the sweet faces of a cow, a pig, and a horse poked over top of a fence and puffy white clouds traveled across a blue sky. A faint rainbow arced over the sky, the daylight scene gradually shifting toward a twilight tone to the right. In the upper right corner hung the moon, with a small, distant cow just visible jumping over it.

Meanwhile, the rest of the room looked fancier than she'd ever seen it. Each wooden table was now draped in yellow cloth, with a small white bucket holding colorful blooms decorating each top. A long, slender sideboard had been pulled close to the mural, and it was piled high with wrapped presents of every size and color, accented with bright ribbons in perky bows and trailing curls. On the left side of the long bar, a buffet of platters arrayed what appeared to be several kinds of finger sandwiches, arranged in elaborately swirled patterns. On the right side, trays of sweets offered brownies and cookies, plus two tall piles of scones beside a bowl of clotted cream and another of strawberry jam.

Sally and June must have been up all night to get all this done! But I hope Sally wasn't, not in her condition! Just then, Miranda overhead a deep voice.

"Uh oh!" sang Tony from the kitchen's open door. "The celebration person is here!"

Miranda giggled.

Sally now poked her head over Tony's where he sat in is wheelchair. "OOO-Eee!" She called.

"Oh, Sally! This is just unbelievable! I'm glad I brought my camera! How in the world did you do all this?"

"Well, I had some expert help," she admitted.

"Not hardly," Tony said under his breath.

"Aha, your secret weapon," Miranda observed. Standing there, looking at her dear friend with her beautifully big belly, the man she loved close at hand, the specially prepared room, the gifts she hadn't expected, the food fit for a queen . . . her eyes began to fill.

"Now, Miranda, don't you be startin' that! If you start to blubberin', I'll just be a goner!"

"Okay. I know. I'll try to keep it together at least for now!"

The two women laughed, which helped Miranda suppress the tears for the moment.

"What can I do to help?" Miranda asked.

"Nothin' at all," Sally insisted. "I've got my helpers, and all we need to do is bring out the hot water dispenser. People should be comin right quick."

Just then, the screen door screeched and Shelley Larrup walked in. "Oh, Bonzer! This place looks incredible!" She exclaimed in her Australian accent.

Behind her arrived Nicole from the gallery, two women who worked at the grocery market, and one of Sally's helpers from her Burn-It-Off workout facility. A moment later, Samantha arrived, deposited another gift on the long table, and made her way past the others to hug Miranda.

Sam glanced around apparently looking for Sally, who wasn't her favorite person. She nodded at the other woman though, a courtesy she rarely afforded. *Good*, Miranda thought. *They're both on their best behavior for my sake.*

Several minutes later, the room now filled with friends, Sally invited everyone to help themselves to the buffet, then take a seat at one of the tables. Miranda held back, chatting with some of the women as they made their way to the line and soaking in all the fellowship swirling through the room.

She glanced over at Sally, standing just behind the bar. Tony lurked close by her, a slight expression of concern on his handsome features. He seemed ready either to help her or get her to sit down. Either way, Sally certainly now had an advocate and supportive partner, which added to the happiness of the day.

Sally had watched from her perch on one of the bar stools, where she sat at Tony's insistence, as the guests filled their plates, the small tables, and their stomachs. He'd made up a small plate for her to enjoy a couple of sandwiches and had asked June to bring her a cup of decaffeinated tea.

Her friend Miranda was glowing. There was no other way to describe how she looked, and Sally had never seen the like. *What it's all about,* she mused, *when you're as happy as she is.*

She herself knew the feeling—almost. Course, she didn't have a wedding on the horizon and didn't know whether that would ever happen. After all, she was carrying the child of a man other than the one she was now seeing. But there was no doubt she loved Tony and treasured his presence in her life at long last. He might just turn out to be her most cherished friend. He was already that. Would he ever be more? Perhaps that would be too much to hope for. *Best to stay in my grateful place, she* told herself.

Grateful indeed that she'd asked four of the girls from the local sophomore class to help with today's activities, she watched as June directed them to clear the tables. Then the girls brought forth the boxes of invitations and envelopes the shower guests would help assemble for mailing.

When the guests saw that Miranda's wedding invitations were actually some of the beautiful postcards featuring one of her signature coastal landscape paintings, they ooed and ahhed.

"Oh! This is Ragged Point, n'est pas?" Nicole asked.

"You guessed it," Miranda confirmed.

"And that's where the wedding will be," Shelley observed. "Perfect!"

Miranda smiled.

"That's how Miranda always plans things," Samantha commented. "She coordinates her paintings with her life, with her community, and with her friends," she added, nodding toward Sally's new mural.

Miranda blushed, and Sally felt a moment of surprised gratitude for Sam's gracious comment. While she herself had been making an effort to get along better for Miranda's sake, perhaps Samantha was doing the same. Trying not to let the tears beginning to pool in her eyes run down her face, she glanced over at her new mural. *When the right folks get married, their happiness puts a rainbow in the sky for everyone.*

Samantha arrived home after Miranda's wedding shower imbued with a nostalgic mix of joy and sadness.

If Sam had ever had a daughter of her own, she'd like to think she'd have been like Miranda. Indeed, she'd been realizing lately that she felt Miranda was more than a close friend but was the daughter she'd never had.

Like herself, the young woman had a passion for the environment. Though she didn't work in the sciences, her wildlife and landscape painting required research and a spirit of adventure they shared. They also had a core ethic in common, a sense that authenticity and equity were important.

What Miranda still had was something Sam had lost: a sense of possibility. Through the younger woman, Sam could feel herself experiencing pockets of hope for the first time in years and could sense some of her own jaded cynicism diminishing.

Sam had worn a lovely pantsuit to the party, and she slid the matching soft burnt-orange shawl off her shoulders but felt a chill. After putting her kettle on to boil, she went to her closet to change into flannel pajamas and fuzzy slippers. By the time she returned to the kitchen, the water was ready to pour over a bag of Earl Gray tea she'd placed in a large pottery mug Miranda'd made for her.

This is one of our movie night outfits, she realized. In the colder months, the two friends would plan evenings to share hot soup and crusty bread, followed by a private viewing from her own large collection of films on both VHS tapes and DVDs. A film buff, Sam would sometimes show vintage films and regale her guest with behind-the-scenes tales she'd learned from friends in "the business." But just as often, they'd watch documentaries, which never failed to inspire. *In Celebration of Trees,* that film by Al Giddings; *The Steel Reefs,* by Stan Waterman. Both filmmakers were acquaintances Sam had met through her environmental work, and their films were landmarks in helping the public understand more about the wonders of the planet.

After the movie, sometimes Miranda would stay in Sam's guest room rather than driving home late at night. *But with her new status, that won't happen anymore.* Sam let the sadness wash over her like one of the waves in Stan's film. *This must be what every parent feels when their child grows up. What do they call it? Empty nest syndrome. Not that Miranda ever actually lived with me.*

Miranda's own mother must be feeling all this like a tidal wave, she mused. Her lovely daughter who'd flown the nest to create a life separate from the one envisioned by her parents... that must've been difficult to understand, perhaps hard to bear. According to all that Miranda had shared, her parents loved her but kept waiting for her to find her "real job." Imagine their surprise at discovering Miranda'd been right all along to pursue her own talent. The girl had followed her heart, and it'd taken her where neither parents nor that manager of hers could have foreseen.

How did they feel about Cornelius? Sam imagined she'd find out at the upcoming festivities. And how would they feel about her and her special relationship with their daughter? Sam reminded herself again that she'd need to be careful around Veri so as not to ignite even the tiniest spark of jealousy.

Miranda tends to be so at ease with me, perhaps more so than with her mother. I'll need to keep things a bit more formal than usual. Sam never could, nor would she ever want to, replace Miranda's parent. But she smiled at the nickname her friend sometimes used, calling Sam her Other Mother. *We should keep that one private while her folks are here.*

Most important of all was the fact so clearly in evidence: her dear daughter-friend was deeply happy, and her joy was spreading through their small community like watercolors suffusing one of Miranda's canvases.

This was the function of joy, and when Sam let herself, she could even feel memories of happier times with Jack from years earlier leaking under the doors she had closed so tightly long ago.

So now, rather than being swept away by the thought of losing the special times she'd shared with Miranda, she could instead let herself ride the wave of joy Miranda and her fiancé were eager to share.

Chapter 17

Tony blinked in the dark late Saturday night.

Supine in his bed, he once again began at the letter *Z* and started reciting backwards. But after twice more through the alphabet, his eyes remained open, staring into the gloom.

"Well, this ain't workin'," he said to the darkened ceiling. *Wonder if Sal's awake too? Or is it only me?*

He moved his large hand till it hovered over the phone, which suddenly rang, startling him. He snatched it up during the first ring. "Yeah."

"Land sakes! You picked up that phone fast as a tomcat pouncin' on a mouse."

Tony felt a laugh rumbling up through his chest. But something didn't seem quite right. *Her voice—it's tense. What if her Mama took a turn for the worse?*

"You . . . I . . ." she stammered. "I was worried I'd wake you—"

"Wide awake. Just layin' here countin' backwards." *She doesn't even sound like herself.* "Sal, you okay?" *Seven months along in her pregnancy. What if—*

"I...I..."

"Sally. Breathe!"

"I don't know why but I—"

He heard the hitch in her breathing, the rising panic in her voice. "Sal, it'll be okay. Hear me? I'm coming over. Right now."

Sally put down the phone. Despite the calm in Tony's voice, fear pumped a shot of adrenaline into her heart and a sickening weakness spread down her legs. *Oh, God. What if Mama really did hurt herself? What if she's ill? What if she dies on me all of a quick, just like Daddy did?*

Her rational side reminded her that Mama had already nearly recovered from this current mishap. But at the moment, Sally's head wasn't speaking to the rest of her body, which seemed to want to convulse. *I do not think I should still be feelin' sick this late in the pregnancy!*

But sure enough, a wave of nausea hit her, and she waddled to the bathroom, where she managed to lift the toilet seat just in time to retch. Afterward, her hands shaking, she rinsed her mouth, washed her face with cold water, patted herself dry, then stood bracing against the sink to catch her breath.

Okay, Baby. I know you're okay in there. Sorry about that little upset. Can't seem to help it. She rubbed her hand around the huge circle of her belly, as if to soothe the child—or herself.

Tony said he was comin' over. But what if he forgot to set the brake and his wheelchair rolled away from the side of his bed? What if he can't get to his car? What if—No! She wasn't going to listen to her own irrational fears. "He's just fine, Baby," she spoke aloud. "Knowing him, he'll be here any minute. Whatta ya bet?"

She told herself the running patter was to reassure the fetus. At more than seven months—thirty-two weeks, to be exact—she knew the baby could hear sounds. She was convinced emotions traveled directly through her own system and into the baby's: love and acceptance, joy . . . and fear. *So if talking to myself calms my own nerves, so much the better for both of us.*

She glanced at her watch. *How long since I called Tony? Seems like forever. He did say he'd be right here—but he's not. Maybe I should go check on him.* Galvanized by the thought that somehow he might be hurt, she felt in the dark for the oversized pair of sweats she wore around the house these days and slid into the soft flats that were the only shoes she could still wear.

"Here we go, Baby, to Daddy Tony's house. Time to make sure he's okay, even though we *know* he is, of course." She permitted herself a tiny smile at how she now called Tony the father of her child. Technically, it wasn't true, but in every way that mattered, he was. *And God knows, I love him, body and soul.*

With the seat in her ten-year-old Toyota pushed all the way back, she managed to slide into the driver's side. She started the car and began to back out of her carport but was stopped by headlights pouring into her rear window.

"Is that him?" she asked herself.

"Sally!"

Her heart leapt when she heard his voice. Throwing the gearshift into Park, she switched off the motor, pushed herself out of the car, and hurried as fast as she could to the driver's side of his van.

His voice hoarse, he begged, "You all right?"

The strain in his face nearly broke her heart. "Yes, Tony, I'm fine. I was just comin' to you. I mean, to see if you were okay and everything."

He shook his head stoically.

She smiled at him. "Wanna come in? I can put up some coffee."

"Can't," he said curtly.

"Oh? Well, Tony, it's not even four in the mornin' yet. We don't have to get on the road to Arkansas for another couple o' hours, do we?"

"Not ready," he said, facing forward.

Stepping up with one foot on the running board, she brought herself to his eye level. "Tony, what . . . ?" Her voice trailed off. "Forgot to put your shirt on, did you?" His face remained so serious, she suppressed a grin.

"That's not all," he said, beginning to chew his lip.

Sally looked down over the edge of the window. In the dim glow from the dashboard, she made out the shape of a towel on his lap. She began to giggle, her knuckles turning white as she clung to the side of the van's door. Daring to meet his eyes, she saw his determined look, and another ripple of laughter escaped her lips.

"Personally, I don't see what's so funny."

Nearly losing her purchase on the door, Sally choked on the laugh erupting from her throat.

"Don't you be falling down, now, in your condition. Till I'm dressed, I'm not climbing out to save you, Miss O'Mally."

Gasping now, Sally let go of the door, stepped down, clutched at her swollen belly and put up a hand to beg for mercy.

"I can see you are not in need of my services at this time. Best I go home and shake a leg."

"Not without me," Sally pleaded. Fast-walking as best she could, she hurried to Tony's passenger side. Opening it, she climbed in and swiped at the laugh-tears leaking from her eyes.

Still looking straight ahead, Tony said simply, "I know it'll be a stretch, but fasten your seatbelt, now."

"Okay, I will," she said in a voice weakened by laughter.

Backing out of her driveway, Tony drove slowly down the deserted street in the predawn darkness.

Sally glanced over at him, and laughter tried to start again.

"That's about enough outta you, young lady."

"Yes, sir." Sally tried, and failed, for some contrition. "I love you, you know."

"I love you too, you know."

"Ye-yus," she said, accentuating her Southern drawl.

Tony disappeared into his bathroom the moment they arrived at his house, and the sound of the shower started. Sally went right to the kitchen, where she saw his one suitcase on the floor by the back door. Already neatly packed, it apparently only needed to be zipped. *Maybe he'll be puttin' in one more thing.*

She busied herself making coffee, then searched in vain for any other ingredients she recognized as breakfast items, but the fridge was nearly empty. *Well, I'll make us somethin' at the rest'rnt as we start our trip.*

Pulling out the one chair from under the low peninsula that separated the kitchen from the living room, she sat down and rubbed her belly. The fit of laughter over Tony's naked rescue mission had swept away the fear brought on by her concern for Mama. Now she marveled at the depth of her own connection with the man. *His first instinct was to come help me. He didn't even pause long enough to dress.*

Tony rolled into the kitchen looking refreshed and groomed, a green polo shirt pulled down smartly over just-washed jeans.

"Coffee?" she asked.

"You bet," he answered, giving her a smile at last.

She melted at the sight of him and came into his arms, sitting across his lap more awkwardly than she had even a month earlier. "Oh, Tony, thank you for comin' to get me." The memory of the panic shuddered through her.

Stroking her hair and back, he said simply, "Hush, now. Everything's okay."

Pulling back, she looked at him eye-to-eye. "Why, Tony—why exactly—did you come with no clothes?"

"It wasn't important to be dressed. It was only important to get there, get you help, if you needed it." He paused for a moment. "One thing you can't be doing now is lifting heavy objects. I thought you might try to lift your suitcase. But I can do that. If I can get leverage, I can lift just fine."

Squeezing his shoulders and arms, she said, "Ooo-eee, I should say so, with those big muscles of yours. Mine are just pathetic."

He pinched her arm gently at her prodding. "You can change that, if you like."

"Maybe after the baby comes. My whole body's gonna need an overhaul then."

He smiled at her, the warmth of it filling her up. Inhaling, she braced herself against his big chest.

"What, Sal?" He scrutinized her. "Go ahead."

Apparently, she could keep nothing from him. "Okay. . . Tony, I don't want us sleeping apart anymore."

He took a sharp breath.

"I didn't like waking up without you. I don't want to be alone anymore."

Stroking her cheek, he closed his eyes for a moment and took a long, deep breath, then let it out with a sigh. "I thought the same thing, Sweet. You know I'm ready, as long as you are."

Brightening, she beamed at him. "Okay, then. I guess we got some movin' to do when we get back. What do you think? Your place, or mine?"

"Have to be mine, I'd say. Can't get into your bathroom—"

"—bathroom, right. Okay by me." Looking around, she added, "This place of yours could use some help."

"Here we go," he said, a hint of alarm in his voice.

"Well, you know, a person needs some furniture. I got plenty for the both of us."

"Uh-huh." Tony sighed. "Just leave me a little room to wheel around, okay?"

"Okay." She grinned. Looking past him out the window, she saw traces of dawn touching the sky. "Land sakes, we gotta get a move on."

"Still feel up to it?"

Without hesitation she answered, "I *gotta* get to Mama."

"Ten-four."

Sally looked down at herself. "And I gotta get home, take a shower, and get some clothes on."

"I'll run you home." He steadied her as she slid off his lap. "And while you're getting ready, I'll look around your living room to see what we can throw away."

"Tony!"

"Just kidding with you."

"You better be."

"Sort of."

She gave him a scowl. But it couldn't hide the smile beneath.

Tony had made quick work when he returned from running Sally home. Within the hour he'd closed both his suitcase and his house, and had driven back to fetch Sally. With her few things added to his own in the van, they were nearly ready to skip town.

Their one remaining stop was at her restaurant, and they pulled into her parking spot in the rear of the building. Between her short stature and the size of her belly, it was no easy matter for her to climb in and out of his high vehicle. So he recommended she make careful use of the running board that served as a step.

Tony watched as she used it now, half-sliding to her feet. *Wish I could help her—but I gotta get my own sorry ass out of the van before I can do anything for her.* Where had his sudden sarcasm come from? This was not how he wanted to start his first driving trip with Sal. *But she doesn't know what she's in for. This is just the beginning.*

Stifling the dire prediction as best he could, he watched as she unlocked the rear door of the restaurant, then went ahead inside as he'd requested. June would arrive in moments, and the two of them would cook up some bacon-and-egg sandwiches for their breakfast-to-go, then pack some turkey-pastrami and provolone on rye sandwiches for them to have later for lunch. *By then we'll be in Nevada . . . maybe even Arizona.*

Now he rotated his driver's seat ninety degrees, bringing himself alongside the wheelchair parked behind. Placing his hands flat on his seat at either side of his hips, he used his strong arms to heft himself into the adjacent chair. Next he wheeled to the center of the platform that would lower him to ground level with the flick of a switch, at which point the van's side doors opened automatically.

Sally's seen me do this. But not eight times a day. He knew it would be all right. Sally was no wimp when it came to the tougher issues of life. And, so far at least, she'd been fearless in the face of his disability.

But this drive—this would be the test. *Is that why I wanted to do it?* No, he argued. They *had* to drive. This late in the pregnancy, she shouldn't be getting on an airplane.

Perhaps, then, this was the universe testing their strength. If so, the test came at a good time. *With the baby almost here, it's time for certainties, not guessing games.* If he and this woman were going to climb in a little boat and make a go of family life, their journey wouldn't all be flowing gently-down-the-stream. Sooner or later they were bound to hit some rapids.

You can deal, Sal. I know you can. I'm countin' on it. But something told him they'd soon be in over their heads.

Chapter 18

Jack Sawyer spent the wee hours of the morning traversing the terrain of his bed. His legs wrapped in the sheets; he kicked them free, his body mimicking what his sleeping mind dictated till the motions woke him.

Strangely, what dream he'd been having deposited him at the edge of memories of his honeymoon. He remembered with no fondness how he'd shocked his young bride. Startled awake each night, she'd stroked his face in the dark till he woke embarrassed and apologetic. "But what if this is a *good* thing?" she'd speculated. "Maybe you're working something out." Though in his view Samantha was wrong about most things, in this case he'd grudgingly admitted she was right. *At least I got something useful out of that doomed marriage.*

Over the many years since his divorce, this behavior had chased several would-be sleeping companions from his bedroom. But he counted this as no great loss, particularly when weighed against the knowledge that his sleep-state was where he did his most concentrated problem-solving.

When he'd been a younger man, doing more of the hard physical labor of construction, he'd actually spoken in his sleep, sometimes so loudly he'd scared women from the room. Since starting his own company and placing himself in charge, sometimes of several projects at once, he'd graduated to a mostly silent form of processing.

Women who'd attempted to interrupt him by waking him from his supposed-nightmares had paid the price: they were never invited back. Sally, whom he'd dated for all those months, had been stoically patient with his nocturnal fits.

But she'd betrayed him. After all their conversations about offspring, after their agreement *not* to have a child, after her swearing up and down she would *not* get pregnant—she'd presented him with her little "problem."

Well, she was gone now, and good riddance. Jack was a single-minded man, devoted to his projects. This was obvious to anyone when he was awake. To him, this was even more so when he slept.

Jack watched in distress as a gust of wind swept through the open window in his office, swept a stack of plans off his desk and scattered them across the small, disorderly room.

He flailed his arms in a futile attempt to capture the papers before they disappeared. He leapt up and began grabbing at the oversized sheets whisking by him. As though performing a mad jig, he kicked at the air and stomped his boots, trying to snag even one corner. But the plans swirled merrily, eluding his every attempt at capture.

He stopped abruptly at the thought his muddy boots might smudge them. It was only the tiny infinity mark that distinguished the real from the phony set of plans to the Clarke house, and he could ill afford to confuse the two.

Then, like a quick dissolve in a film, the scene suddenly shifted. He found himself at the house itself, dictating an inventory of his own infractions. First, there was the set-back distance: the real plans called for a hundred yards; in the phony set, the distance had been amended to two hundred feet—not much to the eye, but it allowed for the expanded deck the client wanted without completely redoing the foundation at the front.

Then there was the substitution of the floor joist material. The two-by-tens had worked in scores of houses before. The foundation hadn't been poured exactly as engineered, but even the bribed inspector had agreed the original plan's rebar requirement was overkill and the foundation would certainly be strong enough.

The rest of his list seemed to expand around him, then lift and fill like a sail billowing in the wind. The dream swept him along as the ground seemed to sway under his feet. The house was now a ship, its floor developing a camber as bow and stern raised off the ground. The S.S. Clarke sailed off the cliff, heading out to sea. No! Jack wanted to cry. She's not sea-worthy! Beware those shoals! Beware the depths! Now he found his voice. "Look out!"

The first thing Jack heard as he startled himself awake was the sound of his own voice shouting.

"Damnation!" he muttered in the dark. "What was I dreaming about this time?"

Something told him to avoid the remembrance, outrun it by switching on the light. Yet, he knew better than to suppress dreams, for they often provided useful information. The deficit he paid in lost sleep was often worth the profit gained in insights—

and even the solutions to pesky problems. So he forced a deep breath and stilled his still-quivering muscles.

The final images of the dream rose like an apparition. *A grand ship . . . but foundering in coastal waters.* He tried to make sense of the nautical image but knew thinking about it too directly sometimes only chased the memory away. *Can't catch a wave on the sand. But if I'm patient, the next wave may bring what I'm trying to remember.* For that process, he'd need a little help.

Rising, he thrust his arms into his frayed bathrobe and yanked it around his middle, tying its soft belt. Then he poked his feet into worn slippers and shuffled off down the hall. His poison of choice for the wee hours was nicotine. *Not as good as smoking after sex but a close second.*

He didn't want coffee yet. The process of making it might wake him up too much. But smoking seemed to enhance whatever thought process was currently occurring, and he wanted to induce a session that would welcome back the bizarre dream images still lurking at the edges of his brain. *This should be a good one,* he mused. Nightmares or fantasies—they were all grist for the proverbial mill.

Using only the night-light, to avoid waking himself fully, Jack rummaged in the cupboard over the refrigerator for the half-empty carton of smokes he customarily hid from himself. *Not that it actually keeps me from the nasty habit.*

But the carton was empty. Irritated, he yanked open a kitchen drawer, finding in its depth a pack with three cigarettes left. Immensely satisfied with the discovery, he snatched one Marlboro, tightened the belt of his robe, and slid open the door to his small balcony, taking his customary seat on one of the battered deck chairs.

Jack struck a match, and its sudden light illuminated the porch like the flash of a camera. Two eyes sparked red in the startled face of some creature. Caught in the act of crossing the railing, it scuttled away. *A rat?* Jack wondered. He shivered, and now watched as the end of his cigarette glowed red like a single eye glaring back at whatever visitor might dare intrude again.

As his own eyes grew accustomed to the dark, he watched plumes of the burning tobacco rise and disappear. He sat perfectly still, waiting for the wraiths from his dream to tiptoe out of the woods. He heard something. *Was that coming from the trees? Or did I imagine it?* His body tensed as he braced for an encounter.

He heard the sound again—small, persistent scratching punctuated by snapping twigs. He stared into the adjacent woods, squinting at faint flashes of red, almost convincing himself eyes were now everywhere, blinking, staring. Then a dark shape seemed to move across the open space toward his house. *Is there another critter out there? Or is someone actually stalking me?* For a moment, he fancied himself grabbing a weapon. *I've got that old baseball bat I keep handy.* But then he felt ridiculous, a man afraid of his shadow, swiping at ghosts.

Still sitting, he gripped the edge of his chair, his breath coming hard, his pulse thumping in his chest. *What the hell?*

Then, with the nasty sensation that he was being watched, he *knew* what had crept out of the woods. They were the ghosts of his good intentions: the integrity he'd meant to provide his clients; the tenderness he'd thought of giving to Sally; the love he'd lost with Sam. They all seemed to join in a macabre celebration now, singing a dissonant chorus, writhing in a painful dance. They rushed at him, coiling around his body, singeing his lungs. What rose from the deck was the acrid stink of his own smoldering conscience.

Jack leapt from his chair, knocking it backwards. *I'm having an attack of guilt? Of all the stupid—!*

He opened the door, charged inside, and slid it shut again with such force he nearly shattered the glass, then stood shaking. Guilt was the most useless thing Jack could imagine. *I have no time for it. No time at all.*

Jack greeted Sunday morning in what had almost become a custom: tousled in tangled sheets, desperate to feed his caffeine and nicotine addictions. He dismissed the bizarre apparitions of the wee hours. Instead, he worried about two things: the Clarke house and the son he'd never known existed.

Ignorance was bliss. Not knowing about the boy, he'd escaped the angst of parenthood. But he'd also missed its joys and challenges. *How might being a father have changed me? Who would I be now? What would I be doing?*

Perhaps his passion for architecture might never have drained away to be replaced by a jaded sense of boredom with the repetition of erecting similar structures, the enervation of compliance with absurd regulations.

Speaking of passion, what would it be like if Samantha'd never left him? Couldn't she have completed her PhD program while still being married? Many people did. Was it that professor of hers who seduced her away? Or was she just fickle? Maybe the woman had always been incapable of seeing things through. After all, she deserted not only him, but their child. *Who does that?*

Infuriated all over again, Jack swung his legs out, nearly tripping when a foot caught in a twisted sheet. Then, thrusting his arms into his threadbare robe, he pounded down the hallway to the kitchen for his ritual reheating of the huge to-go cup of coffee he'd brought home from Sally's restaurant.

He began to reach again for the old pack of cigarettes he kept secreted in the inconvenient cupboard over the fridge, but then stopped himself. *I don't have to start smoking again. I don't. I can do better. Maybe I even have a reason to do better now.*

The thought surprised him. Really? Did he care that he now had a son, a grown man walking the earth somewhere? Would they ever meet? If they did, what would the boy think of him? *Well, he won't be able to think anything if I'm dead.*

Mortality. That was a new slap in the face. He'd been in denial for so long, the concept had become unfamiliar. Jack took for granted his own muscular strength, his seemingly endless energy, the fact that he walked miles every day—at job sites, and on the local trails and streets, inspecting the terrain, the properties both developed and waiting for development.

Jack took his coffee outside to sit on his weathered balcony. The only view was of trees shrouded in early morning fog. As he sat looking at them, the conifers seemed to represent the thoughts he'd ignored for so long. His core values were still sturdy and straight but were now crusted with bark thick enough to make them impenetrable. *That's what keeps the trees safe. Are the things that matter to me protected too?*

He took another sip of his bitter brew, his gaze sharper as he noticed the moss draping from limb to limb. He'd thought for years this was Spanish moss and had gone along with the common belief that it caused harm, blocking sunlight and killing off the host. Instead, he'd learned these trees were draped with lace lichen that hung like elaborate reticulated nets.

The mosses caused no harm, he'd learned, and as he thought about the lacy structures in front of him, he glimpsed the mastery of their design, imagining they represented the complex network of relationships a person might weave over the years. *There's more to my own network now. What will I do about it?*

Jack took his feet off the railing where they'd been resting and stood abruptly, trying to figure out why the hell he'd spent his coffee time waxing poetic. *Must be the fog*, he thought.

Yet, as he returned inside to prepare for the day, a vague awareness of new thoughts seemed to cling to him as relentlessly as the fog clung to the trees.

Susan took another sip of her tea as Kevin's faded red Ford F-150 trundled down Highway 1.

I knew Kevin would take care of me. She glanced over at her friend, all 6-foot-8 of him, calm and competent behind the wheel of the truck. He was comfortable anywhere, she reflected, except in fancy surroundings. That didn't matter at all.

But when he glanced over at her, she knew the questions were about to come.

"Okay, tell me about it. Where were you? At the Clarke house, right?"

Susan's eyes opened wide. "How'd you know?"

"Two and two is four," he stated. "One, you asked for a tour. Two, you wanted to go last night."

"Yeah," she admitted. "I went ahead. Sorry. I figured I could be careful."

"Job sites are for people who do site jobs," he said, as though pronouncing a maxim.

"Then why did you say you'd give me a tour?"

"To stop you from going on your own!" He said this with a raised voice, something Susan had never before heard from him.

"I—I'm really sorry, Kevin. I didn't mean to get you in trouble or anything."

"This isn't about me! You got hurt!"

"Okay, okay," she said, trying to make herself smaller in her seat. "I won't do it again."

Kevin, feeling reassured, helped Susan back into his truck. "It coulda been a whole lot worse," he commented as he pulled out of the hospital ER parking area.

"That shot really hurt," Susan said in a small voice. "And now I've got this humongous bandage."

"True. But you could've broken your leg or something, if you'd actually fallen all the way down into that basement hole."

Susan sighed.

"I think we both need some breakfast," he declared. "Let's stop at Carla's in Morro Bay."

"Never been there."

"You'll love it. My treat."

Kevin upended his coffee mug to enjoy a final sip, then used his paper napkin to wipe his mouth.

He nodded at their waitress, who cheerily delivered their check and thanked them for coming. Though he always enjoyed Sally's, he also felt glad to be away from the tension of sharing meals with Jack Sawyer. He enjoyed Carla's Country Kitchen all the more because it felt like a private getaway.

Susan, who never seemed to eat much, had managed to polish off some scrambled eggs and half a piece of toast. Color had returned to her cheeks, and he felt reassured she'd be fine—if she could manage not to tear the stitches out of her hand nor allow the wound to get infected.

He'd been considering the situation she'd mentioned about needing help with her rent, as well as the promise he'd made to do some repairs. *Might as well see if any repairs are actually needed.*

"Let's head over to your place," he suggested. "I can check out the place for work that might need to be done. That way, it'll be honest when I make the offer to your landlord."

Susan suddenly appeared anxious again. "I really don't need any help. Just drive to your place so I can get my car."

"Not gonna work," he said. "You're not supposed to drive with the pain med they gave you. Anyway, you *do* need help with the rent, right? I gotta check out the premises."

Apparently resigned, she pushed back from the table and then remained silent while they drove the thirty minutes up the highway to Milford-Haven. He opened the passenger side of his truck to help her out, and the two of them climbed the long exterior staircase to her small abode, perched precariously at the uppermost slope of a hill.

This place could be cute, he thought. *I'd wanna check out the supports under the front edge of the structure, though. Then have a termite inspection, mold inspection . . . I doubt Leo Hudson's kept up with any of that, knowing him, but I have people who can do it.*

Kevin's musings came to an abrupt halt when Susan opened her front door and walked inside. "Holy crap!" he said, regretting he'd spoken aloud.

"What?" she asked testily.

"Well, I mean . . ." Temporarily at a loss for words and not wanting to hurt her feelings, Kevin finally asked, "Doesn't Leo even give you curtains or blinds?"

Susan chortled without humor. "Never crossed his mind. The sheet's okay."

Kevin drew his gaze across the stained, bedraggled linen draped from a sagging curtain rod. "Not really. Your place overlooks the street down below. You need more privacy than that." He grabbed the measuring tape clipped to his belt and walked to the window, quickly measuring its full width. Then from the pocket protector that always rode in his front shirt pocket, he withdrew a pencil and a small pad. "I know where to get a set of blinds that'll fit," he said as he jotted a quick note. When he glanced down at the filthy window sill, he poked at with his pencil, dismayed to see the weather stripping had disintegrated almost the point of being powder. He then noticed a water stain below, that likely meant water had intruded inside the wall and by now would be causing mold. *If this is bad, what else has Leo led slide?* At a glance, he saw the edges of the kitchen area linoleum lifting, the bathroom door hanging slightly askew, and another water stain under the kitchen window.

Focusing on the deleterious condition of the building had provided a momentary distraction, but now he took in the full details of Susan's use of the one-room dwelling. Kevin couldn't stand a mess. He considered his own home as a peaceful sanctuary, with organization being a key component. At work, he kept the larger offices at Sawyer Construction in order and could hardly stand to look at Jack's desk. He made sure that all reference materials and client files were kept in place, dreading when something got left on Jack's desk, lest it be lost forever, and sneaking into the relatively private space to recapture and file important documents.

The mess in Susan's space was next level, not so much because she had too much stuff, but because none of it had a place to belong. Clothes were strewn across the floor, shoes lay scattered and not paired. Dishes had toppled over in and next to the sink. Boxes were shoved along one wall. A mattress lay on the floor at an odd angle, a lamp without a shade standing next to it. There was no place to sit other than the one chair and the one small table, and neither seemed to be level. One nice sling-chair stood as the room's only anomaly.

He stood, breathing harder than usual, as his disciplined mind tried to reshape the chaos. *Something else is weird too*, he noticed. The space wasn't aligned. Neither the sink nor the window were placed in the middle of their respective walls. He shook his head, as though this might correct the room. He longed to reach for a sheet of drafting paper to redesign the entire space.

Susan had begun pacing, he saw, obviously made nervous by Kevin's discomfort, which he'd made little effort to conceal. "Sorry," he said. "Uh, this place could really be nice," he offered.

"Like . . . how?" she asked.

"I think for starters, we should probably do a cleaning. You should probably sit, keep you hand elevated a little, like the doctor said. I'm gonna get some stuff from my place. Be right back."

He made his escape, leaving Susan standing mid-room, mouth agape.

Kevin muttered to himself about the deplorable condition of Leo's rental unit as he gathered what he'd need at home. He returned half an hour later with a broom and mop, bucket and sponges, and a bottle of industrial cleaner.

"Okay," he announced on his return. "I'll get started." He began by putting the bucket into the shower, since it wouldn't fit in the kitchen sink. *I could swap that sink out*, he thought, *but while I'm at it I may as well put in a whole new counter.* He paused for a moment, then took the hammer from his tool box and swung it at the sink, which developed an immediate crack.

"What the?" Susan cried.

"Ooops!" Kevin said. "Oh well. Guess it'll have to be replaced."

"Leo will never go for that," Susan complained.

"Oh, he won't have any choice. Apartments have to have working sinks."

"Whatever," Susan said, already drifting back into her nap.

While she slept, Kevin scrubbed the bathroom and kitchen, then mopped the floor. And while she slept on, he made a run to the Home Depot in SLO, bought a kitchen counter complete with a sink, new faucet, and a new disposal for good measure.

When he returned two hours later, he started making a lot of noise. But when Susan woke, she headed for her boom box, inserted some of her favorite heavy metal, and hit play. The cacophony of the two kinds of noise canceled each other well enough to keep them both happy. By the end of the afternoon, Susan had a new kitchen and a clean apartment.

"Well, it's a good start," Kevin commented. *And Leo's gonna reimburse me for everything I've done so far, and more, unless he wants to be written up with code violations.* "Next weekend we can go to Ikea to find a wall unit with shelves and drawers. You'll have a place to put your clothes, and we can get rid of the boxes. There can even be a place to put your boom box and tapes."

Susan looked around at her place as though the tornado had just delivered her to the land of Oz. After a long moment she said, "I have some frozen pizza in the fridge. Can I fix it for you?"

Chapter 19

Tony noticed the round yellow neon sign the moment it popped into view—a miniature, artificial sun in a pitch-dark night. Slowing the van, he pulled to the front door of the Travel Time Motel.

"Ooo-eee." Sally sighed, blinking in the glare.

Tony glanced at his watch. *Midnight, California time. That makes it one a.m. here in Albuquerque.* "Sal," he said quietly. "Before I get my keester outta this seat, do me a favor?"

"Okay."

"Go inside, check with the front desk to make sure they *do* have a handicap room."

"Good idea." Sally opened the passenger door, swung her legs to the side and slid her body carefully to the van's mounting step. When she was safely on the ground, she closed the door and waddled toward the motel's entrance.

Tony closed his eyes and waited, not allowing himself to dream of clean sheets and a dark room—not until he was sure this place could accommodate them. It seemed only a moment later, Sally was knocking on his window, and he saw her nod. *Thank God for not-so-small favors.*

He switched on the ignition and rolled down the window. "Can you handle the check-in, Doll?"

"Ye-yus."

Reaching into his small leather pack, he pulled out his credit card and handed it down to her. "All they'll need is an imprint for now. Make sure to ask for a shower bench."

"Shower bench. Got it."

Sally waddled away again, returning several minutes later with a room key. "I think I'll jest walk over there, Tony."

"Good." Giving her a head start, Tony drove the van slowly down the length of the long, single-story building, then pulled into the lone handicap parking spot. This time when he turned off the engine, he flipped the switch to open the side door and initiate the unfolding of the elevator platform.

Rotating his shoulders and neck wearily, he pressed a release, allowing the driver's seat to slide away from the dashboard, then rotate to the right. He paused a moment to gather what little strength he had left, then—with a grunt—hefted himself into his wheelchair.

He looked out the now-open double side doors of the van to see Sally watching him, as though memorizing his moves. "You could go ahead, you know. I might be a little while."

She nodded, grabbed her small overnight bag from the back of the van, then—still clutching the motel key on its yellow plastic tag—used it to open their door. She fumbled a hand inside to flip on a light switch, then walked in.

Tony reached for his small leather pack, his cell phone, and a fresh bottle of water, placing them in the pocket below his wheelchair seat. Then he hit the mechanism that lowered him to the pavement. Rolling backward off the platform, he used the remote attached to his keys to initiate the retracting of the platform and the closure of the van's side doors. Then he rolled to the back, plucked his own overnight bag from the rear compartment, closed and locked the vehicle.

With his bag on his lap, he moved toward the motel door, where he met his first obstacle. The chair would barely fit through the opening. He sighed, gritted his teeth, and assessed the geometry of wheels and frame, then began a series of oscillations that allowed him to pass into the room.

Sally stood by the one queen-size bed, watching him in silence, eyes big with concern. Glancing at her, he moved immediately to the bathroom, hissing out a sigh at what he saw—*or what I don't see*, he corrected himself. To Sally he said, "Before you get settled, go back to the front desk, will you, Doll? Ask again for that bench."

"But they said there *was* a bench," she protested.

"Yeah." He paused. "They're gonna try to give you a footstool. Tell them that won't work. I need something tall enough that I can make the transfer."

"Oh, you mean slide from the wheelchair onto it just like you would a regular chair?"

"You got it. The stall in there is okay—no lip in the way, handheld shower—but right now the only way I can get a shower is to douse the wheelchair too."

"Oh! Okay. On my way."

He watched her stride purposefully out the door, heard her footsteps on the long exterior corridor. *This is the hard part,* he reminded himself. *Just do the job. Don't fret. Waste of energy.*

Sally was back. "So, um, Tony?" He heard the tremor in her voice. "They say the closest they can come to a bench is a deck chair for around the pool?"

Tony took a deep inhalation. "Okay. You make yourself comfortable, Sal, I'll be right back."

"Well, I—"

"Never mind, Sal, believe me, I've been this route before. You get settled and try to get some shut-eye. Might have to ask you to do some of the driving tomorrow."

"Okay, Tony."

Sally worried as he wiggled the chair back and forth until he could exit the room. *Poor man is bone-tired and mind-weary.* She sensed a dark mood might be gathering too. To ward it off, she thought she better not countermand his wishes.

I have the room key, so I best not lock this door. She pushed their door closed till the metal touched. Unpacking only what she'd need—clean underwear, her few toiletries, nightgown, and her thin terry robe—she slipped off her cotton dress and hung it in the tiny closet, then stripped, dropping today's underthings in a small plastic laundry bag.

Maybe I can get a quick shower. She went into the bathroom, hung her robe on the door hook and stepped into the unusual shower stall. *No lip to hold back the water . . . it's gonna dribble all across the floor—'less I'm quick.* Turning on the spigot, she waited as the stream vacillated from freezing to boiling, and winced as it touched her hand.

When she finally balanced the temperature to a tolerable degree, she flipped the hand-held-shower nozzle switch, not noticing that it was unsecured. A geyser shot up to the ceiling, then aimed for the mirror above the sink, finally hitting Sally full in the face.

Eyes closed and mouth sputtering, she felt her way down the jet of gyrating water till she captured the snaking hose and aimed the nozzle toward the drain. At last, she managed to turn it off.

Well, that's one way to take a quick shower. She stood there, dripping onto the floor. *Not that it matters much now.* She surveyed the damage. The entire bathroom was drenched, along with every towel, bathmat and even her robe.

"Disastardly," she said to herself. It seemed pointless even to cry.

Shaking her limbs, she tiptoed back into the bedroom and stood dripping by the phone, dialing the front desk. "Hello? When Mr. Fiorentino gets there, would you give him some extra towels? We will be needin' several."

"Well, he's right here and—"

"Just have him to bring them."

"Yes, M'am."

Replacing the phone, Sally went to see what she could accomplish by using wet towels to swab the bathroom.

Tony rolled up to the front desk where he rang the countertop bell, startling the young male attendant awake.

"Excuse me. I need some *service.*"

"Yes, sir," said the clerk. "You want to check in?"

"I've already checked in. Problem is, the room does not have all the amenities I require." Tony over-enunciated, as though the young man couldn't speak very good English.

"Yeah?" The young clerk seemed irritated at having his nap interrupted. "Well, like, the rooms come fully equipped."

"The rooms may be *like* equipped," said Tony slowly, "but, in fact, for a wheelchair *like* person, you need a wheelchair bench for the shower, or it's, *like*, not usable."

"Other customers—"

"Other customers may have brought their own. I did not. Therefore, I require the use of a bench belonging to your hotel."

"As I told the lady—" The phone rang, and the clerk seemed relieved to answer it. "Well, he's right here and—"

Sally must have discovered something else is missing. This guy's just gonna have to . . . like . . . deal with us.

"Yes, M'am." The clerk said reluctantly, hanging up the phone.

"What else does the young lady need?"

"Oh, she said she needs extra towels."

"Fine, you can give them to me. Now, you told the young lady you had a pool chair," Tony continued. "A pool chair will not suffice in this instance."

"Well, sir, I don't think—"

"I'm sure, since it's required by *law* to provide for disabled persons, that somewhere in the closets of this establishment you can—and, in fact, *will*—find a bench. This would be a waterproof seat, made of some kind of plastic material, possibly with metal legs. Is this beginning to sound familiar?"

The young man answered sullenly, "Maybe." He turned his back, then disappeared into the supply closet behind the back office. When he emerged, he bore in his hands the very item Tony required, along with two fresh sets of towels.

"Thank you," Tony said. "I'll take them." Balancing the upside -down bench—towels stacked inside—on his lap, Tony began the slow journey back to his room.

When he pushed open the motel room door, he was greeted by a bedraggled Sally. "It went kerplunky," she said, pointing to the shower.

He pressed his lips together, completely out of words. At the edges of his mind, Tony sensed some laughing—not his own, but that of some cosmic observers. They seemed to sit like crows on a distant branch, cackling at his continued misfortune. *Things just don't go right for me. And now it's happening to Sal.*

He angled into the room and delivered the bench and towels just inside the bathroom—which looked presentable, if somewhat damp.

Sally stood in her nightgown. "Think you can get your shower now?" she asked.

He nodded.

"It's shutters and bye-bye for me."

He looked at her quizzically.

"Tuckered. I'm gonna get in bed."

He nodded again, then rolled into the bathroom and gently closed the door. After stripping and transferring himself to the bench, he showered, the hot water seeping into the gaps of fatigue, tacking him together with a temporary glue.

He turned off the water, dried himself, then draped a dry towel over the seat of his chair. Transferring, he rolled himself to the side of the bed, then hefted himself to sit on the edge of the mattress, which sagged with his weight.

"Son of a bitch," he whispered under his breath.

Jostled, Sally asked sleepily, "What?"

"He had the bench all along. I fucking *hate* that. I hate it when people not only don't do their jobs—they make assumptions, they don't bother to find out what's really going on and what people need and don't need. They don't care, and they don't step up. And after all that—they pretend nothing's happened; they pretend they're not responsible. He even tried to shine you on."

"Oh, Tony, it don't make no never-mind; you got what you need now."

"Well, it may make no never-mind to you, but it bothers the shit out of me." He chewed his lip in the dark. "He doesn't think it's difficult enough for a person to drive into a place, late at night, tired? Maybe he might think about someone *else*, for a change."

"Well, after this, I 'spect-a-reckon he will."

"I hope so."

Saying nothing, he used his arms to guide his legs to the mattress, then stretched himself the length of the bed. The over-soft bedding sank even further, rolling Sally toward him till she bumped against his side.

"Mind if I get closer?"

Though he heard the attempt at levity, he felt unable to share the joke. "If you can handle it."

She lurched her bulging body next to his and settled into the crook of his arm. But no sooner had she laid her forearm across him, than his abdomen convulsed.

Sally recoiled and struggled to push herself up against the soft bedding. "Tony, what's wrong?"

"Muscle spasm. Comes with the territory."

"Comes with *what* territory?"

His breath jerked out of him in the dark. "When muscles don't get to work the way they should, they try to work anyway. That's my read on it."

"How awful." She ran what she hoped was a soothing touch down the length of his arm, while the spasms continued unabated.

"Sorry to say this." His voice was low and hoarse. "But I think your touching me only makes it worse."

"Oh! Oh, I see, I'm sorry, I—"

"I'll be okay in a while."

"Right." Miserable now, and filled with a sense of failure, Sally did her best to ignore the spasms racking his body. He, on the other hand, seemed to bear it with infinite patience, as though he knew there was no other way down the mountain.

After several minutes, he spoke again. "Well, this ain't exactly a barrel of laughs."

"What ain't?"

"I've asked you to go gallivanting across the country with a gimpy guy in a bad mood on a pain-in-the-ass trip. And you're not even married to him."

"'Scuse me?" Sally sat up and propped herself against the pillows. "What are you tryin' to say to me, Tony?"

She heard his teeth grind in the dark. "I think what I'm sayin' is, this ain't exactly what you expected, is it?"

"I didn't expect *nothin'*, Tony, 'cept to be with you."

"If we're really going to be together, I need to know something. Are you—not that I *could* at this moment—are you scared of making love with a gimp the rest of your life?"

She bit her lip. "A little."

"This is the time, Sal. Speak up now."

Sally brushed away a hot tear. "I'm scared of not pleasing you, not knowin' how to do it." She heard him sigh. *Was that relief? Or was it more anger?* "Mostly, I'm scared to lose you again."

"Why would you be scared of *that*?"

He still sounds angry, but I've gotta say it. She inhaled, exhaled. "There's somethin' I ain't told you yet. Seein' as how we're puttin' cards on the table, and all."

"Like I said, speak up."

"The father of this baby is . . . and you pro'bly know him . . . J-Jack Sawyer. I don't love him, and for sure he don't love me. I fooled myself about the whole thing for a while. Lookin' back, I think I wanted help buildin' onto my rest'rnt so bad, and he coulda done it. Promised he would. He still comes in ta eat, and I can't barely stand the sight o' him. But the baby . . . well, the baby—" She felt the bed shake as she gasped out a sob.

"The baby's all good," Tony said, covering her belly with his big hand. "I didn't need to know," he said quietly. "But I appreciate it."

She swiped at another tear. "That man ain't important to me. But I don't never want *you* to be at a disadvantage."

"Real good." Tony put out a long arm to cradle Sally, then waited till her body stilled and her breathing steadied. "It don't change a thing between you and me."

She unclenched the hand she'd laid on his chest, then felt his muscles relax as her own anxiety melted away in the reassurance of his embrace. Moments later, they both fell into exhausted sleep.

Chapter 20

Tony had continued to lay still, sagged in the bed. *Has to be 6 a.m. in California, I reckon. And it's Monday morning. Time to shake a leg.* In any case, a shaft of light cracked through the plastic-coated curtains that didn't quite meet in the middle, making it impossible for either of them to sleep any longer.

He gave Sally a gentle shove as she struggled to roll away from him, then watched as she managed to stand and make her way to the bathroom. While she did her thing, Tony made the transfer to his chair.

"Sleep any?" she asked when she walked the three steps back into their room.

"Not hardly," he answered, rolling past her. "A little, though. After I throw some water on my face, I'm gonna dress and go pay the bill. Here are the car keys. Meet you in the van."

"Okay."

Tony saw she was straightening the sheets on their miserable excuse for a bed, wondering why she bothered. *But that's Sal,* he thought, *leavin' it better than she found it.*

By the time he got to his van, he confirmed she'd tucked their bags neatly into the back, draped her still-damp robe across them, and gotten herself situated in the passenger seat.

By 6:30, they were trolling for a decent coffee shop along the highway, after which they'd press on for Arkansas.

Tony's van had been on the road for hours and was burning up Interstate Highway 40.

The bright sun that had lanced into his eyes for hours was finally overhead, and—lulled by the hum of tires and the striation of white-lines-on-blacktop—he found himself settling into the zen of driving.

Sally's voice broke into his meditation. "Hope I packed enough food."

He glanced over at her pert profile. "Good Lord, woman, if this ain't enough, I hate to think what is!"

"Well, I like to be prepared, is all."

"A Girl Scout at heart."

She chuckled. "Oh, you don't *know* how true that is! 'Be prepared.' I surely did take it to heart. Never went to school 'less I took everything I might need: an apple for the teacher, extra pencils and a clean pair of underpants."

Tony waggled his eyebrows. "Now we're gettin' to the good part." Out of the corner of his eye he saw her blush, and laughed. "You were one of those *good* girls who never got in trouble."

"Well, not till later. Thing is, when I was a kid and I *did* do somethin' wrong, I had to just blurt it out to Mama the minute I got home. I always had such a conscience . . . I couldn't keep *nothin'* from her."

"If your Mama bribes me with a piece of her pie, I won't be able to keep anything from her either."

Sally chuckled again. "Speakin' of food, ready for a snack?"

"Not really hungry, but my eyes are gettin' droopy."

Sally leaned over, opened the lid of the large cooler between their two seats, and rummaged for a moment. "Apple slices?"

"That'd do the trick."

Sally opened the top of a small, round plastic container and placed it in Tony's cupholder. He popped a slice into his mouth, the crisp fruit deliciously tart. "How come these didn't turn brown?"

"Drizzled them with lemon juice after I sliced 'em," she explained. "Want a little cheddar to go with that?"

"Mph-hmph," he replied.

She placed some sliced cheese in his cup, then closed the cooler lid. "How 'bout some music?"

"Yeah," he agreed. "Got my tunes packed in that black bag behind my seat. It's about the size of a shoebox, zipped all the way around." He waited while she leaned over to look for it. "Find it?"

"Ye-yus." She put the durable black canvas on her lap and unzipped it, revealing the built-in rack for cassettes, each space filled.

Tony glanced over at it. "That side has the Oldies. They're alphabetical."

"That a Boy Scout thing?" she teased.

"More like a Marines thing, probably. Hey, Doll, you got some gum?" *How long has it been since I called her that?*

"Ye-yus. Spearmint or cinnamon?"

"Cinnamon."

She peeled a stick from its wrapper and leaned over to put it in his mouth, then turned her attention back to the cassettes. "Alphabetical . . ." she mused as her fingers walked over the colorful cassette spines. "Let's start with James Brown."

"Real good."

Sally pushed the *Best of James Brown* cassette into the player, pressed herself back into her seat. "Oww!" the singer shouted, the sound booming through the van's multiple speakers. She jumped, then looked over to see Tony laugh.

Now she laughed too, the giggles coursing through her body till her sides ached and her eyes streamed with tears.

"Oww," Tony repeated, raising and lowering his shoulders to the music.

This sparked her next round of laughter, and by the time she could hear the music again, the refrain had come true. "I feel good," the singer chanted, "I knew that I would now."

Yeah, I knew it too, she thought. *Knew I'd feel good traveling' with this man, no matter where we'd go.* She looked over at his profile: strong nose, trim black beard outlining a sculpted jawline. *And here we are together again. Feels so right! I never thought it'd happen.* Her mind started to run back to their earlier days and to their missing chapters. *We gotta lot o' catchin' up to do. Until we first saw each other again last winter at that concert, I hadn't seen him since before he went overseas.*

"Say, what didya take with you to Vietnam?"

Tony shot a startled look at her. "Now, there's a segue."

"What? Oh . . . sorry, I guess my in-loud talk got to be my out-loud talk without my noticing.'"

Tony gave her a smile. "I like that. Means you feel comfortable with me."

Sally could feel her cheeks warm. "Ye-yes, you might say so." She grinned at him.

"What did I take? You pretty much take what they issue to you: rucksack, poncho, towel, flashlight, compass, canteen. . . ."

As Tony continued with his list, James Brown began to sing "This is a man's world/ This is a man's world/ But it wouldn't be nothing/ Nothing without a woman or a girl. . . ."

As if on cue, Tony said, "I did take a few personal things." He kept his gaze steadfast on the road.

"Oh, yeah?" Sally made sure her tone was light. "Like what? No, lemme guess. Um . . . a picture of your mama?"

"Oh, yeah, I took a picture of my mom." Tony darted a look at her and clacked his gum. "I took a picture of you."

Sally looked forward at the desert floor spreading out before them. "Which one?"

"Our prom picture, what else?" He clacked some more. "Kind o' helped me out sometimes, seeing us all dressed up, fresh faced and innocent."

Sally reached into her voluminous purse, dug into a hidden compartment of her battered wallet, and withdrew a slightly creased, dog-eared photograph. "This the one?"

Glancing over at it, Tony inhaled. "That's the one."

"Funny, ain't it? I was carryin' the same thing. I've always kept it in my wallet. Kind of a picture of hope or somethin'."

"Yeah. A picture of hope." He gazed at her so long Sally worried he'd drive off the road. To her relief he flicked a glance forward before saying, "I got different hopes now than I did six months ago, I'll tell ya."

Sally lifted her eyebrows and turned more toward him. "Like what?"

"Till then I would o' said just maintaining. Just keeping on with the discipline of living, you know?"

"Ye-yus."

"I like to take my time in the morning. I like those quiet hours before the light comes. Before the birds sing. Before the phone rings."

She sighed. "Sounds real good."

"I go over to the standing frame. You know, the thing in the corner of my bedroom?"

"Oh, I didn't understand what that was, Tony."

"I roll over to it and transfer into it, like I would into a regular chair. And then I strap myself in and hit the controls, and it slowly stands me up to my full height. Taller, actually, because I've got a little bit of a platform under my feet."

"Oooh. That must feel good."

"Oh, yeah. It releases tension down the back of my legs, and I can feel my whole back stretching. If I don't do it, I can feel myself drawing up, and that's not good. Stretching is really important."

"Oh!" she exclaimed. "I know, I love to stretch too. One of the things that's gotten a little hard these days." Wistful, she continued, "Can't hardly bend over at all."

Tony chuckled. "That's okay, Sweet. You will."

"'Spect-a-reckon. Okay, so, you stand up and then . . . how long do you do that?"

"I might stay in the frame for an hour."

"Lordy, you just stand there and sort o' meditate-like for an hour?"

Tony burst out laughing. "Okay, if you want this much detail, let me back up. I wake up, I wheel myself down the hall, go out the front door and pick up my paper."

"In your PJs?"

"Sal, I don't wear nothin' to sleep in."

"Oh. I thought that was maybe only when, well, you know."

He leered at her suggestively then clacked his gum as he refocused on the road. "No, I never wear pajamas, just don't like 'em."

"Mmm." She felt her face grow warm again. "Okay, so you put on a robe or somethin', and you—"

"I shouldn't be tellin' you *all* my secrets, but I don't wear no robe when I go out for the paper."

"Well, moon in the mornin'!"

"I guess you could say that, although no one gets a good look at my keester since it's slammed down in my chair."

Letting go with a high trill of giggles, Sally said, "No, no, I didn't mean it . . . not literal, like, it's just somethin' I say."

"An O'Mally-ism."

"Ye-yus. So I guess spinnin' down the road in your altogether is a habit with you, is that right?"

"Not a *habit,*" he protested. "I just go out my front door when it's still dark and pick up my paper. I'm sure my neighbors have all seen a naked man before."

"Ooo-eee. And what about drivin' over to go visitin' like you did in your altogether? That a habit too?"

"No, I save that for special occasions, like when there's reason to worry about a parent, and the one who's worrying is the woman I love."

Sally curled her toes and felt her innards run together like melted butter.

"That's a good one," Tony crooned.

"What?"

"That face. Save that one for me."

Blushing, Sally stifled a grin and pulled at her cotton cardigan, which would no longer stretch across her belly. "Okay, I interrupted you. You get your paper. Then what?"

"I get my coffee, stand up, and read my paper. And then I head to the shower, get myself cleaned up. Whole thing takes a couple of hours. But it kinda sets me up for the day, and then I feel ready, feel like I can think clearly, see what the day might bring, see how I can maybe help somebody."

Reflecting for a moment, Sally said, "You think about that a lot, don't you Tony? You think how you can help *other* folks. Boy, I almost don't *never* think about how I can help somebody else."

"Sally, you *serve* other people all day."

"Oh, yes, but that's just the rest'rnt. I don't really feel like I truly help other people."

"But you *do*. Sorry, Sal, I gotta pull over. I gotta pee."

She glanced both north and south along I-40, able to see only scrub brush leading as far as the eye could see to distant mountains. "But Tony, there's nothin' out here."

"I don't need anything."

She peered ahead to the east. "I see some trees up yonder."

"Time is of the essence—I don't have the control to wait."

"Oh, all right then."

Tony slowed the van, pulled over onto the shoulder and used his plastic urinal, covering himself with a towel.

"'Least you don't have to wait for the amenities."

"There are some advantages to being male."

"Must be nice," Sally said.

"Well, it's not nice. It's not nice to be sitting here pissing in front of somebody."

Startled at the sudden vehemence in his voice, Sally stopped looking out the window and turned to him.

"I'd rather jump out of this van and go stand over there in the bushes." Tension continued to mount in his voice. "There's nothing *nice* about it. It's what I have to do. Damn it!"

Sally pressed herself against the door.

"I hate it when I do that!"

"What?"

"I spilled some!"

"Want some help cleaning up?"

"I think I've been dealing with my own piss for quite a while now. I do *not* need your help."

"I . . . I didn't mean . . . I only meant. . . ." Sally fell silent, trying to make herself small in the passenger seat.

"Okay, I'm going to leave a little piss here along this scenic highway," he said with an edge to his voice. "I'm sure the desert could use another few ounces. And then we'll go."

"Okay," she answered in a tiny voice. *Lordy, what did I do? What did I say? We was havin' such a good time and then . . . I must'o made him angry. I wouldn't mind spendin' a penny myself, but I don't dare to mention it right now.* When they'd been rolling again for several minutes, Sally asked timidly, "Mad at me?"

"*You?*" he said with unmistakable hostility. "No, why would I be mad at *you?*"

The James Brown song seemed to have lost its relevance, and Sally punched the Eject button. She turned her body as much as possible to the right and watched out the window as they passed signs for a river. She turned to face forward again and sneaked a glance in his direction, but he was keeping his thoughts to himself, squinting at the road and chewing hard on his gum.

How do I get us back to the good time we were havin'? She watched the landscape as though scanning for ideas as they traveled along in an uneasy silence. She made a point of studying tufts of brown grass, scoops of gray gravel and the distant hills, which looked as jagged as a graph of her emotions. After a time, she braved another sentence. "So, Tony, if you could do your favorite thing right now, what would it be?"

"My favorite thing? Take a leak."

"Oh, piddle."

"Exactly."

Laughing in spite of herself, she glanced at him sideways, and watched, intrigued, as he suppressed the laugh that was quivering at the edge of his mouth. "Tony Fiorentino, sometimes you're the most *exasperatin'* man!"

"That's right, I *am.* What are you gonna do about it?"

"What I'm gonna do about it is jest . . . tell you what I think!"

"Is *that* all?"

"Ye-yus!"

"Wouldn't you wanna change me in some way?" He clacked his gum.

"No!"

"Good!"

Pulling out the map, she opened it, the rattling paper filling the void left by their fallen conversation. Tony chewed on his gum and worked his lip with his big teeth. "Sally, I really can't see the road very well when you have the map open like that, so as soon as you get done with it, would you mind?"

She folded it slowly, deliberately, without comment. Five minutes later, she summoned the courage for another foray into conversation. "So anyway, Tony, you were tellin' me about when you went to Vietnam, what you took with you. You took my picture, you told me that. What else?"

"I'll tell you something I didn't take. I didn't take underwear."

"Really? Why?"

"One less thing. One less thing to carry, one less thing to wash, to worry about. Between the plastic poncho, the helmet, the socks, the uniforms, the ammo, the weapon, you're carrying a minimum of twenty pounds. You're walking through the steaming jungle . . . the less you have to carry the better. What you really want to carry is water and bug repellant."

"I've heard that men make really good friendships when they're at war. That true?"

"Made a real good friend with Ron. Made some other good friends. Had to watch 'em die."

Sally grimaced and squinted into the sun as it edged toward the horizon. She pulled the cassette carrier back onto her lap, then pulled out the next plastic case. They rode without speaking for a while as they listened to Bob Dylan.

"She aches just like a woman, yes, she does," the songwriter wailed mournfully. "But she breaks just like a little girl."

Is that what he's waitin' for me to do—break? Well then, he's got another think comin'. Sally considered this man she loved so much. *I don't wanna rub salt in his wounds—he's salty enough today. But I don't wanna pretend anything either.*

She picked up the Dylan cassette cover and read the titles. *Before we get to* "Sad-Eyed Lady of the Lowlands" *I better switch to somethin' more cheerful.* An Earth, Wind & Fire album was the next in sequence, and she exchanged it for the Dylan, carefully putting *Blonde On Blonde* back into the case.

She found it interesting to observe her own behavior. *If Jack Sawyer had spoken to me the way Tony did a few minutes back, I'd a' given him a piece of my mind, and then some.* But with Tony, it was different. She sensed his intention. *He wants to show himself to me—warts and all.* Though he was making this as raw and painful as he could, still, she wanted to honor his process. Somewhere inside her, there was a well of patience she'd never tapped before.

Looking at the ribbon of highway stretching out ahead, she thought of the long road they'd traveled and of the road ahead of them, which she hoped would be longer than anything they'd traveled so far.

She looked at Tony as he gazed toward the distant mountains. Gesturing with his eyebrows, he motioned for her to look at what he was observing: a tall column of swirling dust.

"'A pillar of cloud by day,'" Sally said quietly.

"What'd you say?"

"You know, that led the people in the Bible? Night time it was a pillar of fire."

"That's no cloud," he pointed out. That's just a bunch of dust."

"The dust just means you can see it real plain in the daylight. If you had to follow it, you could."

"You believe in that kind of thing?"

"I believe in guidance, yes. I don't know that I hear the Lord's voice real clear too often. But when I *really, really* need to know, I always seem to get my answer. I don't ask for a lot o' help. Jest some guidance, sometimes. I figure it's up to me to choose my way."

They listened to the tires drone over the hot pavement for a few minutes, then Sally clicked the Play button on the cassette deck. "Looking back, we've touched on sorrowful days," sang Earth, Wind & Fire." *Those days really have disappeared. We just have to let 'em go.*

"You will find peace of mind/ If you look way down in your heart and soul." The music with its inspiring words rang through the van. But Tony's resolute face stayed focused forward, squinting against the glare coming through the windshield.

"Do you think it might be time for lunch?" Sally ventured.

"I don't feel like stopping, Sal. Just wanna keep going."

"Oh, I have plenty of goodies right here in the van. But I would *not* mind stoppin' for a ladies' room, though."

"No problem."

It was the first time she'd heard a positive sentence from him in what seemed like hours. At least that was a forward step. *For now, I best be grateful for small favors.* Arkansas was still a long way off.

Sally rubbed her eyes as Tony pulled into Glenda O'Mally's driveway, noting that the dashboard clock—still on Pacific time—read 9:13 p.m. But after their thirty-hour trip and a shift to East Coast time, Sally couldn't decide whether it was early or late.

Tony let the van idle for a moment, while he adjusted his watch to read 12:13 a.m., then turned off the motor and the headlights. In the sudden quiet, Sally could hear a light wind rustling leaves in the tall maples. *That's a home sound*, she thought, letting it seep into tired muscles.

She looked over at Tony, reading residual tension in his face, and feeling it in her own. *We react to so many things the same way. There are ties that bind us and always have.* Across the miles, she'd felt him straining at those ties like a rowboat tethered to a dock in a rising storm. Now as she sensed an approaching calm, she wanted only to be tender with him, to let the boat settle until it rested in a safe haven.

She opened her door and sat there inhaling the rich, moist scent of summer as it swirled into the van. She heard Tony inhale too and stretch his torso upward. Feeling the caress of the cool night air, she closed her eyes.

"Best not fall asleep just yet," Tony said quietly.

Her eyes popping open, Sally answered, "You're right." She picked up her purse and looked around her seat at the debris of snacks and paper cups. "Shall I go on in, then?"

"Yep. Let me know about access."

"Right." Sliding down from her high perch—grateful she could still just see her feet over her expanding belly—Sally touched the ground and walked stiffly up to Mama's back door.

It was unlocked, as she knew it would be. Stepping inside, she found a note on the kitchen table.

Aunt Ida's old room in the pouting house is all fixed for Tony. Your room is ready for you. See you both in the morning. Night-night. Mama

Mama's thought of everything. She always does. Sally walked back outside and motioned Tony to follow her. She heard him start the van again, then guide it slowly behind her down the length of the driveway, passing the main house. What they called the "pouting house" stood adjacent and had a garage of its own. She gestured for him to pull in alongside the white 1955 Chevy pickup truck. *Well, I'll be a double moon pie. Here's Daddy's truck and Tony's van settin' together like two boats on the lake. Who'd a' thought?*

She patted her own cheek to wake herself from the reverie, then walked to the van's side doors, which Tony'd already opened. "Want help with carryin'?"

He waved her off. "We'll get the rest tomorrow, Sal. I gotta hit the rack."

"Everything's ready, Tony. Mama has it all fixed."

"That's what I've been hopin'."

"I'll just turn on a coupla lights while you get yourself in your chair." She crossed the garage and through the wide door leading to the small apartment, where she could see a light already glowed. *This was a good idea, Mama.* From here, the ramp they'd had built for her aunt to use during a convalescence some years back would allow Tony access to the main house without having to negotiate the front steps.

The poutin' house looks jest the same. This separate building —with its affectionate family name—was a stroke of genius from the first day it was built. Huge double garage and workshop on one side, small apartment on the other, complete with its own bedroom, shower, and kitchenette. "Got to get away sometimes," her father used to say, "but not *too* far."

Tony rolled through the door, his large eyes looking sunken with fatigue.

"Bed's this way," she pointed. "Bathroom's right over there. Kitchenette has sodas and some goodies Mama left." She kissed him on the forehead and walked back toward the garage to close its door for the night. "Need anythin' else?"

"Not a thing." Even with the rasp of fatigue, his voice sounded gentle. "You rest well, now."

"I will. You too, Tony."

It took ten minutes for Sally to retrieve her small overnight bag, tiptoe through the main house to her old room, brush her teeth and change into her nightgown. It took her only ten seconds to fall asleep in the peaceful Arkansas night.

Chapter 21

Miranda and Cornelius had one more day before they'd move part of their belongings into the adjacent unit, and she couldn't figure out whether this would create more or less chaos.

Ultimately, of course, things would be more orderly, they'd each have more space, and they'd settle in for the next few months. Meanwhile, she didn't want Cornelius to feel he was being banished next door.

To help sort all this, she'd enlisted the aid of her future mother-in-law, who'd arrive in a couple of hours. Not that she wanted Cornelius' parents to do any heavy lifting! But she thought asking for ideas would be helpful and create a lovely opportunity for including them. *Also, they could keep an eye on things while C and I are in Alaska.*

For now, Miranda had to focus in her studio, making sure she was organized for three of the biggest events of her life: her job at University of Alaska Fairbanks; her rehearsal dinner; and her wedding!

She started by reviewing her preparations for the UAF. She'd already submitted a list of materials that they'd assemble for her. She planned to take her portable easel, the small kit she used for carrying brushes and tools, paints and pallets. And she'd put together a notebook with curricular outlines for each teaching day.

Last week, she'd had a call from Zelda that'd added to the already busy Fairbanks schedule. She laughed, thinking back to Zelda's usual dictatorial style. "After I heard about your teaching job in Alaska, I found you a *professional* job as well."

"But Zelda, my teaching job *is* professional."

"You know what I mean, an actual painting commission. It seems there's a fine museum in Fairbanks and one of their displays has been damaged. This will earn you both points *and* money. They require a wildlife artist, and when they heard you were going to be at the school, they agreed this would work perfectly. They have dioramas with wildlife figures in front of murals that must be redone. At the University of Alaska Museum, you're to speak with a Ms. Rensworth." Adding murals to her work at UAF did sound perfect, and she'd fit it into her schedule somehow.

For clothing, she'd been advised to plan for rain and sun, with waterproof pants and jacket. Lifting stacks of colorful T-shirts from her drawers, she placed them on the bed and followed these with a short pile of folded jeans, then underwear and socks. Because she'd read it could get chilly—even in summer—she added two long-sleeved cotton shirts and a fleece zippered jacket. *A couple of baseball caps,* she thought. *I'll need those. And hiking boots. Since it'll be light all the time, I should pack eye masks for us.*

Then there was the matter of decent clothes for attending whatever faculty events might come up. There might be a reception or even a dinner. She reached for a dark green broomstick skirt that hung on the bottom rail. It folded down to nothing and was already wrinkled by design. Then she found a couple of stretch tops to go with it and pulled out a simple black blazer she could travel in and use for functions. Realizing she'd need something other than hiking boots to wear with her better clothes, she reached for her black travel flats. *Will I need a bathing suit?* It was possible. She grabbed her one-piece and threw goggles on the bed as well.

Then, deciding she did want one nice outfit to wear with Cornelius—*after all, it'll be our honeymoon! I need something I can roll up*— she thought immediately of her trusty green jersey dress, adding it to her list. *Accessories? Brush and comb, sunscreen and lipbalm, hair ties and clips.* Just the basics. She had a small toiletries kit she used for camping and that'd work.

Once they finished their respective UAF jobs, the rest of their trip would be a combination of camping and staying at wilderness lodges. They'd decided two oversized duffles would work, one for camping gear, the other for their personal stuff.

Fortunately, there was virtually no overlap between what she'd need for Alaska, and what she needed for the wedding weekend. She chuckled at that. Though being held at an outdoor venue her mother would consider "rustic," their nuptials *would* be fancy.

She flashed forward to future celebrations, starting with the one her parents would arrange at their home in Belvedere sometime after they returned from their trip. Of course, it would include jewels and high heels, silks and satins, and probably at least one tuxedo appearance. *Oh my God, it's all so exciting. I'm so grateful!* She pulled back from her reverie, knowing that if she went down that rabbit hole it'd take hours to climb out again.

After a few more minute's review, she declared the Alaska list complete and moved on to what she'd need for the wedding. Mother'd sent her some heavenly underwear: a bra designed to work with her dress, silky no-line panties, a garter to keep that tradition. Rather than write these things down, she retrieved the medium-sized suitcase from the hall closet, then took it down the stairs to her bedroom and flung it open on the bed. Into a small, flexible zippered bag she placed all the underwear she'd need, then assembled the full array of makeup, skincare, and hair accessories, including a beautiful comb festooned with shells and ribbons created by her friend Shelley.

For the ceremony, she'd want her new white leather sandals, so she slipped them into a soft shoe-sock. She was about to put her green flats into the wedding suitcase when she realized she'd need them in Alaska, as she'd be taking that forest green dress. Well, the dress she'd found for the rehearsal was also green, but it was peridot to match her birthstone. With its sweetheart neckline, cap sleeves, a side slit in the mid-length skirt, it was stunning, especially with the pashmina she'd found—peridot, with a subtle paisley pattern woven along its length. The scarf was also shot with silver, and she remembered silver sandals were what she'd chosen for the outfit, along with her broad silver barrette, all of which she added to the bag.

Though her mother'd objected, Miranda didn't need a "going away" outfit. After their reception, they'd simply wander off to their suite at Ragged Point for their wedding night. *Oh! I need the beautiful peignoir Mother bought for me!* She unearthed the box from the bottom of her closet floor and folded back the tissue paper to gaze at the creamy georgette fabric, its slightly puckered surface translucent, the bodice finished with some delicate beading.

Wonder how long I'll actually be wearing it? Heat rose into her cheeks. *Don't think about that now!* Back to the timeline . . .

the next morning, a limo would pick them up, bring them home to change clothes, exchange luggage, then take them to the airport for their flight to Alaska.

A few more things had to be added to this suitcase—flip flops and a comfy outfit for their ride home after the wedding, all the bridesmaid gifts she'd made and still had to wrap, the special notes she'd written to her parents and to his. But Miranda heaved a sigh of relief, feeling better organized for the big events. Now, she had to think about the everyday belongings so as to figure out what stayed put and what moved next door.

Charles Jones had finished breakfast with his wife, enjoying their small table in the solarium that protruded from the library out into the garden. The room, made mostly of glass, allowed them to feel they were almost sitting in Veri's flower beds, while keeping them warm from the chilly June mornings.

"I do so want Miranda to paint *trompe l'oeil* climbing vines at the corners," his wife chattered. "I'll put real pots in front of them, and they'll look so realistic with her deft hand." Veri took a sip of her coffee. "Should they be morning glories? Yes! That'll be perfect."

Giving her a perfunctory kiss on the cheek, he took his coffee cup and headed upstairs to his home office. He had always worried about his younger daughter. Miranda was a dreamer and always had been—head in the clouds, feet unshod while traipsing through the woods or across the sand, talking to animals, forgetting import-ant social obligations, and excited about things that baffled him.

As if all that weren't enough, there was her utter disregard of money. IF she earned any, it was spent before it arrived in her bank account. The rest of the family had no idea how many times he'd spoken with their private banker to sort out her finances or even to bail her out a couple of times—something else he'd never mentioned to her.

This was all the more confusing to him because his first child was a genius with finance, so much so that she'd made buckets of money, invested wisely, and founded her own firm. He'd never had to explain one thing to Meredith about fiscal responsibility because it was a language both of them spoke. She had good mentors and colleagues, excellent clients, and quite a head for figures.

Veri understood both their daughters, bless her. She tirelessly explained Miranda to him, for all the good it did. "Just love her, darling. That's all that really matters."

He knew his wife was right. It's just that Miranda had made it hard for him all her life, And then, she'd come home with a scientist character, flashing a rather insignificant ring and claiming to be engaged. The man in question was polite enough, good looking in a slightly unkempt way, and had even requested a private audience to ask for his daughter's hand. *After the fact*. He could hardly grant permission for something that'd already taken place.

Veri talked about "the light in Miranda's eyes" and "how devoted Cornelius seems." These distinctions were far too ephemeral for Charles, who was more interested in employment and assets. After all, if this man couldn't support Miranda, that responsibility would continue to fall to *him* and now that he was retired, he had other plans for his money.

He hadn't quite finished musing—or grousing—about this situation when Veri arrived with a fresh pot of decaf and the morning mail. "Here you are, dear," she'd said brightly. "Don't forget we have a luncheon at the museum today." After a peck on the cheek, she'd hurried off.

He poured himself a cup of their housekeeper Pilar's superb coffee—even if it did lack the caffeine—then glanced through the newly arrived post. *Bills, mostly*, he confirmed, placing them in the "to be paid" caddy on his desk. But one seemed to be a letter with an unfamiliar return address.

"C. Smith," it read, followed by "Tangle, 1 Lighthouse Way, Milford-Haven." *Well, this has to be from Miranda's friend,* he thought, still not fully accepting his status, though he knew wedding plans were well under way.

He slit open the plain white envelop with his silver letter opener and was surprised when a check slid out onto the desk. But he wanted to read the letter first, certain it would provide an explanation.

> Dear Mr. Jones,
>
> Enclosed please find payment in full for the balance owed on the property at 2060 Jones Street, San Francisco. Miranda has allowed me to be the one to pay this as a wedding gift to her.
>
> Thank you again for our wonderful visit last April. We're making progress with the wedding plans, the house renovation is coming along, and we're prepping for Alaska.
>
> Kind regards to you and Mrs. Jones,
>
> Cornelius Smith

Charles snatched up the check and peered at the numbers. The very *substantial* numbers. The full amount still owed on the house Miranda and Meredith had once shared, where Meredith still lived. The house Veri had found for them.

It had been an excellent investment, a point on which the whole family had agreed. But while Meredith had been able to pay her half without difficulty, Miranda had not, so Veri had said the senior Joneses would carry a note for their younger daughter. "This way both girls will be in a safe neighborhood, in a lovely home. Miranda will catch up."

Miranda had, in fact, been making regular payments both during and after her residence at the house, and even while establishing herself in her new little town down the coast. But at the rate she was paying, Charles would be a hundred and ten before the debt was paid off.

Well, not anymore! He couldn't suppress the grin that spread across his face. Then he looked more closely at the check. "Cornelius Smith, PhD" it read. *Did I know he was a PhD? So his name is Doctor Cornelius Smith*, he reflected. *That makes it more palatable. Too bad it's such a common name.* The last time he'd mentioned that, his wife had laughed out loud. "And Jones isn't?" She'd asked. And he'd felt himself blush, sputtering about his proud Welsh heritage.

So how does a scientist with a part time job at NASA afford to write a check of this size? Jesus, I hope this doesn't put them further into the hole.

Zelda McIntyre glanced at her gold Piaget wristwatch. *Only mid-morning, and already the day is shaping up beautifully.*

Looking down at her list of calls to make, she picked up the phone and dialed the Bluewater Press in Milford-Haven. When she'd placed the order for one thousand of the new promotional post-cards to be shipped to her in Santa Barbara, she hung up the phone.

Zelda found an important part of managing careers was creating—and maintaining—momentum. While a client like young

Miranda used to be perfectly happy to crawl into a figurative hole and paint for months with no thought for marketing or exhibiting her work, Zelda had always known better and had trained Miranda well. Last spring she'd arranged a fabulous gallery showing for her client in the artist's own hometown of Milford-Haven, boosting considerably both sales and Central Coast recognition.

She'd arrange for future showings somewhere along the coast, possibly right here in Santa Barbara. Meanwhile, it was vital to both notify and expand the client base, and for this, the marketing postcards were just the right tool.

Miranda's life used to have its complexities. Last year she'd been pursued by Zackery Calvin. In theory, the potential match had had some merit, in that both young people were from privileged backgrounds. Yet, Zelda had been equally aware that it was Cynthia whom Zackery had been publicly courting here in town. That'd put Zelda in an awkward position, particularly when the in-town girlfriend had purchased a painting by the out-of-town girlfriend, facilitated by Zelda herself. *Not my finest hour*, she admitted to no one but herself. Now she had to swap that painting for another, but she was turning that to her advantage. Joseph had seen his son's poor reaction to that first piece and had said he'd be happy to take another one in trade without even mentioning it to Zackery. They'd agreed this was the best plan.

Joseph Calvin glanced at the clock on his dashboard. *Not quite 7p.m.—so I'll be just a few minutes late. Good. Wouldn't want to make this too easy for her.*

He chuckled at the thought. By now he'd given up his annoyance at Zelda's obvious manipulation to get him to her apartment, deciding instead to be flattered by it. He rounded the corner onto Victoria Street and began looking for her address. *Great area . . . one of my favorites near downtown.*

Last winter, she'd invited him to that Doobie Brothers concert. Though he'd agreed mostly because his son was one of the organizers—and he was curious to get a glimpse into what was then a hidden part of Zack's life—he had to admit his evening with Zelda had been fun. But since then . . . he'd been busy. But now here he was, about to spend either a few minutes, or a few hours, with Zelda. He did have some curiosity about seeing the woman in her own place. *Is this an errand—or a date? I guess I'll find out.*

Pulling the BMW into the *porte cochre* as instructed, he stepped out, leaving the car running. Tugging at the waistband of his navy slacks, he handed his keys to the valet. He gave his name to the doorman, listened as his arrival was announced over Zelda's intercom, then walked through the courtyard. Inviting in its privacy, its ingenious *trompe l'oeil* had him fooled for a moment. *Is that a real staircase behind the potted jasmine, or is it just cleverly painted?* He found the elevator and pressed the Three button. When the doors opened again, he faced a small marble entrance hall. Looking across it, he saw Zelda open her front door and smile at him.

God! Is that dress transparent? The amethyst-colored gown draped over her ample cleavage, clung appealingly at the waist, then seemed to float over her hips. *So I'm* not *here on an errand*, he thought as his foot touched the marble. *It's a date.*

His foot suddenly seemed to detach itself from his body and fly forward of its own accord. Though he managed to prevent himself from performing a perfect split, in stopping his momentum, he went down on one side.

Zelda gasped, scarcely believing her eyes. One moment Joseph was walking toward her, the next he was full-length on the hard floor. *That horrific sound—his body smacking the stone! And did I also hear something rip?* "Oh, my heavens!" she shrieked. "Joseph! Are you all right?"

"Argh," he groaned, rolling away from the hip on which he'd landed.

Looking down at her two-inch heels and the slick surface, she whipped off her shoes, reached him and bent down. "What can I do, Joseph? Can I help you up?"

"Oh, that smarts. Just give me a moment."

"Certainly! Oh, I've told her and told her *not* to wax this floor! I don't come up this way myself, you see. I come in the back way, and I had *no* idea! Oh, I'm terribly sorry!"

"Zelda, just . . . okay, so far so good." He'd managed to raise himself to all fours. "Give me a hand, will you?" He pulled himself to both knees. "Now can you give me a shoulder? I'll see if I can stand." Leaning on her heavily, he tried putting weight on his right leg, wincing at the effort. "Okay," he said, breathing heavily.

"Oh, for heaven's sake, be careful!"

Taking small, cautious steps, they made it to her front door and stepped onto carpeting.

"The sofa isn't far, Joseph. Let's just get you comfortable."

Joseph seemed to have the stoicism of an athlete, only wincing slightly as he limped across the room. "Ugh," he grunted as he sat. Leaning against the suede, he then began feeling the hip. "Everything still seems to be in one place," he said. "And the pain, thank God, is subsiding."

"At the very least, we should put some ice on that immediately," Zelda told him. "I'll get some."

"If you've got frozen peas or corn in a bag, that works best," Joseph called after her.

"Right," she said and returned momentarily with four bags of baby peas. "You'll have to take off those slacks, I'm afraid. And I imagine you'd want to anyway, with that rip."

"What?" Inspecting himself, Joseph realized the crotch of the pants was ripped at the seam, his royal blue boxers peeking through. "Oh, for God's sake!"

"I have an expert seamstress who can fix those. Now, would you like help removing them?"

"Zelda, I should just go."

"Oh, really? As the swelling begins, you'd like to renegotiate the marble, and then try driving?" She stood staring down at him in her bare feet, shifting the freezing bags of peas from one hand to the other.

"Oh, for heaven's sake. I suppose not. Here, hand me those."

She did and managed to refrain from laughing as she watched him try to squeeze the packets of frozen vegetables into his pants—gasping at the cold, grunting at the effort. When that didn't work, he looked up.

"Well, I'll have to undo the waistband, I suppose."

Zelda dropped to her knees front of him, unclasped his belt and unzipped the pants.

Joseph thought, *This is either my worst nightmare or my greatest fantasy. What do I do now?* Her scent wafted up to him. *Like roses . . . but it's earthy too . . .with a hint of something like . . . clove. And does that jasmine come from her or from the garden?* He let his eyes follow the line of her neck down into her blouse where her full breasts seemed to glow through the thin fabric. He felt a swelling in his boxers. *Not now!* That prayer was answered when she placed the frozen peas against his hip.

"Agh!" he inhaled sharply. "Cold!"

"That's the idea, Joseph." Withdrawing her hands, she looked up at him. "Sure you want to keep the pants on?"

Clenching his teeth, Joseph said, "For now, I think everything's just peachy."

"Then how about a drink?"

"Make it a Scotch," he said without hesitation. "Neat."

After delivering his drink, Zelda returned with a thick towel. "While you may not mind soaking those divine raw silk slacks, I'm not keen on doing the same to my sofa," she explained. "Mind rolling to one side for a moment?"

"No problem," he said, though he winced as he came back to center.

"My cook has everything ready."

"Really, Zelda, I don't need anything."

"You don't want that Scotch to rest on an empty stomach. I'll be right back with a tray."

As sounds and smells emerged from her kitchen, he decided he was feeling hungry after all. In a few moments, she placed a large linen napkin on his lap, and followed it with a lacquer tray and a plate full of *pasta carbonara*. It smelled divine.

"Aren't you joining me?" he asked, staring at the plate.

"Won't be a moment."

When she returned with her own tray, she sat a little too close to him and tucked his napkin into his shirt.

"Really, Zelda, you needn't do that."

"Since we've had one disaster with the pants, we might as well try to save the shirt."

"Mmm," he savored the bite. "This is great."

Beaming, she said, "So glad you're enjoying it" and took a small bite of her own.

She seemed quite content to eat without talking, and he appreciated the chance to savor his food in silence. When their pasta was finished, she served small plates of mixed greens with balsamic vinaigrette. Next she whisked the trays away and Joseph could hear her talking to the cook in the kitchen, followed by the hissing of an espresso machine. Zelda reappeared with two small dishes of raspberry sorbet, crisp wedges of cookie protruding from their tops.

"Lovely meal, Zelda. Very kind of you."

"It was my pleasure." She turned her head to look at him. "I'll just get our espressos."

"I don't know if I need the jolt of—"

"Not to worry. Decaf."

Joseph leaned away from the package of cold peas, then relaxed against the sofa cushions. "I think that's enough of the ice treatment."

"I agree." There was a twinkle in her eye as she took the peas from him. Zelda returned with two *demitasses* and sat comfortably beside him. He stared for a moment at her hands—graceful and manicured but with rather short nails. And below her hands, a sculpted leg shot through a slit in the drape of her skirt. *Don't stare at that—not with the crotch of your pants ripped open.* Taking the coffee from her, he looked away. "So, Zelda, have you got the painting for me?"

"Of course." Placing her cup on the coffee table, she reached for a letter of agreement and handed him a pen. "As you'll see, this indicates you've received a painting of equal value to the one exchanged."

Joseph raised his eyebrows. *Trust Zelda to be ready, document and all.* Putting his cup down, he reached into his shirt pocket for his glasses, then reviewed the document. "And do I get to see the new painting before signing?"

Zelda rose, walked across the carpet to a closed door, opened it and disappeared. When she returned—walking sideways in order to carry a large canvas—she paused for a moment before rotating to show him the painting head-on.

It was like looking out a window into a familiar world—coastline trailing northward, pines clinging to steep ridges. But the image leapt into three dimensions, belying its two-dimensional physical reality. As though individual objects had been delicately painted on separate layers, the images seemed to be a series of gauze curtains: hazy mist roiling through a vale on one, windswept pines suspended on the next.

"I like it," he confirmed. "Excellent choice."

"I thought you would." Zelda carried it toward the front door, leaning it carefully against the wall. As she walked back to him, she added, "I do have a special box that will protect it."

Joseph reviewed the letter again. "Seems fine." He signed it, put away his glasses and looked at Zelda. "Very prepared, as usual."

Twisting her Cross pen, Zelda said, "Of course."

His gaze dropped to her bottom lip—no longer outlined and colored in that tint perfectly matching her outfit. Now the deep natural hue showed.

A noise from the kitchen woke him from the mesmeric reverie. "So . . . the painting." He cleared his throat. "Can your doorman get it downstairs and into my car?"

"Certainly."

"Thanks for the unveiling." Joseph watched Zelda's eyes widen while her lips twitched into a grin. He could feel the heat rush up his neck. *I don't think I've blushed this much since high school.* "I meant . . . the painting."

"Of course you did." She sank into the sofa beside him.

"Well." He put his hand on Zelda's, not trusting himself to touch her anywhere else. "That was a sensational dinner. Despite my mishap, it's been a nice evening. I better get home and get started with repairs."

"You should do whatever you think is best, Joseph. But my seamstress can repair the pants immediately. Why not at least let her take a look?"

"She's here, you mean? It's the same woman who works in your kitchen?"

"She goes off duty shortly and can take the pants with her. She's highly skilled, I assure you."

Thinking for another moment, Joseph relented. "Just give me a moment. I'll hand them to you."

Smiling, Zelda stood. She started across the room but hurried back when she heard him inhale sharply.

"It's okay, Zelda. I've got it."

"Right." She left again to give him his privacy. After a moment she returned to find him sitting on the sofa, the linen napkin that he'd kept from dinner now strategically placed. She picked up his slacks. "I'll just show these to her."

Joseph watched Zelda's hips sway as she left, carrying away his pants. Summoning as much dignified nonchalance as he could, he glanced at the coffee table, noting the magazines neatly fanned at one end—*Art + Auction* and *Art In America*—and tried to over-hear as the two women conferred in the kitchen. When Zelda reappeared, she asked, "What time would you like to leave in the morning, Joseph?"

"In the morning? No, no, I need to be getting back."

"She's the best, Joseph. You don't want to rush her."

Joseph stewed for a moment. "Fine. I need to leave by 7:30."

"Very good."

Joseph overheard a back door close.

When Zelda returned, she looked down at him. "I do have a more comfortable place for you to recline."

Smiling, he answered, "I was hoping you'd say that." With an effort, he pushed himself to the edge of the sofa and stood carefully. "Well, everything seems to be in working order."

"Oh, *good,*" she remarked.

He laughed. "Just answer me one thing. You didn't wax that floor yourself, did you?"

"I swear, I—" she protested.

"Okay," he said, putting an arm around her. "Funny how things work out sometimes."

"*Isn't* it?"

Joseph let her guide him down a hallway hung with paintings and into her bedroom. Against a rich purple wall stood a four-poster bed, covered and pillowed in layers of color from the softest lavenders and grays to the amethyst of her outfit. Pushing him gently down onto the bed, she plumped pillows behind him and pulled the napkin away.

"The night is young," she said. "We'll have to devise some engaging way of spending the hours." With that, she unzipped her dress and let it slide to the floor, revealing the most interesting underwear he'd seen since his last trip to Paris.

Chapter 22

Tony Fiorentino startled awake at a disorienting sound. Eyes wide, he lay alone diagonally across the double bed and listened. A car drew closer, then its sound dopplered away, but what he'd heard a moment before was not a traffic noise. Then it came again. *I'll be damned.* He smiled. Cows! The lowing must have drifted from the nearby pasture, a sonic portrait of peace.

It all flowed back into his mind: the long drive, the brutal exhaustion, and the arrival at the O'Mally homestead. With it came the grinding awareness of his own testy attitude during the trip. *And she was nothin' but sweetness.*

His gaze scanned the room, which was spacious but sparsely furnished. A square table and four chairs seemed perfect for burgers or for card games. Peach-and-white-checked gingham curtains hung at either side of the glass sliders, a now-rumpled matching comforter covered the bed where he rested. He craned his neck to see the framed picture hanging over his head. Actually, it was elaborately needle-pointed words: "Do unto others as you would have them do unto you."

The slogan stung like a slap. *I've come all this way for my own selfish reasons, pretending it was all out of kindness to Sal.* He wanted to wallow in his self-reproach. But the day with its new potential seemed to nudge, calling to him as insistently as the little yellow bird sitting on a branch outside.

As if to echo the bird and sweep away the last traces of his bad mood, lemon yellow light spilled through those sliding-glass doors that formed one wall of this so-called "pouting house." *What time is it?* He snatched up the watch he'd put on the bedside table. *8:15 already? Geez, I gotta get a move on.* Glancing again at the night stand, he saw a note. *She must've snuck in here. Amazing I slept on through.*

> Gone to take Mama to the doctor. Then we'll go shop-
> ping. Your breakfast's on the stove. See you later.
>   xoxo Sally

Tony pushed himself up, sidled toward the edge of the bed, and transferred to his chair. *Wonder when that was written?* He rolled to the bathroom and took a quick visual inventory: wide door that permitted easy access; handicap shower stall with no barrier; plastic shower bench; even a toilet seat with a frame stood in place.

Touched by the preparations—which were not only thought-ful but thorough and correct—Tony sat for a moment abashed. He realized now he'd been assuming everything at her mother's house would be inaccessible. *Just shows how wrong a chump can be.*

Stripping off yesterday's underwear, Tony slid himself onto the bench and reveled in a long shower. While the hot needles prickled his skin, he resolved to rediscover the Golden Rule for himself.

Tony's transformation to grateful guest was completed by his enjoyment of country ham, scrambled eggs, and fresh homemade biscuits. Having eaten alone in the tidy kitchen, he washed his dishes and placed them carefully in the dish rack to dry.

The window above the sink overlooked the backyard at right angles to the pouting house, both structures overhung by the majestic maple that now dwarfed the property, dappling light in a canopy of palm-sized green leaves. But even this early, no breeze disturbed the window's cheerful yellow-and-white- checked curtains, and Tony could feel heat rising from the moist earth.

He looked around for something to do to make himself useful. *Everything's clean as a hospital, so I guess I won't be scrubbing anything. That's a mercy.* But surely a woman living alone had things in need of fixing here and there. With a handyman's trained eye, he scanned the kitchen. One lower cabinet door seemed to hang slightly crooked, a fact he quickly confirmed by rolling over to it.

Weren't there tools in the garage workshop? He thought he'd noticed some through the haze of his fatigue the night before. He rolled out of the kitchen, down the back ramp, then proceeded through his own guest quarters and entered the garage that housed his van and that ancient truck. There, along the back wall, was a workshop almost as well stocked as his own—if considerably more buried in dust.

Looks like I found my job for the day. Plucking a screwdriver from the array, he made a quick round trip to the kitchen to tighten the screws on all Mrs. O'Mally's cabinet doors. Then he returned to the garage, where he assembled cleaning supplies and committed himself to uncovering the workshop that lay hidden under years of settled dust.

Tony was shooed out of the kitchen the moment dinner was finished. "Land sakes," Sally's mother exclaimed. "You've done the work of four men today. You leave the cleanin' up to the womenfolk."

With a smile at Mrs. O'Mally's profuse and multiple expressions of thanks, Tony excused himself and retired to his quarters.

His own reunion with the dear woman had been tender in its own way. She apparently remembered everything she'd ever known about him in his high school days—including, he had to assume, some of the details of his intimate relationship with her daughter. Mrs. O had a way about her that made a person want to confess. She'd gone so far as to say, "We all get caught up in fool-ishness during our high school days. If we live a good life later, it makes no never-mind."

He responded with a "Thank you, M'am."

After that, they could look each other in the eye without flinching. She'd expressed her regrets upon learning about his own mother—who'd been confined to a home, no longer cognizant of friends or loved ones in the last years before she'd passed on. Then Mrs. O asked kindly about his time in the service, his injuries, and his recovery.

He'd asked about her visit to the doctor and received a dis-missive report, and later a detailed one from Sally. Though she'd gotten a severe bruise, there was no fracture. The fall itself was apparently nothing more than a random accident, and she was al-ready on the mend. Tony'd seen the relief on Sally's face and knew that tangible reassurance was worth the effort of the trip.

Now, half an hour later, the women were still finishing the dishes. The sound of sink water and clattering plates bounced through the kitchen window across the back lawn and into the pouting house.

Alone with his thoughts—and full of O'Mally cooking—Tony felt enveloped in a sense of new possibilities that lurked just over his heart's horizon.

Was it true? Did he deserve happiness? He'd shoved it away in despair for a time. But then he'd decided to look for it and had waited with dogged determination. It was time to reach for it. *Grab the woman and get while the gettin' is good.*

Now that he'd allowed Sally into his life—and she'd allowed him into hers—he *needed* her. That need had started with sentimental stirrings, then deepened, becoming a profound cellular yearning.

He thought of the child she carried. He exhaled. *That child should've been mine.* Once upon a time, when life seemed endless with youthful immortality, they'd had their chance at biological parenthood. Though it still caused him pain to think such an opportunity had been taken from him, he didn't blame Sally.

He breathed in, then out.

Now—when they'd found each other again after all these years—he probably couldn't give her a child, no matter how dear a wish it might be. *But, miraculously, someone else had.*

Tony wanted to hate the man, to vent an envious rage and thereby exorcize the demon of jealousy. But he couldn't. Jack had never truly *had*—or really touched—Sally in any way that mattered. One look in her eyes when she spoke about him told Tony that much. *If Jack ever tries to hurt her again, he'll have to deal with me.* Tony knew that—if given the chance—he himself would gratefully rear Jack's biological child as his own.

That brought Tony back to the matter at hand. During his long drive with Sally, neither his sour moods nor his vicious complaints had shut her down. *Have I revealed enough to her? Does she really know what she's gettin' into?*

What does she see when she looks at me? Some dream from the past? Or does she actually see me as I am?

Tony leaned aside to look up at the full moon, then followed where its silver beams passed through the old screen door and settled on furniture so long undisturbed. *Didn't me and Sal sit in this very room all those times back in the day? Mightn't we still someday sit here with a family of our own?*

Despite his limitations, he knew he could provide. His hands had been his salvation as a worker, his dexterity with wood and tools a sure means of survival. Though access to building sites was problematic, from his own workshop he'd learned to produce quality cabinetry, finding help with installations.

He'd finally gotten around to confronting most of his demons, doing the work of facing up to reality. He'd even developed a modicum of patience. His accounts settled with the universe, he felt ready for the next chapter.

Tony sat quietly, the big maple's trunk barely visible against the night. He'd pulled the wide screen sliders shut to keep out the insects, but he could hear clearly the women's laughter as it rolled from the kitchen window toward him across the back lawn. He could call to Sally, tell her of his impatience to see her, to touch her face, to tell her his secret. But because he loved lurking in the shadows of her heart, he waited for her to choose the time she'd come to him.

A few minutes later, he heard the gentle rasp of the kitchen's screen door. A crack of yellow light spilled across the yard to mingle with the moon's silver rays. Sally's footsteps approached the door of the pouting house.

"Hey," she said softly, the moonlight forming a halo through her gold hair. The sliding screen door whispered as she opened it and came in.

"Hey, your own self," he said in a low voice. He felt her quiver at his touch, the spark between them electric. He used his hand to explore hers, then moved it to palm her swollen belly, need swirling through him at the sound of her quiet moan. He cleared his throat, then asked, "Can you sit with me a moment?"

"Ye-yus." She turned one of the chairs to face his. "Been doin' some thinkin' out here?"

"Just thinkin' about the apology I owe you."

"What about?"

"My ugly manners on our trip."

"I know things is hard on you sometimes, Tony."

"That may be, but that's no excuse. I *am* sorry, Sal. Apology accepted?"

"Ye-yus." She smiled. "Accepted."

"After all your patience and grace, I'd say I love you more than ever." Taking her hand, he pulled her to him, then settled her across his lap.

With her legs trailing to one side, she turned her upper body to him as best she could, then pressed her lips to his.

With his teeth, he gently took hold of her lower lip. Feeling her yield, he pried her mouth open with his tongue, lapping at the nectar he found pooled just inside.

Sally lost track of time and place, aware only that the silk of Tony's beard was caressing her skin and that the satin vortex of his mouth was sucking her under. *His love's like a tidal wave*, she thought. He pulled at her, a powerful current rushing from the shore, then rising back up to shower her with tenderness. His hands were everywhere—cascading down her back, swirling over her belly, sliding up her thighs. Whatever barriers might have been in place between them even moments ago, melted in the surging tide, and she let her heart swamp, tip, overflow, then fill up again. She inhaled his scent, twined her arms around his neck, and held on. *Maybe love really is a day at the beach.*

When the petting reached its failsafe point, Tony pulled back, and his big eyes were watching hers when she opened them. "As you can tell," he said in that low, sultry voice, "I've been thinkin' how hungry I am."

"Hungry?" she gasped. "Land sakes! After all that dinner Mama made for us?!"

"Not that kind of hunger, Sal," he whispered into her ear. "The kind that makes a man weak in the knees."

"Oh," she said. "Oooh," she sang, feeling herself melt still further.

The sexual energy now hummed in the background like power-lines hung at a safe height. They sat in the amber glow of the porch light, listening as a slight breeze stirred the leaves in the tall maple.

Sally looked out the window. "Sometimes I worry I'm not big enough for you, Tony."

Looking down and touching her belly, he said, "You're gettin' there."

Lightly slapping away his hand, she laughed. "Tony Fiorentino, I don't mean that!"

He chuckled. "What *do* you mean, then?"

"Well, I mean, after all the things you've seen—travelin' over-seas, livin' in New York City and all—I'm afraid I won't give you a big enough life. I'm just a little gal from a little farm with a little restaurant in a little town."

Tony stroked her hair. "Power is usually delivered in small packages."

Sally shook her head. "Tony, you're doing riddle-speak again."

He thought for a moment as the breeze riffled the curtains. "Think of a mustard seed—that's better. Like that story in the Bible. It's one of the tiniest seeds of any plant, but it grew into a big tree. It just seems to work that way in the universe. Like . . . well, there are all kinds of stones. Think of one kind."

Sometimes he does this poetry-speak, way over my head "Oh, Tony," she said, leaning against his chest, "You and your riddles."

"Come on," he said in a singsong voice. "Play nice."

Sitting up, she said, "Okay, granite?"

He chuckled again. "Think of one that's more rare."

Sally considered. "Okay, how about opals?"

"All right. So if you have a slab of granite and a chunk of opal, which one do you think is more valuable?"

"Well . . . I expect the opal costs more money, if that's what you mean."

"Even if it's a smaller piece?"

"Ye-yus. It could be a real small piece, even somethin' small enough to fit into a ring, and it'd still be valuable if it was opal."

"Yup. And some stones don't have any color at all, but they're the ones that have the most value."

Sally felt something tickle her left hand. She looked down to see a slender gold band with a small, perfect diamond sliding onto her finger. She blinked, not trusting her eyes. She brought the hand to her face and blinked again, then touched it with her right index finger.

"Sally O," he rasped. "Will you marry me?"

I think he jest said the words. No . . . I must be dreamin'. She peered closely into his face.

"Sal, I'm waitin' here, balancin' on a wire. Will you, or what?"

"Yes!" she shouted, barely noticing Tony's wince at the unexpected volume. "Ooo-eee!"

"Thank God." Tony exhaled, resting his forehead against hers.

But she pulled back to let out a yell. "Wa-hoo!"

"Girl, you're gonna frighten those cows away and scare the daylights outta your mama." Sure enough, the kitchen door opened, pouring illumination through the screens of the pouting house. "Now you've done it," Tony kidded.

"Everything all right out there?" they heard Mama's voice calling.

"Mama!" Sally yelled back. "Wait'll you—"

But with Tony's mouth suddenly over hers, she couldn't finish her sentence.

Glenda O'Mally lay smiling under her light summer quilt in the still-quiet moments just before dawn.

She couldn't be absolutely *for sure* what had transpired in the pouting house the night before. But she had a mighty powerful suspicion. *Was it when that boy was lookin' up at me with doe eyes, talkin' about my Sally girl? Ye-yus. I 'spect that's when I knew the truth of why he came all the way to Arkansas just at this moment.*

Why Glenda knew things ahead of time, she couldn't say. Pictures, words, or feelings just came to her. All day yesterday she'd sensed Tony was ready to bust, trying so hard to keep his big secret to himself.

Glenda kept her eyes closed and drifted into a memory of her own courting days. Simple and honest, her George had been—but as thrilling to her as Prince Charming was to Cinderella at the ball. Glenda couldn't help but smile at their own trysting times in that same old pouting house. *Oooh, if my own Mama'd known about those fancy kisses, she'd ha' tanned my hide.* She chuckled to herself. *But it all worked out in the end. He was the right one for me. And Tony is the right one for Sally. Always was.* Of course, she'd let them tell her in their own time—which she imagined would be right soon.

Just then a yeasty aroma drifted into her room. *Sally bakin' somethin'?* She inhaled thoughtfully. One thing she knew about her daughter was that when she was happy, she cooked. Of course, being the owner of a restaurant, she cooked at other times too. Come hell or high water, she had to feed her customers. But getting up before the sun and baking—that was either to work out a problem or to celebrate. Given the hoopla she'd heard last night, Glenda knew which it was.

Forgetting about the sore hip, Glenda rolled to one side and nearly cried out in pain. *Lordy, I'll have t' remember t' favor that side for a while yet.* She managed to climb out of bed stiffly and do some quick ablutions. *Can't go greetin' the family in my gowntail.* Searching through the overburdened hooks on the back of her bedroom door, she found the good pink cotton robe and pulled it on, tied the fabric belt, then slid into her pink slippers.

Opening her door and looking down the hall, she saw the kitchen light was already on. And she was right—she *did* smell biscuits. Glenda scuffed to the open kitchen door and watched in silence for a moment as Sally and Tony hummed along in a harmony of domestic activity. Tony was slowly stirring eggs in the iron skillet with one hand and playing with Sally's apron string with the other.

Sally had bacon going and was keeping an eye on the biscuits in the oven.

"Mornin', you two," Glenda said.

They both turned their heads to face her.

"Mornin', Mama! How long you been standin' there?"

"Oh, jest a minute or two. I'd ask if you want help, but I think I'm too late!"

"Have a seat, Mrs. O," Tony invited, pulling out a chair for her at the kitchen table.

"Why, thank you, sir." *Surely is a treat to be served in my own home.* "Smells awful good."

"Least we could do, after that dinner last night. That was primo, Mrs. O." Tony smacked his lips on his fingers, then fanned his hand in Glenda's direction.

"Glad you enjoyed it," Glenda replied. In her effort to keep from reacting to their news until they actually *told* it to her, she felt a smirk play at the corners of her mouth. Doing her best to conceal it, she coughed. *I heard that goldfinch singin' his tee-yee song last night and this mornin'. Figured I knew what it meant.*

Pulling the golden biscuits from the oven, Sally placed them in a basket and served the bacon onto three plates, leaving them near the stove for Tony to add the eggs. When the plates were ready, she brought them to the table.

As Sally's hand passed the basket, Mama had her chance. "Somethin' mighty shiny on that finger."

"Eee!" Sally squealed, as though once again a seven-year-old showing her mother a prize she'd won at school.

Glenda looked at her daughter's beaming face, then at her bulging belly. *Not a moment too soon,* she thought. And then reminded herself that these things had their own right time. Tony loved her daughter heart-and-soul, and her daughter loved him back the same. *And that's as it should be.*

"That is *very* pretty," Glenda said, examining the ring closely. "Jest the thing." She beamed at Tony. "Done yourself proud." Then she told Sally, "You've got yourself a fine man there, girl. I'd say y'all should try to be happy." Her voice began to quaver. "But I can see you already are." Tears sprang into her eyes and spilled down her cheeks.

"Oh, Mama, don't you get me started!" Sally wailed, swiping at tears that now ran down her own face.

Glenda grabbed her paper napkin and wiped her cheeks. The next thing she knew, she was being hugged—daughter on one side, future son-in-law on the other. Patting their arms, Glenda rose and said, "Gotta get some hankies." After a quick trip to her bedroom, she returned and handed a plain handkerchief to Sally. But then she held out another delicately embroidered cloth to her. "It's gotten a little yellowed by now, but that's the one I carried when I walked down the aisle to marry your daddy."

"Oh, Mama!" Sally sobbed. "It'll be my 'somethin' old'!"

Tony sat quietly waiting till the crying subsided. Then he said, "Breakfast's gettin' cold. Anyone hungry?"

Both women nodded as they blew their noses, and he used his long arms to move the plates from the kitchen counter to the table. The three ate in companionable silence for a few moments. Then Tony said, "I have a question for you, Mrs. O."

Glenda had just covered half a biscuit with strawberry jam and was about to take a bite. Biscuit midair, she answered, "Ye-yes?"

"Any reason Sal and I shouldn't get married this week?"

Glenda put down the biscuit, then schooled herself *not* to glance at her daughter's swollen belly. Instead, her eyes locked on Tony's.

"First off, lemme say I think it's a *fine* idea." Glenda heard a sigh escape from each of her tablemates. "Now there *is* two parts to this, you know: the religious and the legal. Seems to me there's no waitin' period in Arkansas, but you'll have to check."

Tony set his coffee cup down. "I already tried callin' this morning, Too early. I'll call again here shortly. And as to the religious part, if you have a local minister—somebody who's a friend of the family—"

"And if there *is* a problem with the legal part," Sally chimed in, "We could have a small religious ceremony jest for us and Aunt Ida."

"Then we could drive through Nevada on the way home and make it legal." Tony's big, brown eyes bore into Sally's, and she grinned from ear to ear.

"Well, if that's the way you two would like to do it, no reason I can't do my part. You lemme know about your phone calls, Tony. Then I'll commence to make a couple o' my own."

For a long moment the only sound in the kitchen was birdsong from the yard. Then conversation erupted, everyone speaking at once.

"I've gotta get me a dress!"

"What in tarnation am I gonna tell Ida?"

"How far's the County Courthouse?"

Outside the kitchen window, the goldfinch perched on his branch listening to the babble of voices—one high, one higher, one deep—pouring through the open window into his yard. Fluttering his wings to let more air into his lungs, he opened wide his mouth and trilled his best courting song.

Chapter 23

Zack Calvin stood from his desk to stretch, hoping to relieve some of his growing tension.

He'd just gotten off the phone with Ron Godfrey, who'd reported from the Guerdon. Pressure in the line had fluctuated again. Though there was still "nothing to worry about," both Ron and Zack knew better. Something had Ron's antennae up, and in Zack's experience that never meant "nothing."

Zack grabbed a chilled bottle of water from the mini fridge and looked out the window at the spectacular view. Sumptuous estates punctuated the landscape on the mountainside to his right—his own among them. The curving coastline contained the proliferation of bungalows piled up the hillsides. Down below, the pier angled out into the sparkling Pacific. And in the distance, he could just make out the parade of offshore oil rigs, with Calvin Oil's Guerdon marching along obediently.

The appearance of perfection, he thought. *But how much of it is real?* He allowed himself to think about that for a moment. *The real. Is that what I've been looking for?* He wondered whether his angst could be traced to something so simple. He also wondered why he'd actually been feeling better recently. His only answer was Meredith, who seemed more "real" to him than any woman ever had.

From the first moment he'd clapped eyes on her, he'd been interested. *Nah, that's not the word. That's far too tame a word to use describing her. Ruthlessly beautiful, recklessly brave, brutally honest. Yes, those were the right words for her.*

He still found it hard to believe she'd grown up in the same household as Miranda, their personalities were so entirely different. He'd only believed it possible because of the physical resemblance. They did both have that fluidity of motion, the dark hair, the musical laugh. But that's where the similarities ended.

Meredith was a fox. *Oh, brother, is she!* Wily, furtive, clever, surreptitious, and highly effective: she knew exactly when to pounce, when to come in for the kill. Otherwise, she'd never have risen through the ranks of that huge financial advisory firm, then outgrown it all together to found and fund her own firm.

Could I do as much? Not even his MBA from Harvard could have provided the skill set she seemed to possess naturally. She gave credit to her dad—a man he definitely wanted to meet, when the time was right. And Meredith would decide when that was.

She'd already met *his* dad, though. They'd all met that same night, at Miranda's art show in Milford-Haven. He'd gone because he'd been looking for answers, and he'd found a lot more than he'd bargained for when Meredith had come bubbling into the gallery, proudly taking credit for the ruse she'd perpetrated on both him and her sister. *Yeah, recklessly brave. But you wouldn't want to be on her bad side.*

Zack glanced at his Rolex: 2:49 p.m. Ten minutes to go before he'd be hearing the voice of the very woman who occupied so many of his thoughts these days. They'd been discussing the geographical issue, and when she floated the idea of finding clients here, he'd offered to help. He'd found her a likely prospect. They'd also decided this would be a perfect opportunity to use the latest tech to demonstrate that physical distance need not create a business limitation.

Zack was in charge of a lot of things at the company, technology and communications among them. He'd hired a geek who loved tracking and figuring out the latest and greatest gadgets. It was Phil who'd located a phone that could be installed in his car, making Zack an early adopter of tech that he figured would quickly become *de rigueur* for anyone who planned to continue working at the speed of business.

When he'd asked Phil to investigate video conferencing, he'd been startled to find out some form of the technology had been around for decades. Phil-the-Geek had happily given him a history lesson. The most basic video communications, he explained, requires four interrelated components: audio transmission, wire or radio channels, image capture, and a display system. And all this has to exist on both ends of the communication.

At that point Zack, standing in the break room with Phil, decided he'd better sit down. So he'd grabbed two mugs of coffee and asked his employee to bring him up to speed.

AT&T Bell Telephone Labs, Phil explained, created the first working TV communication complex, called Two-Way TV, and Herbert Hoover's live moving image in Washington was transmitted via cable to New York in 1927. At the 1964 World's Fair, AT&T's Picturephone Mod I was displayed. In 1986 the Mitsubishi Luma

Two-way Picture Phone hit the market, but it cost $1,500. In 1991 IBM introduced its PictureTel, the first PC-based video conferencing, and it allowed sixteen users to run eight video conferences at the same time. In 1992, the system cost $20,000.

Zack whistled. "Wow. Not sure I can justify that kind of expense."

"Everyone else agreed with you," Phil confirmed. "About that time, a guy named Tim Dorsey at Cornell wrote a program called *CU-SeeMe* and it became the first desktop video conferencing platform."

When Phil first brought all this to Zack's attention in 1996, Calvin Oil still didn't have any such system. That was quickly remedied, and now they used Connectix QuickCam as their own version of ship-to-shore between the office and the Guerdon, but they also used it to communicate more effectively with partners and colleagues around the world. Somehow a face on a screen—even if it was tiny and in black and white—gave him and everyone else in the firm a more authentic sense of what was really happening at the other end.

Zack had subjected Meredith to a short version of this story. She, in turn, had successfully sold the idea to her mentor Ron Mansfield, who'd purchased a system he allowed her to use. Even though technically she was no longer his employee, her offices were on the same floor and there seemed to be a fair amount of cross traffic between her small firm and Ron's larger one.

Mary Meeks, the secretary who'd been with his dad for so long that she was Zack's "work-mother," beeped through on his intercom. "Your call with Ms. Meredith Jones is coming through, Mr. Zackery," she said in that elder voice of hers.

"Okay, thanks Mary," he said.

Switching on the video unit, he waited till the screen warmed enough to show an image. And what an image it was that pixilated itself into view. *The beautiful Meredith Jones in the flesh, I wish.*

"Hi, Zack," she said. "Okay, I think we're all set on this end. Audio and video seem to be working fine."

"Yes, here too. Our guest is waiting in the lobby. I'll have Mary bring him in."

"Okay. Here goes nothing," she said with a confident smile.

Meredith punched in Zack's car phone number four hours later, pleased when he picked up on the second ring. "That went well," she said.

Zack chortled into the phone. "It did," he agreed. "Josh was impressed with your presentation and wants to give your services a try."

"Great! And thank you."

"My pleasure."

Through her phone, Mer overheard the slight screech of Calma's iron gates opening.

"Just getting home?" she asked

"Yeah," he said, "after a trying day."

"And what were you trying?" she quipped

Zack laughed again. "Oh, I needed that."

"What, the laugh or the pun?"

"Neither. It's your voice I needed to hear."

Meredith smiled to herself. "Is that so? And how would you feel about hearing it up close and personal?"

"Oh, I can hardly wait for Saturday. I've got plans for you all weekend."

Meredith's heart thudded. "I'm counting on that. But, uh, what if I were to show up a bit early?"

"I should be so—"

"Lucky? You're right."

"Really?"

"Just getting off at the Patterson exit now."

"This really is my lucky day! So you're taking that earlier exit to avoid the traffic at Fairview. Okay, I'll fling things around in the cottage before you get here."

Then it was Meredith's turn to laugh.

She replaced her own car phone in its holder and enjoyed the frisson of anticipation she always felt before she and Zack Calvin got together. Their long-distance dating was both thrilling and maddening.

Is the frustration due only to the distance? She asked herself for the hundredth time. With her in San Francisco and him in Santa Barbara, it was scarcely possible to get together spontaneously, which is why tonight was so special. She didn't really want it to be special, she wanted it to be casual, so they could spend relaxed time together and not be on their best behavior.

She drove along Cathedral Oaks Road, then took San Marcos toward Calma, the Calvin family estate. But there was some other element of the frustration as well, some sense that she still lacked access to a part of him. *Does he have access to it himself?* That was the real question.

She pulled to a stop at Calma's iron gates, rolled down her window, and announced herself over the intercom. "Meredith Jones to see Zackery," she said.

"Very good," she heard James their butler pronounce, no more warmly than he had last time.

She'd have to work on James. But she didn't look forward to that nearly as much as she looked forward to working on Zack.

Zack did indeed have plans for Meredith. Memorial weekend was starting. His dad had made arrangements to spend it on Catalina Island, staying in the family bungalow and playing golf at his club there. His cronies were looking forward to gathering, and Joseph could hardly wait for the respite from work. Along with golfing, he'd likely take his boat out on the water and hunker down at home to catch up on his reading.

After reassuring his father that he wouldn't feel deserted, he'd invited Meredith to join him at the estate, which they'd have to themselves, except for James, who'd prepare a couple of meals for them, but then take some time off himself.

This would be Mer's initiation into the property. He looked forward to showing her the main house, the grounds, and the neighborhood, that is, if they could stay out of his bedroom long enough. *Hold on. Get to that later,* he admonished himself. *There's more to this woman than sex.*

Meredith was delighted that Zack's impromptu plan for Friday night was to stay at home, eat in the kitchen, and watch a movie in the den. It was no surprise that the Calvins already had one of the newly created DVD players for home use. Mer and her family were still watching VHS tapes.

Zack requested that James, the utterly charming house master, make pizza for them. After offering Zackery—as he called him—and his guest an array of possible ingredients, they'd opted for one heaped with vegetables, the other sinful with pepperoni. They'd washed it all down with sodas, and Zack had reached over with a paper napkin to wipe an oily drip from Meredith's chin.

"Wish *Air Force One* were already out," Mer complained.

"Not till July," Zack confirmed, "and only in theaters. We have a decent one, though, if you like thrillers."

"What is it?"

"*Basic Instinct* with Sharon Stone and Michael Douglas. It came out in '92, but just made it to DVD."

"I'd missed it. Sounds great," she enthused.

But though the film had its compelling moments, the best part of watching it in the masculinely attractive den was that she discovered Zack gave excellent foot rubs—even though they tended to overshadow whatever was happening on screen.

What also surprised her was that when they repaired to his cozy cottage and hit the bed, she fell into an exhausted sleep before their usual intimacies took hold. She'd never felt more at home.

Zack took Mer to the yacht club, and they were soon out on the water in the Kipling III, the family sailboat.

It'd turned into a beautiful sunny day, with just the right amount of bluster coming off the water. She seemed perfectly at home aboard, and after they'd cleared the harbor and were comfortably sailing, Zack popped open a couple of sodas for them.

"Not your first regatta, eh?" he asked, speaking loudly enough to be heard over the wind.

"Nope, not my first. I was part of the Optimist Fleet at the Belvedere Sailing Club, I'll have you know."

Zack laughed. "Me too! Well, I was in the Optimist program at Santa Barbara Youth Sailing Foundation. They started us young with those cute little boats."

Meredith nodded. "So smart."

"Yeah, then we graduated to FJs—Flying Juniors—then I had a Sunfish. They were teaching sportsmanship, teamwork, safety, a lot of good skills whether kids ended up loving the sport or not."

"Was your mom still with you then?" she asked. "Was she the sailor?"

"No. She was gone by then. I figure Dad signed me up as a distraction, mostly. But he loved the sport and still does, and I do too. We've always had a boat," he explained.

"You've certainly graduated since then. This vessel . . . thirty-five, forty feet?" she asked.

"Forty-five, with a draft of about eight feet. She can sail in most weather conditions, with plenty of sail area for light winds, and easy reefing for when it pipes up. Very comfortable for two. We could head out to the Channel Islands sometime and stay the night."

"Kipling I and Kipling II?"

"Yup. We still have Kipling II. She's a little smaller, but she's moored at Catalina."

"So your dad might be aboard right now," Mer suggested.

"He might at that, unless he's on the links. So, what about you? Your whole family sailors? Mom? Sis?"

"Mother enjoys being aboard a yacht or a cruise ship just fine, but nothing shorter than fifty feet. Mandy always preferred kayaking. Too much work, if you ask me."

"And too slow. I prefer getting there."

"Yes, I know," Mer offered suggestively.

"Oh, do you now," Zack said, putting an arm around her and pulling her closer.

They sailed on, enjoying the view of the escarpment with its UCSB building marching along top. He didn't plan to go too far, however, since this was a leisure excursion without a specific destination.

"I haven't thought of those days in forever. There was one of those races where I remember one of the guys in our fleet got dumped overboard. Rumor had it a girl from Belvedere took him out. I was too far away to see it happen but always wish I had."

He looked over at Meredith, noticing what he thought might be a blush, though in the wind and sun, it was hard to tell. "What?" he asked. "You remember that too?"

"Uh, well, was the guy named Beaseley?"

"Beeze! Right! Don't tell me . . ."

"Ya, it was me."

Zack laughed. "You gotta tell me what happened."

"Well, there we were, partnered randomly by the committee, doing our best to get along as unfamiliar partners."

"You didn't get along?"

"I mean . . . he was kinda cute, and I may have been a little bit . . . flirty."

"Just a little bit?"

"Everything was fine until—"

"—the wind died down," Zack continued. "We were all becalmed for a while."

"Right, and there was nothing we could do. We chitchatted about some inane stuff. I mean, we were kids, feeling awkward. I was trying to be nice. Really!"

"And . . ."

"All of a sudden this dork says, 'You know, you like me too much.' What the hell! All I wanted to do was get out of there, but with no wind, we were stuck. So I asked him, 'What does *that* mean?'"

Zack didn't miss the irony laced through her tone, which he imagined had been equally potent when Mer was just a teen.

"Idiot-boy tries to explain. He can *tell* because I keep looking at him longingly, I bat my eyelashes, I wiggle my butt. On and on he goes. After about five minutes of this, I've had enough. I shove him overboard, figuring he can climb back aboard. But just then the wind picks up. Ooops! Too bad he has to swim for the life saver I threw after him."

Zack, managing not to laugh out loud again, simply said, "Well, I'm glad it wasn't me. Remind me not to get on your bad side."

Chapter 24

Meredith slept in Saturday morning, then rolled over to discover Zack was already up and had gone somewhere. She plumped her pillows to consider for a moment. *Our paths crossed when we were teenagers! Just as well we didn't meet back then. We weren't ready for each other. Still . . . it's pretty amazing.*

She found a note inviting her to join Zack in the main house. After a quick shower, she pulled on a comfy long-sleeved velour house dress and hugged herself against the morning chill as she followed the path from his cottage.

In the kitchen, she was greeted by James. "Breakfast is on the patio, Ms. Jones."

"Please call me Meredith," she corrected. "Something I can carry out?"

"Uh . . . yes, do take this tray with the croissants, butter, and jam."

"Mmm, my favorites!"

She arrived outside to find Zack reading his paper, sipping his coffee. He stood when she arrived to set the tray on their table. *So much to be said for being with an actual gentleman,* she thought. *And it's not just the manners.* Despite her disheveled appearance, he gave her an appreciative gaze.

She dug into the sinful treat, sipped at the freshly-squeezed orange juice, then poured herself a cup of coffee.

Zack pushed the *Santa Barbara News Press* in her direction, muttering "There's no *Wall Street—*"

"*Journal?*"

"We take it at the office, so it's not here."

"And you'll have less catching up to do since it doesn't publish on Sunday or Memorial Day."

"Of course, you know that," he said, still hidden behind his *L.A. Times.*

Accustomed as she was to reading the *Journal* and the *Chronicle,* she looked curiously through the unfamiliar paper, which landed somewhere between a major and a minor but all in all seemed to offer excellent coverage of national and local items. After a while, she put down the paper and looked around to enjoy the surroundings. "You've got a Belvedere," she said.

"What?"

"A belvedere. It means 'beautiful view' in Italian, and you certainly have that."

"Bel ve-de-re," Zack pronounced. "I never knew that."

"And it's also an architectural feature. You have that too: a roof but open on at least one side. This part of your patio qualifies."

Zack glanced upward. "Learn something every day, oh wise one. We have a cupola, too, but it's not visible from this vantage point."

"I saw it as I drove in. They're roof lanterns, bringing in light but not weather. Sort of a skylight with a cup-shaped roof."

"Architecture was your minor?"

"Just a hobby picked up traveling. I love the fancy buildings in Europe."

"Italy?" he asked.

"For sure. But London too. So much variety, you can read every historical period in the bones of the buildings."

"And you can read them in English," he pointed out.

She giggled. "Exactly!"

"We should go sometime," he suggested.

"Tell me when to pack a bag," she offered.

He held her gaze for a lovely moment, but she sensed some distraction.

"Hey, do you want to get a little work done?"

"Thanks. I do have to make one call, out to the Guerdon. But then I'm all yours, ready or not."

"Ready when you are," she said.

Zack did a little more work than he'd expected to, then went looking for her when James offered soup and salad for lunch. He and James each carried a tray into the den, where she'd been reading through a stack of papers she'd evidently brought along.

Relieved and comforted that she'd been working too, he watched as she brightened, and they enjoyed their meal. After lunch, he led her back to the cottage.

They were at ease, he was discovering, whether recreating or working, serious or light-hearted, clothed or naked. If he were honest with himself, and God, he was working on that, this was all a revelation—that he could be this comfortable with someone, not need to edge away, declare a moratorium, reclaim his space.

So now, while they were casual and at home, while they had daylight, and while he still had the courage, he invited her to sit in one of the two comfortable chairs facing his small fireplace.

"Something on your mind?" she asked, almost too perceptively.

He took a breath. "Yeah. I had this . . . thing with a woman named Cynthia."

"The gorgeous blonde in the newspapers," she stated, rather than asked.

"That's her," he said tersely.

"Serious?" Mer asked.

"As a heart attack—in bed, anyway."

"I'm so jealous I could scream," Mer complained.

"No. That's not why I'm telling you. It's because my behavior was bad. I went along for the ride, pretended that's all she wanted too."

"So you can be a heartless bastard. Okay. What else?"

Zack felt himself shrink as though his skin were receding. "I was still seeing Cyn on and off when I met Miranda."

"Oh! So you not only dated my sister, you also cheated on her."

Zack sighed. "I would have been, had I actually been dating your sister. Still, it wasn't honest. And I'm done with that."

Meredith sat silently for so long that he began to fear she was rethinking their relationship. He realized he was holding his breath.

"Thank you," she said quietly. "That must've been hard. I appreciate your telling me. I'm sorry, if there was pain involved. I mean, there always is, when something ends. But I'm glad, too."

Zack exhaled. "Thank God."

They looked into one another allowing their silence to communicate trust, letting the comfort return.

Mer looked away, then said, "Since we're doing true confessions, you're not the only one whose made mistakes."

"You don't have to—"

But she put up a hand, then continued. "There was a guy I met at a conference. We were going to connect, then we didn't, then some time passed as we ran into each other again. When he finally got around to asking me out, it was a spectacular date."

Zack huffed out a breath.

"I didn't hear from him right away afterwards and figured he was traveling again. But I got a surprise visit one day at work."

"He just, what, arrived at your office?"

"No. His wife did."

"Oh. Oh, God."

"I hadn't known. I'd had absolutely no clue. Talk about feeling stupid."

"Talk about being sideswiped and double-crossed."

"After she left, I immediately took this to my boss, and he put legal on it. He pointed out that the whole thing could have been a setup, something else that hadn't occurred to me."

"Jesus. Anything further?"

"Absolutely nothing. If either of them try to get in touch, there'll be an immediate restraining order."

"So sorry that happened."

She nodded. "The thing is . . . it's made it hard to trust again. So the one thing I need above all else is no secrets."

"Got it," he said. "I can promise that, with one exception."

"Like what?"

"Can I surprise you with something nice sometimes?"

"For that, you have my permission," she said. Then she climbed into his lap and kissed him.

Zack took her out for a nice dinner at Citronelle at the Santa Barbara Inn. He'd booked a table days earlier, requesting the upstairs dining room. Windows lined the wall facing the ocean, and the view seemed to be decorated with palm trees that began to silhouette against a sky painted orange by the early evening sun.

Meredith seemed charmed as they were seated. "This is almost Caribbean," she said, stroking her cane back chair. "Look at that waiter's tie, every color of the rainbow. I almost feel like we're on a cruise."

We're on a voyage all right, he thought. *Going places I never thought I could go.* She wore an aqua silk dress that set off her eyes and was somehow both demure and sexy. Earrings sparkled that were probably aquamarines, but might've been tourmalines or even zircons, according to his recent research. He cleared his throat. "You look beautiful, Mer."

"And you look so handsome," she said, both accepting and deflecting the compliment.

"The chef here is excellent," he offered.

"Would you order for us?"

He chose the Norwegian salmon dish, baked with a leek crust and topped with a light chive sauce, so delicious they savored every bite.

The waiter with his brightly colored tie headed in their direction with another menu, but she leaned in for a quiet comment.

"What?" Zack asked.

She whispered, "The only dessert I want is you."

Meredith luxuriated in the sensations Zack had offered her, waking her a second time with amorous arousal. After a while, sated and dreamy, she said, "You know what they say about blue-eyed people."

"Hmm, not really."

"That they have a deficiency."

Zack huffed out a laugh. "Not so's you'd notice."

She slapped at him playfully.

"Ow! No, seriously, I've never heard of that."

"That's because you didn't live in Japan two generations ago."

"No, I sure didn't." He adjusted their pillows so they could lean and talk more comfortably. "I did overhear once in a while that I was a blue-eyed boy."

"The favored son. Of course, you are." She poked at him.

"Hey, watch it."

"Oddly, although the deficiency thing was purely a racist attitude, there actually is a scientific basis, which they probably didn't realize."

"Sounds like you've made a study."

"Of course. Okay, so it has to do with the amount of melanin stored in the front layers of the iris. People with brown eyes have a high amount of melanin; green eyes have a moderate amount; and blue eyes a minimal amount."

"Kind of a stretch to say that's a 'deficiency.'"

"Unless people latch onto it to confirm racist theories."

"Absurd. Of more interest is how blue eyes are passed along. I remember reading once that it's complicated."

"Yeah, it is. Here goes. It all depends on the pairing of genes passed on from each parent, and the different variants are known as alleles. The one for brown eyes is the most dominant, always superseding others; the green eye allele is always dominant over blue, which is always recessive."

"Does that mean parents who have the same eye color, say they're both blue-eyed, could actually produce a different eye color in their child?"

"It does. So Miranda must've gotten a blue allele from either Mom or Dad, but she also got a green one, which dominated, giving her the green eyes," Mer theorized.

"Well, that explains her eye color, but not yours. I mean, your dad has blue eyes, but your original mother in Japan didn't. So how did—" Zack mused.

"How did I get the dreaded blue eyes?" Mer broke in.

"The gorgeous, compelling, sparkling, haunting, exotic, enticing—"

She put a hand softly across his mouth. "Okay, okay, if I'm honest, I like the blue eyes. They make me the rebel I was born to be."

Zack laughed, then kissed her, then said, "You were about the answer a fascinating question. I really do want to know."

"You and generations of scientists who study genetics." She took a breath. "I read that some scientists think the blue-eyed allele OCA2 had a single origin in Europe as long as 10,000 years ago. But my ancestor could be a lot more recent, given the contact between Asians and Europeans through trade, wars, you name it. I overheard Dad on the phone one time, years ago. Evidently, the person he was talking to said something about a grandfather with mixed south Asian heritage. So if that grandfather, whoever he was, gave me one allele and Dad gave me the other, boom, the blue-eyed baby."

"The genetic stars were aligned," he observed. "And the legacy could continue. If we have a kid he'd have blue eyes."

Meredith's breath caught. *Did he really just say that?* To keep the moment light, she said, "They say *all* blue-eyed people may have a common ancestor."

"So . . . you and I are related?"

Mer giggled. "Well, we might be some day."

"We might," he confirmed. "Which is why I got you this." He produced a small box.

"What the—" she whispered. When he nodded, she opened it to find a sparkling blue-green pendant. Its gold chain was delicate, but the stone was large.

Her heart beating fast, she gazed at the gorgeous gem. "This matches . . ."

". . . your eyes."

She brought her lips to his and melted when he kissed away her tears.

Meredith tiptoed away from his bed Sunday morning, dressed casually, and slipped out to head for the main house.

Greeted by two trays with fresh fruit and cold cereal James must have left for them, she poured bran flakes into one of the bowls and pressed the Brew button on the coffee maker, already set up.

While she munched cereal on the patio, she began to plan a partial day on her own. *All this togetherness is amazing, but I don't want to overstay my welcome. Besides, I should get to know this town a bit more. State Street has some nice clothing shops, a couple of bookstores and cafés. Maybe I'll have lunch some place.*

When she got back to the cottage, Zack had showered and dressed. "Hey, mind if I do some errands downtown?" she asked.

"Anything you like," he offered. "Want to meet for lunch?"

"I'll be back in time for dinner," she countered. "Would you mind?"

"God, it's so easy to be with you," he said. "I could stand to do a little work, maybe catch a ball game on TV. Dinner here?"

"Perfect," she said, thinking, *I was right, he needs some alone time too.*

Meredith wandered down El Paseo, with its charming stores. She bought a beautiful blouse at Nordstrom, then popped it back into her car before browsing through Barnes & Noble. She bought a copy of the new bestseller *Memoirs of a Geisha*, which she could hardly wait to read. She also picked up *The Four Agreements* by Miguel Ruiz, which promised it was all about "self-limiting beliefs," thinking that might lead to some interesting discussions with Zack. *Love that I can talk with him about anything and everything.*

She made her way kitty-corner across the street to Borders, with its two-story-high front windows, and perused the front tables. *Into Thin Air* looked like a harrowing tale by Jon Krakauer and *Killing Floor* by Lee Child would apparently launch a new series about a character named Jack Reacher. *Maybe Zack would like one of those for Christmas.*

For now, she picked up a copy of the *Santa Barbara Independent*, ordered a latte, and found a comfy place to sit. She was just reading the front page when she saw a blonde step up to the café counter, then turn back to speak to a man behind her. *Something about her looks familiar. Oh my God! I think that's Cynthia!* Mer had seen her in a couple of photos when she'd looked up old issues of the society pages. *She is gorgeous, dammit.*

Meredith quickly raised the newspaper to hide herself but then realized the other woman would have no reason to recognize her. She lowered the paper and watched as a handsome Hispanic man joined her, his black hair gleaming, his hand placed at the small of Cynthia's back. *They seem to be together . . . and happy.* The couple left, carrying their drinks and holding hands.

Mer let her pulse settle and smiled as relief washed over her. *Does Zack know she's seeing someone else? Should I ask him? Why not? It might be a good test to see how he reacts.*

Maybe making a list would help me get a grip on this. All the synchronicities were getting too woo-woo, like something that would happen to Miranda but not to her. She was the elder, the logical, the solid sister.

She began turning pages, but her thoughts stayed on Zack, and she began to enumerate the parallels.

Item number one: they were both adopted. *Well, sort of.* She had grown up with her real father. But Mother was actually her step-mother, not that she'd ever be able to think of her that way. She was the only mother she'd ever known. Her birth mother was a shadowy figure who'd put herself in harm's way, rather than prioritize her family. Zack, who'd been adopted by Joseph and his late wife, had no idea who his birth parents were. Still, she and Zack both had this twist in their birth stories.

Item number two: he had sent lilies, she now remembered. He'd sent them when he'd been trying to date Miranda, and they'd arrived at Miranda's when Mer was visiting. *But those are my favorite flowers, not hers.* Miranda had even given them to her sister.

Item number three: they had recognized each other before they met. That accidental phone conversation . . . they both had known it then. But (a) since that had made no sense and (b) other people's feelings had been involved, they'd ignore it. *Well, not really.*

For her, the pull had been consistent and insistent. Evidently, it'd been the same for him. That was actually why he'd driven all the way to Milford-Haven for Miranda's art show: to find out why she had flirted with him revealing a side he didn't know she had. Of course, it'd been Meredith's own wild side that'd drawn him. She'd seen it in his eyes at the gallery that night, seen the puzzle piece drop into place.

Item number four: each of them had a somewhat messy situation with an ex. If she spent more time in Santa Barbara, she'd likely run into Cynthia again. And what about Peter in San Francisco? Though she hoped *never* to see that man again, was it possible Zack and he would come across each other? They were both in upper levels of business in California. That made it almost inevitable. *Does it actually matter? No.*

Item number five was what *did* matter: he'd invited her to spend the long weekend exactly when she herself had felt the need to spend time with him, more than a night or two between work weeks.

Item number six: he'd given her the spectacular pendant that matched not only her eyes but those favorite earrings she'd worn to their dinner. *He had to have bought it before he saw the jewelry I already have. Is he that tuned in?*

She was beginning to think he was.

Part III

Have & Hold

"To have and to hold from this day forward. . ."
– Traditional wedding vows

"It is not in the stars to hold our destiny
but in ourselves."
– William Shakespeare

Chapter 25

Glenda woke up on her daughter's wedding day, excited and frantic.

She'd risen before dawn to shampoo her hair and set it in rollers. Now her rose-colored silk dress needed attention. *Well, it's not real silk. Jest rayon made to look like silk. A good thing too, lest I perspire and ruin it in the heat.*

She opened the front door quietly, sniffing at the air. *Oh, my Lordy, it* will *be a hot one,* she concluded. *But it'll be bright and pretty too.* Closing the door again, she walked into her cramped laundry room, took the ironing board from its rack and winced as its edge touched her sore hip.

"Okay, Lord," she said quietly. "You're gonna have to help me with the pain today. I don't want nothin' to interfere with my hearin' their weddin' vows." She paused a moment, poured distilled water from its jug into the iron, then plugged it in.

It had not escaped her notice that this was Memorial Day weekend and that her daughter was marrying a brave, decorated veteran. She couldn't doubt his courage, but they might have some tough times ahead.

"Lord," she resumed. "While we're havin' this little conversation, I need some help with somethin' else too. Not to say he isn't capable as all get-out, strong, independent as he can be. But I worry about him handling all he has to do and then carin' for Sally and the baby. Jest help me let go of these fears. Let me be in your church today with a whole heart, trusting your Providence and guidance. For sure as I stand here, I do see your hand in all this, and I thank you, Lord, for answering the prayers of my young 'uns."

She exhaled and let the peace that always came with praying settle over her. Spreading out the dress, she smoothed the front of the skirt over the board's cotton padding. When she grasped the handle of the iron, it hissed as she drew it carefully over the creases of the dress that'd hung so long unused, waiting for a special day.

Her task complete, she carried the dress to her bedroom and laid it carefully across the already-made bed. Glancing in the carved mirror attached to her tall oak dresser, she was startled to see a bespectacled apparition whose head sprouted pink plastic rows. *Don't I jest look a sight!* She decided a little powder and rouge were in order for the occasion. While she rubbed and patted at her face, the to-do list played through her mind.

Got us some nice flowers—even if that Wilbur did try over-chargin' at first. But it was right nice, what he did in the end, giftin' us the altar arrangement. Daisies woulda been nice, but those fancy calla lilies is right elegant. Weddin' cake is settin' in the icebox at Ida's. Outdid myself this time, if I do say so. She sighed at the thought of her sister-in-law. *A good woman but the nosiest body I've ever like to know'd.*

The only way she'd managed to settle Ida down was by making her a coconspirator. The fact was Sally was pregnant before being married. Now that Ida'd been let in on the secret wedding, she'd dropped some of her judgmental commentary. *'Course lettin' Ida know a secret only meant word would spread double-fast. But now it'll be the news they wanted spread abroad that everyone would hear.*

Ida Sue was playing a vital role in these nuptials: she was the one who found Sally's dress. *And it's the perfect weddin' dress. Not only that, she lent Sally the blue garter from her own weddin', so now my girl has her somethin' that's both borrowed and blue. The hankie's old and, o' course, her dress is new. So my girl's all set.*

Glenda carefully pulled the rollers from her hair and combed through the tight curls until they relaxed into a silver halo. She struggled to yank on her support hose—ignoring the pain in her hip—wriggled into her slip, then slid into her dress, grateful she was still able to do her own zipper.

She opened the worn leather jewelry box. *There they are—my pearls with their matchin' earrings.* After fastening the necklace by feel, she peered into the mirror closely to adjust the pearl studs. Then she looked at her hand with its thin gold band, knowing she wouldn't be the only one in the family wearing one before the day was over. She slid on her own engagement ring. *Glad I cleaned it yesterday. Now it sparkles jest like it did the first day you gave it to me, George. You stick by me today, y'hear? I'm gonna need you, and so's our girl.*

Tony Fiorentino faced the mirror and fussed with his blue and brown tie. It'd been so long since he'd worn one, he couldn't seem to master tying the knot. "Har har," he said to his reflection. "That's one thing you are gonna master, chump, and you're gonna to it now!"

He gave himself a foolish grin. *I don't feel like a chump today. I feel good. Real good. The only thing that would make it better is if my buddy Mac could be here as my best man.*

There was still the matter of the tie. Nothing would dissuade him from wearing it, since Sally'd given him a special gift last night. Opening a small, faded brown box, she'd handed him a gold tie clasp. It had been Mr. George O'Mally's, and now it was *his.*

Though Sally didn't know it yet, he'd brought her a gift too. Years ago his own mother had given him a pair of small, gold earrings that dangled pearls. "I want you to have them while I still remember," she'd said, "I hope one day you'll have a wife to enjoy them." Tony inhaled and, rummaging through his shaving kit, he withdrew the small, velvet earring pouch.

With another yank or two, Tony decided the tie looked accept-able. He glanced around the pouting house. *Bed's made, bathroom's cleaned up, didn't use the kitchenette.* He patted his suit jacket to make sure the words he'd written down were in his pocket. Then he wheeled out the sliding door, closed it behind him, and made his way down the path and up the ramp to the main house.

Everything seemed quiet. He wheeled down the hall to Sally's room and knocked on the door. "Almost ready?"

"Don't come in!" Sally called. "Not supposed to see the bride!"

Chuckling, Tony said through the door, "Okay, then." He turned and knocked on the facing door. "Mrs. O?"

Glenda opened her bedroom door. "Ye-yus? Oh, my! Don't you look handsome in your navy suit!"

Tony felt himself blush. He watched as she reached out to touch her late husband's gleaming tie clasp, saw her eyes go misty. "Uh, Mrs. O, I—"

"Need the tie straightened?"

At his nod, she pulled the tie slightly to one side, adjusted the knot, then smoothed his collar. "All set," she said.

"Great. Thanks." He took a breath. "Give these to Sally for me, will you? I'm gonna go ahead to the preacher's, get all set up."

"That's good, Tony. I'll bring Sally right along. Ida Sue will meet us there."

Leaving the women to their preparations, Tony touched his tie one final time and headed to his van. He found his way easily to the Faith Community Church. Perched on a grassy green knoll, its red brick walls and white-trimmed windows seemed picture perfect. At street level, a sign was fashioned as a changeable billboard. Today it said: "Our king is not Elvis, and he hasn't left the building."

Chuckling to himself, Tony parked the van in one of the three handicap spots and, as quickly as he could, made his way to the preacher's office. An hour later, he and the Reverend Tobias had become allies. Retired several years earlier, this preacher—it'd been determined by Glenda—was the one who deserved to marry off her girl. Not only was he a long-time family friend, he could also be counted on for discretion and, for now, would keep his mouth shut about the nuptials. Glenda would print a notice in the paper soon enough. News traveled like heat lightning in the little town of Sweetwater. Glenda had told the preacher, "I don't want to be hearin' about my own daughter's weddin' while I'm on my way to the church!"

Tony waited for the rest of the celebrants in a private anteroom. *The wedding sure will be small. But these women have their reasons.*

He thought back to the family "scheme." The plan was to say he and Sal had been married some months ago in a California civil ceremony, but that Sally had wanted the wedding "blessed" in her own home town, in her own family church. Neither Glenda nor the formidable Aunt Ida Sue was comfortable with a pregnant Sally getting married at the last minute. As to actually celebrating with local family and friends, they'd plan that for some future visit, at which time folks could meet both the groom and the new baby. It all seemed a bit complex to him. *But whatever makes my new family happy is all good.*

Tony glanced at his watch. *It's time.* Sure enough, he heard a car pull up outside, heard the motor stop, the doors slam. *Wish I could get my heart to stop racing.*

Reverend Tobias poked his head around the door. "Ready, son?"

"Yes, sir." Following the preacher, he wheeled himself down a long corridor and into the sanctuary. *This is where I'll be takin' my vows.* Nervously, he fingered the wedding ring in his pocket. He glanced off to the right and was surprised to see a white-haired lady in a flower-printed dress sit down at a small electric organ. *What do you know! I guess we're gonna have music.* He glanced over at the preacher—who stood in perfect serenity, reading his Bible—and then at Sally's aunt, who already was dabbing at tears with an oversized tissue.

The music began. At the far end of the small church a head appeared in the doorway. Glenda said, "Mornin', Reverend. May we enter?"

"Come on down," the Preacher called.

Glenda's head disappeared, then the whole person came through the door, walking in stately fashion to the front of the church and taking her place in the pew next to Ida. Tony gave each of the women a smile.

At the sound of the door opening again, Tony looked up to see a silhouette haloed in sunshine. Then the church door closed, and he saw that Sally herself seemed to radiate light. He swallowed the lump that'd formed in his throat.

Now Tony could see Wilbur Thompson, who'd waited just inside to walk her up the aisle. The suit appeared to be left over from the man's high school days, but—despite bulging buttons on his jacket—he beamed a wide smile and walked with a steady gait. *He seemed mighty eager to help with the wedding. I bet Wilbur has a thing for Mrs. O.* The thought flashed through Tony's mind, then disappeared as he caught the full view of his bride.

Her blond curls were pulled up, away from her face, fastened with beautiful white flowers that matched those she carried. Her shoulders were bare, and the dress seemed to frame her in ivory satin.

She was everything he'd ever wanted. *Pretty as when she was my prom queen.* He remembered being the gangly senior picking up the shy sophomore—easily the best looking girl there, yet the most unassuming. She was all potential, then. *Now look at her. She's in full bloom.*

She'd traveled half the distance down the aisle by now, and his gaze scanned her finery. *Would you call those pleats?* It looked as though two fans were opened, then fastened between her breasts. From there, two creased panels of shimmering fabric fell to the floor, leaving a gap inside of which the round belly could hide. *Somethin' sweet about the baby bein' here for this. But to see Sal in that dress, you'd never know.*

She looked him in the eyes now and used her free hand to touch one of the dangling pearl earrings. *She wore them, so my mom is here too.* He could feel tears welling. *Not now! Keep it together, man!*

He appreciated having a moment to collect himself as he watched a side drama in the front row. Sally handed the flowers to her mother. Then Glenda, focusing on her daughter, was flustered when Wilbur Thompson squeezed himself into the pew next to her. Glenda, an appalled expression on her face, made a show of resettling herself and pushing against Ida Sue, whose pinched face showed a similar disapproval of Mr. Thompson.

Tony suppressed a laugh, then felt all the air go out of his lungs when Sally stepped up. Tony rotated his chair and now they both faced Reverend Tobias. *With my tall torso and her short stature, we're almost shoulder to shoulder.*

He tried to listen intently to the preacher's words. He got as far as "Dearly Beloved" when a movie of his entire life began to play through his head. And then the moment for the rings arrived. Tony slid a wide, gold band onto Sally's quivering finger. Then, to his surprise, Sally had one for him too. *When did she have time to get me a ring?* Watching her slide it onto his finger, he smiled when it fit him perfectly.

The next thing he knew, the preacher was pronouncing them husband and wife in God's eyes, and saying, "You may kiss the bride." Tony reached his long arms to Sally's face and tasted the sweetness of his wife's lips.

Chapter 26

Glenda was grateful Mrs. Ballard struck up a chord on the electric organ just at that moment, for it masked the sob she was unable to suppress. Dabbing at her face with her hankie, she looked up just in time to catch Sally's eyes on hers.

She stood—ignoring Wilbur as he leapt up beside her—and watched as her radiant daughter closed the distance between them to give her a fierce hug. As their embrace ended, Glenda inspected Sally's face. Then, finding a dry spot on the hankie, used it to repair the fresh streaks in her daughter's makeup.

"Now, Sally-girl, you want to look pretty for your photos, don't you?"

Sally could only nod, happy tears still glistening in her eyes.

"Ahem." Wilbur cleared his throat as though to make an announcement. "Let's have the bride and groom front and center."

Glenda's eyebrows shot up. "Wilbur?"

"You *did* say you wanted photos, didn't you?"

"Well, I did, but I—"

"I've got my finger on the trigger, ready to shoot."

Tony's head whipped around, and he dropped Preacher Tobias's hand that he'd been shaking.

For just a moment, Glenda caught the wild flash in his eyes as he moved instinctively toward Sally. *His first thought is to protect her.* As Tony reached them, Glenda touched his shoulder and said, "He means he's ready for photos, honey."

She watched as Tony's large brown eyes lifted to hers and softened. The endearment had slipped out before she could even think. But now she could see it'd settled and reassured him. "Yes, M'am," he said, reaching for the hand of his bride.

Glenda noticed Wilbur fussing with his camera. *If he's gonna use that thing, a body would think he already knew how!*

She glanced at Ida, who stood up and walked over to join the rest of the party. "Nothin' like a weddin'," Ida sniffled, choking back sudden tears.

Glenda hugged her briefly. "Oh, Ida, we surely couldn'ta had our bride lookin' so beautiful without all your help!"

A look of such surprise lit Ida's face, it was all Glenda could do not to laugh. Instead, she patted the hand of her long-suffering sister-in-law and asked, "You think you could fix Sally's gown a bit? It has to hang right for the pictures."

A purposefulness now came over Ida's expression, and she bustled over to Sally to tug on the gleaming satin, making it swirl at Sally's feet and ensuring the front pleat concealed the round belly in its folds. Next she tissued away the last of Sally's tears, then spit on her finger and used it to plaster one stray hair on the bride's temple. Glenda stifled a laugh, seeing Sally's determination not to flinch from her aunt's ministrations. But it was hard not to guffaw when Ida made a similar attempt on Tony's hairdo—an attempt he deflected with a piercing look. By the time Ida rejoined her on the pew, Glenda had her amusement well reined in.

She turned her head to nod at Wilbur that he should begin, but he now seemed engrossed in camera angles. He closed one eye and used his hands to frame an imaginary shot. He lifted the camera, and she heard the shutter click six times in rapid succession.

"Excellent!" he proclaimed. "Now, Sally, could you tilt your head just a little to your left?"

Glenda felt a twinge of annoyance. *Here he is, tellin' my girl how to hold her head. As if he knowd anything about makin' pictures!* Leaning over to whisper at Ida, she said, "He is bound and determined t'make himself useful today."

Ida raised her eyebrows. "Well, then, let him."

No one escaped Wilbur's camera. Apparently drunk with a newfound sense of purpose, the shutterbug had chronicled the bride-and-groom, the bride-without-groom and the groom-without-bride.

"Why do we need a picture of my mug without Sal?" Tony had protested. But his objection had been waved off, and Wilbur had resumed: bride-with-mother; bride-with-mother-and-aunt; preacher-with-newlyweds; and finally, he'd asked the preacher to take the camera in order to chronicle his *own* self as a member of the wedding party.

The moment the photos were done, Mrs. Ballard—who'd slid out from behind the organ and was watching the proceedings with interest—toddled over to Glenda to compliment her on all the "weddin' fixin's." On and on she'd went, admiring Sally's dress—for which Glenda took no credit, giving it all to Ida.

Then she'd asked about the flowers, and Glenda'd watched as Wilbur rapidly switched hats, returning to his original role as florist.

"Oh, the bride's bouquet—the white roses, of course, with just a hint of baby's breath!"

Glenda had fidgeted at the mention. *Sally and I decided that was the perfect way to honor the baby—and it's our little secret.*

Mrs. Ballard exclaimed, "And the big arrangement of those calla lilies just matched the lines of that dress like nobody's business!"

Yes, and this weddin' is just that—nobody's business! Glenda had wanted to remind the preacher. No one had mentioned the organist would be there. But the wedding would've been sadly lacking without music, so how could she complain?

Glenda lingered while the others left the sanctuary to enjoy a small reception in the chancery. She knew what they'd find there: the platters she'd fixed earlier, then sealed in plastic wrap. For those who wanted a savory bite, there were sections of vine-ripened tomatoes paired with slices of yellow cheese and crisp wheat crackers. And, of course, she'd made Sally's favorite family recipe: Green Salad. *Well, it's green all right, but I don't know as other folks would think it's really a salad.* She'd had to round up the special ingredients: pineapple chunks, cottage cheese, walnuts, all held together with lime Jell-o. *Some think it's tart; I think it's sweet, myself.* Then, to go with the cake, there were plump strawberries and two bottles of chilled non-alcoholic champagne.

Land sakes, this little ol' group is makin' enough noise, you'da thought we invited all the relations. But before she joined the others, Glenda wanted to hold this moment to herself. Sunlight poured into the sanctuary through the stained-glass window, tinting the room rose. She looked up at the familiar surroundings: the carved altar with the tiny chip on one edge; the pews polished to a sheen mostly by the frequent slidings of parishioners; the well-worn blue carpet that ran down the central aisle. But now, the dear place looked new again. For her, it would always be the chapel where she'd sat at her daughter's wedding.

Feeling the gold band on her own finger—worn, now, and thin—she thought how happy her late husband would have been to see Sally married at last to her Tony. He'd always liked the young man. Her husband would've approved of the vows spoken today. Perhaps, wherever he was now, he could gather a measure of peace from his daughter's happiness. *I felt a presence. I think you paid a visit durin' the ceremony, George.*

A sudden uprising of happy voices reached her from the other room, and she heard Sally say, "That's the most beautiful cake I ever saw! Where's Mama?"

Glenda stood, ready now to join the group. She walked closer to the front of the church, and her gaze lifted to the lectern where preacher Tobias had placed a glass of water for himself. Now the water seemed rose-colored. *Is it the light from the window? I don't b'lieve so.* Though she couldn't prove it, she swore the water'd turned to wine.

Chapter 27

Delmar could feel the gears not only turning, but beginning to mesh.

He loved it when a case reached this point. But he had to ask himself, what case was he thinking about?

That was the weird thing. The missing journalist case hadn't truly been part of his assigned work—not until that car had been discovered.

Now, as though a huge hobbing machine had been milling in the background all along, cutting the gears, sprockets, and splines, one case was beginning to turn the gears of another, and perhaps yet another beyond that.

Christine had followed an earlier lead and found an alternate set of plans for the Clarke house at Sawyer Construction. Surveillance had confirmed clandestine activities at Clarke Shipping. Stacey Chernak was being abused by her husband Wilhelm, who had been caught on tape apparently taking orders from Clarke. And he himself had seen the man with the large mole at the Clarke house construction site.

Now that Gladys was safely away from Clarke Shipping and they had an undercover agent in place, he knew they'd discover more clues there. But Stacey was still at risk, as he hadn't yet contrived a way to get her away from the dangerous man for whom she worked, nor the abuser with whom she lived.

He needed to give this more thought. *Either that or find a way to remember my dreams.* Del knew his subconscious was hard at work on these interconnected cases, which wouldn't leave him alone. *Who knew I'd encounter the most complex case of my career when I moved to this seemingly quieter part of the state?*

One of his recurring nightmares had to do with the deserted shack he'd found near the site where Christine's SUV had been discovered. As soon as he could take a day, he planned to hike that entire region and explore that structure. Something might've been left there that could provide a clue.

Was that place the reason the car had been near Lake Nacimiento? Had it been a kind of way station for hikers? Perhaps even part of a hut-to-hut hike? For that, he could check with back-country organizations.

Meanwhile, something else preyed on his mind: Russell Clarke's taped remark about "adding someone to this shipment." He ran a shipping firm, and purportedly his primary product was oil. But what did he mean by having someone "dispatched?" Was this a cold-blooded reference to murder? Or had Del stumbled across a trafficking ring?

If so, this was well above Del's pay grade, and he'd need bigger guns and a more powerful team. For all he knew, he might've tripped across a long-standing case already underway by the FBI. Or since Clarke Shipping sent vessels to international ports, perhaps this would involve the clandestine services.

No wonder I can't get a good night's sleep. There was plenty to keep him on tenterhooks.

Stacey had endured another horrible evening with Wilhelm. But it wasn't as bad as the one a couple of weeks earlier.

That'd been one of the worst beatings, in a series of escalating attacks. *How much longer can I manage to stay?* She asked herself the same question so frequently, it'd become rhetorical.

But the previous night had brought a different sort of worry. Wilhelm had been eerily calm when he got home, a mood that sometimes presaged his particular brand of violence.

But this time, he had told her she would need to attend a special meeting that would take place on the docks.

At first, this had not been a concern. She'd often been used as an errand girl or courier. The waterfront of Morro Bay was both charming and familiar, and she'd pictured being able to grab a hot lunch of fish and chips from a local vendor.

That idea was quashed when he mentioned the meeting would take place at night.

"At night?" she queried. "But Wilhelm, nothing is open at that time. There are not even very many lights. Why must it be so late?"

Wilhelm had given her one of his joyless grins. "No one is to know about zis meeting, Liebshen. You see, Gladys was going to take this meeting for us, but as you know, she has a sick aunt and has left town. So you will fill in for her."

But Stacey had *not* known Gladys had a sick aunt. When she'd asked after her friend, the temp sitting in for her had only said she'd be back soon.

Now she put two and two together. Gladys was gone. For how long, Stacey had no idea, but she suspected her friend might never return.

Fear raced up and down her spine with a velocity she'd never experienced. She knew she was in danger. And she knew she must not go to the docks for this supposed meeting.

There was only one thing left to do: make contact with Deputy Delmar.

Meredith felt a longing that had her on a rollercoaster, and she wasn't sure she liked the sensation.

Her work continued to go well, for which she was immensely grateful. That part of her brain remained mercifully on terra firma. But the rest, from her solar plexus to the tips of her toes, seemed to belong somewhere outside her body. If she had to name the current location of these important parts, it would be the back pocket of one Zack Calvin.

Oh, she had it bad. And as it did in the jazz world, bad meant good.

She laughed at that, but it was more out of nerves than actual humor. She wanted to see him. She *needed* to see him, but felt uncertain how much of this need to reveal. *Yet, I've already revealed more to him than to anyone else. Now that the dam is broken, I doubt I can stop the flow.*

Mer sat with this for a moment. How had Zack managed to open her so easily? Well, if she were honest with herself, it might at least partially be because she was the one who'd initiated the relationship, which had made her feel she was in control. *That's about the last time I've felt any real control, that night I asked him to take me for a drive,* she admitted.

But why had she not clammed up as she usually did? Why had her sometimes secretive nature been so disarmed as to leave the door unlocked for him?

Each of them had taken a big step forward by spending their weekend together over Memorial Day. *So many heartfelt discussions, admissions, confessions.* It'd also been a chance to find a daily rhythm, even if temporarily. Piecing together their months of weekend visits and their long weekend at his homestead, she'd gotten a clear picture of what their life together might be like.

Evidently he had too. He'd made a few comments about how they should spend a lot more time together. He'd asked a zillion questions about her life, her work, and her family. And he'd given her a serious piece of jewelry.

She'd known these were not the actions of a man trying to keep his distance. But then he'd taken things a step further.

"You've got one client here now," he pointed out. "You'll get more. You're good at what you do."

She'd flushed at the wonderful compliment from someone whose business acumen she respected. "Well, I'm not gonna be a mogul any time soon, but I do enjoy working through problems with my clients."

"I get that. So if you want to develop these contacts, what would you say to allocating more of your schedule to Santa Barbara?"

She was stumped for a moment. *Is he making a business proposition? Or is he asking something else?*

He'd instantly sensed her confusion and walked to her, taking her face in his hands. "I'm sorry. That was clumsy. Here's what I'm really asking. Would you consider moving in with me?"

Her heart had started to hammer so loud she thought he'd hear it.

"Take your time," he'd said gently. "We could even say it's temporary, if that feels more comfortable."

"It's a big step," she'd said in a quiet voice.

"Think about it. I know there are logistics to work out. We could try it for six months."

When she continued to hesitate, he brought up the most important thing. "You know I love you very much."

That's when she'd stopped breathing for a moment. Then she'd leapt into his arms and said, "I love you too."

Meredith was doing her utmost to keep her feet on the ground, all except for that leap.

There was so much to think about, so much to plan, she hardly knew where to begin.

For now, she was not making plans to close her San Francisco office. It was much too soon for that, and she had no intention of letting down her existing clients.

But what about the house? She was thinking about this as she pulled to the sidewalk at her own address. She wanted to quickly change out of her business suit, then make a run to grab some groceries.

As she came back out her front door, she was appalled to see a familiar figure standing beside her car. *What the hell?*

The woman who'd claimed to be the wife of Peter Sylvester, a man she'd thought she was dating; the woman who'd walked boldly into Meredith's office demanding she stay away from the husband Mer hadn't known he was: she was now at the front of her property.

"What the hell are you doing here?" she demanded.

"Giving you fair warning," the woman said with an evil glare.

"You already did that, didn't you?" Meredith was reaching for her phone to call her friend and mentor Ron. Clearly, it was time to inform their legal department that this troublemaker had resurfaced.

"Here's the thing," the woman interrupted. "There's a restraining order against you."

"You have that backwards," Meredith countered.

"Oh, don't worry. I have no intention of coming to your workplace ever again. But you are not allowed within fifty yards of that door," she said, pointing to the adjacent property.

Outrage boiled through Meredith, but she kept her tone even. "That's impossible. That's Nora's place, and she's been my neighbor and friend for the whole time that I've owned this building. Obviously, I can't keep that far away from a building that's immediately next door."

"Well, good luck with that," the woman gloated. "Didn't Nora tell you? She'll be in Italy for six months. For the duration, I'm your *new* neighbor."

Meredith stalked back inside, grocery shopping forgotten.

First, she completed the call to the office and left an urgent message for the legal department.

Next, she called the realtor her mother had used when she found this house. Mrs. Rimaldi answered immediately.

"Oh, Miss Meredith! How are you? How are you enjoying your beautiful house?"

"Very much," Mer replied. "But it turns out I may need to be away for about six months. I hate to leave it empty all that time. Would you know anything about the possibility of renting it out?"

"Well, this is not usually my specialty, but I do have a partner who can help. Of course, you would want a very good monthly fee for such a beautiful property."

"I would, yes. But It might also be a little bit urgent to get it rented."

After a slight pause, the agent said, "I see, yes. I will do some work about this. May I call you tomorrow?"

"That would be excellent," Mer confirmed.

This is one hell of an accelerated schedule. But maybe it's all to the good.

Chapter 28

Miranda sat at the artist's desk in her studio, gazing out the window but not seeing what was actually in front of her.

In the three weeks since Memorial Day, most of June had whipped by, so full of events she could hardly imagine they were all true.

Sally had returned from Arkansas married! She and Tony seemed to glow as brightly as their shiny new wedding rings, sharing stories every chance they got, and full of plans for their future together.

Sally, more pregnant than ever, would still be at Miranda's wedding, but now Tony would come too. *Have to add him to the guest list for the caterers. Just as well Sally opted out of being a bridesmaid, cuz now she'd be a brides-matron or something like that.*

Miranda chuckled as she jotted down the note about one more guest. She riffled through the planner pages for the last weeks, grateful she'd completed more work than she'd thought possible, readied for her summer teaching job in Alaska, packed for their honeymoon, and prepared all the gifts for her bridesmaids, family, and new in-laws.

Her day-planner overflowed with sticky-notes, scribbles, and reminders. "Solstice" was circled in bright green and next to it were the words "our wedding."

And that's tomorrow! As though hearing her excited inner voice, Shadow tiptoed over to bump her face against Miranda's cheek. "It's true, kitty. We're getting married!"

Tonight was the easy part, at least as far as she was concerned. The rehearsal and the dinner afterward would be casual and fun. Cornelius and his folks had done all the planning and she hadn't had to lift a finger. *I'll make up for it tomorrow. But tonight, all I have to do is enjoy.*

Zelda sat at the desk in her Santa Barbara office with her Montblanc poised over her Filofax. From her cup of Melior pressed coffee an aromatic steam arose, but rather than taking her first sip, she continued to pause.

Miranda's wedding would take place tomorrow. Though Zelda had originally judged the match to be beneath her young client because the groom was home-grown in that little coastal town where both now lived. But she'd relented upon learning that Cornelius had both a reputation as a local genius working for NASA, and a bank account that seemed to far exceed the usual bounds of scientists who generally lived from one grant to the next.

Good for her, she thought again, happy for the girl. She did still worry to what extent this would place Miranda even further out of sync with her own family. She knew Mr. And Mrs. Jones had harbored similar reservations to her own. The upcoming nuptials had created a significant realignment both inside and beyond the familial structure.

In addition to the fact the groom was not a man of business, there was the sister factor. Not only was Meredith the maid of honor; she was also now dating Zackery, the bride's former boyfriend. The previous romantic entanglement—if it actually ever was romantic—had disentangled itself nicely. But as one couple tied the knot, she wondered how many loopholes Meredith and Zackery would have to slip through to find their own secure mooring.

Enough with the rope metaphors, she thought impatiently, reaching at last for her coffee. But as she replaced the cup in its saucer, she thought about how close to home these complexities had come. Joseph now occupied her thoughts quite often. The thought of him brought instant heat, along with fantasies about their next assignation.

She reveled in the thought of planning their visits as carefully as she would a gallery event, choreographing what he would experience from the moment of his arrival. She'd delight in each detail, from the fresh flowers to the cooking aromas, from the lighting to the outfits. She'd allow time for cocktails and light conversation, wonderful meals that weren't too heavy, and of course the tableau with herself at the center.

How she loved presenting herself to him, loved how his gaze consumed her. At last she had arrived in a relationship where her pulchritude was an asset, not a liability. He treated every part of her as though her entire being were a feast he could enjoy again . . . and again. Her breasts began to ache as she remembered. Zelda picked up a sheaf of papers to fan herself. *Good Lord. I can't even take down some simple notes without overheating!*

This was a critically important time, she knew, as the wedding would likely stir memories and ignite expectations. Did he feel sorry that Zackery had missed his chance with Miranda? Or was Joseph impressed with Meredith? Zelda would talk with him about it tomorrow night, in bed, after sex, when he'd be comfortable, satiated, and relaxed. That's when she would get his honest impressions of how his son was responding to this new woman.

Zelda would be all ears, genuinely interested in his feelings. She was beginning to enjoy both kinds of intimacy—the physical and the emotional.

Miranda felt the accusatory stare of her cat radiating from inside her carrier, which rested on the passenger seat.

"I know, pookalu, it's just terrible that we have to leave you while we go to Alaska. And you can't even be at our wedding!" Miranda sighed, regretful to have to leave her beloved pet, while at the same knowing Shadow would have a wonderful time with Kevin. She always did. So did he, for that matter. A true animal whisperer, her friend Kevin always seemed to welcome the chance to cat-sit.

Miranda pulled into Kevin's driveway and, after turning off her motor, walked around to the passenger door. Kevin was already there, however, lifting out the cat's carrier and speaking softly to the feline, whose language he seemed to know.

"Made some tea. Want some?" He asked.

"Would love it," she replied, following her tall friend into his rustic home. Like her rental, his was made of redwood, which harmonized with its forested surroundings. Also similar to hers, his was situated on a steep hillside, with the main floor kitchen hovering over a downstairs bedroom. From his kitchen balcony he could see into a dense stand of pines. And from stories he had shared, he'd befriended a jay, a squirrel, and an opossum, all of whom made regular visits to receive treats. Protocols recommended not feeding wildlife, but Miranda didn't have the heart to criticize Kevin. For the most part, animals were his only friends.

She, however, considered him to be both friend and family, and Cornelius now felt the same. "We really appreciate this, Kev," she said, taking one of the two chairs at his kitchen table.

"Of course," he said. "No problem."

"I've got a month's worth of her food in the car, but I know you'll add some treats. Keep track of what you spend so we can reimburse you."

"K," he said, setting two steaming mugs on the table.

"She always loves staying with you."

"It's mutual."

"How are things with Jack?" She asked, dunking her tea bag in and out of the hot water.

"Oh, you know, the usual."

"Overworked and underpaid? And I don't mean him."

Kevin chortled. "Yeah, pretty much. Thing is, if he'd ever leave me alone I could actually get a bunch of work done. He keeps interrupting my work flow."

"Oh, that would drive me nuts."

"Cornelius doesn't? Interrupt, I mean."

"He makes an effort not to," Miranda said, drizzling honey into her tea. "Still, it's different, you know? I mean, I sense that he's there, and I know it's the same for him. He's worked alone for years, up all night while everyone else sleeps."

"Awesome."

"Speaking of which, I haven't had a chance to tell you—he got the permit to build his planetarium."

"Wow! Very cool."

"He's excited because he can teach small groups—kids of course, but adults too. Maybe even I'll learn to recognize a few constellations."

"I'll sign up. I'd really like to learn to navigate. But I suppose to teach that, he'd have to have an observatory."

"Oh, and that's next on his list. Well, after getting married and getting our house built, of course."

The two friends laughed.

"And thanks so much again for agreeing to be one of the groomsmen. We're so glad you'll be in the wedding party."

Kevin's smile began to overtake his face.

"Me too. So, you excited about Alaska?"

"Yes. Nervous too. I mean I love teaching, but I want to do a really good job, you know?"

"You will. And then there's the other stuff: whales, eagles, grizzlies. . . ."

"Yeah, that last thing makes me really nervous!"

Kevin stared out the window for a moment while in inhaled. "Yeah. You're gonna have to be alert. But you know how to listen for the cues the animals give."

Miranda nodded. "I like to think so." She stood and took her mug to his kitchen sink. "I have to get home and get changed for the rehearsal dinner. I'm gonna slip out so Shadow doesn't make a fuss. See you there!"

Phyllis and George Smith had spent some consternation choosing a venue for their only son's only rehearsal dinner. Ultimately, knowing that coastal locations were the theme of his future residence and wedding, they'd chosen a beautiful but unelaborate hotel in San Simeon.

A two-story rancher, the Cavalier Inn spread out over a treeless swath and boasted the only waterfront location in the town just north of Milford-Haven. The Smiths had known the Victors, who'd built their hotel and added to it over the years. Phyllis had always liked the place and been quite smitten with the dining room's floor-to-ceiling windows that showed a wide expanse of the Pacific.

George liked the firepit, imagining the party could have s'mores for dessert. And he liked the pool, envisioning a mini-vacation for himself and his Mrs. Accordingly, he'd booked their room for two nights and insisted they stay there after the wedding, rather than driving all the way home—even though this would only save them ten extra miles.

From George's perspective, San Simeon had always seemed to have more history than future. In the 1830s, a mission was established, and twenty years later a whaling station was built at San Simeon Point to take advantage of the grey whale migration. He was sure Miranda would not approve of this appalling practice, which ultimately declined and faded away. The Hearst family then began purchasing local land and the rest was . . . history. In recent decades, they had not done anything to develop the ocean side of Highway 1. The Smiths and all their friends preferred it that way, leaving the Bay Pier and the Cove to be enjoyed as part of the Hearst State Park Beach.

After much conversation, it was decided that the rehearsal dinner could be "casual"—a word Phyllis's soon-to-be sister-in-law Veri Jones found confusing, when Phyllis called to discuss the gathering with her.

"Is it a golf resort?" Veri asked.

"Well, they do have miniature golf," Phyllis replied.

"Hmm, I'm not sure that's quite the same thing. Will we have cocktails on a patio?"

"Excellent idea. I know they have a pool."

There had then been a moment of silence before Veri asked, "Shall the ladies wear skirts? Or should I plan on some linen slacks?"

Phyllis didn't own anything made of linen, but she did have a nice pair of peach polyester pants with a matching jacket. "Slacks sounds just right," she confirmed.

"Fine. Jackets but no ties for the gents?"

Phyllis hadn't seen either her husband or her son in a tie in some years but knew they'd both be suited up for the wedding. That was about all she could expect from either of them, and she didn't want to push her luck. "No ties, no. But a jacket would be smart. It can get a might chilly with breezes off the water in the evening."

"Oh, yes, of course," Veri had agreed.

"Uh, one more thing," Phyllis ventured. "George is thinking it'd be fun to make s'mores at the firepit by the pool after dinner. What would you think of that idea?"

Veri had laughed. "As long as there are plenty of napkins, I think that sounds like fun."

Cornelius led Jameson and his two other groomsmen to their places near the pool. *Glad this isn't a hard-drinking crowd. Otherwise, someone might land in the water.*

He felt a bit tired, he admitted, having stayed up late to edit his vows. He and Miranda had both wanted to end with the same phrase, but the rest they wrote separately. He'd wished he had the skill to write a proper prothalamion, but he was certainly no poet, and it was more important that he sound like himself. In any case, what he'd written was simple and heartfelt and, he realized, words he longed to say to the woman he loved. He shook his head as if to come fully awake.

He'd invited one fellow astronomer, who'd driven down from NASA Ames, and another long-time friend from Cal Poly days. Both were good sports and seemed to be enjoying themselves.

He'd kept a close eye on Miranda's friend Sally as she neared the pool. In her condition, she could hardly see where her feet were landing, and a fall would be disastrous. The woman seemed lit with a special beauty, and he found himself wondering what Miranda would look like if and when she was gravid with a future child of theirs. One glance at Sally's new husband showed him exactly how he'd feel.

After the wedding party had laughed their way through the mock ceremony, all the guests had taken their seats and the speeches had begun, all of them mercifully short, lest they be here all night.

A disposable camera sat on each table—an idea of his mom's —and guests were encouraged to snap photos at will, since no formal shots would be taken this evening.

His parents had outdone themselves with this lovely gathering, and he felt both grateful and proud. Somehow they'd struck just the right tone and made everyone feel welcome. Even Mr. and Mrs.

Jones had gradually relaxed their stiff postures and gotten into the mood of the party.

A few gifts were placed on a side table, and Miranda started passing them out as dinner plates were being cleared. The women friends who'd be part of the wedding were first, and as they began opening their small, wrapped boxes, miniature hinged frames held two images each. On the right, a smaller version of the wedding invitation postcard showed the Ragged Point location. On the left, Miranda'd done a watercolor of each bridesmaid's dress. *Thoughtful and creative as always*, Cornelius thought when Sally showed her gift.

Cornelius had purchased for his pals small framed images of a luminous moon of Uranus set against a black background. Silver lettering under each read, "Fortunately, Miranda's orbit inclined toward me." Of course, Michael from NASA got it right away, laughing out loud and explaining that Miranda was the name of this particular moon with an "inclined" orbit.

At this point he gave his own short speech, which included what he thought would be another astronomy joke. He figured he might as well make these himself, as everyone else certainly was. When he said the words, though, he found himself getting choked up—a common occurrence when he thought about his bride. "Fortunately I was paying attention when Miranda's orbit arrived at perigee," he said. "When she came nearest, I was waiting."

"It was a heavenly convergence!" his friend Michael called out, and the group laughter allowed Cornelius a moment to recover.

"I have small gifts too," Veri piped up, carrying two beautifully wrapped boxes to the bride and groom.

"Mother!" Miranda exclaimed when she opened hers. "You remembered! The stardust sweater from Gump's!" She held up a soft black cardigan covered with white disks, each raining down a sparkle of white stars.

Cornelius appeared stunned when he opened his small box, which held a tie clasp enameled with images.

"For the few times you wear a tie," Charles commented.

"Amazing," Cornelius said, holding it up. "The planets aligned." He planted a kiss on Veri's cheek. "Couldn't be more perfect."

Veri appeared to blush with pleasure.

"I guess we all know this love affair is astronomical!"

"A heavenly match!" another guest called out.

"The stars are aligned!" said Jameson.

"Speaking of which," Cornelius said, bringing a slender box to Miranda.

She opened it to find a necklace featuring all the planets, plus the sun and moon. "I love it!" she exclaimed, then added, "My Very Excellent Mom Just Served Us Noodles."

"What in the world?" Veri asked.

"Cornelius taught it to me, a mnemonic for remembering planetary order."

"I guess this means you're officially over the moon," added Charles, which caused a light-hearted groan to ripple through the room.

Glasses were raised as toasts were made, some sentimental, most humorously filled with puns or jokes, and Jameson offered a limerick. Miranda shared a gratitude list, managing not to cry. Cornelius went last.

"We're here to celebrate syzygy," he began.

"Doesn't he mean synergy?" Charles asked his wife.

Laughter rolled across the tables.

"There is great synergy here, yes, Mr. Jones," Cornelius allowed. "But syzygy is the conjunction of two paired, corresponding things, like a groom and his bride." His gaze caught Miranda's and they held for a moment before he continued. "Syzygy is also the alignment of three celestial objects, like sun, earth, and moon. All of you here this evening are our closest people. Miranda and I want you to know we deeply appreciate your aligning with us. We'll be counting on you."

As twilight offered the last of the light, guests gathered by the firepit and began roasting their confections.

"They look like meteorites streaking low across the sky," Miranda commented, standing with Cornelius at her back, his arms keeping her warm.

Holding her tight, he added, "Not even the Leonid Shower could make this night brighter."

Chapter 29

Cornelius woke in the guest room of their new addition. That's how they referred to it for now, at least, though this other side of their rental had stood there all along. Now it was no longer empty, and both of them were enjoying the additional space.

For one thing, it'd given them this guest suite—a mirror to the master suite they used in the other side. He knew it would come in handy. He hadn't suspected he'd be the first "guest" to use it, though. Miranda, upon the admonitions of her mother, had suggested they shouldn't wake up together on their wedding day. Indeed, he'd been forbidden from seeing her today at all, until he stood at the alter to watch the bridal procession.

Cornelius squeezed his eyes shut and spent a moment imagining it, his beautiful Miranda walking toward him in her finery, taking her place beside him. *Where she belongs, thank God.* He opened his eyes and stepped from the room out onto the lower-level deck, letting the ocean breeze brush over his skin. Clutching the railing, he bent his head to pray, but there was nothing left to ask for; there was only his prayer of gratitude.

Both humbled and energized, he headed back inside to shower and dress. Jameson would be here soon to drive with him up the coast to Ragged Point. His friend would be the best man, carrying boutonnieres for the two of them and carrying the ring—a simple band that matched not only her engagement ring, but the colored-stone rings he planned to give her over the rest of the year. He grinned to think of her delight when he doled out his surprises. But for today, only one ring mattered: the one he'd be slipping on her finger during the ceremony.

Zack pulled into the Raged Point parking lot, got out of his Mercedes, and straightened his tie. He faced a series of buildings and was unsure where to go. *Meredith will have gotten here a couple of hours ago, but she'll be sequestered with the bride.*

The bride. Miranda. The woman for whom he now had sisterly feelings. *If I'm honest, that's probably how I always felt about her.* He smiled, realizing his being here for her wedding was the first— or second—step as their friendship reached its new definition.

Zack saw a pathway ahead that seemed to lead to a garden. A series of lovely, blooming, raised beds gradually gave way to a spectacular ocean view. Overlooking it, stood a pergola decorated with more flowers. *This must be the spot*, he thought. *And it's perfect for her. Nature at its most welcoming and stunning, a landscape just like one she would paint, and probably will, if she hasn't already.*

A feeling of happiness washed over him as he stood there. *This is right. This is perfect for her. And it must be right for Cornelius too.* Zack inhaled while his gaze swept across the view. *And it's only right for me to be a guest here. The woman I really love is waiting for me to escort her as the maid of honor.*

Veri fingered the pearls that rested perfectly just at the edge of her collar bone, then glanced at herself once more in the mirror of the wedding venue's dressing room. *Eyeliner not smudged, not yet at least. Lipstick perfect. Hair all in place.* She checked her handbag one more time to make sure she had enough tissues tucked away. She had to admit, the sea foam organza did look lovely. *Miranda and her painter's eye, her sense of color. She may not have the fashion sense her sister has, but with those color skills and a little help from me, she didn't need it.*

Veri's knee bounced for a moment, a small eruption of the nerves she still worked to suppress. It all felt a bit out of control for her taste. This setting, while picturesque, was certainly more rustic than anything she could have imagined. The musicians had somehow gotten lost somewhere along Highway 1 and ended up too far north but were now on their way. Thank goodness the June Gloom had lifted, and for the most part, they had sunshine. The wedding party hadn't managed a formal rehearsal at the venue but had done a mockup of the ceremony at the Cavalier. *More joking and laughter than real rehearsing.* She supposed that didn't really matter, so long as Mandy was happy. And Oh, Lord, it was abundantly clear that she was happy, more so than she'd ever seen her younger daughter. Veri smiled and felt tears began to well. *No! Stop that! Plenty of time for that later,* she admonished herself.

She stood, fluffed the fabric of her dress and faced the mirror one more time. *Time to be mother of the bride! And almost time for Charles to walk daughter number two down the aisle.*

Delmar had barely had time to change out of his uniform before hitting the road again. As he fought to keep just a couple of miles over the speed limit on Highway 1, he imagined Emily Wilkins would by now have saved him a seat.

Suddenly, it struck him as odd that two of the women to whom he felt closest in his new Central Coast home were both journalists. *Christine isn't really a friend, but I feel I've gotten to know her well enough that she would be.*

Emily was still something of an enigma but a very interesting one. He enjoyed her pithy writing style and sometimes couldn't imagine how she managed to attend so many local events to cover them for the *Milford-Haven News*. She'd lived in the region for quite a while but was originally from South Africa, and that'd led to some interesting discussions about apartheid.

Finally, the turnoff for Ragged Point came into view. *So kind of Miranda to send me an invitation, and I certainly don't want to be late.*

A few minutes later, he saw the men and women of the wedding party had already arrived at the portico. *Hard to miss Kevin towering over the others.* Relieved the ceremony had not yet started, he found Emily and took the empty chair next to her. "Thanks," he said quietly.

"Of course," she said with a welcoming smile. "Isn't this lovely?"

"It truly is," Del replied, hoping the peaceful setting would stay that way.

Miranda lifted her hand to fiddle again with her hair, but Meredith stopped her.

"It looks beautiful Mandy. Leave it."

"Okay," Miranda replied. She looked at her sister in whose eyes she saw, for once, gentle reassurance. "Mer, I so appreciate your being here with me," she said, grabbing her hand. "I love that I get to share this special time with you, just like we imagined when we were little."

Meredith laughed, which was her default response to anything sentimental. Then she said, "I'm glad too, kiddo. I like your man. He's good for you. And I think you're good for him too. You're both lucky."

"We're blessed. That's how I see it."

"Then it's true. True for you," Meredith added.

The sisters were quiet for a long moment, then both began speaking at once.

"You look gorgeous," Miranda commented.

"*You* look gorgeous," Meredith proclaimed.

Then they both laughed. From outside, they heard music begin to play, and a light murmuring of voices carried on the breezes. They stood, straightening their dresses. "You two ready in there?" came their father's voice.

"Ready!" Meredith answered.

Miranda took a deep breath. "Guess it's time."

"See you out there," Meredith said, heading outside.

Miranda watched as her sister began the stately walk in cadence with the music. Her teal dress fluttered in the breeze, and through the edges of the arbor she could see her bridesmaids flanking the portico, a different shade for each dress. *Like a watercolor palette, just as I imagined.*

Then it was her turn. She looked over at her father and took his arm, noticing he suddenly looked proud, an awareness of the moment settling over his features. She gave him her broadest smile but then turned to look again toward the portico, where the handsomest, most incredible man in the universe stood waiting for her.

Taking a jagged breath, she stepped forward and gasped. Just beyond Cornelius and the wedding party, a storm cloud had scudded across the sky, leaving in its wake a perfect rainbow whose two ends floated on the surface of the sea.

"Look!" she said, but not loudly enough to be heard. For a hush came over her, a sense of the miraculous touching down to bless her wedding to the one she loved.

Samantha walked with the other guests toward the reception. The ceremony had been perfect as far as Sam could tell, and her young friend seemed to quiver and then float with joy.

She smiled at the thought, replaying the lovely tableau that looked exactly like one of Miranda's own paintings. Now she caught a glimpse of herself in a wall of glass alongside the walkway. The forest green, silk, layered pantsuit she'd chosen certainly complemented the surroundings. And though it had asymmetrical hems cascading from hip to thigh, with hems that hovered over her matching sandals, the outfit wasn't exactly formal.

Sam arrived at the dining room and waved when she saw Delmar. She began looking for the table number she'd seen listed as she entered, and as she navigated through the room, she looked approvingly at the neutral tones of the stone pillars echoed by the warm wood flooring and the paneling that formed a partial wall. Clerestory windows let in light that washed over the room brightly but would turn to amber as their guests enjoyed the wedding feast. Round tables were draped with white cloths that matched the white folding chairs, but across the tables, wide fabric runners picked up the floral tones: lush green Amaranthus; Hilltop Stella Dahlias, vivid red at their centers, their petals shifting to white tips; delicate orange poppies to celebrate California; vivid petunias in deep purple and yellow; and white gardenias for their beauty and fragrance.

This couldn't be more different than the runaway wedding Jack and I had all those years ago, she reflected. *Miranda and Cornelius truly have the blessings of their community. Maybe that's what it takes to sustain a marriage.*

Phyllis thought the decor, the menu, the service, the setting, and all the guests were entirely perfect, and she couldn't imagine how her new daughter-in-law had managed to arrange it all. Even the wedding cake was perfect! The icing seemed to be made of Miranda's own watercolors. The bottom tier, blue-green with images of coastal pines ringing the base, blended into the a delicate aqua tone with white sea shells climbing upward toward the white top tier, where two sea stars danced with heart cockles at their feet.

Somehow her scientist-son had found himself a visual poet, and Phyllis felt breathless at the new energy cascading into their lives.

Zelda had chosen a plum confection to wear to Miranda's wedding. She'd decided upon a cocktail-length lace chiffon dress, with an asymmetrical floaty hem, its bodice covered demurely with sequined lace and modestly ruffled elbow-length sleeves.

The muted amethyst color would be no surprise to the bride, who knew her artist's rep favored every shade of purple. Still, Zelda had given the choice quite a bit of thought. She wanted to honor her client, not compete with the bride's mother, fit in well with other guests, and represent herself properly. If she were honest, she had also dressed to please Joseph.

She thought about their storied recent past. She'd first met him when pitching her corporate art services in his office, and there'd been an unmistakable spark. Then she'd attended a fabulous soiree at his estate and saved the day when Zackery's former girlfriend had a meltdown afterward. But since then, their busy lives had only crossed intermittently, until three weeks ago. He'd been busy at work since, but when Zelda had invited him to her young client's wedding, he'd accepted.

Lifting her napkin to press the corners of her mouth, she glanced across the table where Joseph caught her gaze. The dance floor was beginning to fill, and he raised his eyebrows in invitation. Zelda's reply was to nod slightly, whereupon he came over to pull back her chair and offer his hand. Once in his embrace, she inhaled his spicy scent and pressed her breasts against his chest, enjoying his unmistakable response. *Oh, I've missed this*, she thought, letting her body conform to his and follow his lead.

Veri watched Miranda dance with her new husband, yet it was more of a rhythmic embrace than a pattern of steps. They'd done the fancy footwork earlier and now, as the party began to wind down, their private celebration seemed to be calling to them.

Looking around at the guests, she saw one glancing at his watch, another fix a stray hair back into place, and yet another reviewing the paper program left on the table. The cake had been cut, desserts enjoyed, speeches given, dances shared. Much as she didn't want this night to end, it was time to see the new couple off with the planned fanfare.

Leaning toward Charles, whose eyes had glassed over, she murmured, "Time to go, dear."

"Thank you," he mumbled.

"First, they have to throw the flowers and the garter, then we have to throw the rice," she reminded him.

Puckering slightly as the realization hit him that his youngest was about to slip completely out of his grasp, he nodded and took his wife's hand.

Veri caught Miranda's eye as they began to head toward the door, and her daughter nodded. A moment later, Meredith's voice rang out over the PA to invite the men to gather on one side of the dance floor, the women on the other.

A wonderful hubbub erupted as the single women positioned themselves behind Miranda who now held her bouquet aloft. "One, two, three!" they sang in unison, and the bright blooms flew directly into Meredith's bodice, despite the slack hands at her sides. Reflexively, she grasped the flowers before they could fall, and everyone cheered. Veri, standing and clapping with the surrounding guests, caught Meri's expression of alarm, then saw it shift to a shy grin. Veri darted a glance in the direction of Meredith's gaze to find Zack laser-focused on Meri. *Oh, my*, she thought. *Things have been progressing.*

Meredith straightened the back of her sister's gown one final time as her hand was grasped by her handsome new husband.

Surprised by her own sentimentality, she'd had to brush away a tear or two at their obvious joy. Though technically this was the start of the new couple's life together, Mer felt they'd been together for ages. Now she realized with some relief that there were absolutely no further strings attaching her sister to Zack, except for the developing familial ones.

Miranda had held her sister for a moment while guests were dancing. "Oh, Mer, I'm over the moon." Of course, they both had to laugh at the joke that would likely pursue her and her astronomer mate. "I mean, I feel like I'm on a spaceship, and the universe is opening for us. It's beyond amazing. Wish I could explain it."

Meri had held her sister's shoulders and looked into her radiant face. "You don't have to. I can tell." After a pause she'd added, "Hope I get there someday, too. Though for me it's more likely to be train than a spaceship."

"Hmm, I like that," Mandy reflected. "Wherever it goes, you'll be riding in First Class." After another chuckle, she added. "Not to make assumptions, but I don't think you're that far behind us."

Meri tried pulling back, making some sort of denial noise, but Mandy wouldn't let her.

"You're the one he needs. And you need him too. Embrace it. You deserve it."

Her sister gave her one more quick squeeze, then flitted off to connect with other guests. Meredith felt herself take a breath. *She's right.* The words came unbidden but welcome.

Finding Zack chatting with her father, she broke into a broad smile. "Great," she said. "When the happy couple departs, how about if the four of us have a nightcap? There's a beautiful bar here, and they're keeping it open for us."

"Splendid," Charles enthused.

The three of them went to find Veri and stake out a foursome of leather chairs that surrounded a gas fireplace with a handsome stone mantle and hearth.

Veri had joined the others to throw birdseed and joyful wishes as the bride and groom walked under the beautifully decorated arbor to follow a path that disappeared into the Ragged Point property.

Just slightly teary, she'd patted her face with the monogrammed handkerchief she kept in her evening bag, then accepted the invitation to visit with the other young couple in their lives. *It'll be a good distraction,* she thought. *And maybe I'll learn a thing or two.*

They ordered brandy, and Veri could suddenly envision all of them gathered around her own fireplace in Belvedere, serving her lovely family members brandy in her own crystal snifters, pulling out photo albums to embarrass her daughters, and welcoming their partners into the fold.

I'm getting ahead of myself, she admonished. *But not by much.*

Later, when she and Charles were in their suite, nearly ready for bed, Veri was about to pack her evening purse when she realized it contained an envelop she hadn't seen. Pulling it out, she recognized

Miranda's handwriting. "Mother and Dad," it said in her lovely cursive. She opened the note which simply said, "Thank you for everything. Love, Mandy."

Inside the note was a printed paper, folded to fit the notecard. Veri opened it, then let the tears flow as she read:

Miranda & Cornelius wedding vows

Miranda to Cornelius:

My path was leading me to you long before I knew it was. You were a fantasy man I could only try to imagine enough to paint as a dreamscape. If I had continued to look at life from my head perspective, I would have missed seeing you. You were so far above where I was looking, I had to elevate my understanding even to catch a glimpse of you. But it was when I learned to look from my heart perspective that I saw you.

It's not that you complete me, but that I recognized you because I saw my own completeness, and I know that's also why you recognized me, You have made me realize that if we trust in the Universe, it will conspire to give us exactly what is right for us, bring us to the right place at the right time, aligned with what we hold most dear.

Who you are aligns with my best sense of who I hope to be. As I promise to be true to you, I am also making a promise to be true to myself.

I love you with my whole mind and with my whole heart. I love you now, and I know this is only a foretaste of how much I will love you in the years to come.

From now on, you are the one I promise to have and to hold.

Cornelius to Miranda:

You're too good for me the same way a star is too good for the telescope through which it can barely be seen, for in every constellation you are my lucida, the brightest star.

You're too good for me the way quantum entanglement is too good for explanations and descriptions. Yet, there is nothing I can do to diminished our entanglement because it is bigger than both of us squared.

You're too good for me the way mathematics is too good for those of us who stand at the blackboard. Yet in the perfection of calculation, you are my reciprocal, so as we are multiplied, we equal one.

You are the one for me. I will love and cherish you always, into the infinity I can imagine because of you. You are the one I promise to have and to hold.

Chapter 30

from Samantha Hugo's Journal
(Volume 50, maroon cloth cover)
Ragged Point Resort

Miranda and Cornelius . . . my heart is full after attending their beautiful wedding!

The setting was so perfect for them; it was as if Miranda created one of her beautiful canvases, then had all of us step into it. The bridesmaids' dresses seemed to flow as part of the watercolor, the handsome men stood tall, and a rainbow touched down to frame the tableau.

Guests couldn't hear the vows, what with the sound of waves and the breezes off the ocean. But that was fine. The moment for the two celebrants was sacred and private, even though taking place in the sight of God and family and friends. That hush that's supposed to happen was there, and everyone seemed to feel it.

During the reception, I had a lovely talk with Miranda's mother, who asked that I call her by her nickname Veri, so I asked her to *call me Sam. She's a great beauty, so it's clear where Miranda gets her looks. Her sister Meredith, too, another beauty, whom I met at Miranda's art show last spring.*

She was paired with Zack Calvin. At first I was quite surprised to see him at Miranda's wedding, given that they knew each other first. It became evident that he is now dating Meredith, which didn't seem to present a problem for the bride or the groom, and Zack seemed quite taken with the elder Jones sister.

It was good to see Joseph too, and we had a nice talk, though it was cut short when Zelda hovered. Perhaps they've become an item? It seemed that way. In any case, she was there for Miranda, who is still her client.

There's obviously something in the air this summer. Milford-Haven is abuzz with romantic news. It's as though everyone in town has a contact high, even those who don't actually know the bride.

I should say brides plural, because Sally O. got married too. I saw her at Miranda's wedding and recognized the man she was with, then she walked—or waddled, in her pregnant state—right over to me and introduced him as her husband. That was nice of her, and they both seemed very happy. I have to admit, what I've heard of their story is inspirational. The man she loved when they were both young who became an injured war veteran, now back in her life. He moved across the country to start a new life for himself, hoping they could at least be friends. And now they're married at last, and he's about to be a stepfather.

I must say I don't quite know how to think about Jack having fathered another child he won't be rearing. I didn't give him the chance with Gregory, but according to Miranda, Sally gave him every opportunity. That door is firmly closed for him now. I wonder whether he'll try to assert parental rights. If Gregory is ever found, I wonder the same thing.

I feel the son I barely knew must be close, though this isn't proven by any stretch and perhaps not rational. Nothing about the "case" is. It wasn't rational to give him up, though it seemed so at the time. Trying to find him now might not be either. But knowing how old he would be, this is the time in his life he'd likely be finding his own mate. He might be marrying, might be having a first child.

I keep asking myself what I truly want. Do I want to disrupt his life to ensure he has a fuller picture of his history? Would he even be interested? Or did he adjust to not knowing his biological lineage years ago?

Do I instead want to become a voyeur in his life, observe some of his activities but then leave him alone? Would I be able to resist the temptation to reveal my identity?

If only I knew whether or not he's looking for me. If he were, perhaps each of us could accelerate the process . . . though I don't know how.

Here's an irony I've been considering. My career is about avoiding or repairing damage to the planet. Yet, my actions regarding my son have likely caused damage I cannot undo. How can a person be forgiven for abandonment? How can I forgive myself? This will take a lot of work from my side, and I'm aware that I want to get started on it. I need to find a program, a counselor, some kind of guidance. I'm certainly not the only one to tread this path.

And while I wonder about damage, I sure have a good example of it in Susan. That girl! Some days I can see her intelligence, her progress, her willingness to learn. Other days I see her close down, and it seems to take very little to tip the balance toward the negative.

She mumbled something in my office yesterday, and when I asked her to speak up, she said Kevin had helped her.

"With what?" I wanted to know.

"With my apartment," she replied. Apparently, some repairs were needed, and that dear man did them for free. I'm glad she has at least one good friend, as she'll seldom let me get close. Everything I suggest is construed as a judgment, and really, I can't blame her for that. I do come down hard on her sometimes but always because I want her to do better and succeed.

The thing is, I wasn't damaged in my youth. So when mentors, teachers, coaches, professors insisted I work harder, I generally took it as a sign that they cared and that they knew something I didn't know. If they said I'd succeed if I did more work, I believed them.

But if I say the same thing to Susan, she thinks I'm only criticizing her. I wish I could be more nurturing. Perhaps that's one of the many things I failed to learn because of giving up my son too early.

After a conversation with Miranda a few weeks ago—when we were discussing the concept for the painting she did as Cornelius' wedding present—I've thought a lot more about alignment. She made such an interesting point: that you can only see certain things from a specific vantage point.

POV, which stands for point of view—that's what my friends in the film business call it. It's pertinent for the writers but also for the directors and cinematographers. Their job is to serve the story, letting the audience in at exactly the point they want to present, and that applies to the physical angle, the character, and to the chronological moment.

If I try to view parts of my life as though it were a film, there are plenty of times when the thing I wanted to see was obscured. Sometimes Jack was in my way; sometimes it was my own self judgment that prevented me from seeing clearly. I like to think I'm now able to see past so many of these obstacles. I think Cornelius would say my goal was occulted, the way one heavenly body can cover up another in its line of sight.

What's so interesting is that it only takes moving to one side or the other, and sometimes only a small movement, to see past the occultation. Miranda always talks about head and heart. If the head is seeing from one perspective and the heart from another, they're not aligned.

Alignment . . . occulting . . . rather metaphysical subjects for a wedding, but then, consider the deeply thoughtful bride and her brilliant groom. Indeed, he brought up one more concept I find intriguing, one I haven't thought about in a while. At the rehearsal dinner, where everyone had a chance to share thoughts more informally, he talked about syzygy. I had to look that word up again to remind myself of the definition. Of course, Cornelius used it in an astronomical sense as in "the planets were aligned in syzygy."

From this wider, more cosmic view, nothing is hidden, or occulted, and the alignment of different elements becomes visible, as though viewing from a spacecraft the Sun, moon, and earth, all in a line.

In a psychological context, Carl Jung used the word to describe "a union of opposites" like animus and anima. In this usage, it sounds like a perfect word to describe Jack and me. We certainly are opposites, as we prove every time we have a discussion about environmental matters. But our opposition goes back much farther and also goes deeper.

If it's true that opposites attract, that law of attraction was operating from the moment we met. And rather than repel us away from one anther, it drew us together, apparently proving Jung's theory. A little more research revealed that Gnostics believed the whole universe was brought into being through the interaction of *cosmological opposites. That hints at the incredibly creative energy Jack and I used to feel as we talked about our plans when we were first married. And though neither of us acknowledged it then, that energy created a child.*

I've been avoiding this fact for years. But it's become clear that I can't continue to pretend that I'm alone, unaffected by the forces in which I live. Several months ago I studied spring and neap tides. I remember now, when the sun and moon are in syzygy, their tidal forces act to reinforce each other, causing the ocean to rise higher and fall lower than at average times. It's as though I've become aware enough to feel these forces pulling on me.

What that means is that I already live in syzygy; I just had't allowed myself to recognize it until now. If this is true for me, it's true for all. This is a force entirely larger than any one self, the very rhythm and flow of energy and awareness governing the universe. Where we belong, and with whom, then, isn't a matter of personal will but a universal law leading to the integration and wholeness of being. Only from this higher perspective will I be able to discern . . . whose hearts align.

Cast of Characters

Joseph Calvin: mid-60s, 6'1, gray eyes, steel-gray hair, clean-shaven, lean, handsome; CEO of Santa Barbara's Calvin Oil; eligible widower; dates several women, including Christine Christian and Zelda McIntyre.

Zackery Calvin: mid-30s, 6'2, blue eyes, dark blond hair, handsome, lean, athletic; VP of Calvin Oil, works with his father; popular bachelor; dating Meredith Jones.

Nicole Champagne: mid-20s, 5'5, brown eyes, brunette, chic dresser; runs Milford-Haven's Finders Gallery; sells Miranda Jones's and other artists' work with skill; originally from Montreal, Quebec, and speaks with a French-Canadian accent.

Stacey Chernak: late-40s, 5'6, blue eyes, blond hair, kind, submissive, speaks with a Swiss-German accent; married to abusive Wilhelm Chernak; works full time as Clarke Shipping secretary, and works part-time for Chernak Agency.

Wilhelm Chernak: mid-60s, 6', deep-set black eyes, silvered hair and beard, low resonant voice, a Swiss citizen who still carries an accent from his native Germany; capable of fierce and sudden anger; started the Chernak Agency, a service for locating adopted children; abuses his wife Stacey.

Christine Christian: missing; a former special investigative reporter for Satellite-News TV station KOST-SATV; is being investigated by Deputy Delmar Johnson.

Russell Clarke: early-60s, 6'3, coal black eyes, dazzling white teeth, dusky skin, deceptively strong, by turns charming and stern, adopted, has unknown mixed lineage; owner of Clarke Shipping; Stacey Chernak's employer; business associate of Joseph Calvin; commissions Jack Sawyer to build him Milford-Haven's most magnificent seaside mansion.

Tony Fiorentino: early-40s, 6'4, brown eyes, black hair, athletic wheelchair paraplegic, recipient of Veterans Assistance Award; has moved from New York City to Milford-Haven; high school boyfriend of Sally O'Mally who marries her with her Mama's blessing in Arkansas.

Ralph Hargraves: late-70s, 6', blue eyes, gray hair, a face seamed with smile lines, pleasant disposition; a fixture in Milford-Haven, owner of Hargraves Hardware.

James Hughes: early-60s, 5'11, brown eyes, thinning gray hair, soft-spoken with a mid-Atlantic accent; the fiercely loyal butler at the Calvin estate, Calma.

Samantha Hugo: early-50s, 5'9, cognac-brown eyes, redhead, statuesque, sharp dresser; director of Milford-Haven's Environmental Planning Commission; Miranda's friend; Jack Sawyer's former wife; a journal writer.

Deputy Delmar Johnson: early-40s, 6'2, brown eyes, black hair, handsome, muscular, African American; with the San Luis Obispo County Sheriff's Department, assigned to the Special Problems Unit; originally from South Central Los Angeles. Committed to his investigation of missing journalist Christine Christian.

Charles and Veronica "Veri" Jones: late-50s, parents of Meredith and Miranda, elegant members of Bay Area elite society; long-ago friends to Joseph Calvin and his late wife.

Meredith Jones: mid-30s, 5'8, teal eyes, silky, long brunette hair, Eurasian, beautiful, exotic, shapely, athletic; San Francisco financial advisor; Miranda's half-sister, raised as her sister. Has new clients in Santa Barbara; dating Zack Calvin.

Miranda Jones: early-30s, 5'9, green eyes, long brunette hair, beautiful, lean, athletic; fine artist specializing in watercolors and murals; a staunch environmentalist whose paintings often depict endangered species; loves her adopted town of Milford-Haven; in love with local astronomer Cornelius Smith to whom she is recently engaged.

Michelle "Shelly" Larrup: mid-40s, 5'6, hazel eyes, bobbed burgundy hair, well-toned dancer's body, flamboyant dresser; originally from Australia and speaks with the accent; owner of Shell Shock in Milford-Haven.

June Magliati: mid-40s, 5'2, brown eyes, dark brown curly hair, no-nonsense expression that goes well with her thick Brooklyn accent; Sally O'Mally's trusted friend and employee at the restaurant.

Zelda McIntyre: early-50s, 5'1, violet eyes, wavy black hair, voluptuous, dramatic and striking; owner of private firm Artist Representations in Santa Barbara; Miranda's artist's rep; corporate art buyer; has designs on Joseph Calvin.

Sally O'Mally: early-40s, 5'3, blue eyes, blond curly hair, perfectly proportioned; owner of Sally's Restaurant; owner of Burn-It-Off; born and reared in Arkansas; Miranda's friend; dislikes Samantha; pregnant by Jack Sawyer; in love with high school sweetheart Tony Fiorentino, and just married him at last.

Cynthia Radcliffe: early-30s, 5'8, amber-brown eyes, blond, shapely, gorgeous; passionate, petulant, persuasive; Santa Barbara social climber; Zackery Calvin's previous girlfriend.

Kevin Ransom: late-20s, 6'8, hazel eyes, sandy hair, strong jawline, lean, muscular; foreman at Sawyer Construction; innocent, naive, kind; tuned in to animals; technologically adept; highly intuitive; has longings for Susan Winslow.

Jack Sawyer: mid-50s, 6', blue eyes, salt-and-pepper hair and mustache, barrel-chested, solidly muscular; Milford-Haven contractor-builder; Samantha Hugo's former husband; secretly dated Sally O'Mally but broke up with her on learning she was pregnant.

Cornelius Smith: late-30s, 6'1, indigo-blue eyes, black hair, handsome, lean; grew up in Milford-Haven where his parents still live; a professional astronomer who works part time at NASA Ames and plans to build an observatory in Milford-Haven; a loner, an eccentric; in love with Miranda and recently married her.

Gladys Wilson: mid-50s, 5'9, heavyset, long-limbed, short black hair, African American; Director of Safe Haven; a former victim of domestic violence who uses her wisdom and compassion to help other victims.

Susan Winslow: mid-20s, 5'4, black eyes, long black hair, rail-thin, attractive but sullen, Chumash Native American; Samantha's assistant at the EPC; avid rock star fan; victim of traumatic childhood; feels trapped in Milford-Haven; defensive about her heritage; toys with Kevin; friends with Ken "Notes" Kasmalia.

Milford-Haven Recipes

Pilar's French Toast
(As prepared for the Jones family in Belvedere
on Miranda's wedding shower weekend)

Serves 4

Ingredients:

    2 baguettes of French bread, sliced 1" thick (16 pieces)

    8 eggs, separated

    ¼ c half-and-half

    2 sticks cinnamon

    ¼ t vanilla

Preparation:
Beat the egg whites until almost stiff. Beat the egg yokes, adding
half-and-half and vanilla. Fold in the egg whites. Pour liquid mixture into a wide, flat pan. Place the pieces of bread into the pan,
allow the liquid to be soaked up on one side, then the other.

Place the soaked bread pieces onto a buttered griddle or pan
and allow to brown. Finish the bread pieces in an oven or toaster
oven until they puff slightly, an indication the center is cooked
and no longer raw.

Sauce: maple syrup warmed with raisins added until they're
slightly plump. Serve the French toast pieces with the warmed
syrup and raisins.

Optional serving suggestion: Add some crunchy almond pieces.

Provided by Mara Purl and Tamako Hasumi

Milford-Haven Recipes

Carla's Country Kitchen
Pooney Scramble
(As provided by Carla Wixom)*

Serves 6
Ingredients:

>   12 eggs

>   1 rasher of bacon, cooked and choped

>   8 oz. grated cheddar & jack cheese

>   8 oz. cream cheese

>   1 bunch fresh spinach (remove stems)

>   1/2 lb. mushrooms, sliced

>   Green onions (optional)

Preparation:
Add all ingredients to skillet with 3 tablespoons cooking oil.

Cook on medium heat

Scramble and serve.

Enjoy!

*This is a family recipe. My mother-in-law's nickname was Pooney
This is our most popular dish!" – Carla

James Hughes's Baked Salmon en Croute
(Adapted from Zack's description of a similar dish
served at Citronelle in Santa Barbara)

Serves 2

Ingredients:.

> 1 kilogram salmon (whole side)
>
> 500 grams puff pastry (or use 2 ready rolled sheets)
>
> 180 grams cream cheese
>
> 150 grams spinach (chopped)
>
> 1 shallot (chopped)
>
> 1 egg for egg wash only
>
> 10 grams butter
>
> salt and pepper

Preparation - Filling

1. Saute chopped shallot in butter over medium heat until translucent, then add the chopped spinach leaves.

2. Turn the heat down to low and cook until the moisture has completely evaporated before removing it from the heat and allowing it to cool completely.

3. Blend the sauteed spinach and shallot with cream cheese in a food processor until smooth and all incorporated. Season to taste with salt and pepper and a squeeze of lemon juice and set to one side.

Assembling and baking salmon en croute

1. Skin and trim the salmon to the right size for the puff pastry sheets

2. Preheat oven to 400 degrees

3. Line a baking tray with parchment paper and grease it with butter. Lay one of the puff pastry sheets on top.

4. Lay the salmon on top of the piece of puff pastry and smooth the cream cheese and spinach filling over the top using a spatula.

5. Brush an egg wash around the edges of the puff pastry and lay the second sheet on top of the fish and filling. Press it down around the salmon and use a fork to crimp the edges together, sealing them.

6. Using a sharp knife, gently score a fish scale pattern into the surface of the puff pastry, making sure you don't cut all the way through it.

7. Brush the egg wash over the whole salmon en croute, and bake in the oven for 30 minutes until golden brown and glossy. Rest for 5 minutes before serving.

Provided by Mara Purl, adapted from Rosanna Stevens @ Rosanna Etc.

Milford-Haven Recipes

Dill Cream Sauce
(For Salmon en Croute)

Make the sauce while salmon is baking.

Ingredients:

    400 ml double cream

    250 ml white wine

    1 shallot (diced)

    10 grams butter

    2 T parsley

    2 T dill

    1 T Dijon mustard

    ½ lemon

    salt and pepper

1. Heat butter in a pan over medium heat; saute the diced shallot until translucent

2. Add the white wine and bring it to a boil, allowing it to cook down by two-thirds in volume (about 10 minutes)

3. Add the double cream and turn the heat down to medium-low before bringing it back to a simmer. Cook 5 to10 more minutes to thicken

4. Add the Dijon mustard, lemon juice, and season with salt and pepper to taste before stirring through the fresh herbs

5. Serve the dill cream cause with the salmon en croute

Return soon to . . .
Milford-Haven!
Available now . . .

Mara Purl's
When Hearts Heal

Book Four

in the exciting Milford-Haven saga

Here's an excerpt from
the Prologue . . .

Prologue

Senior Deputy Delmar Johnson leapt out of a deep sleep at full alert, springing from his bed in one fluid motion. Swaying, he jerked his head from side to side in the dark, looking for the slightest glint of the man who'd shaken his mattress. *Probably a perp tripping as he tried to exit the room.*

Still struggling to determine who'd invaded his bedroom, Del's lightning reflexes brought his gun to hand even before he slapped his thigh to switch on the sound-activated light. The light didn't work. Staggering slightly, he ran into the empty living room. It was when he saw the dining room lamp swinging from the ceiling that he realized it wasn't an intruder who'd disturbed his sleep. *It's been a long time since an earthquake threw me out of bed.*

The first image that sprang into his mind was that the looting would start as soon as it was light. As a beat cop, he'd soon be called in as reinforcement for crowd control. As quickly as these thoughts crowded into his mind, he arrested them, locking them in a cell with the other memories burned into him by his years in South Central Los Angeles.

This was the Central Coast, and things like looting and pilfering didn't happen here. Even so, he felt uncomfortably vulnerable fumbling for his flashlight and looking for some underwear.

Yanking on his uniform trousers and snapping his holster into place, he reminded himself he was now a senior deputy with the San Luis Obispo Sheriff's Department. As such, his job was mostly to protect the good citizens—among whom he now lived—from crimes of a more subtle nature.

As his pulse slowed, Del stood, feeling the floor for the tell-tale vibrations of aftershocks. This hadn't been a major seismic event. Back in L.A., he'd been through bigger quakes in the early 1970s and the early 1990s. More significantly, there's been the societal "quakes" in the South Central of his youth and early professional years. There, generation upon generation of welfare, neighborhood gangs, and blighted opportunity had created a society of lack.

He'd sensed his people were angry even when they didn't know they were, and when some so-called act of God came along —anything from a hot-summer power brownout to the Rodney King verdict—that anger erupted with the sudden vehemence of pent-up frustration and seething disappointment.

Where other segments of society might pull together in an emergency, there every day was a crisis of its own, setting the stage for disaster as inexorably as drought sets the stage for wildfire. Only through an exquisite clarity of faith did people thrive in such a setting, and that accounted for the miraculous life his own mother had led.

For as long as he could remember, Ruby'd fed the neighborhood children and handed out oversized helpings of Christian virtue with every bite of delicious home cooking. There was no such thing as lack in Ruby's world: the Lord provided. During services at the AME Church at the end of their street, the congregation swayed and sang rousing hymns, all the while their mouths watering from the aromas wafting up from the basement kitchen where Ruby was cooking breakfast.

The memory brought him up short, and Del realized he was hungry. There'd be no stop at Sally's this morning for a homemade biscuit. Switching on his flashlight, he headed for his own kitchen to search for something to eat.

Pulling open the refrigerator door, he saw a carton of orange juice and a box of stale donuts—a law enforcement cliché, but they'd do. Pulling out his kitchen chair, he sat and munched the donuts, chasing them with a few swigs from the half-empty carton.

The overhead lamp in Del's dining room was no longer swinging, and the earth seemed to have settled—for the moment. He'd never been through a quake in this area. If looting wouldn't be the local reaction, what would be? Had there been serious damage somewhere? Was anyone hurt? Jumping to his feet, Del hastened to finish dressing and went to check in with base.

Del completed a slow scrutiny of the Touchstone Beach area before dawn broke over the eastern hills.

Its row of charming motels stood with their signs eerily unlit. Seeing a group of people standing outside the main entrance of the Belhaven, he stopped in and chatted briefly with Mr. Connor. No damage to the motel, the owner'd said, reassuring the restless group of tousled guests. Those who hadn't already decided to pack up and leave the area were standing in their robes and slippers, shuffling against the chill air. With the gas burner in the motel office kitchen, Mrs. Connor had made a fresh pot of coffee. Thanking her, Del gratefully accepted a small Styrofoam cupful.

Now he sipped the hot liquid, edging his SUV across Highway 1, and turned down Main Street. Training the car's searchlight along the southwest side of the street, he balanced his coffee in one hand and turned the wheel with the other. A severe bump sloshed coffee across his hand. "Damn!" he said to the dark, pulling the car over.

Licking the hot liquid from his skin, he turned to see what had caused the bump—a dead animal, perhaps, though he hoped not. He could see nothing but the double yellow line painted down the middle of the road. But the line seemed broken.

"Doesn't make sense," he muttered to himself, placing his cup in the holder and stepping outside. He remembered the paint had recently been redone. Clicking on his portable flashlight, he trained it on the median line. "Good Lord."

The once-solid double yellow line was now interrupted and continued on the other side of a small sink hole—one he knew hadn't been there two days before.

His heart thumping in his chest, Del stood and felt concern seep into him, just as water now intruded into that new hole in the road. For the second time that morning, he was feeling vulnerable.

COLOPHON

The print version of this book is set in the Cambria font, released in 2004 by Microsoft, as a formal, solid font to be equally readable in print and on screens. It was designed by Jelle Bosma, Steve Matteson, and Robin Nicholas.

The name Cambria is the classical name for Wales, the Latin form of the Welsh name for Wales, *Cymru*. The etymology of *Cymru* is *combrog*, meaning "compatriot."

The California town of Cambria is named for its resemblance to the southwestern coast of Wales, where the town of Milford Haven has existed since before ancient Roman times and is mentioned in William Shakespeare's *Cymbeline*.

The dingbat is the keyhole limpet shell drawn by artist Mary Helsaple. The keyhole limpet, or fissurellidae, is a marine gastropod mollusk. Their common name derives from the small hole in the apex of their cone-shaped shells. Their conical shape and low profile allow them to withstand wave intrusions on exposed rocks, to which they firmly attach with their muscular foot. The shell varies in both color and pattern but is recognized by its strong radial ribs.

As its physical qualities of strength and steadfast adherence imply, the keyhole limpet symbolizes persistence, stability, and safety. The hole, which allows the creature to breathe underwater, implies adaptability and resilience. The architectural structure is essentially triangular, making this shell a foundational part of sacred geometry.

PIEDRAS BLANCAS LIGHTHOUSE

Each of the Milford-Haven Novels features a real lighthouse. The Piedras Blancas Lighthouse has been featured previously in the Milford-Haven series, as it is the anchor lighthouse for the Central Coast.

Like all lighthouses, this one has an interesting history. Though it still serves the coastline in this region, its light shining outward twenty-five miles, the original Fresnel lens has been replaced by a flashing beacon. The flasher sits atop the sturdy base that once supported the Fresnel and its multi-windowed superstructure, giving this lighthouse an unusual profile resembling a rook chess piece. The lighthouse and its peninsula are situated just north of San Simeon and are named for the white rocks located just offshore.

The lighthouse was operated by the U.S. Lighthouse Service until 1939, when the U.S. Coast Guard assumed jurisdiction. The Coast Guard staffed the lighthouse until 1975, at which time the tower was automated and the station unmanned.

In 2001 management was transferred to the Bureau of Land Management, which has already extensively reclaimed native plants and has plans to restore the upper portion of the tower and replicate the original light. The original lens, slated for destruction, was saved by the Lion's Club, the Coast Guard, and the community of Cambria, where the lens is on display on Main Street.

Funds are being raised by local community groups to restore the lighthouse. Visit www.piedrasblancas.org for information or tours.

Secret of the Shells

*Special Messages about a Woman and Her Self,
and about Discovering the Next Chapter . . . of Her Life*

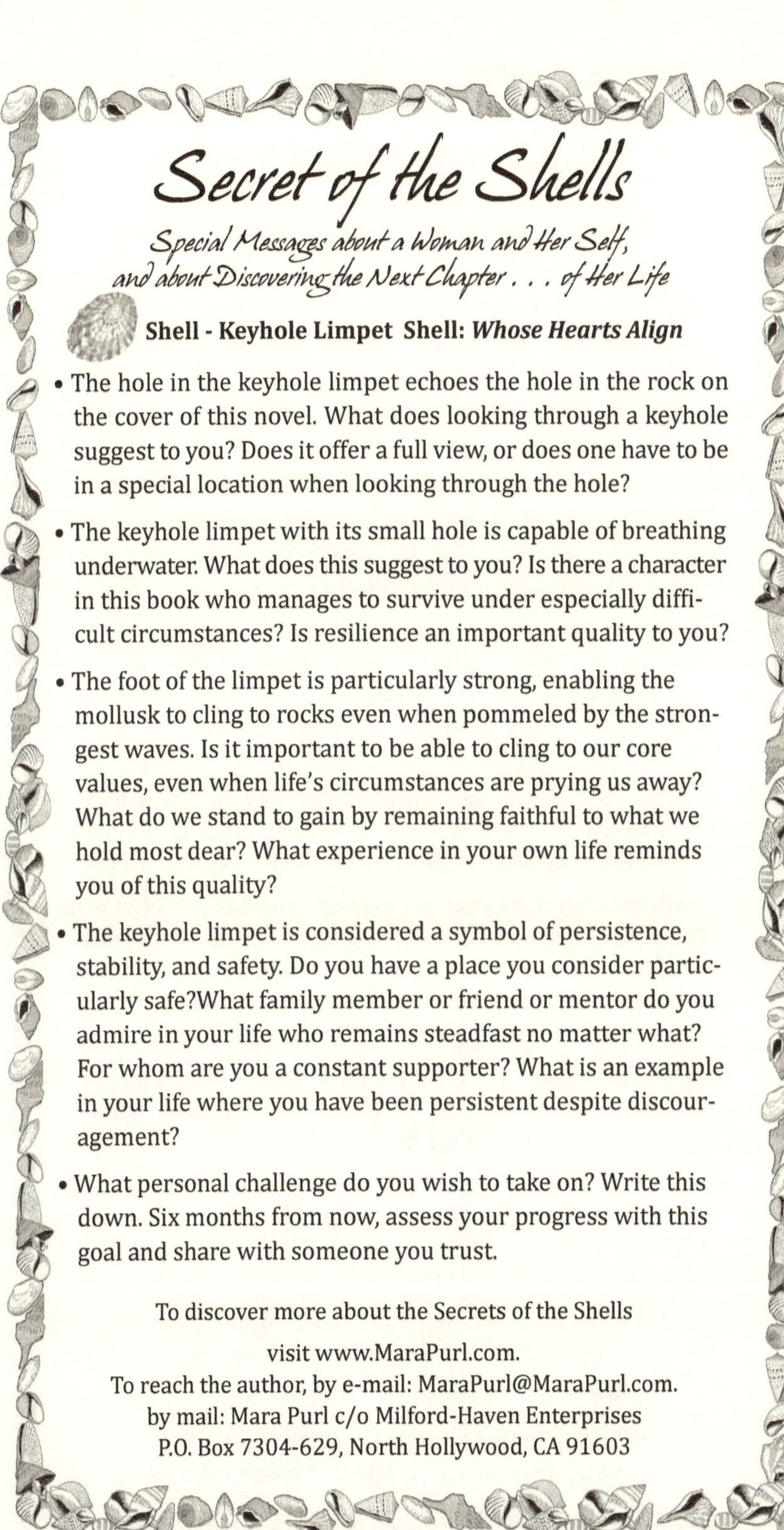

Shell - Keyhole Limpet Shell: *Whose Hearts Align*

- The hole in the keyhole limpet echoes the hole in the rock on the cover of this novel. What does looking through a keyhole suggest to you? Does it offer a full view, or does one have to be in a special location when looking through the hole?

- The keyhole limpet with its small hole is capable of breathing underwater. What does this suggest to you? Is there a character in this book who manages to survive under especially difficult circumstances? Is resilience an important quality to you?

- The foot of the limpet is particularly strong, enabling the mollusk to cling to rocks even when pommeled by the strongest waves. Is it important to be able to cling to our core values, even when life's circumstances are prying us away? What do we stand to gain by remaining faithful to what we hold most dear? What experience in your own life reminds you of this quality?

- The keyhole limpet is considered a symbol of persistence, stability, and safety. Do you have a place you consider particularly safe?What family member or friend or mentor do you admire in your life who remains steadfast no matter what? For whom are you a constant supporter? What is an example in your life where you have been persistent despite discouragement?

- What personal challenge do you wish to take on? Write this down. Six months from now, assess your progress with this goal and share with someone you trust.

To discover more about the Secrets of the Shells

visit www.MaraPurl.com.
To reach the author, by e-mail: MaraPurl@MaraPurl.com.
by mail: Mara Purl c/o Milford-Haven Enterprises
P.O. Box 7304-629, North Hollywood, CA 91603

Whose Hearts Align

Reading Group Topics for Discussion

1. This is the fourth novel in the Milford-Haven series, and there are novellas and novelettes that are also part of the saga. Since this is the penultimate book in the novel pentalogy, it includes the continuation of several plotlines. How do you feel about this?

2. Protagonist Miranda and Cornelius are "over the moon" about their wedding and upcoming honeymoon in Alaska. Do you feel they're right for one another? Do you expect theirs to be a happy marriage?

3. Miranda and Cornelius as artist and astronomer have two demanding careers and their respective families are quite different from one another. How are they navigating these challenges so far?

4. This novel includes a major focus on Miranda's sister Meredith and her relationship with Zack Calvin. Do you worry about Zack's previous liaisons? What do these two have in common that he didn't share with the other women he dated? Do you feel they might be right for each other?

5. How do you feel about Sally O'Mally? Were you surprised by her sudden marriage to Tony Fiorentino? Are they headed for trouble as live in the same town where Sally's baby's father lives?

6. Deputy Delmar Johnson is still investigating missing journalist Christine Christian. (There is more of their story in the novella What the Soul Suspects.) But in this book he discovers a conspiracy involving Wilhelm Chernak and Russell Clarke that is putting two Clarke Shipping employees in danger. How has he made these connections?

7. A protagonist should have some solid recurring qualities, but also should grow and learn from her experiences. In this book, Miranda "finds her alignment." What does that mean?

8. Author Mara Purl has now won more than seventy awards for her series. Before then, she created a hit radio drama for the BBC. What do you consider to be her strengths as a writer? What other parts of her series do you wish she would write?

9. Why is this book called Whose Hearts Align? Which characters are aligned with one another? With what core values are some of the characters aligned?

To share or print these discussion points please visit:
http://marapurl.com/books/why-hearts-keep-secrets

SALLY'S
WING DINGS
FINDERS

MARA PURL

the Milford-Haven Saga

Saga Chronology at MaraPurl.com/Books

Mara Purl, author of the best-selling and critically acclaimed *Milford-Haven Novels, Novellas & Novelettes,* pioneered small-town fiction for women.

Mara's beloved fictitious town has been delighting audiences since 1992, when it first appeared as *Milford-Haven, U.S.A.©*—the first American radio drama ever licensed and broadcast by the BBC. The show reached an audience of 4.5 million listeners in the U.K. In the U.S., it was the 1994 Finalist for the New York Festivals World's Best Radio Programs.

Mara was named the Top Female Author for Fiction by The Authors Show, and to date, her books have won more than seventy book awards, including the American Fiction, Benjamin Franklin, National Indie Excellence, USA Book News Best Books, and ForeWord Books of the Year.

The *Milford-Haven Novels,* set in the late 1990s, capture the spirit of adventure and the soul of small-town life, interweaving the tales of three multi-generational women who find romance, friendship and success on California's gorgeous Central Coast.

Mara's other writing credits include plays, screenplays, scripts for *Guiding Light,* cover stories for *Rolling Stone,* staff writing with the *Financial Times (of London),* and the Associated Press. She is the co-author (with Erin Gray) of *Act Right: A Manual for the On-Camera Actor.*

As an actress, Mara was "Darla Cook" on *Days Of Our Lives.* For the one-woman show *Mary Shelley: In Her Own Words*—which Mara performs and co-wrote (with Sydney Swire)—she earned a Peak Award. She has co-starred in multiple productions of *Sea Marks* and plays the title role in *Becoming Julia Morgan.* She was named one of twelve Women of the Year by the Los Angeles County Commission for Women.

Mara is married to Dr. Larry Norfleet and lives in Los Angeles and in Colorado Springs.

Visit her website at *www.MaraPurl.com* where you can subscribe to her newsletter and link to her social media sites.

She welcomes email at *MaraPurl@MaraPurl.com.*

www.ingramcontent.com/pod-product-compliance
Lightning Source LLC
Chambersburg PA
CBHW021922220726
48287CB00019B/1338